THE PRAIRIE AHEAD OF THEM DIDN'T LOOK
HALF BAD, BUT . . .

"There are cutbank streams, some of them running
down small canyons, to work past," Mister Skye warned.
"And Indians. This is game country—buffalo, antelope,
deer, bear. They come here to hunt—Cheyenne, Sioux,
Arapaho mainly, but also Crow, Shoshone, Gros Ventres,
Assiniboin, and sometimes others."

"It looks like it'll swallow armies. Like it'd be sheer
chance if our tiny caravan might be discovered," said
Cecil.

"We'll be found and watched. Probably are already,
mate."

"Are you expecting a fight?"

"I always expect a fight. Especially here."

# SKYE'S WEST:
## SUN RIVER

### RICHARD S. WHEELER

TOR

A TOM DOHERTY ASSOCIATES BOOK
NEW YORK

SUN RIVER

Copyright © 1989 by Richard S. Wheeler

A TOR Book
Published by Tom Doherty Associates, Inc.
49 West 24 Street
New York, NY 10010

Cover art by Royo

ISBN: 0-812-51073-9     Can. ISBN: 0-812-51074-7

First edition: July 1989

Printed in the United States of America

0  9  8  7  6  5  4  3  2

*For Win and Martha Blevins*

# Chapter 1

Eager for information, the Reverend Cecil J. B. Rathbone hurried diagonally across the dusty parade ground of Fort Laramie, past the two-storied officers' quarters known as Old Bedlam, and on to the sutler's store at the far corner.

Inside that low, wide building, and hovering amidst the piles of tarpaulins and ropes and clothing and barrels of foodstuffs, lurked a sallow clerk. That would not do, Rathbone thought. He wished to speak to Bullock himself.

"Where, sir, might I find the sutler?" he asked.

The clerk said nothing, but gestured toward a far corner. The Reverend Mister Rathbone nodded, and found a bearded man there doing his accounts at a crude plank desk.

"Mr. Bullock, sir."

"Why yes," said the man. "May I be of service?"

A southerner, the reverend supposed.

"I am told on good authority that you can direct me to a certain Barnaby Skye. The guide."

"Mister Skye," said Bullock.

"Why yes, Barnaby Skye."

"*Mister* Skye," the sutler repeated. "He permits no other address." He carefully blotted ink from his nib pen, and set it on a lined ledger. Then he rose, a tall and courtly man. "I am Colonel Bullock," he said. "And whom do I have the honor of addressing?"

"Cecil Rathbone. I'm a clergyman. My party and I wish to employ Mister Skye to take us to the Blackfeet."

"Blackfeet? Bug's Boys?" The sutler was visibly startled.

Rathbone grinned. "Scares the bejabbers out of me, too."

Bullock stared out of his small window toward the low June-greened bluffs that rimmed the Platte Valley. "Skye won't take you. I can tell you that now. There are certain Blackfeet who'd kill him on sight. Old blood, bad blood . . . Maybe I can find you someone else to transport you to your doom."

Cecil J. B. Rathbone laughed. "I say we'll prosper. We made it this far, haven't we? In spite of the troubles?"

The sutler glared at him fiercely. "Indeed you have, suh. The work of innocents or fools or madmen. I suppose you're with the wagon train that just rolled in. Probably the only one we'll see in 1855, with the Sioux in an uproar and Harney gearing up to a fight . . . not to mention bloody troubles in Oregon, and all the rest. I must say, suh, you and your good missionaries took a desperate risk. And the worst is yet to come."

Rathbone laughed easily. "It's been a perfect trip. Lots of grass because there is no one ahead of us. No waiting at the fords and ferries."

"I can imagine," said the sutler dryly. "The luck of the innocent. An odd year. Last year we counted over five thousand wagons. But that was before that popinjay, Lieutenant Grattan, got himself slaughtered."

Time was wasting, Rathbone thought. "Now then,

Colonel, if you'd be so kind as to steer me toward Mister Skye . . . ?''

"How many are in your party?" Bullock asked.

"Ten. Five men, three women, two children. Four wagons."

"Wagons? There's no road whatsoever to the Blackfoot country. You can't take wagons. You can't take women or children either."

"We intend to," said Rathbone. "Now, sir, if you could direct me?"

Back in Independence they had told him that Bullock was the man who'd put him in touch with Skye. He felt a little irked. What was it about being a missionary that caused people to assume he was fragile as an egg?

"Far as I know, Mister Skye's available. No one's hired him this year. He came in a few days ago. Bought a new slant-breech Sharps. But I can tell you, Reverend, you'll have no more chance of engaging him than a snowball in, ah . . ."

"His whereabouts, Colonel Bullock?"

"Why, he keeps a lodge up the Platte some. Two, three miles above Squaw Town. Beside a stand of cottonwoods."

"Thank you kindly, Colonel," said Rathbone, offering his big, frontier-hardened hand. The trader pumped it, shaking his head.

The reverend walked quickly through the store and out into the blinding sun of the parade. God love 'em, they all thought that Indians were unteachable; that the savages would sooner or later be exterminated, and probably sooner, to make way for settlement. And any attempt by missionaries to civilize and settle the tribes must be the work of muddleheads, fools, and religious crackpots. Cecil Rathbone intended to show them otherwise. His plan had seemed hopeful and plausible enough to persuade the Methodist Board of Missions to approve, and spring a few miserable dollars.

He liked Fort Laramie, but he knew no one else in the party would. It was, really, a desolate outpost, many hundreds of weary miles beyond the Missouri frontier, bleak and almost treeless, set improbably at the juncture of the Platte and Laramie rivers, a fur-trade post until 1849. Now it baked in a late spring sun, its bunch grass greening early in the arid climate. The bedraggled adobe fur-trade stockade still stood, a magazine and storage area now. And the army was desultorily building around the parade. Long barracks. Cavalry stables. Married officers' quarters. Innumerable outbuildings, thrown up crudely. The commanding officer had been a green West Point brevet lieutenant—until the Grattan affair last year. That woke up the army, and now an experienced officer, Brevet Lt. Colonel William Hoffman, commanded, and the post flexed its muscles for war.

Unlike most clerics, the Reverend Mister Rathbone paid heed to all of that, noting the sentries, the two howitzers and their limbers strategically placed to protect the weak fort with a wall of grape since it lacked a stockade. Mister Rathbone approved. It seemed an unfinished place, like the business of life, with some buildings started, and others half raised.

Mister Skye, he thought, lived well beyond the fort's protection, alone in a skin lodge up the river. And between him and the fort lay Squaw Town, the camp of the loafers and ne'er-do-wells and—he thought piously— those squaws sunk in vice. Most of them were Oglala Sioux, he'd heard, but some were Brulés, the very band Grattan had tangled with; the band General Harney was preparing to punish.

Skye was plainly a man to reckon with, living beyond safety like that. It jibed with everything he'd heard about him, too. He had made inquiries back east in St. Louis and Independence and St. Jo. Who could take his party, his wagons, his women and children, safely to the Blackfeet? No one can, was the answer. Veteran fur traders along the Missouri frontier looked at him aghast even for asking the question. And had smirked. But even as he had asked, the name Skye emerged. One man, one man alone, a legend of a man, Barnaby Skye, might do it.

Not that Skye would consent to such folly, they had hastily added. But he could do it. He could even move missionaries.

Rathbone grinned at the memory. Moving missionaries was a sort of ultimate wilderness test. And Mister Skye would be the man to do it. On lanky legs the reverend raced on down past the fort to the meadow beside the trail where the wagons were parked. In normal years it was bare, littered ground, every blade of grass mashed under by a thousand wagons and oxen and mules and horses and hordes of people heading west. But this year it remained lush, and the missionary herds—oxen, horses, mules, milch cows—grazed contentedly.

Cecil Rathbone managed to wear his black broadcloth suit through most of the journey, as a sort of badge of office, although he felt more comfortable in homespuns, and the lean hard legs that had walked him from frontier Illinois to the Wesleyan college in Boston were more at home in soft denim britches and big square-toed boots. He would saddle up the mare and ride out to Mister Skye. Persuading Mister Skye did not worry him. Paying Mister Skye did. There really were no other candidates. He had noted how trappers' eyes softened at the name: Skye? Ah, yes, Mister Skye. How well I remember . . .

The reverend wondered whether the man was real, or merely a legend, another frontier tall story, the sort of yarn old Jim Bridger loved to spin for greenhorns. He'd find out soon enough. Mountain men had peculiar notions, and some of their raucous kind were esteemed not because of any known virtue, but because they had survived in a brutal wilderness. Skye might be that type—a lout in stinking, dirty buckskins, a man so murderous that he thrived on terror. The thought made Cecil Rathbone uneasy. He did not want to employ a guide so repellent that he outraged his own party of missionaries, or violated its ideals, nor ride into the northern Blackfoot land in the company of a man who personified evil among them. On the other hand—and this was where Cecil Rathbone believed he differed from the others in his party—one had to be flexible, and manage the practical compromises that would ensure success. Where would Mister Skye fit?

The wagon train slouched haphazardly in the meadow, all discipline broken down in the safe lee of the fort. There were twenty-eight wagons, of which four belonged to his missionary group. The rest were owned by men— there were no women this wartorn year, save for the missionary wives—bound for golden California beyond the far western mountains, or Oregon and the Willamette Valley where, people said, anyone could grow anything in such abundance that it staggered the imagination to think of it. How often he had listened to them, and their shining dreams and great hopes, on the trail! After some rest and refitting at the fort, those wagons would lumber up the Oregon Trail. These were small wagons mostly, the sun-bleached canvas stretched and sagging over the bows, and the undercarriage and boxes showing wear and grit. Many of the owners had drifted to the fort, the sutler's store in particular, seeking news and companionship and sometimes supplies, or a trade or two. Worn oxen for fresh, a heavy bedstead or dresser for a barrel of flour; two saddlesore gaunt horses for a rested fat one.

The three wagons and light carriage of his own party looked even less trailworthy than those of the others, for there had been little money, and the missionaries had acquired the oldest and meanest available, and had prayed that they would do; that the battered hubs and spokes and wheel-rim felloes and tongues and axletrees would somehow last them. Cecil Rathbone was not content with prayer. He held that God always demanded the best from his people. So Cecil had pulled out his broadaxe, his draw knife, his saws and chisels, and had set to work on the old wagons, replacing weak wood with fine strong hickory or ash or birch, and somehow the wagons had survived. The rest of the party had thanked God, and attributed a minor miracle to him. Cecil thanked God too, and smiled as he touched the new spokes and axles he had hewn and cut and shaved.

The Newtons in particular had thanked God, rather than Cecil. And that was good enough, thought Cecil Rathbone. Henrietta Newton was his daughter; Alexander, his son-in-law. He loved them, but knew their narrow letter-perfect faith was radically different from his own. The pair of them was pious, intense, and—the Reverend Mister Rathbone sighed—sour-natured. It worried him. How would they react to the savage Blackfeet? Still, he loved them, and they had bravely joined the Rathbones in this great enterprise.

He looked among the wagons for his own Esmerelda, and didn't find her. Like the rest, she had drifted off to the fort, no doubt, in her black skirts, to gaze upon this place of war and arms with good-humored prudishness. But the Newtons lounged beside their wagon, resting in camp chairs and flapping small folding fans. It amused Cecil to see them thus. He and his brown-eyed Esmerelda were thin as sticks, while his daughter Henrietta and her husband Alex were plump as autumn turkeys, and both sandy-haired and freckled.

"Have you seen the Samples?" asked Alexander in his nasal voice that could rattle the back wall of a cathedral. "It's past the nooning and the Samples have drifted off."

"Around the fort, I'm sure," said Cecil amiably. "You might fetch your own meal this time." Clay Sample, his wife Alice, and two children had come along to launch the mission farm and eventually to teach agriculture to their charges. Cecil admired them as he did all Yankee yeomen of hearty and courageous manner. On the trail Henrietta and Alexander, pleading exhaustion, had soon taken to sharing the Samples' table, and now had come to expect it.

"That's the trouble with the world and the thing we must preach against," added Henrietta. "People running off, not caring about the needs of others, selfish in their own pursuits, heedless of want. I wish we had brought a more responsible couple."

Cecil didn't like the drift of this. "It's a holiday," he

said. "A celebration; the end of the first great leg of the Oregon Trail. Why don't you make a holiday of it yourself? I hear the sutler has a splendid eggnog."

"Daddy, it's too hot. And besides, I'm unwell," she added pointedly, referring to her delicate condition.

"The Samples will have to contribute more to the mission if they want my esteem. We've no room for ne'er-do-wells in a hard wilderness," Alexander said. "And they scarcely even understand Methodism. God relies on us to spread his message; and we are forced to rely on the Samples for better or worse."

All of this stretched Cecil's patience. Prior to this long hard journey he'd scarcely given a second thought to the character of his daughter and son-in-law. But now, far removed from the world they all had known, he was discovering—or perhaps they were first revealing—traits that disturbed him.

"Good news," he said cheerily. "Skye's available, the sutler thinks. I shall go find him. He lives in a skin teepee out beyond Squaw Town a couple of miles."

"I've heard about Squaw Town," said Alexander. "May God smite them all, with their unspeakable vices, and I suppose this famous guide is a part of it, in his filthy buckskins."

"I don't think so," said Cecil mildly.

"I think we should have an army escort take us. The Republic owes it to the missionaries who bring light to the savage breast," said Henrietta. "I have no stomach for a hard journey led by some barbaric pig of a man."

Cecil smiled again. "Perhaps it would be best to withhold judgment," he said mildly, and chastised himself for not adding that Christian charity might help.

"Yes of course. You don't need to lecture, daddy," she said. "And if you see the Samples, direct them here at once."

The Reverend Cecil Rathbone ignored his daughter and set off to find his horse, a ribby bay mare, gaunt across the haunches, and venerable of age, if Cecil was any judge. Still, she had come this distance and had not become sorefooted. He had ridden her as much as possible to take the strain off the oxen dragging the overburdened wagon.

He found her in the loose herd of the wagon train, several hundred yards east, where grass grew lush and green. There was no guard whatsoever—the entire complement of the train had bolted toward the fort, leaving no on to watch the herd, a laxity that worried and astonished him. He had been too long on the frontier of western Illinois to suppose such a thing didn't invite trouble. The Newtons were on hand; perhaps he could prevail upon Alexander. But then he thought better of it. The Reverend Alexander would not be prevailed upon. Cecil threaded casually through the oxen and milch cows and mules, until he came nigh to the mare, but at the last second she spun away.

"Blast it, Magdelene, are we going to go through this again?" he muttered, easing after her. He thought perhaps if he paused and invited the Lord to stop Magdelene in her tracks, he might catch her, but he scorned that. He'd do his wily best first, and only after that, if all else failed, would Cecil J. B. Rathbone bend a petitioning knee.

"Come along, Magdelene," he crowed amiably, with a tone of voice he reserved professionally for recent widows. And he laughed. Her name was his delight, mainly because it had shocked the Newtons, and had even troubled his dear wife Esmerelda. A preacher riding a horse named Magdelene indeed! A school for scandal. "Come along now, Magdelene," he repeated in a quavering funereal basso that caught her ear. She paused delicately. He haltered her and led her back to his wagon, where a tattered saddle and battered bridle with woven horsehair reins awaited.

"It gets harder and harder to catch Magdelene," he said in passing to the Reverend Alexander Newton.

Newton sniffed knowingly.

"The herd is quite unguarded. I don't suppose, from

Christian duty, you'd care to walk over there and keep a watchful eye, Alexander?''

He looked remarkably pained. It was like asking him to wash dishes. "I don't suppose anyone will take them," he replied. "But I will petition God about it.''

Cecil Rathbone nodded, and turned the mare toward Skye.

# Chapter 2

The way threaded through Squaw Town, which turned out to be a chaotic jumble of lodges, crude huts, brush arbors, and makeshift livestock pens lying loosely along the riverbank on a meadow hemmed by cottonwoods. The Reverend Mister Rathbone stared, curious and appalled, at bronze women with bold stares, drunken men, naked brown children with moon faces, and gaunt hard-used Indian ponies. Here troopers and infantrymen could find most anything, from women to buffalo robes and winter capotes. Here were the Laramie loafers he'd heard of, the fort's own Sioux, who ran errands, guided, sometimes supplied buffalo meat and hides, worked in menial jobs at the fort, and made small livings from it, which they exchanged for powder and lead and strong spirits. The place was a fact of life, and did not dismay Cecil, though he pitied its dissolute denizens.

But he knew the others in his party, the Newtons, and Silas Potter who had come west to teach, would find it loathsome and stark proof of the damnation of the red races. Cecil sighed, wondering how the mission would fare if its staff harbored such obdurate contempt of the people whose lives and souls they hoped to change. There were noisome odors here, and lurking disease, and no doubt some of his fine white colleagues would hold it all against the redmen, not understanding that this degradation was a product of a white man's fort. In their distant villages the Sioux did not live like this.

After a few minutes Cecil found himself on the far side of Squaw Town, on open meadow uninhabited save for some loose Indian ponies in various colors, paints, brindles, roans, spotted animals, buckskins and bays and whites and blacks, and some boy herders.

Leisurely he threaded up the river, in a wide sunny valley dotted with stands of cottonwood. The fort disappeared from sight as he rounded a broad curve, along with Squaw Town. The missionary was quite alone in a wilderness six or seven hundred miles from the frontier. Then at last he spotted a solitary lodge of buffalo hide, its smokehole and flaps blackened by long hard use. As he approached he realized it was a small lodge, perhaps ten feet at its base, as if its owner was a man on the move and wanted no roots. Grazing beyond the lodge was a small herd, consisting of two heavy ebony mules in good flesh; several nondescript Indian ponies of varied hue, and a monster of a horse, a giant blue roan that struck Cecil Rathbone as the ugliest brute he had ever seen. Closer to the lodge, a fresh-killed mule deer carcass hung from a limb. He saw a pleasant brush arbor supplying shade. And under it, the figure of an Indian woman in buckskin, working a hide. Just what she looked like he couldn't say; she was too far away for his poor eyes.

As he approached, a man emerged from the lodge. At least, Cecil thought, it appeared to be a man, for indeed it was the strangest apparition imaginable, and gave him a fright that not even all his frontier experience could allay. As he drew up Magdelene he found himself gaping at a veritable Falstaff, a man of great height, built like a hogshead. From top to bottom the man looked bizarre.

He wore his iron-gray hair loose and shoulder length, in the manner of the mountain men, which the reverend had anticipated. But on top of his head sat a black silk stovepipe hat, jammed down hard and dimpled from hard use. It rested slightly akilter, to portside, making him look unballasted and likely to list in a hurricane.

In the center of all this was a square beardless face, with a massive, pulpy, twisted nose of a magnitude beyond the experience of Cecil Rathbone; a majestic prow that had obviously been smashed and mauled in a thousand brawls. From behind this formidable stem stared two small, icy eyes, perhaps blue but so buried in folds and creases of flesh that the reverend couldn't tell. A jagged white scar ripped across his right cheek, and a pucker scar dug into his forehead above his nose. Cecil thought that if God wanted him to hire this man, God had better send a sign.

At the base of a thick neck a fine buckskin shirt with fringes on its sleeves barely contained the barrel staves of the man. All this mass rested on stout, slightly bowed legs, encased in fringed leggins and a red-beaded breechclout. On his feet were not moccasins, but heavy, worn, square-toed boots largely hidden by the leggins. Only then did the reverend notice a shining new rifle resting easily in brutish brown hands the size of summer squash. So electrifying was all this that he scarcely glanced at the woman who placidly scraped hide under the brush arbor. This was, he thought wildly, a most alarming sight, half devil and half Viking berserker, and not fitting for ladies or gentlefolk. Surely this could not be the man . . .

"Mister Skye?" he croaked.

"Yaas?" thundered the man. With one word he had sounded like a den of grizzlies, whose shiny gray claws indeed he wore in a necklace.

"You are Mister Skye, the guide?"

"I am Mister Skye," the man said in a voice that rumbled like an earthquake. "May I be of service to you?"

The question—or rather the elegance of it—startled Cecil Rathbone. Was this brute educated? Housebroken? "Why . . . why, I believe you can. I'm, the, ah, Reverend Cecil J. B. Rathbone."

"Ah," said Mister Skye, "a divine. One who does not wear the collar of Rome. You have come west to tamper with the heathen."

"Methodist," said Rathbone shortly. He had detected something—was it mockery?—in Skye's comment. He would turn around right now and hire a human rather than a grizzly, he thought. This man would be utterly impossible, especially among the women of the mission. "I was, ah, looking for a guide, but I don't think—"

"To where?" asked Mister Skye.

"To the Blackfeet."

"For what?" demanded Mister Skye.

"Why . . . why . . ."

"To turn them into white men. And probably do a bloody poor job of it."

"Not exactly," Cecil stammered. "All by degrees. A farm. A school. Practical things first . . ." Cecil began to warm to his topic, his vision. "Christian religion doesn't catch in a savage. They have been vaccinated against it . . . by savage living . . . We have to civilize them first and then they'll understand religion."

"The Blackfeet are nomads and roam a land the size of several New Englands," said Mister Skye. "Will you roam with them?"

"No, no, not at all. We've heard of a place called Sun River. Wide, flat, fertile valley east of the Rockies some; a place to set up our farm, our school, our headquarters. The advice we got was Sun River, and we'd like to employ you to take us there."

Mister Skye stared up at the reverend, and then at his gaunt horse. "I will consider it," he said at last. "How many are there of you?"

"Ten. Five men, three women, a boy of fourteen and a girl of eleven. Three wagons and one carriage. Some oxen, mules, and two milch cows."

"Wagons," said Mister Skye.

But he said no more, and Rathbone was surprised.

The man studied Cecil. "What did you say your name is?"

"Cecil J. B. Rathbone."

"What does the J. B. stand for?"

Cecil felt skewered, and hastily blurted his response. "Nothing. Nothing at all. I added it when I entered the ministry. Ah, just vanity. When I entered Wesleyan, I was plain Cecil, from Galena, Illinois. When I graduated and was ordained, I became Cecil J. B.—John Burnside, I tell people. More clerical, I fancy."

For the first time Mister Skye grinned. Cecil felt nonplussed. He had confessed something that not even dear Esmerelda knew, his own little pettifoggery and conceit. What sort of man was this, who elicited such things? A dangerous one, surely.

"And who are the others?"

The Reverend Rathbone felt rattled. "My daughter Henrietta, ah, now Newton. Married to the Reverend Alex Newton. Ah, Silas Potter, a lay brother and divinity student—our teacher. James, a mulatto escaped slave from Louisiana. Fine strong fellow. Ah, the Samples. Clay Sample, good Yankee yeoman who'll tend our farm. His wife Alice, sturdy stock. Their son Alfred, almost a man. And a daughter, Miriam, old enough to help with everything."

Mister Skye waited, disconcertingly, for the reverend to continue, but Cecil had already blabbered more than he intended. Then the giant nodded. "This is Victoria," he said. "She is a woman of the Absaroka, the Raven people, the Crow. I named her for the Queen, God save her bloody life. She has another name in her own tongue. She tends the camp, tans fine buffalo robes, makes the elkskin clothes I wear, guards the horses, fetches wood, shoots her percussion lock rifle better than I can, takes scalps, mutilates the enemy"—Mister Skye's eyes glinted at that—"swears bloody oaths, tells bawdy jokes that make preachers swoon, makes spirit medicine to heathen gods, is a real medicine woman and healer of the Crow people, builds my sweat lodges, rides buffalo ponies, and is second-in-command when I'm, ah, incapacitated.''

Cecil turned for the first time to look at her. So galvanizing had Mister Skye been that he had quite forgotten she was present. She was tall and gaunt and her black hair was well shot with gray. Though her walnut flesh was withered, she looked almost as strong as her consort. She smiled gently, and turned back to the hide scraping, which she did with a curious black iron and wood tool. Could she really do all those appalling things, or was the guide funning him? Cecil suspected that the woman could and would do everything on that dismaying list.

Cecil grinned back, and nodded to her.

''She also swears like a bloody sailor, and if you don't do what she says, mate, she'll turn you into a tenor.''

Cecil nodded. Take orders? From her . . . ?

''Do you shoot?'' asked Mister Skye abruptly. ''I see no arms at hand.''

''I do,'' said Cecil. ''I have fed our party this trip, in fact. Pronghorn, deer, several rabbits.''

Cecil expected him to ask whether the missionary would shoot at humans, at redmen, in self-defense, but the question never came, and Cecil felt vaguely relieved.

Instead, Mister Skye said, ''My fee would be five hundred dollars in advance—if I accept, which I have not made up my mind to do.''

Cecil was stricken. ''Why, sir, that is what a man makes in a year!''

Mister Skye nodded almost imperceptibly.

''We haven't it,'' Cecil said, relief flooding through him. ''We reserved two hundred maximum, a draft on the Methodist Board of Missions, but hoped to do for less.''

Cecil felt giddy with escape, and turned Magdelene to go.

"Wait," said Mister Sky. "I will go with you. I never make up my mind until I have examined the party."

"But we can't possibly afford you!"

"We shall see," said Mister Skye. "Belay yourself. I'll gather my horse and be with you right smartly."

He whistled in some earsplitting fashion, and that terrible blue roan's head lifted and he trotted toward his master.

"I can pipe him in," Mister Skye said amiably. "His name is Jawbone."

"Were you perhaps a sailor, Mister Skye?"

"I was. Royal Navy. Pressed in, until I deserted."

"I have it that you were a brigade leader with Astor's American Fur."

"That too, Mister Rathbone."

If Mister Skye was an apparition, Jawbone was twice an apparition to Cecil Rathbone. Never in a life spent among horses had he seen such an animal as this. Jawbone was a horse sired by the devil on Moloch, and the reverend piously resisted the impulse to cross himself or run.

Never had an uglier horse been spawned among the gentle creatures of earth. Jawbone towered seventeen hands but looked lean as a starved wolf. His enormous bones projected through flesh everywhere, making him all ridges and bumps. He stared at the world with cruel, intelligent yellow eyes set narrowly on a long Roman nose that rivaled his master's. An ear was half torn off. Everywhere, his battered blue and white hair bore the scars of a thousand battles. Across his chest lay a long puckered slash. In a dozen places were hairless circles where arrows had buried themselves. His rump was concave and laced with ridged, proud flesh, sites of countless blows from lances and knives. His legs looked straight but battered and knotted. Long sinewy muscles rippled and corded through his stifle and shoulder, suggesting raw strength. Even as the reverend gaped, horrified, Jawbone bared his long, cruel teeth. He clacked his molars resoundingly, and Cecil Rathbone felt faint.

But at bottom it was not the physical aspects of this monster that appalled the reverend; it was his malevolence, burning in his eyes from the throne of hell with an intelligence that was almost human—or demonic.

"Where . . . where did you get a horse like that?"

"Pulled him from a dying mare, suckled him on a she-bear, raised him the way I wanted," Mister Skye replied as he threw an apishamore over the stallion's back, and then cinched down a light battered rawhide thing that could be called a saddle.

Mister Skye looped a horsehair rope loosely over the monster's nose and knotted it underneath, a single line of it running back along the neck.

"Better stand back, mate. You and your party must never come closer than ten or twelve feet."

"Does he kick?" asked Cecil.

"No, he kills."

Involuntarily Cecil Rathbone edged Magdelene back. Jawbone clacked his teeth from the sheer joy of it.

"How—how can you steer a horse with only one rein?"

"He knows."

With that, Mister Skye bounded effortlessly into his saddle, lifting his vast weight the seventeen hands as easily as stepping over a hound, and holding that gleaming new rifle to boot. Then they rode off, Mister Skye taking the lead, straight through Squaw Town, parting its gaping denizens like a bow wave, while Mister Rathbone on Magdelene trailed like a dinghy in the wake. Squaws and squaw men and breeds stared, half afraid, and Cecil Rathbone saw respect and more. There in Skye's wake, he never felt safer. That was a novelty: he hadn't felt truly safe, this year of wars, ever since they had left Independence.

On the meadow at Fort Laramie a squad of infantrymen were practicing with their bayonets, learning to feint and stab while a drill sergeant with a long staff tutored. As Mister Skye approached they stopped and stared, resting the butts of their Springfields in the battered grass.

Who was this to make the United States Army gawk? Cecil asked himself. Then they rounded the north corner of the parade, and Cecil saw the wagons.

"Over there." He pointed toward the knot of wheels and canvas and people comprising his missionary group. It looked from that distance like his party had returned from the fort and the sutler's, though with his infernally bad eyes he couldn't be sure.

Mister Skye nodded and imperceptibly steered Jawbone in that direction, while Cecil's nerves tightened. What on earth would they think of a man such as this? It was not going to be easy. Could they understand that here was not menace, but safety?

A sharp breeze lifted Cecil's hair, and he wondered whether it would pluck Mister Skye's black silk hat and set it sailing. But it didn't, and the hat, still askew, seemed anchored to his skull over his flowing white-shot hair.

Then they were there. Mister Skye reined up Jawbone, and stared, first at the assembled missionaries, one by one, from eyes so small and buried that no one could meet his gaze. Then his eyes raked the equipment. The horses and mules and oxen first, and then the wagons, lingering on the hubs, spokes, hounds, felloes, axles, tongues, and singletrees. Then at last he smiled. Jawbone raised his head to the heavens, bared his terrible teeth, and screeched. Several people jumped.

In all this awful silence Rathbone's party stared back, dismayed and alarmed, their eyes darting from man to horse, resting on Mister Skye's awesome nose, studying the scars on his weathered face, darting to the wounds and lumps and ridges of the horse he sat, peering disapprovingly at the bit of brown thigh flesh between Mister Skye's beaded breechclout and his leggins. Miriam Sample, pale and toothy and thin, slid around behind her mother and hid but young Alfred stood his ground bravely. No sissy was he.

The Reverend Cecil Rathbone thought that the stretching silence had gone on long enough. He cleared his throat. "I would like you . . ." he rasped, "I would like you to meet Mister Skye, who may become our guide to the Blackfeet."

Mister Skye nodded amiably.

Cecil continued bravely. "This is my daughter Henrietta and her husband, the Reverend Alexander Newton."

The pair nodded curtly, indignation rising in their plump soft cheeks.

"Next to them, my dear wife Esmerelda."

She managed a darting smile, and Cecil was pleased.

"Over there now is James, James Method," Cecil continued, nodding toward a powerfully built tall mulatto of perhaps thirty, with tawny flesh and yellow eyes. "He fled his native Louisiana, and we have taken him in. We don't hold with slavery here. A good man, and a fine addition to our party. We gave him the surname, Method."

James Method grinned easily. He alone was not dismayed by the barbaric power of the guide. He stood easily, muscles rippling through his homespun shirt that was tucked into denim britches. "Ah think you'll do in a tribulation, Mister Skye," he said. "You look like safety itself."

The mountain man stared, smiled, and nodded. "Likewise," he rumbled. "You remind me a heap of Jim Beckwourth, a trapper friend of your color, and an adopted Crow headman."

"And these are the Samples. Clay here, who can make things grow in deserts; Alice, his wife, and the young 'uns, Alfred and Miriam."

They too managed smiles. Mister Skye's eyes lingered on Clay in particular, and then the others, and he nodded.

"And lastly, our fine teacher, Silas Potter. William and Mary College and Dartmouth too, before he began his studies at Wesleyan for the missionary field."

Silas Potter was frail, pale even after weeks on the trail, and nearsighted. He wore gold-rimmed spectacles.

Now he stood rigidly, his soft young lips drawn into a pout, his eyebrows furrowed into contempt.

Silas Potter swallowed, and his Adam's apple bobbed up and down. Then he said, "I will not travel a mile with this unholy barbarian. We are people of God, not the devil."

# Chapter 3

Mister Skye had a way of sizing men up in a hurry. He had refined that gift as a brigade leader in his trapping years when his very life depended on the sort of men he had around him. He knew at once that he would take this group up to the Blackfeet. What might happen to them after that was not his business, but he would get them there.

Now, as he eyed the group, Jawbone restless under him, he turned again to James Method, and liked what he saw. The ex-slave had seen the worst of life, and the worst of human nature, and that made him a realist. But one who had not gone sour or stoked his soul on hate. That sort of embittered man could be a menace in the wilderness, where sticking together often meant the difference between life and going under. He was muscular too, and probably had a journeyman's skills with tools as a result of his slave chores. Strong. He would do in a corner.

"You can shoot that?" he asked, alluding to a battered percussion lock rifle lying easy in the man's hands.

"Ah thought you might ask whether ah could aim it," James replied. "Do you want to see?"

"You'll do," said Mister Skye.

Even while the rest of them wrangled about him, he surveyed them one by one. Clay Sample would do, too, but seemed less bright and in need of a leader. The Reverend Rathbone was made of sturdy stuff, frontier stuff, and would be an asset, unless attacked by some sort of scruples. So would his doughty wife.

The Newtons were a question mark. Soft, arrogant, disdainful on the one hand, but with strong wills. They might shape up. He'd reserve his opinion of them. And then there was Potter. A loss and liability out in the wilds. But every brigade and caravan had a few of those, he thought. The man's flapping mouth would be the problem, rather than his physical frailty. That mouth could breed dissension, division, hatred, and weakness. As for the rest, Mrs. Sample and her children, assets.

"Mister Method," he said. "Are you as handy with a shovel as you are with that rifle? We have roads to make, cutbank streams to cross."

The man grinned.

"It doesn't matter whether he is or not," Silas Potter snapped. "We have decided not to employ you."

"I have decided to take you," said Mister Skye. He addressed Cecil Rathbone. "Reverend, you just hand me that letter of credit on your mission board, and we'll be off."

"Why, I was about to do it."

"Daddy, I do believe this requires more discussion," broke in Henrietta Newton.

"It's all discussed," said Cecil. "You might bend a knee about it, however."

"I think we're being hasty. We'll let you know in the morning, Skye. We have other candidates to interview—" said Alexander Newton.

"Mister Skye."

"Well, whatever it is."

"Newton. All the years I was a slave on a British man-o'-war I was Skye. Now I'm mister. Have we come to an agreement about that? Yes, Newton?''

James Method grinned.

They fell to wrangling again, and Mister Skye watched them, learning much. Cecil Rathbone was the senior man, and in command, in some fashion. And that was good. If Newton or Potter had been senior, he would have long since turned his back. But Rathbone was a man to reckon with, plain enough.

The money wasn't much. He'd turn the letter of credit over to the sutler, who'd collect, and put it on account meanwhile, so he could draw on it. There were no other prospects this year, with the Sioux aflame across the prairies. Two hundred would do. It would mean only a little less strong spirits, he thought ruefully. Even so, the two hundred would buy him a cask.

He addressed Potter. ''What is it about me that offends you, mate?''

''Why . . . why, your immodesty for one. You haven't the decency to wear britches, and your exposed limbs are a disgrace. In front of women, too.''

''And what else?''

''Why—you have a squaw. You live in sin with a woman of the red race.''

''You don't know the half of it,'' said Mister Skye. ''And what else?''

''Why—you are the very apparition of war, and we come in peace and brotherhood. Your very presence among us belies our entire mission and purpose.''

Mister Skye smiled. ''Your peaceful presence, Mister Potter, will assure you of a peaceful journey through the lands of the peaceful Sioux and Cheyenne and Crow and Blackfeet.''

''My faith is in God's providence, and not that instrument of murder in your hands.''

Mister Skye understood the silence that followed. Potter had evoked the sword of God, and that meant much to these people. He didn't scorn it. Indeed, at sea as well as in this ocean of wilderness, there had been the inexplicable, the unexpected succor, the safe passage through the bowels of hell. No, far be it from him to scorn it.

"We'll meet you here at dawn." he said quietly, "and be off after breaking the fast. You'll have the rest of this day to reoutfit, rest your stock, trade off the gaunted ones. We'll be making road where there is none, so I'll want a shovel for every man, woman, and child. A pike pole and a sledge would help."

"We haven't the means," said Cecil.

"Find the means. Or forget your wagons and walk. I'll collect that letter of credit now, Reverend."

"Surely," said Cecil eagerly. He hastened to his wagon, found a black pigskin valise, extracted it, and started to hand it to Mister Skye.

"Don't step closer," said the guide sharply. He slid off Jawbone, who stood stock still, ears laid back, and collected the letter from the minister, glancing at it briefly.

"We are agreed then. Be ready at first light."

"But—" said Silas Potter. The word died in the breeze.

Cecil J. B. Rathbone looked pleased.

"Be ready," said Skye, touching Jawbone's flanks. The horse knew he was going to the sutler, and took him there. Jawbone was not a horse to tie to a hitchrail, and not a horse to leave in any intimate proximity with other beasts, two- or four-footed. So Mister Skye simply dismounted and left Jawbone to his fate. Jawbone, in turn, turned rump toward the store, stood guard, and eyed the world murderously, as Skye knew he would.

He found Colonel Bullock at his desk, and with a carrot-haired visitor wearing the collar of Rome and a suit of black broadcloth. He handed the letter to Bullock, who read it slowly.

"They've engaged you, then."

Mister Skye pondered. "More like I engaged them."

Bullock read it again. "It'll take a half a year to collect this," he said. "But I'll advance you a hundred eighty on account, taking twenty to negotiate this."

"Fair enough," said Mister Skye. "I will make a list. What have you by way of spirits? I am as dry as a Methodist sermon."

The red-haired priest grinned.

"Is it grain alcohol you want, or whiskey?"

This was always a profound dilemma. The grain alcohol, properly diluted, and with a twist of tobacco in it and a few peppers, was the great lubricant of every trappers' rendezvous he had ever attended. It tasted bygod awful, and drove redmen to vast excesses, not to mention white men; but it wasn't the stuff of his parched desire. Good aged corn whiskey was. Alone among life's terrible dilemmas, this one flummoxed Barnaby Skye.

"Well . . . well . . . twenty gallons of alcohol. No! The bloody whiskey, Bullock. A ten-gallon cask if you please. I'll have Mary and Victoria pick it up, and the rest."

"I perceive you have an unrequited thirst, Mistuh Skye," said the sutler.

"I do, I do."

"Let's see here. I have advanced you almost a hundred dollars of credit for the slant-breech Sharps, which this mission draft will cover and leave you with about ninety. The cask will run you twenty-eight. Not much left for a year's outfitting, Mistuh Skye."

Mister Skye groaned.

"But I have, in fact, a bit of business for you." The sutler smiled at Skye through the combed white strands of his full beard. "This, suh, is the Reverend Father Dunstan Kiley of the Society of Jesus. He's headin' your direction."

At that, Skye took a closer look. Father Kiley was a big, rugged, florid, freckled Irishman, perhaps forty, with observant eyes, taking in what there was to take in about the mountain man.

"Where might that be, Father?"

"Why, to the Bitterroot Valley, Mister Skye. To Fort Owen, which used to be St. Mary's Mission, established by my friend and colleague Pierre de Smet some years ago.''

Skye knew of the place. Father de Smet had built it in the 1840s to minister to the Flathead Indians and other nearby tribes. But funds were not available, and it had been closed and sold to David Owen, who had forted up there and become the first white settler in that area.

''But there's nothing of the mission now—''

''Of course, of course. My task is to bring the holy sacraments to our Indian converts there, teach as much as I can this summer, and let them know we'll return when we can.''

''A long dangerous trip for that.''

The priest shrugged. ''Obedience is a Jesuit vow. But I am bringing something precious to people who have asked for it, asked for us to return. And that is reason enough.''

''How'd you get here? You're a long way from the states.''

''I had intended to come with the wagon train—the only one leaving this year. But I was delayed, and came along alone, hoping to catch up. At times these last days it was in sight ahead of me, but I never quite made it.''

''You came all that way alone? Without protection?''

''I am told that we are everywhere respected among the plains Indians. The blackrobes . . .''

Mister Skye laughed.

So did Father Kiley.

''Are you armed?

''I'm armed, but only to make meat. If it's my fate to become a martyr, then that is my fate.''

''How are you traveling, mate?''

''A light cart and a dray. And I'm on a saddle horse. I thought to abandon the cart here, and pack from here on.''

''A sound idea,'' said Mister Skye. He leaned forward. ''Now tell me, Father Kiley, how you will deal with the Methodists, the missionary party I'm guiding.''

The priest turned somber. ''It's in the hands of God,''

he said quietly. "Let us hope for the best. The evening campfire usually draws people close. But if not, holy silence. Perhaps I shall camp apart. Certainly I can manage my own meals. If they object entirely, I will go my way alone. Perhaps you will give me some idea where I am to go?"

"You're coming with me, mate. Objections or not from the Methodists, I'm taking you as far as I can, which means to the Yellowstone and west. I have friends among the Crow you can engage to take you to Bitterroot Valley."

Father Kiley fussed with a pipe, tamped tobacco in it from a black pouch, and lit it with a sulfur match. "We haven't discussed your fee, Mister Skye."

"Nay, we haven't. I usually charge what the traffic will bear."

"And what might that be?"

"Why, a quart of Mister Bullock's finest."

The sutler laughed.

"I fear I would be leading you to perdition, Mister Skye."

"I've already been there and back more times than I can count, Father Kiley."

Father Kiley sucked his pipe noisily a moment. "A most satisfactory arrangement," he said slowly. "But one proviso . . ." He paused, a glint in his eye. "Share and share alike."

"Done!" cried Mister Skye. "A wet Jesuit in a party of dry Methodists. A man of faith and sauce. We shall make the prairies sing, Dunstan Kiley. We shall make the buffalo bulls bellow, the wolves bark, the ducks quack, and the rattlesnakes rattle."

"I *have* led you to perdition," chafed Father Kiley.

"The water's warm there," said Mister Skye. "We are leaving soon after dawn. I'll introduce you then." He arose. "Now I must put my squaws to work. There's a heap to do . . . Colonel, they'll be along presently and strip your shelves."

"That's what I'm afraid of," said Bullock.

"Squaws?" said Father Kiley.

"Mary and Victoria."

The priest stared.


Alexander Newton sat patiently in the chill dawn on the seat of his wagon, waiting for the oatmeal that Alice Sample was boiling up over the morning fire. He scorned coffee as a stimulant of the flesh, and therefore sinful, but the use of it was so common among others that he kept his silence about it. Someday, from a proper pulpit, he'd condemn it. The wagon swayed under him as Henrietta squirmed into her skirts underneath the canvas-covered bows. The air felt moist and sharp here in the bottoms, but he bore that patiently as well, doing his devotions as he waited.

The trip had been just short of an ordeal, and many was the time he wondered why he had volunteered. Perhaps because his father-in-law had been so enthused and persuasive. Neither he nor Henrietta shared that enthusiasm, but they perceived the need for a mission to the Blackfeet, and considered it a matter of high duty. There were benighted souls throughout the wild savage places of the west, and the church's mission was to reach them all.

Unlike his father-in-law, Alexander had no roots in the frontier. Quite the contrary. He had matured in amiable circumstances in Trenton, New Jersey, a settled, shady, civic-minded place. That perhaps was why these hundreds of miles through a desolate prairie in a bouncing wagon had seemed an ordeal. There was not even a privy for comfort and privacy, an ordeal for poor Henrietta. But they had a fiery faith, he and his Henrietta, and the pair of them intended to be torches, beacons, fires upon the hills, for generations to come.

Silently Alice Sample handed him a bowl of oatmeal gruel and a large spoon.

"Thank you, my dear Alice," he said. "You should smile, I think. God has given us a glorious day to begin the next leg of our mighty exodus."

But she didn't smile, and indeed turned her back to him and began to feed Miriam and Alfred, who had helped her gather wood and build the fire and now stood waiting.

"There's no need to be cross," he said. "We must all smile."

Across the meadow the buildings of the fort loomed, misty and lavender in the dawn light. Once in a while, the call of sentries had drifted to them in the night.

At another fire the Rathbones bustled, along with Silas Potter and James Method, and the smell of sizzling side-pork drifted toward him, annoying him because Alice Sample served only gruel, and that without salt or season. He noticed laughter over there too, for the Rathbones were early risers, unlike himself and Henrietta, and came alive almost from the moment they awakened and poured steaming coffee into themselves.

Well, God forgive them such fleshly exuberance, thought Alex. Henrietta emerged, and thumped silently toward the river brush for her necessary needs. Why couldn't man be born without bodies—and just be ethereal spirits? he wondered, puzzling as he often did about disgusting bodily functions that kept the soul from flying freely into the realm of heaven. It was a puzzle, why God fashioned men with bodies that made demands, hurt, required attention.

He finished the oatmeal and silently dropped the bowl and spoon into a kettle of boiling water that Alice Sample had over the coals for that purpose, and stepped down into the dewy grass. Time to find James and have him harness the oxen. There were three yoke to gather. The heavy, carved wooden yokes had to be dropped over the necks of each pair, and then the tugs attached. Alex had tried it once or twice, but it all was beyond him so he had gotten the mulatto to do it. Which was just as well, he thought. It permitted him to engage in spiritual exercises and devotions that, he was sure, brought the whole party closer to the Divine, and kept them all safe in the midst of all sorts of storms. Each to his own best labor.

No sooner had he collared James at his in-laws' campfire and set him to work than he noticed Skye—preposterous of the man to call himself mister, like some lord of the wilderness—and his entourage toiling toward them from out of the dark west. The burly guide he recognized easily enough, astride that terrible blue roan monster. And behind him, riding two ponies, were two Indian women, which surprised him. As they hove close he saw that one was gaunt and gray, while the other one was young and full-figured. Behind her on the little mustang sat a child, a boy he supposed. They sat scandalously astride, with their skirts hiked high and their brown calves brazenly displayed. He decided he'd have a private talk with Skye about that. Such things were not permissible. Behind them came two giant black mules, each heavily laden with canvas manties bulging with supplies, hitched down with taut ropes forming diamond patterns. And bringing up the rear was another pony dragging a travois with some sort of burden of skins tied to it.

Nor was that the whole of this strange parade. Beside Skye rode a man on horseback who looked very like a Romish priest. In fact, he was obviously a priest, in a suit black as sin, and a white collar that could only choke out all goodness. And beneath the flat-crowned, widebrimmed black hat was a florid square face, and a bit of hair as orange as the rising sun. And behind the priest came another packhorse, this one lightly laden.

Skye stopped the infernal blue roan an appropriate distance from the missionary fires, and surveyed the whole party and its preparations.

"I see you are not yet ready," he said. "Very well then. Henceforth at this time, and by this light, we will all be ready."

Alex Newton resented the tone of command in the wildman's rumbling voice.

Skye continued. "These are my wives. The younger is Mary, of the Shoshones, and the older is Victoria, of the Crow. And behind Mary is my son Dirk."

"Oh dear," said Henrietta.

Then the guide's voice rumbled through Alex's reveries again. "And this is the Reverend Father Dunstan Kiley. He's a Jesuit. He will accompany us much of the way and has engaged me as his guide."

A Papist, thought Alexander Newton. A bigamist, if that was the word for living in carnal sin with two squaws. And now a black Papist. The whole mission party would be in the grip of the prince of darkness, he thought wildly.

"I won't move an inch in this company," cried Silas Potter.

But Cecil J. B. Rathbone had started to laugh.

# Chapter 4

For four days Mister Skye led them along the ruts of the Oregon and California Trail, angling ever northwest on the south bank of the Platte. Because of the rampant Sioux, there was no other traffic. Swiftly, under his keen eye, the party had settled into a successful routine.

Mister Skye rode in the lead on his great blue horse, his silk stovepipe a black landmark for all to see. Close to him rode his younger squaw Mary, a striking woman, and with her their four-year-old son Dirk, a burly child like his father but with the warm dark features of his mother. The older squaw, Victoria, scouted lithely on the right flank, often ranging a mile or so from the party, and frequently out of sight. On the left flank, also far removed from the party, rode James Method, recruited by the guide because of his natural wilderness skill and keenly observant eyes. On occasion Mister Skye himself rode ahead to the crest of a hill or beyond, looking for surprises and finding none.

The Reverend Cecil J. B. Rathbone, observing all this as he walked beside his lead yoke of oxen, found himself

satisfied by it. Mister Skye was not for a moment careless, and ceaselessly maintained a casual but potent discipline in his entourage. Cecil was a happy man. With
each step he came closer to bringing Light to the benighted Blackfeet, a tribe that had fascinated him since
his youth because of its ferocious and warlike ways.

Sometimes Esmerelda trudged beside Cecil, lighten-
ing the load in the heavy wagon. She had become as
expert with the bullwhip as he, and could often relieve
him for a spell when he grew weary. She didn't exactly
share Cecil's dreams—what woman would?—but wherever Cecil went, she would go too, and enjoy herself if
she possibly could. If she could no longer entertain
women in sewing circles and reading societies, why, she'd
have the Blackfeet wives over for tea and talk. And perhaps slip into the gossip a word or two about the faith,
and the joy, and important things of life and death. She
might be middle-aged, but she knew she had a gem in
Cecil Rathbone, and her constant concern for his happiness and comfort was a pillar of her life.

The three yoke of oxen tugged a heavy load, the stuff
of Cecil's dreams, for in addition to the necessaries of
the trail, they hauled a new one-bottom plow, scythe and
sickle, and seed—corn, wheat, oats, and all the things
he supposed he would need to teach the Blackfeet about
farming and turn them into civilized sons of the soil. It
pleased him, that vision, and he had chosen his supplies
with care. He even included apple and cherry saplings
that would spring into an orchard, grape cuttings for a
vineyard, and in the loose herd behind, two milch cows
for butter and cheese and cream. These things, leading
to a settled agricultural life, would be the salvation of
the Blackfeet, and wean them from their warlike ways.
As they grew more pastoral, their minds would open to
God, he hoped. Thus it pleased Cecil Rathbone to haul
this precious cargo across an unknown continent, and he
guarded this special load as carefully as if it were the
Ark of the Covenant.

Cecil's wagon was a small one with upright bows, but

the Newtons' wagon, directly behind, was larger, with flared sideboards and bows that overhung the box fore and aft, similar to the majestic Conestoga, but smaller. Henrietta was hauling furniture, unwilling to part with it for the sake of the oxen. Cecil knew that only the mercy of abundant grass this unusual year, keeping the trail-worn oxen in tolerable shape, made it possible to haul that highboy and bedstead and little pump organ. Alex guided his oxen grimly, unrelieved by Henrietta, who mostly lounged inside the wagon or perched on its front seat. Cecil gave him credit for that: it wasn't Alex's nature to walk across a continent beside slow oxen, but he was doing it. Cecil felt faintly ashamed of his own Henrietta. He resolved to speak to her at a proper moment.

Behind the Newtons came the mule-drawn carriage driven by Silas Potter, and carrying the small supplies that he and James Method required. And behind them rolled the Samples' wagon, pulled by three span of big mules. Alice usually drove, handling the jerkline running to the fractious mules as easily as Clay. Their children on foot, as well as Clay on horseback, brought up the rear, herding the loose stock along. They had one spare yoke of oxen, and one spare span of mules among the loosely herded animals. It seemed a good arrangement, Cecil thought, and one that Mister Skye had insisted on.

But that was not the whole of the party, Cecil knew. There remained the alien presence of Father Kiley, the blackrobed Jesuit, in one sense a colleague, but in a more profound sense a rival and a menace. They rarely saw the man, for Skye had made him a hunter and scout. The priest's laden packhorse, following dutifully behind the guide's mules up near the younger squaw Mary, was the only concrete evidence, hour after sunny hour, of the presence of Rome. Cecil felt faintly envious: he would much rather have been out hunting—dangerous as it was in a high prairie that was home to the Sioux—than plodding along beside his lead oxen all the dusty hours of the day. Each day the priest had returned with meat. Once an antelope, and twice doe mule deer, each shot with a single, well-placed bullet and—Cecil supposed—only after a careful survey of the surrounding hills.

Mister Skye knew men, Cecil thought, and it was quite shrewd to keep the priest out beyond the horizons, where his presence would not fester in the minds of the Newtons and Silas Potter, or—Cecil admitted—in himself. For he scorned the Romish persuasion and all its ritual and arrogance, and he scorned above all this order of Kiley's, the Jesuits, that had been so merciless as the soldiers of the pope. He thought of Kiley as an emissary from the old world, a power that had no rightful place in this new one that freemen were creating here on a virgin continent. Still, Cecil thought, the priest had been civil enough, almost a shadow in the evening campfires, withdrawn and buried in his breviary while the long June light held. The truth of it was that he'd like to try his theology on the man, and taste the priest's—but he doubted that Father Kiley would seriously consider any of the ideas that Cecil entertained, and would dismiss him as a heretic. Well, Cecil thought tartly, maybe the Jesuit was the heretic.

It grew hot. Cecil wondered how the priest stood the dry, furnacelike winds in his black broadcloth and tight white collar. Cecil sweated freely in the June sun, his own suitcoat off and great dark patches spreading under his armpits. The oxen slavered and foamed, and sweated heavily over their shoulders, where the cruel wooden yokes dug into their flesh. Far above, an eagle circled, and then glided toward a hazy horizon. The bronze prairie had grown rugged and rocky, cut defiantly by the swift and murky Platte.

Esmerelda joined him, matching his stride with hers, looking cooler in her brown dress and numerous petticoats than he felt wearing half as much. It was her thinness, he supposed.

"You look done in," she said. "I'll drive for a while; lend me the whip. You go fetch a cup from the cask. It's still cool."

"I believe I will."

She took the bullwhip. "Gee!" she cried. "Giddap!"
She cracked the whip smartly, producing an expert pop.
The weary oxen tugged a bit harder.

She grinned ruefully at Cecil. "The teamsters have a
much better vocabulary." she said. "Sometimes I am
envious."

"You probably learned it from me."

He stood gratefully while two yoke of oxen passed by
and the wagon rattled up, and then found the dipper and
lifted mildly alkaline water from the river to his lips. He
was filled with the impulse to thank God for water, the
succor of life itself. Refreshed, he waited quietly for Alex
and his lead yoke, and then paced amiably beside his
sweaty son-in-law.

"Henrietta has the heatsickness," Alex said. "She's
resting. I've never known such heat. You'd think Skye
would stop and have mercy on the beasts. Look at the
poor creatures."

The unfortunate oxen that were dragging Henrietta,
her organ and other furniture, were indeed in trouble,
their tongues lolling out and spraying foam as they went.
They were dehydrated, Cecil judged. Normally three
yoke of oxen could walk, rather than pull. The pulling
had exhausted them. But so heavy was the Newtons'
wagon that these three yoke never stopped pulling, and
Cecil doubted that even four yoke could walk and not
strain into their wooden collars. How the beasts had survived this long he couldn't imagine.

"And what does Skye do? He sends that papist priest
out on easy hunts when the man could be helping, spell-
ing us, doing his share. I say we should get rid of Skye.
This trail's ten yards wide and smooth as a turnpike.
Don't see as we need a guide . . ."

Cecil nodded. It was talk. The Reverend Alexander
Newton knew perfectly well that soon enough they'd leave
the trail and plunge into land known only by mountain
men and guides, and still terra incognita to the United
States Army.

"Even if the road was clear all the way to Sun River,

we'd need Skye, or one like him, to deal with the Indians," Cecil said.

"We can hire someone else. Go on to the Platte River crossing and find someone else, and be done with this devilish bigamist and his wanton women and the half-breed brat. It's a scandal."

Cecil nodded cheerfully. Let the man talk, as long as they were plodding steadily toward the land of the Blackfeet.

"And that priest . . . I've been talking with Silas about it. We think you're playing with fire, Cecil. There are things that godly people don't accept; lines to be drawn. We've stepped across those lines, Cecil, and we can expect the wrath of God upon us. This devilish heat is just the beginning. I say we meet tonight after supper, and vote on it. I think the Samples are with me. I'm sure Henrietta is. James isn't; he is much taken with that barbarian, but he doesn't count."

"If there is a vote, his will be recorded," said Cecil sharply.

They had been climbing slightly, and now they struck a long downgrade into a broad coulee that stretched down toward the Platte. The gulch looked dry now, but could carry a heavy wash when it rained. And down below, the trail dropped into a rocky white streambed, twisted sharply and scaled the far side of the coulee at an angle. Cecil hastened forward to relieve Esmerelda, for steep slopes were tricky and dangerous. Now, instead of dragging the deadweight of the wagons, the oxen would act as brakes, especially the wheel oxen, whose yoke supported the wagon tongue between them. These beasts in particular bore the looming weight of the wagon pressing behind them. Cecil pulled a heavy chain from the wagon box and rough-locked a rear wheel by running the chain between the spokes and hooking it to the undercarriage so that the wheel skidded rather than rotated. With a wheel skidding, the looming wagon no longer pressured the faltering oxen. Sometimes it became necessary to chain some sort of drag, usually a log, behind the wagon to slow its descent or attach a special clawed shoe to the locked wheel. But Cecil judged that the grade would be soft enough this time to handle with a rough lock and the slowest possible traverse.

Esmerelda plucked up another chain and headed for the off side, where she could slip it between the spokes in an emergency, while Cecil gazed at her fondly. Through this whole trip she had been everywhere, contributing quietly to the well-being of all. There was scarcely time to wonder how Alexander was faring, or to hasten Henrietta out of that wagon in case it broke loose. But even as Cecil worried, he saw Mister Skye sitting aboard that terrible horse beside the trail, his gaze raking Cecil's wagon first, and then fixing upon the Newtons'.

"Your wagon's overloaded, mate."

Alex did not deign to answer.

"Lock a wheel while you can."

"I beg you to remember who is employer and who is employee," said Alex irritably.

Skye ignored him and addressed Henrietta, perched on the front seat. "You'd better get off and walk now, and be prepared to lock the wheels."

"I don't know about such things," she replied shortly.

The lead oxen were heading downslope now, the heavy wagon perched on the crest of the grade. Reluctantly Henrietta descended and began to trudge through the fierce heat. Then the groaning wagon rolled onto the downgrade, and pressed at once against the weary oxen, making them mince and drag their hoofs in the dust.

Mister Skye watched, but said nothing.

The locked wheel on Cecil's wagon proved to be the right medicine, and he negotiated the grade successfully. It bottomed with a sharp drop into a sandy streambed, and careened up an equally sharp rise on the far side, even as the trail twisted to the right to traverse the opposite grade obliquely. On the upgrade, past the turn, he unlocked the rear wheel and hung the chain back on its pegs, even as he grew aware that the Newtons' wagon was rolling downslope too fast, the trembling wheel oxen barely holding back their burden. Swiftly Cecil whipped his lead oxen forward, making room on the upslope, and then ran back to the gully to help if he could. The Newtons' wagon was not out of control, but neither was it descending at a safe speed. He saw Henrietta throw a small wooden chock in front of a rear wheel. The wagon tilted, slowed, and then righted itself as the iron wheel rolled over the chock. Then they hit the sandy bottoms, the front wheels bouncing sharply as they dropped into sand, even as the weary lead oxen whipped to the right to ascend the far bank and the angling grade beyond.

The tongue snapped as it was yanked violently to the right. The heavy wagon careened a few more feet into the sand and stopped. The three yoke of oxen, dragging the broken tongue, trotted a few feet up the far grade and stopped, trembling and slavering. The Reverend Alex Newton, red of face but containing his temper, stood staring at the wreckage. Cecil sighed. Mister Skye rode close, surveyed the damage silently, and rode upslope toward his own packmules and the waiting Mary. There he slid off Jawbone, opened a pack, extracted a heavy axe, and rode down the coulee toward the Platte a quarter of a mile distant. There were cottonwoods along its bank.

He will cut a new tongue, Cecil thought. Clay Sample arrived, toting his mechanic's box, and began at once to unbolt the tongue fragment.

"We're lucky the kingpin didn't go," he said as he loosened the shattered piece from the hounds.

"This wouldn't have happened if you had helped us at the top," snapped Henrietta.

Clay paused to stare at her.

"I am sure that Clay had his own problems, Henrietta," Cecil said hastily. "It was up to you and Alex to handle your wagon."

For an answer she clambered into the tilting wagon and pulled the flaps shut.

Cecil stood. "Let us thank God the matter isn't worse," he said gently. This bickering of godly people shamed him.

"It's another warning," cried Silas Potter. "When we traffic with devils, we must expect this and worse."

"Where's James? Why isn't he here helping?" demanded Alex.

Cecil spotted James on the distant ridgetop, sitting easily, rifle across his saddle. And on the rear ridge was gaunt Victoria. The pair of them were their sentries out upon the prairie, now that they were caught in these coulee bottoms.

"Guarding us well, I believe," said Cecil mildly.

"He's loafing is what he is. Turning lazy on us, thanks to your Mister Skye."

Clay Sample hammered the last bolt, and Cecil pounded the splintered tongue free. "Cottonwood won't make much of a tongue, but it's what we have," Clay said as he rolled out from under the wagon. From down on the Platte came the whacks of methodical chopping as Mister Skye felled a cottonwood limb. While they waited for him, Esmerelda circulated among them with a dipper of cool water.

"Alex," said Cecil, "you might profitably drive your yoke down to the river for a drink. Here. I'll help you unhitch the tongue."

"I was just going to," snapped Alex. Together they drove the tired animals down to the riverbank and let them drink their fill. Mister Skye had dropped a well-chosen limb, and was clipping the branches off of it.

"We're just in time to drag that back," Cecil said.

Skye nodded. Sweat blackened his buckskin shirt. He stared long and hard at Alex, but said nothing. Then his gaze roamed the ridges, settling first on James, and then on Victoria, until he seemed satisfied that nothing was amiss. The priest was nowhere in sight.

Mister Skye's silence seemed somehow even worse than his occasional snarls. When the guide issued his quiet commands, the whole party understood him and obeyed. But this silence! It made Cecil shiver. Who knew what somber thoughts Skye was entertaining? The things he did not say to Alex Newton—or perhaps himself—screamed in Cecil's ears.

They chained the cottonwood log to the tugs, and a red-faced Alex Newton hawed the three yoke back up the coulee. In two more hours Clay Sample had expertly barked and squared the limb, hewed it into shape, and bored the bolt holes through it with his auger and bit. In another hour the new tongue was bolted in place and the oxen hooked up. The mishap had cost them half a day, and Cecil supposed they'd camp soon, as they strained their way up the long grade and out upon the high plains again, driving straight into a low and blinding sun.

He worried about the evening's camp. There'd likely be blame and temper, and somehow the whole trouble would be laid to Mister Skye and Mary and Victoria—and the priest. God spare us that, he thought. He intended to use a strong hand if he must, and resort to his rare rebukes. High time this surly group looked up to the great heavens and thanked the good Lord for this Mister Skye.

The supper hour came and went, but Skye pushed on, and they followed in sullen silence. They were all trail-hardened, having come seven hundred miles across empty prairie, and they endured it quietly. Then at last they descended a long grade into the bottoms of the Platte, and a halt was called close to the river. The oxen and mules and horses were set out to graze, with young Alfred Sample detailed to keep an eye on them, and the surrounding hills. Later the beasts would be driven into a rope corral which Skye had devised, with the three wagons and the buggy forming its four corners. That was familiar to them too. In the larger train from Independence the wagons had been formed into a defensive circle each night, and the animals kept within, to keep them from the cunning hands of Omaha and Pawnee horse thieves.

Even as the party plunged wearily into its evening tasks, Father Kiley rode in, this time with the tongue and hump ribs of a buffalo cow wrapped in canvas behind the saddle on his nervous bay horse. There would be a treat for all when the tender hump meat was done. The priest gave meat to Alice Sample and Esmerelda, who did much of the cooking because Henrietta felt indisposed. The rest of the meat he gave to Mary and Victoria, for Skye's mess, which was also his own. He smiled quietly, walked off to the river to wash, and seemed to vanish into the dusk from whence he had appeared minutes before.

When at last the meat had browned and the keen fragrance of dripping fat on the fire wafted through the evening air, Cecil drew them together and blessed the food and praised God for this abundance. Skye, Mary and Victoria, and the priest ate separately, but on this occasion he stood beside the Reverend Mister Rathbone during his grace.

"We're at Bridger's Crossing," Mister Skye said abruptly. "This is where we leave the Oregon Trail. The crossing is no easy matter. The water's high and we may have to build rafts. Or tack canvas or hide over the beds of the wagons and float them. Either way, we have work ahead. From now on, there's no trail. If you insist on taking these wagons, we'll shovel our way down every cutbank, and shovel our way up the other side." He paused, staring at Alex Newton. "Your wagon is overloaded, mate," he continued. "I don't know what's in it, but this is where it stays. We're going out upon a land with no trails, with rocks and holes and gulleys. That wagon won't last ten miles. Your worn-out oxen even less. That ballast must go or we capsize."

"I brought my pump organ, bedstead and highboy seven hundred miles and I'm not going to surrender them now," Henrietta Newton retorted shrilly. "The organ is for the church. I play it; that's my gift to God and the people we will redeem. If it stays on this riverbank, then I . . . why, I must stay.''

Mister Skye didn't argue. He walked back to his own fire, where Mary and Victoria and the priest were waiting.

''It's come to a head,'' whispered Silas Potter. ''Now we will free ourselves of that barbarian.''

# Chapter 5

Silas Potter quietly disapproved of the Reverend Cecil J. B. Rathbone. And Esmerelda Rathbone too. The pair of them were too lax, too spiritually loose, to command an important mission. He had his doubts about the entire mission, and particularly about Rathbone's plan to show the Blackfeet pastoral ways and turn them into civilized and educated farmers before stressing the Gospels.

Silas had been hired as a lay teacher, to instruct the savages in grammar and arithmetic, in reading and writing, and science and the wisdom of Western civilization. That was all well and good, he thought: he had a bachelor's degree that proclaimed his ability to do so. But he also had a year of divinity school, and he regarded himself as a keeper of the faith, destined to celebrate its orthodoxy and drive out heresies and bad thinking. And in his estimation, Cecil Rathbone was trafficking with evil now.

Grudgingly he respected Father Kiley, for he saw in the Jesuit his counterpart, the pope's soldier enforcing the faith. Of course they were corrupt and wrong, those people, and Silas was careful not to carry the analogy too far. Nonetheless, he saw himself as the Methodist Jesuit, his mission to save other Methodists from weakness and sin, and keep the faith pure. Toward this end he studied the Scriptures assiduously, underlining passages, comparing texts. He knew that in theological debate he could be acid and biting, even withering in his contempt for those who strayed.

Potter was a humorless young man, thin and weak, not from illness—he was in blooming health—but because his scholarly life had cloistered him indoors, and his muscles had atrophied. He was fair, and could burn to a crisp in minutes under a summer sun, and this had always been his rationale for avoiding the great outside. At least until now. He wore a broad-brimmed flat hat that kept the sun off his face, and under it small rimless glasses that gave him the distant vision he lacked. Even protected by the hat, his face had grown red and chapped under the fierce western sun and wind.

Unlike the Newtons, who indulged their corpulent flesh and foisted off the labor of the trail on others as much as possible, Silas did his share without complaint, being careful to go a shade beyond what was required of him as a matter of virtue and general principle; he considered sloth a sin. His helpfulness was not inspired by any sympathy for the burdens on others, such as the Samples, but by a sense of sublime duty. To do his share and more was virtue, and the virtuous were close to God. So in all matters he acted with care. He treated James Method cordially, as was his duty. Not that he, a considerable scholar, had anything in common with James, an escaped slave. But Method was a child of God, and therefore worthy of proper treatment. And so the pair of them shared a tent and wagon amicably and politely, though they could scarcely be called friends.

He addressed others gravely, often blinking behind his glasses. So far he had not been smitten by a woman, though he was not immune to their attractions. That had been a matter that troubled him terribly, and led him into

moments of secret despair. For in the night he sometimes
lusted, vague images of feminine faces floating through
his mind, young women he had seen once, or met a time
or two. Worse, in the night his mind turned to their figures, the exquisite forms beneath their petticoats and
skirts, and he knew this to be lust and of a devilish nature, for all the appetites of the flesh were, in his eyes,
sinful and only the things of the spirit were of God. He
prayed he might be free of his body; that it might become an inert thing so that his soul could enjoy the pure
rapture of the spirit. He did not perceive these lusts to
be the natural hungers of a young man, but rather an
alien appetite instilled by the devil, and many a time,
startled awake out of his lustful dreams, he prayed fer-
vently for release from the devil, who plainly possessed
him or a part of him, and was his private torment.

This had happened two nights in a row. His mind, half
asleep, had entertained visions of Skye's young squaw
Mary, dark and comely and voluptuous in the loose
buckskins she wore. She never braided her lustrous blue-
black hair, but let it fall loose over her shoulders and
breasts. Her brown eyes were as warm and inviting as a
doe's. From time to time she had looked thoughtfully at
Silas, sizing him up. She had stared with equal curiosity
and intuition at the other white males, but Silas was certain that he had somehow galvanized her particular interest, and that her interests were wanton. Certainly she
had smiled at him, and had been careless in her dress,
often revealing her young honey-colored arms and neck
and graceful shoulders to him. Perhaps later she would
become stocky, as so many of her people did, but now
she looked lithe and supple and a man's dream of fleshly
paradise. And cheerful as well, with shy smiles toward
them all, and adoration in her eyes when she gazed at
Mister Skye, which Silas often caught her doing, to his
annoyance.

Brazenly she rode her horse astride, exposing smooth
knees, a portion of female limb that Silas had never seen.
It had made his heart pound. In the night, tossing in his

bedroll, he had imagined himself performing the marital act, the sacred business, with her, she beneath him wide-eyed and smiling. It was too much. Trembling, he had awakened and walked through the camp under the icy stars, to purge himself. Now, he knew, he must drive Skye, his dark concubines, and that whore of Rome out of this place, for the sake of them all, or surely God in his wrath would turn this trip into a journey through hell.

Now the chance had come. Skye had issued an ultimatum of sorts about Henrietta Newton's furniture—even the pump organ, which would grace the little church they would erect on Sun River! There would have to be a meeting, apart from the demonic ears of Mister Skye and his women and that priest. And they had to overrule Cecil Rathbone. If not, if the head missionary persisted, Silas intended to take the dissidents—himself, probably the Samples, and surely the Newtons—back to Fort Laramie. They could establish a mission right there in the safe lee of the fort, and there would be work enough for ten missionaries among the soldiers and the lost creatures of Squaw Town. That might be better anyway than this wild plunge into a frightening wilderness to minister to a tribe noted for its ferocity and evil.

After their buffalo hump supper, Silas had demanded a private meeting of the mission group. Surprisingly, Cecil obliged at once: they would gather after the dishes had been washed and the chores done, beyond the herd along the riverbank. Cecil even volunteered to tell Mister Skye of it, and that it would be confined to the missionary party.

In a lavender twilight they gathered quietly, except for the Sample children who had slipped into their bedrolls.

"Pray, what is on your mind, Silas?" asked Cecil amiably. His very kindness enraged Potter. Why couldn't the man simply be unreasonable, instead of merely wrong?

"Some of us feel it's time for changes," he began tartly, his fevered eyes focusing on one and another of them. "Henrietta has brought her organ seven hundred miles, and there is no reason to abandon it now. It's unbearable, this instrument we have brought so far to praise God with song, lying here on the trail, to be smashed to bits by savages.

"Another thing. We must dismiss this wicked and sinful guide and his concubines, and rid ourselves of that priest. We are trafficking in evil. Skye will start wars, murder redmen whenever we meet them. I despise the Jesuit, but he and his kind have roamed the far west in their black robes, unarmed, and have had little trouble with the savages. We don't need guides like Skye. We must establish our peaceful and friendly intent and trust in Divine Providence instead of murderous weapons."

He turned nervously to James Method, wondering whether the African would carry tales back to Skye. "Most of us oppose your policies, Cecil. Perhaps we have more faith than you. We believe we can carry that organ to Sun River, and the rest of Henrietta's furniture too. And we wish to do it without Skye. The longer we keep him near, the more we provoke God and invite his wrath. Already there have been signs, the unnatural heat, the snapped wagon tongue. Much worse might come if we persist in our faithless ways."

There settled an uneasy silence. Silas knew he had not minced words.

"Why, perhaps you're right," said Cecil. "Let us take a silent moment to seek guidance, eh?"

Silas did not pray. He raged at the senior missionary for being all too accommodating. He wanted matters to shatter right then and there, so that he and the Newtons could turn around and head for Fort Laramie, and holy work there.

Then Cecil said, "Alex, how do you and Henrietta feel about this?"

"Why, perhaps Silas has stated it a bit strongly. But something must be done. We would grieve to abandon the organ, and the few small amenities we have hauled so far, through such a terrible wilderness. And of course Skye and the priest trouble us. He parades his sinfulness before our eyes. And issues commands as if we were his servants. Frankly, Cecil, we think he's loathsome. Surely there are other guides within reach.''

"Clay?'' asked the Reverend Mister Rathbone.

"Well, I tell you. We're doing right fine, except some overworked, I reckon. Seems like Mister Skye has got us this far safely. I figure he's right about that extra weight.''

Silas Potter felt betrayed. The trouble with those yeoman farmers was that they never thought for themselves.

"James?''

The black eyed the others nervously. He was not used to being consulted, and it plainly troubled him. "Ah feel safe as a frog on a lilypad with Mister Skye keeping track. If he says we should lighten up the loads, I guess that's what we should do.''

Silas had expected that. The half-civilized African had little sense of sin or virtue, goodness or evil.

"Henrietta?''

"I have no intention of abandoning that organ. Or anything else,'' she said. "Except maybe this hare-brained trip to nowhere. I wish to return to Fort Laramie. There's work for us there.''

Silas Potter felt delighted. He had primed her to say that. Cecil J. B. Rathbone cocked an eyebrow when he heard his most cherished dream being called hare-brained by his own daughter, but he showed no other sign of distress.

"Alice?''

She smiled, making dimples in her cheeks. "I'm in the middle, I guess. I think Mister Skye is really a comfort. But if he's objectionable in some way . . .'' her voice trailed off. "I know how much the furniture means to Mrs. Newton,'' she added, folding and unfolding her hands.

Silas smiled. The woman would accept any course of action.

"And my dear Esmerelda?''

"Why I was thinking we might redistribute things between the wagons, and then Henrietta and Alex could keep the furniture." Mrs. Rathbone's practical bent irritated Silas. Compromisers always ended up compromising their faith.

But Cecil picked up on it. "Well, there's something to it. The wagons are lighter than when we left Independence. Lots of food used up. Suppose we work something out. Mister Skye's quite right, the Newtons won't get ten miles with that load going overland. I imagine, Henrietta, if you abandoned the heavy highboy, and we and the Samples divided the bedstead between us, and we put a hundred pounds or so of the Newtons' supplies on one of the spare mules, we might make a stab at it—"

"I will not surrender anything," snapped Henrietta. "Least of all the highboy."

"My dear, your oxen are near collapse. The spare yoke we've been rotating are trailworn too, gaunted down. There's really not much—"

"If we have faith we'll perform miracles," said Silas Potter.

"Perhaps we could slow down and let the animals graze more. Maybe five miles a day," suggested Alex Newton.

Cecil Rathbone sighed. "It is almost July. We are only halfway. Seven or eight hundred miles more, I reckon. At five miles a day, we'd arrive at Sun River in late November. A northern wilderness devoid of shelter, in late November. It'll be bad enough making a road up there . . ."

Agitated, he paced back and forth, hands clasped behind him. Then he halted.

"We will unload the furniture here. All of it. Perhaps Mister Skye will help us cache it so we can recover it later. There must be ways. Then we'll redouble our efforts. If the oxen tire, we'll abandon a wagon, too. If the oxen die—and they might—we'll pack what we can. We'll do what we must."

Cecil stared at them, waiting for them to defy him and his authority as the senior missionary. No one did.

"Mister Skye is our safe passage across this wild land. Indeed, his conduct is deplorable, and one bridles at his ah . . . peculiar marital circumstances and all the rest. But he's a man, a man to get us through. As for the priest, he's not our business. He's supplied our meat and has been an able scout, keeping watch. He'll be leaving us anyway, on the Yellowstone. I pray that you accept these matters, and tomorrow we'll be on our way."

He was done, then. Silas fashioned a riposte in the silence and nerved himself to begin.

"No," he said. He hated the shrillness of his own voice, which seemed to echo across the murky river to the brown bluffs beyond.

"Unless we discharge Skye and proceed with the furniture, the Newtons and I are going to return to Fort Laramie. They need us there, a mission to the soldiers and the lost souls of Squaw Town. I'm sure the Samples will join us, too. There in the safe valley of the Platte."

"I see," said Cecil slowly. He looked melancholy for a moment, but then he brightened. "Sleep on it, and we'll discuss it in the morning."

"A night won't change anything," Silas cried. "We won't traffic with evil."

Cecil stared at his daughter and son-in-law, and they looked away. He glanced at the Samples, who seemed caught and unable to decide what to do. And then a sadness settled upon the old minister's craggy face. "Perhaps Esmerelda and James and I might go on . . . if James is willing. I have a dream. A dream of a peaceful land, of a people finding God's grace, of farms and fat cattle and tall haystacks and young Blackfeet building a new world . . ."

Nothing more was said, or needed to be said. As the shattered party trudged back to its camp, Silas Potter felt pleased. It had been so easy. James Method walked beside him, back to the tent they shared.

"Reckon we'll be saying goodbye come morning," he

said softly. "Ah'm a man to stay with Mister Skye. And with the Rathbones."

They stood quietly, watching the Samples gather the grazing herd together to contain it for the night in the rope corral. The animals had had less time to graze this evening because Mister Skye had pressed on, almost to sunset. But they were docile, having watered at the riverbank and spread out over the lush grass of the bottoms. Jawbone was not among them. Skye kept that violent animal separate, close to his lodge, where he usually grazed all night. Even in the dusk Silas could see that the oxen and mules looked gaunted. All the more reason to return to Fort Laramie, he thought tartly. Then the last of the stock drifted inside the rope, and Alfred tied the line tautly to the Samples' wagon.

A milch cow bawled once. A horse nickered, and then silence settled. Silas stood outside the tent—he needed to make water but never did so until the others were retired, out of some natural delicacy—and admired the long streak of blue light riding the northwestern horizon, slightly sawtoothed to suggest that there were mountains there, far across the brooding and mysterious high plains. Then he found the moment to relieve himself, and turned in. James Method was already asleep in his roll, breathing through his open mouth. The ground felt hard, but at least dry, and Silas refused to complain. Complaining was an act of self-indulgence. Eight nights, coming across the plains, they had made a wet camp, and set their bedrolls down in soft, cold, damp ground that moistened his blankets and numbed him. Two of those nights had been pouring rain, and there had been nothing for it but to shiver in his sopping roll, and pray for a warm dawn.

He drifted into a troubled sleep. The bare earth always kept him restless, and not even the exertions of the trail, day after weary day, brought him the kind of oblivion at night that he craved. He began to dream again, the sinful images of Mister Skye's squaw, warm-skinned and voluptuous, drifting through his misted soul. She laughed and invited and beckoned, and he grew tempted, though a stern voice from heaven itself warned him, warned him not to surrender—

A rush of hoofs on grass outside his tent awakened him. Then the thunder of a small stampede, squealing horses, bawling oxen, braying mules. And then a piercing "Hiyah, hiyah," the nasal cry less human than animal, and harsh as wilderness. And then a booming shot. The rattle of other shots. A harsh zip as something seared through the canvas above him. Another boom, and Mister Skye's roar, and the crackle of the lighter rifles of the squaws. And then silence.

Silas Potter quaked in his robes. "You all right?" came the soft slur of James. "We been having our stock stole."

Stock? In horror now, Silas pulled his wire-rimmed spectacles over his ears, and peered out, fearing the bash of a tomahawk cleaving his brain. But it was quiet. Dawn light streaked the east, and he supposed it might be four or five, this time of year. In the murky gray light he searched for the stock. He could see not an animal. The corral ropes curled on the grass between the wagons. Every ox, every mule and horse, were gone. He knew instantly what had happened: this was God's punishment upon them for employing Mister Skye. This was exactly what he had warned of, the wrath of God, leaving them out here in these gray wastes, helpless, abandoned, without so much as a pony to take them back to Fort Laramie.

He spotted Cecil standing beside his wagon, disheveled and shocked, in his bare feet and nightshirt.

"I told you so," cried Silas. "I warned you."

Then the rest were up, carrying rifles, nightshirts stuffed into britches, women peering modestly from the puckerstring holes of their wagons. And not a horse in sight.

Out of the gray murk Mister Skye loomed, in his buckskins and some moccasins, oddly calm although his shining new Sharps was crooked in his arm at the ready.

"Gone! The thieving redskins stole our stock," cried Alex in his grating nasal voice.

"We'll get them back," said Skye quietly.

"And how do you propose to do that?" snapped Silas. "Every animal we possess has been stolen. Why weren't you guarding?"

Skye looked surprised. "Should we have posted a guard? Aren't we on a peaceful journey, our intent plain to others? Would you have stood guard, you and Mister Method, and Mister Newton, and Mister Sample, and Mister Rathbone, two hours in the middle of each night? Ready and willing, of course, to shoot raiding Indians on sight?"

"You didn't ask us. You're incompetent as well as immoral."

From beyond the far hills came an unearthly whinny, and Barnaby Skye smiled.

# Chapter 6

The neighing had sounded like the cry of a ghost horse cantering across the sky, but Mister Skye knew it was Jawbone. He could see very little. The sun had not yet torn loose from the shoulders of the prairie to the east, and the gray gloom obscured the terraced bluffs to the south of the river, that still rose step by step into pale night, miles of dark grasses.

The missionary party looked stricken. They wandered disconsolately from wagon to wagon, wagons that seemed anchored to earth like frigates without canvas rocking at the end of a hawser. In a moment of time these schooners had turned into useless hulks. The priest emerged from his small tent, dressed in black as usual, but without his white collar. He had started a beard, and now the red stubble blurred his jawline and made him look disheveled. He stared at the empty animal compound, saw that his horses, too, had been taken, and then trudged toward the river to begin his ablutions.

Again they heard that terrible shriek, the scream of the

ghost horse clattering over the clouds of heaven, making the grassy hills cringe into their rocky bones.

"What was that?" cried Alex Newton.

"Your salvation," rumbled Skye.

"I have never heard a sound so . . . demonic," said the Reverend Rathbone.

Mister Skye laughed. "It's from the devil, all right."

Cecil drew himself up. "Well, Mister Skye, what are we to do? We are marooned in this sea of grass, as surely as sailors on a sandy isle."

"March back to Fort Laramie," snapped Silas Potter. "I warned you of God's wrath. I warned you! Now we have no choice but to walk whatever it is, seventy, a hundred miles."

"More like a Cheyenne horse-stealing party, mate, than the wrath of God. Four or five of them. Not enough to slaughter us in our beds, but enough to snatch a few horses."

"You may see worldly events as merely that, Skye, but I see God's purpose in all things."

"It's Mister Skye, mate."

James Method grinned.

"We need a miracle," Silas Potter said, "and I doubt that you'll supply one."

"We do need that," Cecil agreed somberly. "We are a long way from anywhere. And with women and children in our party."

The northeastern horizon, far across the Platte, vibrated with golden light now, and then the top of the sun emerged like a golden caterpillar crawling along the far blue ridges, throwing long light, slats of fire, across the wide land and into the western dark.

Now Skye saw them, five tiny gold coins cantering over the crest of a hazy ridge miles away, and off to the left, a sixth shining coin he knew, even from that vast expanse, was Jawbone. Then his horse stopped and neighed once again, closer this time, like the shriek of werewolves.

"What *is* that dreadful sound?" cried Henrietta.

It drew their eyes to its source, and now the six running animals became visible, tiny dots of light, now in sight, now plunging into blue coulees not yet lit by the horizontal sun. Closer they came, while mortals stared, fascinated, by the flight, and by the skillful herding of the giant blue roan that drove the rest.

"I don't suppose that's miracle enough for you, mate," said Mister Skye, addressing Silas Potter.

The young man paled. "The Scriptures say that evil spirits can perform wonders."

"Some devil," said Cecil acidly.

Then the animals clambered down a steep slope into the river bottom. They were, precisely, Mister Skye's own creatures: Jawbone, the two giant black mules, and the three wiry Indian ponies. Those, and no other.

Then at last they stood, sweated dark and trembling from long miles of running, while Jawbone slavered and heaved.

"It looks like any miracles you come up with are strictly for yourself, Mister Skye," Alex Newton said.

He ignored the remark. "Start to tar or canvas the wagon boxes," he said. "Get a move on now. We're going to float them across soon."

They gaped at him.

"Get along with you," he growled. "Have faith."

Victoria and Mary slipped horsehair bridles onto two ponies, and led them toward Skye's lodge.

Jawbone stood panting, legs stiff and head lowered. Skye walked to the great horse, who pressed his head into the guide's chest, while the man ran his thick hands down the great roan's knotted neck, beneath his mane. It was a reunion. "Aye, you did it again, lad," whispered Mister Skye into Jawbone's ragged ear. The horse sucked air, and butted him gently.

"Who might they have been, sir?" Cecil asked.

Skye shrugged. "Cheyenne most likely. Sioux. Arapaho."

He hurried toward his lodge, Jawbone following of his own accord, breathing more quietly now. Skye hated to put the sweat-stained animal to work, but there was no helping it. He dropped the apishamore over Jawbone's back, and then the light pad saddle of the Crow people over it, and cinched it tight, and clambered aboard.

The missionaries had done nothing, only gaped at him as he steered Jawbone southward, up the layered land and out of the Platte Valley, into a choppy sea of grass. He was in no hurry, and let the blue horse pick its way easily, resting at a walk. Now the long sun gilded the grasses, cutting shadowed trenches in the prairie, glowing off east-facing bluffs.

Southward he rode, his new rifle cradled loose in his arms, his vision on horizons that receded before him like the very curve of the earth. The oxen would not be far, he knew. They could lumber along only a little, and then would have fallen behind. He hoped only that the horse-stealing party hadn't stopped to slaughter them, driving arrows into the hearts of the white men's buffalo. As for the mules, they'd run longer, be farther along before dropping out, unless the raiders made a point of keeping them. But what warrior of the northern plains lusted for mules? In the end, the raiders would have the horses—the Jesuit's two, and the Methodists' four—the ones ridden by James Method, by Cecil, by Clay Sample, and the spare. He'd get those six too, if he could. They would be needed.

Now the sun brightened the great massif of the Medicine Bows to the west, the first great chain of the Rockies which would ultimately funnel the raiding party south, up and down vast ridges. This land close to the mountains reminded him more of the ocean than did the flatter prairies to the east, as if the mountains were tidal waves, and the great ridges the churning of the mutinous seas. He rode easily, at home in this stretching place. The seas had given him that.

He had been born in England in comfortable circumstances, his father a successful merchant trader who sent his barks to the ports of Portugal and Africa and back. At the age of fourteen, looking ahead to a time at Cambridge and then his father's trading house, he had been idling near the company docks on the Thames when he was suddenly surrounded by several of His Majesty's sailors, rough sorts, who cornered him and pinned him easily.

"Why here's a powder monkey," said one. "Come along, matey."

And they had dragged him bodily, the boy sobbing and fighting, aboard the H.M.S. *Jaguar*, and down into its stinking cramped hold, into a brig so low he couldn't stand up. He never saw his family, or England, again. He didn't even see daylight, or the sun, until the frigate rode the sea, sailing south by southwest, bound for Portugal and a load of limes that the admiralty had belatedly employed to prevent dread scurvy, and on down the coast to South Africa.

A powder monkey he had become, and a roustabout who cleaned slop pails and scoured decks with holystone . . . and starved. For at the mess, larger and meaner men stole his food and laughed, and if he protested at all, cuffed him and sent him sprawling. No one cared, least of all those fancily dressed officers who captained the vessel and seemed to run it with terror and whip and the threat of bodily harm. He weakened and knew he would not last long, and as he performed his bitter chores, wrestling heavy kegs of acrid gunpowder up precarious passageways from the bowels of the ship to the upper decks where cannon filled each port, he did not know whether he cared to live at all. But some youthful spirit raged, a boyish will to live, and one day he walked to mess with a wooden belaying pin wrapped in a sack.

That time, when a particularly brutal sailor and bullyboy named Larch mocked him and grabbed at his gruel, he swung the pin and knocked Larch cold. They leapt on him in an instant, pulverizing him with their horny rope-scarred fists. Even in his weakened condition he clobbered one and another with the belaying pin before they pinned him to the deck and poured slop over him.

But after that no one stole his food. And slowly he filled out, grew burly and strong. There was a lesson in it. From that point on, win or lose—and he lost more often than he won—he fought whenever he felt himself trespassed. He became known as a brawler, and half the time he nursed injuries, a nose mashed and mashed again, torn ears, ripped flesh, bruised kneecaps where belaying pins had shattered them. The officers looked upon him with distaste, and sniffed at the young sailor, and never inquired into his origins or how he came to be aboard King George's vessel of war. He came to know the ship's foul brig intimately, and every cockroach in it. Those above him were called mister and sir and even lord, and wore clean clothing and slept in private quarters, and had property, while he slept in a miserable hammock in the pitching, rocking fo'castle and owned utterly nothing but his own body. Someday he would be mister, like his father, and unlike every humble tar grinding out life in the bowels of the ship.

They knew him for a potential deserter, and never let him off ship at port that first year. Later, when the Royal Navy plunged into the Kaffir War of 1819 against the native Xhosa, Barnaby Skye finally set foot on land, closely watched. He never forgot what it felt like to stand on solid earth, momentarily free from the tyrannical confines of the hull that had oppressed and degraded him. He would be free. The moment didn't come until 1826, when the H.M.S. *Jaguar* braved the dreaded bar of the Columbia River, on the far-off Pacific coast of North America, to visit the new Hudson Bay post, Fort Vancouver. There, in the fog, the powerful man Barnaby Skye had become jumped overboard carrying only a wooden belaying pin, and emerged, dripping, on the cold south bank of the river, in a disputed land the Americans were starting to call Oregon. That belaying pin was all he needed. All his years as a sailor he had brawled with one, and now he could throw it with such accuracy that he could kill small game, and defend himself with it, even against a man with a knife. He survived, found succor, and hated the land of his birth, though not entirely. And from that moment, he permitted no man to address him as Skye. He became Mister Skye, an awesome man of the mountains, harder and more daring than others, cautious, wily, but a terror in war. He soon led the fur brigades of Mister John Jacob Astor, and later Monsieur Pierre Chouteau of St. Louis, becoming, insensibly, a legend among the mountain men, and even more a legend among the Indian tribes that had the misfortune to run into him.

This vast continent was better than the sea. And he steered his own ship, Jawbone beneath him, down the plain trail of broken grasses, hoofprints, and excrement that marked the exodus of the missing animals. A party of young Cheyenne horse stealers, he thought, not knowing why he thought it. He had simply become so alive to the land, so attuned to its spirit and its wild people, that he knew without knowing why he knew.

The carcass of an oxen hulked on a rise, and when he drew close he recognized it as one of those worn hard by the Newtons. The last of its precarious energy had been consumed in this pell-mell run. Over the brow of the next divide he found two more, one dead, the other still alive, breath staggering in and out of its lungs spastically. He let it go. If it got to its feet soon, it might survive the wolves. If not, it might be eaten alive. Three gone. The trail ran relentlessly up and down ridges, crosswise of the water courses, so that he never knew what he would find as he topped each ridge. He held Jawbone to a walk, letting him rest after his long harsh run. He knew approximately what Jawbone had done, herding his own animals away from the flanking braves, and he knew what he might find ahead.

In the next long swale he found the oxen, still dark with sweat and dirtied over from rolling their soaked bodies in dust. Some lay on the ground; others stood still, head down, legs propped, refusing to sink to earth.

One quiet one looked dead or dying. Four gone, two yoke. There in the same swale but farther down were the mules, which had lost ground to the fleeter horses. The run had been easier for them than for the oxen, and now they grazed. Six mules, all belonging to the Samples, all suffering no more than a winding.

Mister Skye did not stop, but let Jawbone carry him farther, over the brow of the next ridge. The trail grew smaller now, but still plain in the early sun, a path of bent and crushed grass leading ever southward. Now he could make sense of it, and thought there were about five raiders, five young warriors on their ponies, several miles ahead. From the crest of the ridge he stared down a long gravelly slope broken by outcrops of layered tan rock and occasional copses of cottonwoods. Jawbone pricked up his battered ears. There down the slope, near the bottom, lay a dark form on harsh fragmented shale rock. It looked human. Now Skye paused and scanned the wide land, dwelling particularly on the copses of cottonwoods and the rocky outcrops that might conceal other life. He took his time. He always took his time, and survived because of it. Beyond the form on the ground, the trail continued onward, broken grasses shining in the slanting sun, over the next long shoulder of sagebrush-covered land. Here is where it had happened; where Jawbone had fought his own war. The horse beneath him seemed to expand at the recollection, some evil pride making him mince as his rider eased him downhill, far more alert for trouble than previously.

It was a young Cheyenne, scarcely sixteen, Mister Skye thought, staring lifelessly at the sky. He had bled to death from a compound fracture of his right leg, and another of his right forearm. Cheyenne fletching of the arrows still in the quiver on the young man's back. Cheyenne warlock. Each tribe had its own way of making moccasins, and these were Cheyenne. Just above the boy's right ankle there were toothmarks, a circle of broken and bloody indentations in his smooth flesh. That was where Jawbone had thundered close and clamped his massive teeth over the leg and had yanked the youth to his doom. This was where Jawbone had made his move, while it remained almost dark and the copses of cottonwoods and the outcrops would enable him to drive Mister Skye's own horses and mules away from the running herd and kill the flanking Cheyenne boy on the left in the process, simultaneously clamping the boy's leg while lunging crazily into the Cheyenne pony, making it stagger and fall, pitching the boy off at a lope or even a gallop.

They might be back at any moment, looking for the boy. Skye walked Jawbone to a thick grove of cottonwoods forty yards distant, slid off Jawbone in deep shade, and waited. The boy had died an honorable death, young but in the midst of a successful horse raid. He would be honored in the lodge of his family, for there was no shame in the accident that killed him. Mister Skye settled down to wait, confident that the whole party would return. Jawbone stood like a gray ghost behind him, head low, dreaming his evil dreams in the shade.

Some while later—he didn't know how long exactly—the rest of the Cheyenne party rode cautiously over the far shoulder single file, looking for the missing boy. Two rode ahead, then the loose horses, and two behind driving them slowly. From the shoulder they spotted the dead boy and wound slowly into the bottoms, negotiating patches of shale and thickets of sagebrush. When they reached the body they stared, and pointed, and looked fearfully at the ridges and the glades, and began to sing sad songs. It saddened Skye as well. For all his brawling, and for all the death he had seen, the death of the boy still saddened him. The boy had probably died on his first horse-stealing raid, at the very dawn of his warrior life. Even as he had died at the very dawn of his own life as a Cambridge scholar and then a merchant in old England.

The boy's pony was missing. Perhaps Jawbone had demolished it, too. These young Cheyenne youth would recruit another horse, one of the stolen ones, to carry the sad burden back to their village. But Mister Skye would prevent that. The horses belonged to his clients.

He slipped onto Jawbone quietly, and rode out of the thicket and was spotted at once. None of them had rifles, but they all swiftly nocked an arrow . . . and then lowered their bows. They knew. Most of the tribes of the plains knew of this man and this demon horse, with a medicine so evil it made them quake inside and hide their eyes from the sight. The blue roan riveted their attention, and Jawbone knew it and responded, baring his terrible teeth and uttering small screeching noises and mincing as he walked forward, murderously alert.

Skye stopped Jawbone and stared, not unkindly, but with the bore of his shining rifle gliding carelessly from man to man. He knew the tongue, and wouldn't need signs this time.

"I am sorry that your brother has died," he said. "It was a good death in a moment of honor. His pony is missing. But I will not give you one. You will have to make a travois and carry him behind one of yours. When you make war, and go to steal ponies, you must pay the price." He stared at them, one by one. "Bury him with honor. Mister Skye has said it."

One, on the far right, meant to try him. There'd be no greater glory for a young warrior than counting coup on Mister Skye or Jawbone. To wound Skye, or kill him, or even touch him, would make any warrior a great man among his people. It came suddenly: the boy whipped his bow back. Mister Skye's Sharps thundered and the boy's hand bloomed red and the bow clattered to earth. He screamed. Jawbone plunged into the others, screeching and biting and flailing with murderous hoofs, even while Mister Skye arced the Sharps, now a terrible club, knocking two more warriors off their plunging ponies as they drew their bows. And then it stopped as fast as it had started, with one gasping at his hand and two more writhing in pain in the dirt.

"Bind up his arm," Skye rasped to the remaining two, who were watching the screeching and plunging Jawbone with terror.

Two of their ponies were limping. One bled hard where

Jawbone had ripped flesh from its chest. The others danced in panic.

Mister Skye reloaded the Sharps as he watched them care for the wounded. In the grass, one of the writhing warriors stopped writhing, and was out cold. The wounded youth, gray from pain and loss of blood, fainted as the others stanched the flow with his buckskin war shirt, and fashioned a tourniquet.

"You will need two travois," said Mister Skye, eyeing the inert one he had clubbed.

They stared a moment, then headed for the cottonwoods to cut poles, while Mister Skye watched. They built two crude travois—the cottonwoods were poor material—loaded up their dead and wounded, rode quietly south, over the shoulder, and were gone. In the bottoms, grazing, were Father Kiley's horses and four more belonging to the missionaries, all sweated black with dirt and drying foam. Leisurely he herded them north.

In the next valley he herded the oxen and mules and began the slow push forward, four miles of walking the exhausted stock. At midday he drove them over the last layering ridge and down into the Platte Valley, and on the riverbank the missionary party gaped. They had never expected to see their stock again.

# Chapter 7

White people were mystifying to Victoria. Even Mister Skye was sometimes mystifying, although she understood him much better than she understood other whites. He was a leader of men, and that made him a chief in her mind, and not a mister. There were lots of misters among them, and none of them a chief.

Even more mystifying were these white medicine men and their wives—Victoria had scarcely seen a white woman before, so they fascinated her and she studied them surreptitiously. Right now, for example, no one made medicine. In fact no one did anything. Jawbone had returned with some horses. Mister Skye had saddled Jawbone and had told them to prepare the wagons for the crossing of the Platte. But now, an hour after he had ridden into the hills, these white people had done nothing. They had not even cooked a morning meal, but stood around with long faces, as uncertain as newly weaned colts. Had not Chief Skye told them to get busy? Had not Chief Skye told them he would bring the wagon cattle back, the lumbering white men's buffalo? And the mules too?

She watched them narrowly as she busied herself around her small fire. The priest, at least, had sense enough to feed himself. As soon as Mayree—the Shoshone wife's name was hard to pronounce in her Crow tongue—had finished spooning the buffalo stew into Dirk, Victoria would clean the pots and load the packhorses and tie the lodgepoles and lodgecover to the travois, and then they'd be ready. And Mayree would have the ponies saddled, and Dirk dressed in soft doeskins and up on a pony's withers, clutching its mane.

What was the matter with these medicine men? The long-robed one, at least, looked ready. But not even he believed he'd ever see his horses again. All of these whites seemed to think that Chief Skye had simply bragged, made giant boasts, when he said he would come back with the stock. It irked her. Not even the sensible one, old Rathbone, seemed to do anything but sit on his wagon seat, as if he had given up his medicine. Didn't these whites believe in their own medicine? Here they had come a long way to bring the medicine to the vile Siksika—the thought appalled her but she kept her silence—and now when trouble came they ignored their own medicine, God they called him. It was odd medicine, asking just one God for different things, when everyone knew that all the spirits had different tasks, and you had to find the right spirit helper to get things done.

She would put a stop to it. Rathbone was the chief medicine man, and she would tell him to get busy. So she went to him.

"Sonofabitch," she said. "How come you ain't doing what Mister Skye says? He says make the wagons float. Get ready. You ain't even cooked the damn stew yet."

He stared at her shocked.

"Get your ass off the seat. You ain't got all day."

From over at the next wagon Alex Newton stared, turned red, and closed his eyes. Henrietta, horrified, ducked into the protective darkness of her wagon.

"If you ain't got medicine, you go home. Beat it from here."

Esmerelda absorbed all this without wincing. "She's right," she said to Cecil. "We must have faith. We must do our chores. We must have our breakfast and prepare, just as if the stock were here."

"Do believe you're right," Cecil said.

"Hey you!" Victoria was yelling at James Method. "How come you ain't guarding? Cheyenne maybe come down the slopes into this here river bottom and kill us all. Just because you ain't got no horse don't mean you stop being the eyes and ears of this here camp."

"Ah think you're right," he said. He picked up his rifle from the plunder scattered around the buggy, and began walking upslope to a crest where he'd have a clear view of the country. "Bring me some of that chow."

Victoria headed for the Samples, singling out Clay. "Hey you," she bellowed. "How come you ain't got them damn wagons ready for floating?" She waggled a finger at him.

Clay brightened. "Don't think it's necessary," he said slowly. "I thought Mister Skye had it wrong, telling us to make the boxes watertight."

"You do what he says. He's the chief."

"No, now wait just a minute, Victoria. Maybe we can block up the boxes and get over. I reckon these wagon bottoms stand about two and a half feet above ground. You figure that river's two and a half feet? I can block them up, too. Lift the box beds up a foot by putting blocks on top of the axles. You think that water's three and a half feet?"

This subdued her. She didn't understand it all. But at least this one was still thinking about the trip and not wandering around like a wrung-necked chicken.

"Hokay, you fix them wagons."

Clay scratched his ear uncertainly. "Sort of need your help," he said. "Need to borry your pony and ride into the river and see how deep she goes. Maybe take a pole."

Victoria grew indignant. "Ain't nobody rides my

pony. Ain't nobody touches my pony. She's big medicine pony, buster.''

''You ride then,'' Clay persisted. ''Go see how deep.''

''All right I will,'' she said. ''Only then you get them wagons fixed up plenty fast, or Chief Skye get mad.''

She spotted Silas, smirking happily near his wagon. ''Hey you!'' she bawled.

''Save your breath,'' he replied. ''I don't intend to do your bidding. We are returning to Fort Laramie, and on foot, and I see no need—''

''You go over there and pull that heavy stuff, that stuff Skye says don't go up the trail—you and that preacher, Newton, you pull it out of that wagon.''

''I have no intention—''

''If you ain't got no intentions, do it anyway.'' She glared at him. ''When Skye comes back, you better be ready, or I make you dance fancy.''

With that the old crone stalked back to her camp, and slid a horsehair Indian bridle over the head of her spotted buckskin and brown pony. Then she pulled her heavy skin skirts high and clambered up on the barebacked horse, turning it toward the river as she settled herself. She steered it toward the turbulent water.

''The river will be cold, Whistling Arrow,'' she said in her own tongue to her horse. ''But you will go in, and we will see how deep.''

The horse entered unhesitatingly, and the flow tugged hard at its slender legs as it stepped carefully, deeper and deeper. At the center of the river the water rippled around its thighs. Victoria kept on. ''You see, Whistling Arrow? It is not so bad. My legs are cold too, but soon they will be warm.''

Then near the far bank they hit the main channel, and the horse plunged suddenly, boiling water edging up on its belly, nearing its withers. But with the next steps, it grew shallower. She turned her pony around and rode back to the deepest part. The water sucked and pushed dangerously at the standing horse, but she took the measure of it, lapping just below the withers, almost to her pad saddle, and then urged the pony back to shore.

"Hey you," she said to Clay. "The water comes upta here." She flattened her hand on the pony's shoulder.

"I dunno," he said slowly. "Wisht you'd taken a measuring stick. But I reckon it'll do. We'll block up the wagons, and save us a big piece of work."

She eyed him narrowly. "You disobey Skye, just to make lazy, and it don't work, I'm gonna make you dance."

"I reckon it'll work," he said. "I'll fetch my double bit, and cut me some blocks."

The women were stirring at last, Alice and Esmerelda building a breakfast fire, the children hunting wood. They found little because emigrants had stripped the whole place bare of it in previous years.

She spotted Silas Potter, lounging beside his buggy, reading his Bible. "Hey you!" she bawled. He looked up calmly. "I tell you to pull that truck outa that wagon, you do it, hokay?"

He blinked at her patiently through his thick spectacles. "You are perfectly rude," he said nastily. "But let me tell you something. I don't know whether it will sink into that wooden head of yours, but I'll try. I have resigned from this party. I don't recognize your authority, or Skye's authority over me. The Newtons have resigned as well. We are going back to Fort Laramie."

Henrietta watched all this from the puckerstring hole in the back of her wagon. "I have no intention of walking a hundred miles back to Fort Laramie," she shrilled. "Not in my condition. I'm staying right here until oxen are brought here and I can ride."

"I don't care what kinda stuff you say. You get your ass over there and pull that plunder from the wagon like Skye says." Victoria squinted at him. "Or else I cut you up," she added, pulling from the folds of her skirt a shining Green River knife. "Slice you good, fingers and toes first, then better stuff." She grinned maliciously.

The knife glinted in the new sun.

Silas stared at it, at her, and then carefully closed his Bible and stood. He looked faintly annoyed.

Cecil approached. "I'm truly sorry that's your decision, Silas. And I grieve that we've lost my own daughter and son-in-law, too. I didn't know things had progressed this far. I imagine I'm to blame, not listening very well . . . I wish you'd reconsider, and seek guidance . . . But until you quit this camp, I reckon you're necessarily under my authority as the senior man here. We cannot permit a camp to tear itself apart in a hostile wilderness. And I've chosen Mister Skye and his people to guide us. So, until you quit us—and I'm sure you'll reconsider, my young friend—until you quit us, we'll have no anarchy here. Understood? . . . She's instructed you to help unload the Newtons' wagon. We're going to do it, you and I."

He turned to Victoria. "We are God's people here, and that knife is not helpful."

There was something in the man, Rathbone, she liked and respected, and she slid her knife into its buffalo-hide sheath at her waist. "I leave him to you. You fix him good, and move all the truck."

Silas fumed. From her pony Victoria could see rage in him, twisting his face, driving his arms and hands in small angry movements. But he was obeying, with a look of long-suffering patience painted falsely on his face, like white victory paint on a warrior after a losing battle. He followed Cecil Rathbone to the Newtons' wagon.

"Alex, please lend a hand. It'll take the three of us to lower these things."

"No!" cried Henrietta. "Daddy, what're you thinking of?"

From her saddle seat Victoria could see that the wagon was chockful of trunks and barrels. The furniture hulked at the rear. Toward the front, on a false floor, lay a straw-filled tick they used as a bed.

Cecil peered in, while Alex watched in icy rage. Then Cecil walked to the rear, undid the puckerstring, and pulled the canvas back until it fell free of the rear bow.

He nodded to the others, and clambered in. The fine black walnut bedstead came easily. Cecil handed the headboard, footboard, and runners to Alex and Silas, who laid them on the grass. The walnut highboy was harder. Even after they had removed the drawers, each stuffed with clothing, it remained a heavy and cumbersome piece. But eventually the two reverends and the teacher eased it to the ground. Irritably Henrietta yanked clothing and linens from the drawers and stuffed it all into gunny sacks.

Then they confronted the organ. As organs went, it was a small one, with foot bellows. But it was a monster on the trail, and filled much of the wagon. Getting it out meant lifting it over the sides of the box and lowering it safely to the ground. And that proved to be plainly impossible, at least until Clay could join them and skids could be built. It was scarcely possible for the three men even to lift the organ for a few moments, much less lower it from the wagon side to the ground.

"This will have to wait," Cecil said to Victoria. He was winded. "I'll have Clay cut some runners. "Perhaps Mister Skye can help us . . . I never imagined the Newtons were carrying this much weight . . . or that it could be dragged this far."

Victoria nodded. She would have pushed the thing, whatever it was, over the side and let it crash. What good was it? It would sit here anyway, until someone busted it up for firewood. But that would not be the way of these people.

"Hokay, I'll have Skye come do the damn thing."

She saw that the white women had a meal ready. "You go eat and then you get them wagons fixed up for the crossing."

From the women at the cookfire she got a small iron pot of oatmeal gruel and a wooden spoon, and then rode up the long rocky slope to the black man's sentry post.

"Here's the slop," she said. "You see nothing?"

James Method shook his head. She didn't trust his vision, so she squinted out across the prairies, spotting several small groups of antelope and some almost invisible mule deer. But the sun-kissed steppes seemed to hold no mortal terror at the moment. Still, she peered again, having lived through murderous ambushes several times. Nothing.

The man downed his oatmeal hastily.

"Slop is what Skye calls it. He tells me don't cook it unless there ain't nothing else to cook."

"Ah've had worse by far," said Method. "Lots of times Ah've had nothing."

"Don't they feed them slaves?"

"Lots of times they don't."

"How come some of them white people got slaves and some don't."

Method shrugged. "In the north they're against having slaves, and in the south they're for it. I got runnin' out of the south."

"We got lotsa damn slaves," she said. "The Absaroka people capture lotsa Siksika women, Lakotah women, make them dandy goddam slaves. I don't know how come them white medicine men are against it."

"Beats me," said James Method. "It's plenty bad for some black men, especially the cotton pickers. They get whipped all the time, and die quick if they run away. I had it easy—what they called domestic service. I just run around and chop wood and haul slop and such. They even taught me reading and writing, and I got to play some with the young masters at first . . ."

"Then how come you ran away?"

Method smiled. "Read too much, I guess."

She sniffed. "Maybe so Skye should make you a slave again. I could use you good."

Method's eyes grew cold. "He monkeys with me, and I'm going to fight. Maybe I'll die trying, but I'll fight."

"You'd make one helluva warrior," said Victoria. "When Skye comes, you tell us. Don't fire that piece, just wave, hokay?"

Victoria rode down the slope, puzzling about white men. In one part of their land they had slaves, and in another part they didn't. And they had longrobes, like that priest she'd been feeding, and shortrobes, like the rest of these medicine men, and they never could agree. The longrobes never touched a woman, and the shortrobes did. It scandalized her that the longrobes scorned women. That was plainly crazy. But maybe it made big medicine. Bigger medicine than the shortrobes had. She didn't know. They were all strange, even Skye.

Back in camp she dropped the empty pot·at the cookfire, and scanned the whites. They were bustling about, and that was good. The big one, Clay Sample, had a wagon bed jacked up and was sliding blocks under it, between the bed and the axle. The women packed their plunder. Even the spectacles one, Potter, packed up his gear. Satisfied, she rode back to her own fire. Mary had long since made ready. They could leave in a minute.

Unless maybe that blackrobe wasn't packed and ready.

She found the priest on the riverbank, fishing with a pole he'd cut, and some string.

"Them fish ain't good to eat. Makes you weak and puts poison in you," she said.

"All the things of the earth are good," he said. "They are given to us by God."

She sniffed. "How come you don't touch no women? Eh? Sonofabitch, you blackrobes are crazy."

His wild orange hair and freckled face fascinated her. She hadn't ever seen freckles. Maybe that was because he had black and white parents, or maybe ones spotted like a trout.

He laughed easily. "It's so that we can give our entire loyalty to our Lord. All our time and effort, instead of looking after a wife."

"Sonofabitch, that's big medicine. Hokay, what do you do when you want to crawl between the robes with a woman. Ain't that a distraction?"

He scanned the horizon dreamily, until she thought he wouldn't answer. "For me, a lass is always a distraction. But I'm a poor priest. For the best, the ones with—

medicine . . . that part of us is dead. The body's dead, and we live a life of pure spirit."

"Ain't that crazy," she muttered. "How come them shortrobes over there don't like you, eh?"

"Who's to say they don't like me, old mother? You must know more than I know."

"I don't know nothing about white man medicine, only Skye, he gets you away from camp, and you eat from our pot."

"It goes back a long time, almost three hundred years . . ." he said, and slipped into silence. The pole twitched, and he lifted it, but nothing had bitten. "We're all fishermen," he said.

There was some shouting behind them. She peered up the slope, and saw the black man waving. Far to the south, she saw a herd of driven animals wend its way down long slopes.

"Sonofabitch, here comes Chief Skye," she said happily. "Now you get your goddam horse back."

He stood slowly, not quite believing, squinting into the glare of the day with the wind riffling his carrot hair.

"I'm a poor priest, mother," he said. "Aye, a poor priest."

# Chapter 8

Somehow, the return of the stock was not an occasion for joy. Shock, rather. No one had expected it. Even as the weary animals spread out to graze along the riverbank, the missionary party stared mutely. Only Father Kiley showed any pleasure. He gathered up his pack and riding horses and curried them.

Cecil J. B. Rathbone felt the pang of guilt. He had been faithless. And the division among them was far from settled. This miraculous recovery of the stock might even make matters worse, he thought.

Mister Skye stared at the camp from his perch on Jawbone, his gaze first upon the blocked-up wagons, and then upon walnut furniture sitting forlornly in the grass, and then upon the carriage, which had been emptied because it rode too low, the few possessions of Silas and James now aboard the Samples' wagon.

Satisfied, he said, "We'll cross now and then rest the stock on the other side. Use the mules, not the oxen, to cross all the wagons."

Cecil realized there were fewer oxen.

Mister Skye caught him staring. "Lost four," he said. "All of them Newtons'. They ran themselves to death. Only two yoke of theirs left and no reserves for them or for you. Your three yoke made it."

The remaining oxen looked desperately weary, and unable to pull wagons a mile farther, but the mules were in good condition.

"We will have to lighten on the other side," Cecil said.

He spotted blood on Jawbone's muzzle, and the sight of it disturbed the preacher.

As if reading his mind, Skye said, "Cheyenne. Five young ones on a horse-stealing raid. Looking for a little glory."

"You met them?"

"Aye, I did."

"And was it peaceable? Did they suffer any . . . losses?"

"Let's get these wagons across, mate."

So then there had been trouble, Cecil thought. Perhaps dead and wounded. For the love of God, he had hoped to avoid that.

The crossing of the north fork of the Platte was routine. The mules did heavy duty, pulling one wagon across, and swimming back for the next until all were over. The oxen were hazed across and swam so wearily that they drifted well downstream before they found footing on the north side. Silas and the Newtons were oddly subdued, offered no resistance, and did not threaten to take themselves and their goods back to Fort Laramie. The loss of so many oxen would have made even that hundred-mile retreat impossible. And in their wagon, bare inches above the lapping water, sat the heavy organ, its fate uncertain.

The far side offered good grass and a better supply of firewood in the river bottoms, and they made a good camp. Cecil wondered, though, if half a day of rest would suffice to strengthen the gaunted oxen and tired horses. But he would leave that to Mister Skye, who seemed more and more to reveal some commanding ability to get along in this vast land. The guide sent Victoria and James Method on long horseback scouts, and detailed the priest to hunting nearby. Skye didn't want any shots fired more than two or three miles from camp. Father Kiley's horse seemed none the worse for wear, and jogged off northwest, out of the bottoms.

"Your woman Victoria is a very effective leader. She had us hustling," said Cecil amiably.

"Aye, and why was it necessary for her to do it?" the guide answered tartly. "And why aren't you out finding a wagon road, mate? There isn't a road over here for wagons. From now on someone's got to hunt out a level path and avoid the worst grades and coulees, and find a way around cutbank streams, and have shovels handy to dig roads past ditches, and axes handy to cut through sagebrush and thickets and all the rest. You thinkin' it'll be easy now, mate? The hard part's scarce begun."

Seven hundred miles left, Cecil thought, and no road. Not even a rut. There'd be dead ends, backtracking, boulder pulling, shoveling crude paths down cutbanks and up the other sides. He shrank from the thought, and wondered what madness had set him upon this endless journey to the lands of dangerous Indians. He suddenly understood the yearnings of the Newtons and Silas Potter to hasten back the way they had come, to some small snatched security and comfort at the fort.

Mister Skye was watching him. The guide hunkered easily, squatting on two feet, a position the mountain men seemed able to enjoy for hours, but one which cut off Cecil's circulation and swiftly made his legs tingle.

"I'll go with you; I don't want you getting too far from camp and picked off by some Sioux. Grab a shovel, mate, and we'll go make a road."

They trudged up a long gentle shoulder with some sort of path on it, whether made by Indians or buffalo or other wild animals the Reverend Rathbone didn't know. He carried a shovel; Mister Skye bore his new Sharps, and a holstered Army .44 Colt as well. At its crest they left the river bottom behind. Ahead rose a vast tawny prairie, fairly flat, and stretching aching distances, clear to the horizon and beyond, to some unknown lip of the world. Far to the northwest lay a low strip of blue mountains, scarcely visible.

"Those are the Big Horns," said Mister Skye. "We'll keep well to the east where the going is easier. Maybe up the Powder. There are creeks all across here, headwaters of rivers that join the Yellowstone. Beyond the Big Horns we'll strike the Yellowstone and follow it west a way, and then cross it, drive north through a gap— Judith Gap—and head northwest toward the Missouri . . . and Sun River."

"Why," exclaimed Cecil, "this doesn't look half bad. Level enough for a road. No trees or brush to cut through."

"There are cutbank streams, some of them running down small canyons, to work past," Mister Skye warned. "And Indians. This is game country—buffalo, antelope, deer, bear. They come here to hunt—Cheyenne, Sioux, Arapaho mainly, but also Crow, Shoshone, Gros Ventres, Assiniboin, and sometimes others."

"It looks like it'll swallow armies. Like it'd be sheer chance if our tiny caravan might be discovered."

"We'll be found and watched," said Mister Skye grimly. "Probably are already, mate."

"Are you expecting a fight?"

"I always expect a fight. Especially here."

"There seems little enough road-building as far ahead as I can see."

Skye grinned. "Wait until we're out in it, Mister Rathbone. The prairie hides its hellholes until you're hard upon them."

Cecil didn't doubt the guide. Far to the west he saw a solitary horseman, who appeared, antlike, along a rise and then disappeared from sight. James Method probably, or the priest. Appearing and disappearing on what seemed to be level prairie. Cecil sat down to rest, and Mister Skye squatted beside him.

"Mister Rathbone, there are things you aren't telling me. Victoria says there's division in your party. I must know of it. I must know everything—for the safety of us all."

Cecil sighed. A division indeed, and there was the other thing too. Weary oxen, enough for one wagon maybe, but not two.

He hemmed around in his mind, backed and filled, softened and harshened, and then settled on plain talk, since honeyed smooth words would clang like cymbals at dawn.

"Mister Skye," he said, "there's some who want us to discharge you, and think you're—ungodly." He smiled wryly. "I didn't put that true. Potter thinks you're the devil's own creature, and maybe the Newtons do too. Lust and blood and bigamy upon you, and a horse that is hell on earth. Maybe I'm not so far from that notion myself, only I got my own reasons . . ."

He waited for some reaction, some disclaimer from Mister Skye, but the guide only nodded.

"They were all set to hightail back. Seventy miles back to Laramie, but they're calling it a hundred. Henrietta's plumb determined to haul that that organ to Sun River, or quit us. That and all her truck."

"Organ?" Mister Skye had forgotten about it.

"Their wagon's got a little pump organ in it. So heavy we couldn't even get it out to ditch it. And she ain't going anywhere without it. Says she'll set it up in our Sun River church and play the daylights outa it."

Unconsciously Cecil had drifted back to a frontier tongue he had abandoned in his youth when he walked east to school.

"The oxen are so worn we hardly got enough for one wagon—five sorry yoke. Some footsore, too. So we've got to ditch a wagon, too. And that means we lose the Newtons. Lose my own daughter. Crack the whole mission apart."

"Well then, let's take the organ," said Mister Skye. "I'm going to deliver one bloody organ to Sun River."

"But . . . but . . ."

"From now on we'll take one ox-drawn wagon. Yours because it's lighter. And it will contain one item—the organ. You and Mrs. Rathbone will ride the buggy. Mister Method is out scouting all day and needs only a tent. Mister Potter will learn to walk. You'll abandon your plunder, except for food and a tent; the Newtons will abandon theirs, except for the bloody organ. And we'll trust that five wornout yoke can haul your lighter wagon with one organ inside of it."

"But that's—mad," Cecil cried. "I'm bringing tools, a plow, seed—to teach . . . I can't leave that, just leave that. It's the heart of the whole dream, the vision—"

Mister Skye shrugged. "You can buy some of that at Fort Benton. Not far from Sun River. That stuff isn't important, mate. That ain't worth a diddlydamn. Now that organ, that's what's important. You get Henrietta pumping that in your mission church, and that'll cure whatever ails the bloody Blackfeet."

"I can't let you do this!" Cecil cried. "I spent months—years—culling and selecting and discarding, until I fitted everything into my wagon—everything to start a farm, teach domestic sciences . . ."

Mister Skye stared. "Everything for a farm, sure enough, mate. And nothing for a mission. We're hauling the bloody organ."

"But that's not the way . . ." Cecil's voice faded. Was this heathen and heretic measuring Cecil's faith and dedication and finding it wanting? The thought tore through him like a barbed arrow. "Oh, Lord," he muttered.

"If I don't get Potter busy pushing his feet forward, he'll cause trouble," Cecil added quietly. "It's all set then."

They turned back then, Mister Skye rolling along with his sailor's gait. The earth could buck and heave under him, and not slow him down a particle. And the Reverend Rathbone behind, once again feeling like a dinghy towed by the man ahead. On the soft zephyrs came a muffled report, far to the west. Mister Skye paused a moment, sorting, and then continued on.

"Father Kiley has a deer," he said mysteriously, and Cecil wondered how he knew. And hoped, for once, Mister Skye might be dead wrong.

Back in the bottoms, the guide explained the new order of things, with a series of short sharp commands, and astonished people hastened to obey. Esmerelda laughed, and pecked Cecil on the cheek. Together they tugged everything out of their wagon until it lay in heaps on the grass, and the wagon bed looked oddly naked. Then she began to sort out the necessaries, with a ruthlessness that Cecil didn't possess, while he groaned silently within, watching his plow and harness and seed and hoe and scythe end up in the discard pile, while food and clothing survived the holocaust.

Over at the Newtons' wagon, a similar process had begun, though more anguished, as they wrangled to hang on to things. Henrietta cried occasionally, and Alex wondered out loud why he did this, why he was here, why he took orders from a brute and a heathen. But it was the organ, the vision of the organ arriving safely on Sun River, that compelled them onward. To get her organ to Sun River, Henrietta would bear any cross.

Silas Potter had withdrawn into a shocked petulance ever since Skye returned with the stock, and in that condition he lacked will. Mindlessly he emptied the buggy of its tent and his few books and clothes, and let Mister Skye show him how to make a mule-pack of them, absorbing the lesson with dull eyes and bare interest. In the grass of the Platte Valley the heap of discarded things grew. It was nothing new. All along the Oregon Trail they had seen remnants such as this. Some had been salvaged by those who came behind, or by Fort Laramie scavengers, who collected it far and wide and took it to the fort for furnishing. But much more lay in ruin beside the great artery across the continent. At least there was one thing that pleased Silas Potter, and he took pains to express his pleasure: the organ would go, and Cecil Rathbone's farm implements wouldn't.

The Samples were unaffected by this great sweat-down, at least until Cecil cornered Clay and begged him to take just one small barrel, containing various seeds, and one little hoe, and a few orchard cuttings. Clay grinned and found room. His mules had weathered the trail well. They looked ribby but trail-hardened, and seemed strong enough. There were ten of them: three span for his wagon, a pair for the carriage, and two spares, which would henceforth be carrying packloads of the Newtons' goods. The spare horses would carry the meager possessions of Silas, and James Method.

"May the Lord bless you," cried Cecil. "And don't tell Mister Skye."

Later, all the men in the camp helped to transfer the organ. They positioned the Rathbone wagon back to back with the Newtons', and rolled the canvas off the bows of both. Then, with Mister Skye and James Method on one end, and Clay, Cecil, Alex, Silas, and young Alfred on the other, they hoisted it over the solid rear wall of the larger wagon, and down into the smaller. They stripped the Newton wagon of its canvas—which would become a tent at Sun River, while they built dwellings—and abandoned it. It sat forlornly, its naked bows hard against the sky. The sight of it saddened Cecil. It had come halfway, sheltering his daughter and Alex and all their worldly goods, which now lay scattered in the tall grasses, unclaimed, for any wild child of the plains to take.

The only thing in Cecil's wagon other than the organ was the Newtons' tick. They would sleep there nights; the tick added nothing much to the weight. Alex stalked the camp, red-faced and angry, while Henrietta pouted and complained that her feet would swell and she wouldn't be able to walk. Cecil had a remedy, if it came to that: Henrietta and her mother would ride in the buggy, and he would ride Magdelene.

Ruefully he gazed at the rear seat of the carriage, piled high now. The canvas salvaged from the Newtons' wagon filled most of it, and what little space was left was given to food and a few items of clothing. He and Esmerelda would arrive at Sun River with scarcely more than the clothing on their backs, an axe, and a few tools.

Esmerelda saw him staring at the small desolate load in the buggy, and knew the thread of his thinking. She took his hand.

"We're going for a walk, you and I, Reverend," she said, and tugged him toward the riverbank, and down the stream through cottonwoods and brush, until the camp disappeared and only the silence of sunny nature lay around them, black and white magpies flitting from tree to tree, and corrugated clouds high overhead to the south. He felt her strong warm hand in his, leading him somewhere, and did not resist, though he worried about slipping too far from the safety of the camp.

Then at last in a sunny glade where the grasses grew emerald and the river gurgled just beyond a wall of brush, she stopped him and turned to him.

"Cecil Rathbone," she said. "We don't have much left, but we have each other." And then she hugged him, and he felt his own hard hands and skinny arms fold around her and pull her lean warm figure tight. They kissed.

"We have that, and we're rich," he said. "Plumb rich."

She smiled, comfortable and warm in his arms. "There's not a dream ever dreamed by mortal man that has not been battered and changed as life went along," she said. "We'll make do with whatever God gives us. Is that not right, Cecil?"

He sighed. "Hate to give up dreams. I get to thinking I'm giving some kind of gift to God, bringing a whole tribe of people to Him, and then He upsets my apple cart."

Cecil Rathbone laughed, and Esmerelda joined him, and they hugged in the quiet, and were reluctant to let go. There had been so few stolen moments clear across the plains.

"The organ won," he said, and they laughed softly together. "But Clay's carrying my seed, and a hoe."

They kissed again, and then walked arm in arm back through the golden quiet, sun filtering through the young cottonwood leaves, aware of each other, and danger out here, and sudden fate.

There had been some imperceptible change in camp. The abandonment of their worldly things had been some sort of shriving that had cleansed them and drawn them closer. Even Silas Potter smiled thinly.

Cecil hunted down their guide, for it somehow was Skye's doing. He found him, and Father Kiley, skinning a doe that hung from a stout cottonwood limb, and taking care about it because Victoria wanted the hide.

Cecil watched awhile. The priest was an expert, peeling and cutting delicately, yanking the hide down in clean, effective jerks.

"Mister Skye," Cecil said at last. "We have the organ, and we've ditched almost everything else except for the clothing on our backs. And I daresay tempers are sweet for a change. Now how is that?"

"Well, mate, it has to do with flags. Do you know about flags?"

"You have me there, Mister Skye."

"During the Kaffir War, the man carrying the Union Jack fell, and fast as he fell, we marines—the bloody Royal Navy turned us into marines for a bit, down there— we fled. It was a godalmighty rout. Until a bloody tar grabbed the Jack and lifted her up, and all the bloody tars saw it again and rallied with a shout that still rattles me ears. And we turned around, mate, and overran them bloody Kaffirs."

"I'm still not following you, Mister Skye."

"Well, Reverend, men will follow flags and guidons through hell on earth. But men ain't going to be brave for the sake of plows and seed and hoes."

"You're saying I failed to inspire my people?"

"No, Mister Rathbone, I ain't saying that at all. What

I'm saying is, that pump organ of Mrs. Newton's—that thing is your flag, and all your folk are rallying to her.''

Father Kiley grinned. And for the first time he and Cecil took amiable measure of each other.

''Perhaps our Lord prefers organs,'' he said, and Cecil chuckled.

# Chapter 9

For nine days they toiled north by northwest, sticking to the ridges and shoulders because they were easier on the wagons, with fewer boulders and gullies. They crossed several small streams without difficulty, finding wide sandy places with easy slopes. Two creeks gave them trouble, and they had to shovel their way down sharp dropoffs and throw earthen ramps together on the far sides, so the wagons could roll up to the grassy slopes again. And uncoiling behind, mile after mile, were the tracks of wagons, cutting grass and indenting the virgin earth, tracks anyone could read.

The exhausted oxen that had dragged the Newtons' heavy wagon clear to the crossing of the Platte were not used at all. The three yoke that had pulled the Rathbone wagon were in better condition, and now they continued to pull it and the organ inside of it. The strife that had torn the Methodist party was gone, or at least much subdued, as far as Father Kiley could see. The ones least equipped for this wilderness travel, the Newtons and young

Potter, were quiet and self-absorbed, perhaps humbled by the vastness of this virgin land.

Dunstan Kiley had been here before, several times, as one of the several Jesuits who had helped Pierre de Smet bring the faith to the northwestern tribes, most particularly at St. Mary's mission in the far Bitterroot Valley. Father Kiley had first seen this incredible land in the fur-trade days, and it awed him no less now than it did then. He imagined, as he rode perhaps three miles ahead and to the west of the missionary party, that it could easily hold the whole population of the earth in one small corner of it. The red-hued earth and limitless land, stretching over the lip of the horizon, contrasted starkly with the verdant, misty, intimate vales of his native Ireland. It had frightened him once, as a man who has never been to sea is frightened when there is no land in sight, and every lapping swell seems a menace. But now he knew precisely where he was and where he would go. Each day the blue bulk of the Big Horns off to the west and north grew larger, and visible now was a vast barrier ridge, dark and foreboding, where God had cleaved the great plains from the mountains.

Everywhere here he found game. Rarely an hour went by that Father Kiley did not see something or other, deer, antelope, elk, and even a bear or two. But these he ignored for the choicer meat of a young buffalo cow. The great brown beasts had not gathered into a giant herd here, but grazed the bottoms in small groups guarded by a fierce old bull or two. Whenever Father Kiley approached the top of a ridge or shoulder, he paused, his head barely above its crest, and he surveyed the open lands beyond not only for succulent buffalo, but for Indians as well. But of the Indians he saw none.

Now, in this cloudless early afternoon, he found what he was looking for, a herd of a dozen buffalo grazing quietly in a shallow dished valley with a small creek and a few cottonwoods lining its bank. The west wind would be ideal, for he was to the east. And the cottonwoods would supply cover enough for him to stalk close and select a good cow with care. He traveled lightly, and without a packhorse. His bay gelding could carry an antelope or even the hind quarters of a doe as well as himself, if the distance to camp wasn't too large. It never quite grew used to the brass smell of blood, and carried its burden with subdued alarm. Buffalo were a different matter. For these he needed a packhorse, and usually went back to the party to fetch his spare, leaving his packload temporarily in the wagon carrying the organ.

Father Kiley rode quietly toward the group, screening himself as much as possible behind the cottonwood groves. The old bull that stood apart from the others, and guarded this group, twisted its massive head until it peered straight into the cottonwoods, and then looked away again. Its weak eyes saw nothing, and the west wind brought him no scent of danger. Even so, he turned his body so as to stare continually toward the copse where Father Kiley sat his horse. Easily the priest slid off and unsheathed the old Hawken percussion lock rifle he had acquired years ago from a young mountain man whose two children he had baptized. It was a good weapon, with a short heavy barrel and a ball large enough to drop a buffalo with one well-placed shot.

But Father Kiley needed to get closer. He crouched two hundred yards distant, and he preferred to shoot from half that. There lay a crease in the sere land that would permit him to edge closer if he crept, and kept his head low. He did not wish to crawl. That would besmudge the heavy black suit he always wore, even now, in the heat and on the hunt. He had learned to carry a smock in his kit, and this he wrapped around him when he butchered or shouldered meat. That suit and its white Roman collar was his badge, his joyous prison.

He selected the cow he wanted and edged closer. But the guardian bull was restless now, and it puzzled Father Kiley, for the bull stared not toward him but toward the east, on his flank. The cow was still too distant, but he decided not to wait. This herd grew restless now, and ready to run. He lined up the sights of the Hawken until he stared at that place behind her shoulder where the ball would tear through lungs and heart and she would take a step or two and drop. And then he felt, as he always did, a grief about the taking of life, for his Irish heart was tender and his spirit exulted in the life he saw in the shining eyes of God's creatures. Even as he aimed he remembered for a moment that some Indians thanked the creature they had slain for the use of its body, and to bless it on its journey to the spirit world. He could not do that; he could not address a prayer to an animal or commune with its spirit, but he wished he could.

He fired. The throaty boom of the Hawken echoed out upon the wide land. The shot went true, and the cow coughed and slowly folded, sinking to the warm earth even as blood frothed from her nostrils. And then another boom erupted, lighter than his Hawken's, and a third, and two other cows were wounded. One began to run, and made twenty yards before she sank to her fore-knees, her head low, refusing to collapse and die for as long as her will permitted. And then she fell. The other cow had collapsed, and now lay on her side, her legs kicking spastically.

Father Kiley was astonished. He stood. And as he stood, mounted Indians poured out of a defile, a crease to the east that the priest scarcely knew was there. More and more of them poured into the valley, until at last he counted twenty, a sizable party, all of them naked on their ponies except for breechclouts and moccasins. They alarmed him, for he had no way to escape. But they were not painted. This was not a war party, as far as he could see. These might be hunters, or more likely, a group out to make mischief, steal horses, count coup wherever there might be enemies . . .

They ignored the three slain buffalo and the retreating herd, and instead rode straight toward the priest, fanning out, arrows nocked in bows, and the black bores of several rifles and fusils pointing at him. Some wore their black hair shoulder length; others wore it in two braids. One wore his long hair in a single braid that fell clear down his back and over the right stifle of his pony. Except for the quivers on their backs and the small medicine bundles hanging from a thong around their necks, they carried nothing. His heart hammered. Sometimes in his fancies he had dreamed of becoming a holy martyr, and going straight to God, in all honor. But now death chilled him. He didn't want to be a martyr, at least not yet, not yet . . .

They studied his black suit, and the white collar tight around his neck, and the small burnished wooden cross hanging on his chest, and then they pointed and gestured and stared. One leapt off his pony and approached, his eyes gleaming like agates, and Father Kiley had no notion what the warrior might do. The priest stood quietly, forcing himself to stand with a calm he didn't feel, while the powerful short warrior stepped close, raised a hand, and then fingered the white Roman collar, feeling the tight fabric that imprisoned the priest's neck. He grunted then, and Father Kiley had no idea what it meant.

They argued among themselves in a language he didn't know. He didn't even know what tribe they were, not having mastered the subtle differences between them, as Mister Skye had done. Father Kiley could recognize Nez Perce, Shoshone, Flatheads, and Blackfeet, all tribes that usually roamed well to the west and north of here. But these Indians were none of those. And yet . . . the headman, the one with the unusually long single braid and a single eagle feather tucked into the top of it, awakened some memory in him, some campfire knowledge exchanged with a hundred men of the mountains he had sojourned with. This one had scars on each arm, torture scars shaped like three chevrons that made puckered white lines in his umber flesh. Like a sergeant's stripes, the priest thought wildly. And if this was the one he had heard of, the one who wore those scars, then this was a subchief of the Cheyenne named Wolf-That-Circles, and a more erratic and sometimes dangerous man did not exist on the prairies. Father Kiley blessed himself. If he was to become a martyr, he hoped he would find the courage within himself to endure it grandly. But oh, God, spare him that . . .

For what seemed an achingly long time to Father Kiley, nothing happened. They stared and muttered and pointed. Then, at a sharp command from the one with the long braid, two of the warriors set off to find the priest's horse, and another was sent to the crest of a nearby hill to act as a sentinel. In short order they found his bay and brought it close. Then the powerfully-built leader—Father Kiley was sure it was Wolf-That-Circles—opened the priest's saddlebags. He found little inside. A white stole, a small tin of wafers not yet sanctified, a flask of oil for anointing, a breviary, a flint and striker for fire-starting, balls, powder, and caps, and some jerky. The chieftain flipped the tissuey pages of the leather-bound breviary, as if to read, and threw it to the ground, a useless thing.

Father Kiley didn't know what else to do, so he talked. "I am Dunstan Kiley, a priest of the Jesuits and a brother of Pierre de Smet, whose name you probably know," he began.

They listened, but without understanding, as far as he could see.

"I'm on my way west, passing through here to go to the mountains, to bring my . . . medicine to tribes there who ask for it."

They watched him talk, even as they pawed through his few simple possessions. One of them took the flint and striker and began to build a fire, gathering dry cottonwood sticks.

"I have killed that cow; you have killed the others. I will butcher mine now, and you can butcher yours. Perhaps we can have a feast, and then I must leave," he said to no one in particular.

He still had his Hawken in hand, but now Wolf-That-Circles wrenched it violently from him. Father Kiley thought to smash the chieftain with his big freckled fist, but thought better of it. He wasn't a bit frail, but neither would he be a match for that war-leader, who'd kill him in an instant.

Instead, he stood upright and made the sign of the cross, knowing in his troubled heart that he was not invoking God's blessings, but employing theater, medicine, to save his life, and he felt ashamed.

They stared. Again he blessed them, this time trying desperately to invoke the blessings he sought.

"You have my rifle now as a gift. I'll just leave now. You have the cow I shot as well," he said, walking hastily toward his bay horse.

But at a barked command, arms grabbed him roughly and spun him to the ground. He grew frightened now but determined not to show it, and again he blessed them with a sweeping slash of his hand, and even from the ground gazed at them steadily, one by one.

He didn't expect what happened next. They undressed him, taking great care not to rip his clothing, as if these items of clothing were medicine itself, and might impart medicine to whoever wore them. The white collar was most prized. Wolf-That-Circles took it and hooked it in place on his own bronzed neck, and paraded happily with it. They took everything from him, and Dunstan Kiley felt violated, naked before his enemies, his freckled white flesh bared to them and the sun. One of them tried on his black broadcloth suitcoat and found that it fit, except that it was too long in the arms. Another pulled on his black clerical shirt. Another his black pants. Another the black-dyed boots he had specially made for this trip into the wilderness.

Then they lashed his hands behind his back, and his legs as well, and left him in the grass. He felt utterly helpless and his heart hammered and he could not pray. At last the Latin seeped back into his brain, and he began to chant it from some wellspring of memory. He recited the Mass.

Several of them were gathering wood, bringing armloads of it from the copses. He supposed they would have a feast of delicious hump ribs and tongue, or liver and boudins, while they decided what to do with him. Where was God? Where had God vanished? His mind riveted upon the preparations before him, and he could not pray.

But there was something wrong with his hopes, for none of them butchered a cow, peeling back hide, cutting out the succulent hump ribs or severing the choice tongue. No, they were gathering long dry sticks and placing them in the fire like the spokes of a wheel, watching their ends flare and burn hot.

And then Father Kiley knew. They would test the medicine of this priest of the whites, this shaman of the whites, with burning brands twisted into his pale flesh, and see for themselves whether this holy man was vulnerable and mortal, or whether he might magically resist, or laugh, or heal himself as fast as the brands were thrust into his flesh.

Father Kiley groaned, a dread engulfing him beyond any dark feeling he had ever experienced, and for a moment he hallucinated, thinking himself back in the cool green vales of his home, seeing his good mother and father at the hearth of their cottage, smiling, seeing the softly smiling Virgin in her niche at his parish church . . .

Wolf-That-Circles eyed him intently, his eyes bright with curiosity. He would begin the honors. From the fire he selected a thick stick, its end a glowing orange coal and blazing. With this in hand he approached the priest, tied hand and foot on the grass. The chieftain had dark gray eyes, and these peered deeply into Father Kiley's own. And then the burning stick drew close, not toward the priest's torso, but toward his face, closer and closer, and then Father Kiley knew. The blazing stick was coming toward his eye, his left eye.

"No!" he shrieked, and twisted violently to one side and the fiery brand drove home. It missed, singeing his ear. He yanked and twisted violently, flipping and jack-knifing on the grass, his mind gone mad with terror. Powerful hands pinioned him from behind, jamming him back to earth, brutal weight across his shoulders. More hands caught his flailing legs and pinioned them. Still more hands caught his writhing body and held it down.

"Mother of God," he cried, imploring.

And then the fiery brand came again, faster and harder now, searing his face, into his eye, burning and grinding unspeakably. White light exploded in his head, white and blackness, the smell of burning flesh, mad pain in his eye, blackness. He screamed and didn't know it. Then the other eye, burning fire, sizzling flesh, white and black light, stars of yellow, sun and midnight, and then blackness. He fainted, then came to, then his spirit wove in and out of himself. Blackness.

But they weren't done. Now smaller brands jabbed into his chest and thighs, convulsing him wherever they touched, stinging pain and ache, mortal ache, and blackness. Then a hot coal touched his private parts and he shrieked and not even ten hands of five powerful warriors could subdue his writhing body. Then the coals touched the bottom of his feet and he flew out of himself into madness, muttering and yowling like a rabid wolf.

A rifle boomed but he scarcely heard it. Blood splattered across his burned and raw chest, but he scarcely felt it. A body fell on him, even as the rifle boomed again, and other rifles, but he scarcely knew of it. The torture stopped but the pain still burst through him, waves of lava that exploded in his head, one after another. Then no one pinioned him. Blackness. He could not see. He hoped he might die fast. His breath came in gasps. His heart pattered, too fast, bursting itself within him. It slowed, and he caught a hoarse breath. More shots, volleys of them. God, let him die, let him die . . .

Someone beside him. "Easy, mate, easy," said Mister Skye. "We chased the scurvy bunch of them. Killed four, bad medicine for them."

"Shoot me," begged Father Kiley.

He felt small feminine hands on him, cutting the thong that bound his arms and legs, and in the midst of his pain he remembered he was naked.

"Cover me," he cried.

"Easy, mate," came Skye's voice. "It's nothing to them and they have washing and salving to do. Mary and Victoria are here; James Method's here. Clay Sample's here. Alfred too. Wagons are on the hill yonder, and the preachers are guarding."

"Where are my clothes?"

"Scattered about, mate. Bad medicine. Three that wore your things died, and Wolf-That-Circles is dead. We took your collar off him."

"Kill me, I beg of you. I cannot see."

"Nay, mate, we'll be doing none of that."

The priest felt a powerful rough hand hold his. Pain lacerated his head and muddled his thoughts, tearing his mind to pieces. He saw God and then he didn't. He touched his brow area and felt wet pulp. His nose was a blistered hill, dripping fluids. The only reality was the ghastly pain, and the big rough hand holding his own in the middle of midnight.

He grew feverish and slipped in and out of awareness. At last he felt a blanket around him, torturing him wherever it rubbed one of his burns, and then strong gentle hands were carrying him, laying him on a tick, covering him.

"You're in the wagon with the organ," Mister Skye said. "Your face is in a bad way, but the rest of you isn't so bad, a dozen burns that'll heal up. Aye, you'll live, Father Kiley, whether you want to or not."

"Pray God that I will not," he begged.

He heard the voice of Cecil Rathbone speaking. "Can't say that it's the end, Father. Can't say that at all. Not from the standpoint of heaven above. Might just be the beginning. Only, was I in your shoes, I'd figure it the end for sure. Don't know how you took it. I'd a gone plumb mad. You got some kind of holy fire burning away in you, I'd say. No, Father, it's no end."

He heard Esmerelda. "Dear Father Kiley," she cried. "How my heart aches for you. How I wish . . . how I wish . . ." She wept. Her hand found his and clutched it.

But he could think of nothing to wish for.

# Chapter 10

For two days Father Kiley was out of his head. The wagons toiled northward over gigantic shoulders of land that reached out from the westward mountains, all the while to the somber groaning and cries and babbling from within the covered wagon. They were all subdued by that ever-present reminder of suffering and terror and the suddenness of death in this wild land.

Mister Skye detailed James Method to provide meat for the small caravan, and to scout as well to the west, or mountain side. They passed close to Pumpkin Buttes to the east, and then struck the Powder River and worked north in its valley a way. In the lush wide valley of the Powder the going was level and the animals rested after the up and down strain of negotiating the surrounding slopes. But the Powder was a favorite place among the hostile Sioux and their allies the Cheyenne, and Mister Skye did not want to tarry there long. Victoria, who became his principal scout, felt nervous all the while. She had seen several smokes, and her keen senses told her they were never far from other parties. Tomorrow they would cut northwest over a high prairie divide, to Crazy Woman Creek.

Each morning and evening Victoria tended the raving man, making poultices of roots and herbs known only to herself, which she collected, ground to powders, and carried with her in small skin sacks. She had dealt with innumerable wounds in her day among her own people as well as Mister Skye and Jawbone, but nothing she had ever seen was as ghastly as the oozing carnage of Father Kiley's eye sockets and the blistered dripping red flesh that surrounded them. Still she cleansed the wounds while the priest raved, and packed in the wet mash of her medicines and then bound his head again. The other burns, while festering and painful, were not mortal or even dangerous unless they infected badly.

For Father Kiley there were no longer days and nights, and he raved and sobbed at odd hours, deep in night as well as noon. Little of it sounded coherent, but Mister Skye thought the priest was addressing, variously, his mother and father, a brother, the Virgin, the founder of his order, St. Ignatius, and others beyond deciphering. In his more rational moments the priest begged to die, prayed God to slay him. And always there was the priest's red pain maddening him; a pain that never lifted. The man was feverish as well, his tortured body hot and dry, and frequently each day Skye stepped off Jawbone and gave the priest a dipper of water. He had seen terrible things in his day, but this was one of the worst, and it built in him an awesome thirst he knew he could not long resist.

Of the others, only Cecil and Esmerelda approached the sickbed. The Newtons somewhat grumpily pulled their tick from the wagon and began to camp outside nights. Alex and Cecil took turns driving the oxen hauling the organ and the priest, but the groaning cargo was more than Alex could endure, and he fled from the task as much as possible. As for Silas Potter, he had a sharp and unsympathetic opinion of the whole matter, and voiced it to anyone within earshot, including Mister Skye.

He pitied the poor priest, blinded forever, but it had clearly been the wrath of God, unloosed upon the minion of Rome among them. Of those who contemplated the priest's suffering, Esmerelda was affected the most, for she had a practical and loving bent that foresaw a bitter life for the blinded man. She would have nursed him but for Victoria, who seemed better able to cope with those ghastly wounds and a raving spirit. And beyond the endless suffering there loomed the question: what would they do with this helpless man out here? Where would they take him? Wilderness stretched in every direction. He could not be dropped off somewhere, turned over to someone's care. This Irishman, this Jesuit who wore the collar of Rome, had suddenly become their burden.

Then, after three days of raving, Father Kiley became himself. Victoria, who was tending him at the time, was the first to know it.

"Is it day or night?" the priest asked. "Who am I talking to?"

She summoned Mister Skye, who was eating buffalo cow ribs succulently prepared by Mary.

"It's evening, mate, and Mister Skye here, and my Victoria."

"I could eat a little," he said. "If I can sit up. I hurt so much I don't know whether . . ."

He started to lift himself up, but fell back weakly.

"You'll be getting well fast now, Father."

The priest sighed. "I don't want to. Forever night. I don't know why . . . Why must I suffer this? It was because I wasn't brave. I didn't have faith; I didn't endure . . . I cried and begged them, most shamefully."

"You have nothing to be ashamed of," Mister Skye retorted harshly.

"I failed in every way a man given to our Lord can fail. They wanted to see whether I had medicine. They tested my medicine. Religion for them is medicine, power. And I had none, none at all, only weakness of body and a faithless soul . . ."

"Father Kiley, I'll not have you torturing yourself,

tormenting your soul along with your body. Let me tell you something, mate. We came over the ridge and saw what it was all about, and began shooting at once. I killed three of them. This new Sharps with its paper cartridges reloads fast, mate. And Victoria killed one, and Mister Method injured two, all before they reacted much. Then they fled. The dead ones were wearing your clothes. Wolf-That-Circles was one, shot through the head. You know what the rest did? They stripped off your priest clothing from the dead. That stuff had medicine, big medicine, bad medicine. The story of that medicine, Father, that story is going to fly from campfire to campfire, to every tribe on the plains, and I doubt that any of your folk, wearing your collar, will ever be menaced again. They hadn't ever seen medicine like that and they aren't going to forget it.''

The priest sighed. ''Medicine. That's not what I came to bring them. Not what I wanted . . . superstition . . . just coincidence that your bullets hit the ones who wore my things—you didn't shoot at them for that reason, did you?''

Mister Skye shook his head, and then realized that the priest couldn't see. ''No, it was just something that happened. But it's big medicine for them. From now on, they'll leave priests alone, mate.''

Father Kiley sighed. ''It means nothing.''

''You're wrong. It means everything. All religion is medicine, the quest for power and control, whether you want to admit it or not.''

The priest didn't respond. Then, ''Are you a believer, Mister Skye?''

''I don't know what I am. I think about it, like most men. Read about it too.''

''You read?''

''Whenever I can lay me hands on a bloody book.''

The priest lay quietly, exhausted even by these few words. Then Victoria returned with warm broth and a horn spoon, and slowly fed the priest a little, then more.

"That's enough," he said. "My head bursts with every swallow."

"I don't know the mystery of religion, Father. I'm too old, and a bloody scoundrel, and beyond knowing, I'd say. But I'll tell you, mate, things happen. Things that can't happen naturally. I've seen strong and haughty men struck down at the height of their power. I've seen weak, miserable, hopeless ones lifted up, find courage, dare the impossible, and succeed. I've seen too much o' that not to respect it. At sea, and here in the wilds. The Indians call it medicine, and I'd call your faith medicine too, but of another kind."

"I can't talk anymore," Father Kiley said. "Even to form words is too much and sets my head afire . . . more than I can bear. Never goes away . . ."

Mister Skye knew what he'd do, then. For himself more than the priest.

"I've got just the painkiller," he said. "The very jug of sour mash you bought at Mister Bullock's."

The priest nodded. "I'll try anything," he said. "Anything to slow this pain down."

Skye clambered from the wagon and lumbered heavily toward the mule-packs beside his lodge. Victoria watched him, knowing. Jawbone watched him, knowing. He yanked the cords loose and rummaged within until he found the brown jug, stoppered with a cork. This he twisted out sharply and threw it aside. This jug would not be returned to its niche in the pack goods half emptied. Then he lifted it, letting the fiery liquid gurgle from the neck and into his mouth until he burned, and his eyes watered, and still he didn't stop. Then finally, a pint later, he wiped tears from his small eyes, stood quietly, the demon pressures gone, and returned to the wagon where Father Kiley lay.

"Try this, captain."

The priest held up his hands feebly, searching for whatever was proffered, and Mister Skye realized he must help the man.

"Right here, captain," he said, placing the jug in Father Kiley's hands.

"Just a little," said the priest. "Enough to stop the pain. Oh God, enough to damp it a wee bit."

The jug was heavy, and he barely managed to lift it, and lift himself up enough to swallow. He coughed. Mister Skye watched him hawklike, ready to catch the jug, ready to snatch the precious juices in it.

"Ah," said the priest. "Ah . . . just a little. I am a weak man, Mister Skye. I should endure all this and more, but I am weak."

He sucked again, and coughed, and Mister Skye rescued the brown jug as it slipped.

"That is enough," Father Kiley said. "I am sinking into the pits."

His body drooped and then relaxed, and his ragged breathing steadied. But Mister Skye scarcely noticed. He lifted his jug regularly, feeling fire in his belly that spread out to limbs and made his head light.

Victoria peered in. "Come to the lodge. Sonofabitch, this here is a granddaddy coming. You git your ass to the lodge. Them missionaries all looking now, too, and ain't that trouble."

Mister Skye did as he was told. He usually managed that, managed to get to the lodge when Victoria demanded it. She would take over, she and Mary and Jawbone, while he took a voyage of his own.

They were staring, he knew, icy glares as he wended his way from the wagon to his lodge, but it didn't matter. Once in a while it was good that nothing mattered. Not anything. Not Methodists for sure, not the priest, or himself. Maybe Dirk, his little son, born of Mary.

He settled back into his buffalo robes and sucked regularly, feeling the warmth spread to his toes and fingers.

"That's the way the stick floats," he muttered. "Here's damp powder and no way to dry it . . ." and then, after a fine satisfying belch, "God save the bloody Queen."

* * *

The priest lay quiet that night, and for that the Reverend Cecil Rathbone felt grateful. For three nights the priest's sobs and groans had rended the dark and spawned terrible night-thoughts in them all, pouncing upon them when their aloneness in the dark lay deepest. On the other hand, from Mister Skye's small lodge there had emitted awful sounds all night, like a bull's bellow or an elk's bugle, and for these Cecil was not grateful. Their guide was drunk. Nay, more than drunk: he had departed from them into some world of his own, bawling like a newly weaned calf.

So the night was sleepless like the previous three, and at dawn the mood turned sullen among them. Even tireless Esmerelda showed signs of strain and fatigue, he thought, watching her as she busied herself at the cookfire.

Alex Newton approached, looking unkempt and haggard. "Your Mister Skye has become a drunken lout, leaving us unprotected and unguided," he said acidly. "We seem to have little choice but to turn back. Preferably alone, leaving that swine and his squaws here to meet their fate."

The thought had occurred to Cecil, but he resisted. He possessed a dream. "Let us wait and see," he replied mildly. "Perhaps this will pass in a day. We could all use some rest, and a quiet day given to repair of ourselves, and given to God—it's Sunday, I believe—might serve us well."

Over at Mister Skye's lodge there erupted a great bellow, and the guide emerged, shaking his head from side to side. He wobbled unsteadily ten yards, and then dug at his breechclout and relieved himself. The white women turned their faces away.

"We cannot permit this," snapped Alex. "The man's everything that is barbaric and pagan and unholy, and now he has offended our womanhood."

Mister Skye rolled unsteadily back to his lodge, but it was no longer there. Victoria had yanked it down and was folding the lodgecover. So he teetered over to Jawbone, but the evil horse laid back its ears and clacked its teeth and then butted Mister Skye, who tumbled to the ground and growled.

"Mercy!" said Esmerelda.

"Now his true character emerges," said Silas Potter coldly. "I saw it from the beginning and tried to warn . . ."

Something in the young man's smugness annoyed Cecil. Something of instant judgment and impossible standards and holy rectitude that felt as cold as a grave.

"I think we should hold a meeting here and now and decide what to do," Silas continued. "We obviously must do something. Skye is scarcely among the living and can't guide us. I don't suppose he could even say which way is north. And no protection at all. What if the savages fell on us? And we have that mad priest to cope with too—"

"He is not mad," said Esmerelda tartly.

Silas Potter stared coldly from behind his thick lenses. "Blinded then. He is now physically what he and all his ilk have always been mentally. I think there is a kind of justice in it. At any rate we have that to deal with, and I suppose we're stuck, unless we simply leave him here with the drunk and his loathsome squaws, and we return to Fort Laramie . . . picking up the other wagon and the Newtons' furnishings, if they haven't been demolished by passing savages. If our party is dirtied, it must wash, and the way to cleanse ourselves is to scrub away the filth and return to holiness."

Both Alex and Henrietta agreed, adamantly. The Samples, as usual, tended to their business and avoided the controversy. James Method was out scouting.

Cecil wasn't ready to surrender. "We'll wait a day. Take your rest today. We will see how things look in the morning. I'm not going to throw away a thousand miles of hard travel just because of a temporary setback. Mister Skye has kept us out of harm's way and delivered us here, and I'll not quit now. I am going to conduct some small Sunday service in an hour, when we are done with chores. I intend to invite Father Kiley to join us.''

The look on Silas's face told Cecil a lot about the young man. Too much. He knew instinctively that he had chosen the wrong man to come west and teach the Blackfeet. The man was a holy hater, without a saving humor, and Cecil went cold at the thought of putting the Blackfeet, who would be both suspicious and eager to absorb the religion of the whites, in daily contact with Silas. And there'd be no help for it. This deep in the wilderness, the die was cast.

He watched Victoria clamber into the wagon to succor the priest. She was burdened with her bag of medicines, an iron pot, and a brown jug. Somehow the woman had brought Father Kiley along, tended to his needs, cleaned him, helped him through his bodily functions, and all of it kinder and more Christian than anyone in his camp. Cecil felt ashamed.

He walked to the wagon and found her spooning a buffalo meat stew into him.

"This is Cecil Rathbone, Father. I trust you are better?"

The priest remained silent. Then, "I couldn't say."

"It's Sunday, and I'm going to have a little service. A psalm, some Scripture, a prayer or two, maybe a little sermon. Thought maybe you'd like to sit in . . .''

He was met with silence.

"Or maybe I could read to you some, from your book, your, eh, breviary . . .''

"No.''

"Well, if I can help—''

"No. I failed and am an outcast. Thrown into the darkest corner of hell, Reverend.''

"Sonofabitch, you're crazy, blackrobe. You just getting your sight now, medicine sight inside. You're gonna be big medicine man before you know. Goddam, you ain't got sense.''

She set the pot aside angrily and began cleaning his wounds.

"You!" she bellowed at Cecil. "You go away. You go get your people ready to move. Too damn much daylight gone by. We're all ready. All set to hop on ponies. Mary, she got us packed up."

"This is our holy day and I've declared a day of rest," said Cecil firmly.

"We ain't gonna stop. This here place ain't safe and we're gonna git out, see?"

"Without Mister Skye?"

"He's going to get on Jawbone. Mary and me, we'll lift him up. He's gone away awhile but he'll come back. Meanwhile, I'm the chief, you see? Sonofabitch, we don't stop for nothing. Me and Mary and Jawbone, we are the chiefs now."

"I think you have your marching orders, Mister Rathbone," said Father Kiley.

"I am going to have my services," said Cecil stubbornly. "But after that we'll go if you insist."

Victoria glared. "Make 'em fast. We got to go. This is a bad place, see? Too damn many Lakotah around the Powder River."

There was something in all this that delighted Cecil, and he agreed. On this day they'd do another fifteen miles or so, trek that much closer to Sun River.

"I will tell them," he said.

"You, blackrobe," said Victoria, proffering a jug to Father Kiley, "you drink some firewater I stole from Skye. Make pain go away. Drink before he come get it."

The priest found the proffered jug, swallowed and coughed, and swallowed again. "It helps," he said softly.

Two hours later the small caravan rolled out of the valley of the Powder and toward some high, rugged prairie ridges. When Cecil told his missionary party that they'd travel that day as usual, immediately following a brief service, they stared back harshly. All except Esmerelda, who laughed with delight. But they had silently packed and prepared, and silently listened when he conducted his service. And before they decamped, Esmerelda, as well as James Method, had stopped at the wagon and quietly held Father Kiley's hands, giving what they could.

Ahead rode Mister Skye, jug in hand, and listing twenty degrees to the right. Cecil Rathbone could not imagine how that black silk hat stayed on the guide's head.

# Chapter 11

They toiled slowly this day because the land was rugged, and the towering shoulders of prairie were riven with gulches and thickets of chokecherry and buffaloberry brush. Victoria watched impatiently as the white medicine men behind her dug the earth with their shovels so the lumbering wagons and the carriage could ease into a dry gulch and groan up the other side. Sweat rivered from them, and their chief, Mister Rathbone, had finally taken off his black clothes and put on faded blue britches.

Victoria did not scout today: it fell to her to lead the caravan, because Mister Skye was in his own world for a while. She sent Mary out to the right, and the powerful black man, James, out to the left, and hoped they would see the world as well as she did. Before her, on the withers of her pony, sat Dirk, as much at home with Victoria as with his mother. She had no doubt about Mary's scouting. Mary had Indian eyes and could see and stay hidden herself. But the black white man, James, she worried about. The whites didn't see. That had become obvious to her over her long life. They could look straight

at trouble and not see it. Often they didn't see it even
when they looked at it through the magic eye-that-makes-
things-bigger. The first time she had looked through
Mister Skye's magic eye, she had jumped. The doe
she stared at was so close she could almost touch it. The
whites had strange and wonderful medicine, and the
magic eye was one of those things. But they had to have
medicine like that because they were so inferior in other
ways. Any Absaroka person could see things that the
white missed.

They were a strange people, the whites. They had lots
of words, but some of them could not be said. She grew
aware that the medicine men and their women recoiled
when she said some things, as if she was saying something terrible. She had learned the English words from
the trappers who stayed with the Crows each winter in
the days of the beaver-catching. Lots of good English
words filled her mouth full and rolled over her tongue
like honey. Sonofabitch! they'd say, and she liked the
sound of it better than the Absaroka. Mister Skye had
lots of words, and she mostly used the ones he used,
which were a little different because he came from across
the big water and the other trappers didn't. She liked his
better. But these medicine whites made sour faces, like
eating green cherries, when she used the words, and so
she knew these whites had good words and bad words.
More than ever, the whites mystified her. These medicine men should be able to use all words, not just some.
The Absaroka used all their words, and the shamans were
the word-givers, not the word-hiders.

Victoria did not relish being in command today, because this was dangerous country, and the Lakotah lurked
everywhere. Some of the Lakotah, the Brulé and Oglalla,
were at war, but some not, but that didn't make much
difference. There were always war parties out this time
of summer, hunting prey, hoping to jump enemy hunting
parties or steal horses from villages. A small party of
whites like this would be great sport for any of them.

Mister Skye would be away from the world for another

sun or two, she knew. He had finished the jug the black-robe had given him, and was now into the ten-gallon cask he had bought from the sutler. He sat on Jawbone swaying gently and hugging his jug. Whenever he listed too far, Jawbone snarled at him, and he set himself right for a while, only to lean the other direction, until Jawbone snarled at him again. Jawbone didn't like to have Mister Skye out of the world, and he walked with his ears laid back and murder in his eyes and was twice as dangerous in these times. He let Mary and Victoria lift Mister Skye on and off his back, but that was all.

The trouble with this land of great shoulders was that whole war parties or villages could be hidden just beyond any ridge, and it worried her. It was ambush country. It would take a dozen scouts, not two, to check all the possibilities for trouble. To make matters worse, the wagons had to travel along the smoother ridges rather than the coulees, so they were visible for miles in these uplands. So Victoria rode, expecting trouble and maybe death at any instant, and constantly seeking out defensive places as they went along, where they could instantly shelter themselves from arrows and the occasional fusil or rifle of the Lakotah or their Cheyenne allies.

When Mister Skye was in the world he would show himself to enemies, and maybe treat with them, and his medicine and Jawbone's medicine were so great that usually there would be no battle. The Indian people of the prairies knew that to fight Mister Skye or Jawbone was to invite death. But they had never caught Mister Skye out of the world as he was now, and Victoria worried that they might at any time, and kill him, and then the rest of the party.

They struggled over the crest of a dry divide in the middle of the gusty day, and stared down upon the long green basin of Crazy Woman Creek miles distant. The going was steep, and they had to lock wheels once again. An hour later they reached a flat filled with shady cottonwoods and watered by a purling spring, and here Victoria called a midday halt to rest and water the animals, and unlock the wheels of the wagons. Mary appeared, but Mister Method did not. Victoria, who was Mister Skye's sits-beside-him wife, listened to Mary detail the dangers ahead. She had seen nothing but she knew there were war parties ahead. It was something she knew. It was something Victoria knew too, and she wished Mister Skye were back in this world. She feared for James Method. He might be caught. He might give away their position to the Lakotah.

But all remained silent. A red-tailed hawk soared above the protected valley. She spotted crows, the symbols of her people, hopping from limb to limb among the cottonwoods. She could feel trouble, but could not see it. Together she and Mary lifted Mister Skye from Jawbone and let the horse graze. Skye relieved himself and sat upon the grasses, muttering and sighing and cradling his shining new Sharps in his big hands, and staring into the prairie hills.

The medicine people busied themselves with the livestock and the wagons and a simple noon meal. They were all quiet, knowing that Mister Skye was not in the world with them. The blackrobe groaned in the wagon, so Victoria took the jug away from Mister Skye and gave some of the spirits to the suffering priest.

"Is this Victoria?" he asked. "I am glad to have a sip. My head, my face . . . everything seems more painful than ever today."

He sucked the raw whiskey and gasped, and sucked again.

"I never knew how it is to be helpless and hopeless and plunged into hell. And to depend utterly on others for everything, the food I eat and the needs of my worthless body," he said. "I wish a good Sioux arrow would take me."

Victoria had no answer for that; there was none.

A half mile to the south James Method burst over a ridge on a sweated horse and raced recklessly downslope to their camp, and Victoria knew that the trouble had come. Jawbone laid his ears back and snarled, and in one gigantic shaking heave pitched Mister Skye's loose-cinched saddle off him and prepared for war. Mister Skye rocked slowly and then stood up, weaving like a dying top.

James Method rode fluidly, staying with the horse even as it plunged down a hard slope creased with gullies. It was no small feat of horsemanship, and Victoria momentarily admired it. But then the ridge above him filled with riders, bronzed warriors naked save for their breechclouts, ponies dancing along the ridge, a great horde of them, twenty, thirty, finally maybe fifty, she thought, all stripped for battle or the hunt. Not painted for war but plainly looking for prey of any sort, the great summer war games of the plains Indians. They lined the ridge, a terrible sight spread far to the left and right, dancing their sweated ponies, taking the measure of the small party below with its astonishing wagons where none had ever rolled before.

They were waiting, plainly, for some signal from the tall warrior who sat his white horse quietly about in the middle of the line. Then some of them were pointing and gesturing at Jawbone, and at Mister Skye, who rotated on his feet and peered at the blur ahead of him. Victoria hoped that it might be enough; that his mere presence and medicine might stop the slaughter. Mary stared, gathered Dirk to her, and began to sing her Shoshone death song. Victoria shuddered. Soon she would sing her own, and then join the others who had gone across to the other side.

But not yet. "Sonofabitch!" she cried. "You!"—she gestured at Cecil Rathbone—"get them damn horses and mules into the cottonwoods. Get them damn rifles out. Get them damn women in the wagons if they ain't gonna shoot. Get them damn wagons rolled around to make a fort along the cottonwoods. You git ready to shoot lotsa Lakotah. Mebbe Sans Arcs, mebbe Minneconjou."

They unfroze and began feverish preparations. Henrietta burst into tears and fled into the wagon. Clay Sample and his son Alfred drew their rifles and found cover in a thicket of cottonwoods. Alice and Miriam Sample shooed the oxen and mules and horses into the woods.

"Oh dear," said Esmerelda. "I think I'm going to find a rifle and I think I am going to shoot."

She did find one in the carriage.

James Method raced up and jumped from his lathered horse.

"They're a-coming," he said to Victoria. "And there's more than I ever seen. I guess I ain't gonna be a freeman very long." Then he grinned. "Bet they ain't ever took a scalp like mine before."

He found an excellent defensive position behind a fallen cottonwood trunk. It even had a notch in it where his blue rifle barrel poked its deadly bore toward the ridge.

"You!" Victoria bellowed at Silas Potter, who blinked whitely behind his spectacles. "You get your rifle and guard the rear. Them Lakotah is going to run to the side, see? You git over to them cottonwoods over there and cut them off, see?"

He stared. "I don't take life. I will retire to the Sample wagon and invoke the divine blessing that will preserve us. Meanwhile, I trust you will proceed to make peace."

"Sonofabitch!" Victoria roared. "You and that other one, Newton. You git your rifles and git into them cottonwoods and see that them Lakotah don't come from the sides."

Red-faced and frightened, Alex Newton demurred. "I think you should treat with them first. You know the hand signs and all . . . Tell them we are missionaries. Medicine men. Peacefully passing through to do the works of God, eh?"

"Sonofabitch, you git them rifles and plenty of powder and ball."

Neither of them did as she bid. And now the leader, up there on the ridge, was putting on his warbonnet. Its white and black eagle feathers caught the sun and whipped in the wind. Its red tradecloth trimming looked as bright as new blood. Its tasseled ermine skins framed the face of the chief. The long bonnet-tail of feathers whipped sideways and fell over the croup of his dancing white pony. But still they pointed and argued up there, and it was Mister Skye's presence they argued about.

For his part Skye yawned, belched, lifted his new Sharps, and fired into the heavens. A hawk plunged to earth, losing feathers as it fell, Victoria gaped. How could he do such a thing? Within seconds he loaded a new paper cartridge and primer. Whites stared. Skye belched.

Above, young warriors were arguing heatedly with the chief, and Victoria knew exactly what they were saying: there is Mister Skye down there, and Jawbone. We are over fifty and they are few. Now at last we can count coup, take the scalp of Skye, kill the terrible horse. And whoever kills Skye will be the greatest warrior on the plains. And each of the young Lakotah, she knew, dreamed the dream of glory, of Skye's scalp on the tip of his war lance. They would come even if the chief forbade it; the young warriors would sweep down and around, seeing only glory against such a puny party below.

And they would succeed, she knew. Who among these missionaries could even shoot straight? Then they stopped arguing, and the warriors on the ridge began a fierce war chant, wheeling their restless ponies, gathering into three attack groups, one for each flank and one down the center, even as the chief directed with sharp strong gestures up there.

Jawbone, ears back, returned the howl, with an unearthly shriek. Mister Skye was not in the world and not in the saddle, so he would need to fight alone. Mister Skye peered boozily up the slope and decided to saddle up. Languorously he lifted his saddle to Jawbone's back and tightened the cinch, fumbling a little. It gave Victoria some small hope. Skye's actions were so deliberate that he seemed contemptuous of danger. From above, where the warriors were milling and watching fascinated, Skye would seem to have a superhuman nonchalance. Still, Victoria thought, it was nothing. Nothing against so many crazed young Lakotah. This would be her death-song day. And all these missionaries, too. They would die whining the way whites usually did.

Behind her Henrietta Newton was doing something crazy, pawing desperately at the puckerstring of the wagon. Then she had the canvas loosened at the rear of the wagon and pulled it over the bows until the organ in the rear of the wagon was in plain sight. It puzzled Victoria. Maybe Henrietta was just showing the warriors on the ridge what useless plunder lay in the wagon, that big wooden thing that did whatever it did. Victoria shrugged.

Then they came. With an ear-shivering howl they flowed down the long grassy slope, shining bronze bodies glinting in the afternoon sun, wild ponies plunging and dancing beneath them, lances in hand, bows nocked with arrows. Above, the chief sat still on his white horse, watching. There were two headmen with him, ready to convey his messages.

Jawbone shrieked but Mister Skye held him, weaving gently in his saddle. Even out of this world, Mister Skye was an awesome force, and with Jawbone beneath him, a danger to the clot of warriors pouring toward him. Victoria knew what Mister Skye would do, and Jawbone knew it too. At the right moment they would plunge up the slope directly toward that war chief on the ridge.

Behind her Henrietta was still fussing with that organ thing. Now she sat before it and pulled out small white-capped things. What a useless business. At least the woman was not cringing in the bed of the wagon the way some white women did in war. Then her hands pressed down on the organ thing, and thunder rose up from it and shivered through the valley. "A Mighty Fortress Is Our God," she sang in a quivery voice even as the organ sent thunder out into the ranks of the howling warriors, now only a hundred yards off.

"Sonofabitch," yelled Victoria.

"Jaysas," muttered Mister Skye.

Several warriors pulled up their ponies and gaped.

Victoria sighted down the barrel of her carbine and squeezed, and one fell off his pony.

The music bellowed out now, as majestic as a cathedral hymn, with Henrietta's tart soprano in accompaniment. What new and terrible medicine was this? Victoria didn't know. Mary, hand to her mouth, peered at the organ wagon, terrified. A shot racketed from James Method's rifle and another warrior who had stopped in his tracks to fathom the thunderous organ fell.

An arrow hissed toward Henrietta but missed. She was oblivious to danger anyway, spellbound by her own recital. Several of the milling Sioux renewed the charge, but Clay Sample's rifle barked and then Alfred's. Esmerelda, crouching behind the carriage, aimed and fired and a pony faltered, sagged and collapsed, the young warrior on it jumping free. And still they milled, terrified of this thunder-music. Some saw that it was only noise and tried to rally their brothers to battle. But others saw the medicine of the sky spirits in this white woman's hands and knew the day would be evil unless they fled at once. More arrows hissed, and one burned past Victoria slicing her sleeve and drawing blood on her arm.

"What's happening?" cried Father Kiley.

"The Sioux are attacking," said Henrietta primly as her hands continued to press the keys.

"I will stand then and pray for an arrow," he said, rising in the wagon beside Henrietta and the organ. He wore his priestly clothes again, which were none the worse for wear except for some bullet holes in them. And then the warriors were pointing at him as well, the man in the black suit and white collar, with a heavy bandage over his eyes, tall and blind and exposed to whatever arrow or bullet came.

Far up on the ridge the chief in the warbonnet barked something to his lieutenants, and the subchiefs rode down the slope, signaling. It seemed all over, at least for the moment. Victoria did not lower her carbine. There might still be some Lakotah warrior itching to count coup against Mister Skye. Jawbone shrilled insanely, pawing the earth.

Henrietta finished "A Mighty Fortress Is Our God," and started "Rock of Ages," still warbling along with the thunderous organ.

"Jaysas," growled Mister Skye. "My head."

Cecil rose from under a wagon. "Henrietta, dear," he said. "I think you have inspired us enough for the moment."

She played on, though, unable to stop, afraid the silence would bring renewed howls of war and death. Father Kiley held his hands to his ears, and then sat down weakly in the wagon again. And then at last Henrietta finished her solemn hymn, and stood, glaring at the world.

"Thank God," said Alex, but he didn't say for what.

From his vantage point high on the ridge, the chief elaborately pointed his rifle into the sky and fired. Then he slowly picked his way down the slope, his powerful bronze torso impressive even from Victoria's distance. His authority lay upon him. A nod, a gesture, won instant respect among his warriors. She knew he was a great chief of the Lakotah, a dread enemy of the Absaroka people. Easily the man rode, straight toward Mister Skye, who squinted through blurred eyes while Jawbone snarled. Mister Skye handed his jug to Victoria, and she knew he would come back into the world again. Jawbone watched Mister Skye pass the jug, and he no longer laid his ears back.

Then, at perhaps fifty yards, he waited. Mister Skye squinted, weaved, and roared like a grizzly.

"Man-Afraid-of-His Horses!" he roared. "It is you."

"And it is you, Mister Skye."

Mister Skye dismounted from Jawbone, who watched the encroaching menace with murderous intent and bared teeth.

But Mister Skye wove forward with open arms now, and the great war chief of the Oglalla Sioux did likewise. And then they were together, Mister Skye quietly pressing the chief's hands, and Man-Afraid-of-His-Horses likewise. From the ridge the Oglalla watched suspiciously, angry about their dead, and from the scattered shelters of the wagons and cottonwoods, the missionary party watched narrowly. What sort of turn of events was this? Victoria lowered her carbine as a sign of peace, but not all the way.

# Chapter 12

Under crisis, Mister Skye's mind cleared swiftly, although he was reluctant to abandon his whiskey-journey. He knew Man-Afraid-of-His-Horses well. Many times the Oglalla chief had come to Fort Laramie, and had visited with Mister Skye. Now they would smoke the pipe, and there would probably be a feast, unless some fool among the missionaries, or some refractory Lakotah warrior, caused trouble.

Even now Man-Afraid-of-His-Horses was pulling the sacred calumet from its soft-tanned bag, and summoning his lieutenants. Mister Skye recognized one of them, a tall craggy warrior in his early thirties named Red Cloud. He stared up at both of them. The Sioux leaders were tall men, though he was wider.

He thought to summon his own lieutenants to this parley. "Mister Rathbone," he called. "Bring Father Kiley, and leave your rifle behind."

He glanced at Victoria, who swiftly concealed the whiskey jug in the mule-packs, and at Jawbone, who had settled into resigned toleration of these enemies. Victoria and Mary would see what lay ahead, and erect the lodge nearby, for this would be an all-night affair.

He spotted James Method standing behind a cottonwood log rampart. "Mister Method, you will join us," he said. "We are going to have a party; lay down your rifles, all of you. Your lives depend on it."

He watched as Clay and Alfred Sample reluctantly slid their rifles into the wagon, and Esmerelda Rathbone lowered hers and grinned. Alex Newton hefted a rifle as well, but seemed almost paralyzed at the sight of so many warriors so close.

"Mister Newton," Skye roared.

Slowly the reverend lowered his weapon, and sought out Silas, who stood stiffly, white and staring, a Bible in hand. Those two would be the ones most likely to cause trouble, Mister Skye thought. He nodded to Victoria, who understood his purpose at once. She always did. She would keep her hawk's-eye on them.

Cecil Rathbone led the priest to the growing circle of headmen sitting in the meadow grass. Even as the priest sat down, shakily, beside Cecil, they were staring and pointing at the priest's bandaged eyes, but also at the bullet holes in his black coat and black shirt. Victoria had washed the priest's garments, purging the bloodstains from them, and Mister Skye knew exactly what the Lakotah were thinking—that the blackrobe's medicine had prevented the bullets from piercing his body. They themselves had sacred war shirts they believed turned bullets. They were almost as fascinated with James Method, although a black man of the whites was not new to them. From the fur-trade days, there had been several, including the dreaded Crow subchief, Jim Beckwourth.

"We shall smoke the pipe," said Man-Afraid-of-His-Horses, tamping tobacco into the bowl and igniting it from a glowing ember one of his warriors brought to him solemnly. The chief held the pipe before him, and then saluted the cardinal directions with it, and Mother Earth, and Wakan Tanka, and puffed solemnly. He passed it first to Mister Skye, who repeated the small ritual, and then passed it around the circle until all present had smoked the pipe of peace, and the charge of tobacco had been entirely consumed. Then he knocked out the ash and leisurely slipped the sacred pipe back into its elaborate pouch.

"Now then, Mister Skye," the chief said in Lakotah, "I will introduce my chiefs and you will do the same, and then we will talk. Our hearts are heavy because two of our young men lie dead, and one horse. Our hearts are afraid because of the bad medicine of the thunder-music-maker. And our hearts are curious about the blackrobe with the bullet holes in his clothing and the bandage upon his eyes, and the black man here, of a kind we have seen only once or twice in all our winters."

Then he introduced his headmen while Mister Skye translated for the whites and James Method. Mister Skye stared at Red Cloud, knowing in his bones that the craggy warrior with the proud demeanor would become a great Sioux war chief, perhaps against the whites someday. Mister Skye then introduced his own men.

"This is the Reverend Cecil Rathbone, a holy man who is taking his medicine people to the north to teach the ways of his medicine.

"And the man without eyes is Father Kiley, of the blackrobes, who is bringing his medicine to the people of the west. He is a brother of the blackrobe you know, Pierre de Smet. A few days ago he was caught by a hunting party headed by Wolf-That-Circles, and they put his eyes out. But Father Kiley's medicine was very large, for no sooner had they done that thing than Wolf-That-Circles died, and so did others among them who had taken his clothing."

The Oglalla headmen gasped. This was news indeed.

"What did you tell them?" asked Cecil Rathbone.

"That Father Kiley is a man of great medicine; that those Cheyenne who took his clothes all died."

"I have no medicine," said Father Kiley wearily. "I didn't want to teach them medicine. I came to bring them other things. You are misleading them, Mister Skye."

The priest spoke in a voice so small and tired that it seemed to fade even as he finished.

"Leave this to me, mate." Mister Skye said. "Who says you haven't got medicine? Will you say it wasn't the hand of God, eh?"

Red Cloud followed the exchange closely, and Mister Skye suspected he knew English.

Man-Afraid-of-His-Horses broke in. "We have two dead and even now I hear my warriors chanting the songs of death behind me. We have a dead pony. What will you pay us for this? We want many horses and powder and lead, and we wish to hear the thunder-music-maker if you will assure us it is not bad medicine."

Mister Skye turned harsh. "You lost your young men in war, attacking us. We did not attack you. They died honorably in battle and will be celebrated in the lodges of the Lakotah for dying bravely. We will give you nothing. We will not reward you for making war upon us. And you must never do it again. If we make the thunder-music you will all fall away like leaves after the frost comes."

The chief nodded solemnly, and then conceded. "It is as you say. Our medicine is bad because of the wagon that makes noise. We are not at war with medicine men. We wish to learn of this thing you have here. We have no word for it."

The priest surprised Mister Skye by responding in a hesitant Sioux tongue. "My good chiefs, it is called an organ, and it has no medicine in it. Only the One Above has medicine. It is the same thing as the flutes you have, only larger. It is used by whites to praise the One Above, mostly, but it is nothing but wood and metal and leather. If Mister Skye tells you it has medicine and you must fear it, then he misleads you."

Mister Skye was astonished.

Man-Afraid-of-His-Horses stared at him sharply, and Red Cloud did also.

"Mister Skye," said Father Kiley in English. "I'm a poor priest. I'd be an even poorer one if I let the Lakotah here believe that the organ has medicine powers for good or ill. I will not encourage them in their idolatry.''

Red Cloud, who seemed to understand some English, listened sharply.

"What is all this about?" asked Cecil Rathbone. "Have you threatened them with the organ?"

"Aye, mate, I have. Medicine is life or death here."

Cecil pondered it. "And so are other things life or death, Mister Skye. Please tell the chiefs and headmen that Henrietta will be pleased to present an organ concert of hymns offered to God.''

Mister Skye did, pondering all the while the strange courage of Father Kiley. And for that matter, the strange courage of Henrietta Newton who responded to bullets and arrows with hymns.

Man-Afraid-of-His-Horses nodded. "We will listen to the woman play the organ." he said. "We will have a feast. We killed two fat buffalo cows and that will be enough. We will listen to the organ make music to Wakan Tanka. And then we Lakotah will dance for Wakan Tanka, so that you may see our music as well. The black-robe, Father Kiley, speaks well and with a good spirit, and has eyes inside of his head that see light. We will honor this blackrobe, Father Kiley, as a friend of Lako-tah, and of the Oglalla people this evening, and we will give him a name. You, Skye, have great medicine, but medicine goes bad, and someday your medicine will not be enough for you.''

Mister Skye translated most of it for Cecil Rathbone and James Method, while Red Cloud watched intently.

The chief stood, and with him his headmen, and with a nod he retreated to his warriors.

Cecil Rathbone helped the priest to his feet. "I don't know what all that was about, not speaking Sioux lingo, but I got the gist of it. Must say, you got courage, pa-dre.''

"No," Kiley said slowly. "It is not that. It is that I have nothing, and therefore have nothing to lose. I would welcome an arrow, Reverend. My Lord has taken everything away from me, and surely I have been punished. I am a poor priest, but I could be a poorer one if I didn't speak out against idols.''

Mister Skye did not have time to ponder the strange turn of events. There was a feast to prepare for, camp to be made. And cobwebs to shake out of his head. Silently Victoria handed him a cup of coffee, and he drank the hot bitter liquid thinking of medicine and power and living and dying, and the warning of Man-Afraid-of-His-Horses.

"Mister Method," he said. "Some of the younger Sioux will no doubt try to steal the horses. They don't care about mules or oxen, though they might drive the mules off just to keep us from going after them. They're likely to try it even though the headmen have smoked the peace pipe. So . . . hobble them. And picket them close to the wagons. And you and the Samples keep guard. Shoot if you must.''

"Ah'll do it.''

"And, Mister Method. They've scarcely seen a black man. They'll be curious. You tell them what you want. They have slaves of their own, so they'll be interested in how you got away.''

"Not very often Ah'm the center of attention.''

"Well, enjoy yourself. They mean no harm.''

Mister Skye wanted to talk with Silas Potter. If this feast under the peace pipe turned into a slaughter, it would be Potter's doing. He found the young man slumped behind the Samples' wagon, staring whitely at the bustling Sioux warriors, jaw clenched.

"Need to talk with you, mate.''

"Are you drunk, Skye?''

"No, but I'm not cold sober either.''

"I do not heed the depraved.''

"You'll listen to me, mate. Your life depends on it. Stand up now. I'll not talk to you sitting down, like a man addressing a mutt.''

"Is that what you think I am, a mutt?''

"Stand up.''

Angrily and deliberately the young teacher stood, contempt written across his face.

"I do not intend to be at this party of yours. I will not watch heathen savages dance to their heathen god. I will not tolerate naked savages in the presence of our women."

Mister Skye scarcely knew where to begin, he had so much to say. He would have preferred a chop to the jaw that would lay the bloody fool down for a few hours.

"I'll start with a little warning, Potter. If you start trouble, any kind of trouble, I'll truss you up and gag your mouth and throw you in a wagon."

"That's about the way I've assumed you'd behave, Skye. All force and power and diabolical strength. No reason, no persuasion, no holy restraint. You're as barbarous as these savages. Do you know what preserved us a few minutes ago? Henrietta's hymns. The invoking of Divine Providence, and not your drunken confrontation with fifty or sixty armed Sioux, with a few rifles here."

"Medicine," replied Mister Skye. "Thunder-music, bad medicine for the Lakotah."

"Henrietta's faith; divine intervention."

Mister Skye was not one to mock God. "Perhaps you are right, Mister Potter."

Self-righteous Silas was not one to be gracious in victory. "Your demon medicine is nothing, and you have no authority over me. I intend to stop the heathen dance to their heathen god."

"Will you listen to reasons and arguments?"

"I've no intention of listening to any of your talk. You are Satan or one of Satan's."

Mister Skye shrugged. "That's what I thought, mate. We'll be watching you."

"Poke my eyes out and jam burning brands into me!"

"You envy Father Kiley, do you?"

Silas Potter looked pained. "The church of Rome is a whore," he said.

Mister Skye shrugged. There were other things to do, and he hunted for Henrietta, who sat quietly with Alex.

"That was a fine brave thing, Mrs. Newton," he said.

"No thanks to you," Alex intervened shortly. "With a drunken guide she had to do something."

"Aye, mate, I was that," Mister Skye agreed. "My women run a camp better than I, and you were bloody fortunate they were in charge."

"I don't believe in guns and war. We would have all been slaughtered," she said. "I played the hymns to rally us, remind us of our purpose, bringing God to the savages rather than fighting them. I played so that our missionary party would lay down our guns and trust in God."

Mister Skye grinned. "It was a brave thing, madam. The Sioux have requested a concert, and I have told them you would oblige. Play what you will, but play."

"I will do that," she said quietly. "Perhaps if they hear sacred music, they will be converted."

"They're going to dance, you know. They want to show us how they dance to Wakan Tanka. They have no drums or rattles, because they're traveling light, for war. Maybe you could do a drumbeat while they dance."

"I don't know—a heathen dance . . ."

"Mrs. Newton, what they call Wakan Tanka is their perception of God. A dance to Wakan Tanka is not the same as their dances to the animal spirits, buffalo dance, deer dance, rain-maker dance, and all the rest."

Henrietta looked at Alex, uncertainly.

"Well . . ." she said.

"I think not," said Alex. "Their nakedness offends our women. They're doing a heathen dance. No, when they start we shall all retire and not witness evil."

"I can scarcely imagine a graver insult to them," said Mister Skye.

"Mister Skye," said Alex in a pained voice. "We are people of God. We don't traffic with heathen things."

Mister Skye sighed. "I don't know what you'll do when you reach the Blackfeet—if you reach them, Reverend."

There was no arguing with them, so he left them. He'd

truss and gag them too, if he had to, if they invited a massacre. Off a little, the Sioux had several cookfires burning. Guards had been posted on a ridge, and herders watched their ponies. He counted fifty-seven of them. One small incident, and he and all his charges would be slaughtered. The warriors had finished skinning the buffalo cows—usually women's work but this was a war party—and brought the prize cuts, hump ribs that tasted better than a beef standing rib roast, to Mary and Victoria and the white women. He hoped the whites understood the courtesy of the Sioux, presenting them with the prize cuts.

The shadows lay long across the hills when at last the buffalo meat was cooked perfectly and the feasting began. There were three feasts, really. One composed of the Sioux warriors, off by themselves, some of them nursing anger toward the whites who had killed two of their number. At another fire sat a smaller gathering of the whites. But around a separate campfire between the others was Man-Afraid-of-His-Horses, his headmen, and invited guests, which included Mister Skye, Father Kiley, James Method, and Cecil Rathbone. Mary, Victoria, and Esmerelda sat outside of this circle, according to Sioux custom.

They ate heartily. The buffalo meat was as tasty as any that Mister Skye could remember. There was little time for talk although the ones next to James Method were curious about him and plied him with questions, which Mister Skye tried to translate from across the circle. The former slave enjoyed the attention. When at last they were all full and heavy in the belly, they wiped their hands in the grasses or at the spring beside the cottonwoods. And then the chief addressed those around his fire, in the twilight.

"I wish to give the blackrobe a Sioux name," he said, while Mister Skye translated. "He has a true tongue and is a brave man who has endured torture and pain. He's worthy of my people. Please bring him forward."

Cecil led the priest around the fire and settled him on the grass before the chief.

"I have decided on a Lakotah name for you," said Man-Afraid-of-His-Horses. "I have chosen a name that describes your great medicine. I will name you Man-That-Sees. From now on, among my people, you will be Man-That-Sees, and you will be welcome in any Lakotah village or camp, and all the Lakotah people will hear of you and know you are a brother."

Father Kiley nodded. "I am honored by the name," he said softly. "You have given me vision again. May I see in your behalf, and may my vision be true and pleasing to the One Above."

One by one the Sioux in the circle clasped his hands and gave him their names, the chief last, and it was done.

"Now we would like to hear the thunder-music again. We would like to see the woman make the music that praises the One Above."

The chief stood and beckoned his warriors, and in time they gathered quietly around the wagon with the organ in it. The canvas had been stripped away from its bows so that all might see Henrietta play. She sat down gravely, choosing a Bach recital first, before the hymns. When the first deep notes thundered into the lavender sky and echoed off the wild lonely hills where no such sound had ever been heard, the Sioux shivered and covered their mouths or held their ears, and even Mister Skye felt an odd twinge as the vibrating music lost itself in the wilds the way the rays of fire were dimmed by distance. Henrietta played determinedly, no longer from the sheet music before her because it was growing dark, a white-faced rigid figure. She did not play particularly well, Mister Skye thought, but with force nonetheless. She turned to her hymns then, all of them majestic and slow. No one sang. The warriors stared, absorbed by this novelty, half afraid at first but gradually relaxing. Across the flickering light Mister Skye watched Silas Potter and Alex Newton carefully, wondering what was going through their heads. And then Henrietta finished. She stood stiffly, bowed slightly, and clambered down from the wagon.

The chief stood. "Now my young men will dance." he said.

Mister Skye waited, on edge. A Sioux dance could involve almost anything, including a display of scalps. That, indeed, proved to be what this dance was about: a scalp dance, invoking the blessings of the One Above in the taking of many scalps from many enemies. The chosen dancers assembled around the fire, each carrying a lance dressed with scalps, or carrying war shields with scalps dangling from them. He saw excited whispering over among the whites, and pointing, and pained expressions, and Mister Skye feared the worst.

He leaned over to the chief. "I believe I can make the organ sound like a drum. Send me a drummer, and we will make the organ thunder like drums, fast or slow as your drummer says."

The chief spoke, and an older warrior, honored by the chief's request, sat down beside Mister Skye on the organ bench. He showed the warrior how to pump the bellows with his feet and how to tap the lower keys, and he returned to his place between the chief and Cecil. Then it began, harsh chanting, pounding organ beat, sticks on logs, and the rhythmic spastic movement of almost naked bronze men circling a fire, waving lances and shields adorned with human hair. Two or three minutes of that were enough for Silas Potter and the Newtons, who stared angrily and turned to leave, herding the Samples with them. That's what Mister Skye had feared, a calculated insult and a deadly gesture. He arose, intending to herd them back again or box them into submission, but Cecil caught his arm.

"Would our Sioux friends mind if I joined the hoedown?" he asked. "I haven't had a chance to kick up my feet since I left Illinois. Methodists frown on dancing, you know, but I feel a bit wicked tonight." He laughed heartily, even as his eyes followed the retreating backs of his missionary party out of the firelight. His eyes were not alone, for now every Sioux watched and muttered.

"Hurry!" said Mister Skye.

Cecil leapt up and headed straight into the circling warriors and began a nimble imitation, as spirited as anything the Sioux did. Laughter and excitement rippled among the Sioux. Cecil was grinning, leaping and dancing in his black suit, enjoying himself. Out at the edge of light, the Newtons and Potter and the Samples gaped, horrified.

Esmerelda stood. "Come, Father Kiley, we shall dance too, and I'll lead you. In their own way, they are dancing to God, and so shall we."

The priest shook his head at first, tired and afraid, but the cataract of her laughter caught him and his face brightened beneath the heavy bandage. He stood, and was led into the firelit circle and gently, with Esmerelda leading the priest, they circled the fire with quiet dignity. The warriors stood and howled with delight. The drummer working the organ speeded up the heartbeat. Man-Afraid-of-His-Horses smiled and leaned over to Mister Skye.

"There are some among your medicine men who are friends of the Lakotah, and some who are not," he said. "And so it shall be, before Wakan Tanka."

# Chapter 13

Crazy Woman Creek proved to be the toughest obstacle they had yet encountered. It ran between cutbanks in a rugged arid prairie valley, and it was running high because of heavy June storms in the Big Horns, combined with the last of the spring snowmelt. James Method rode over a mile in each direction from the point where the small caravan struck the creek, but the best he could come up with was a place somewhat to the north where the east bank was gentle enough to carry the wagons, while on the west side there loomed a ten-foot cutbank of tan gumbo clay. It would mean a lot of shoveling.

For three days after their encounter with the Sioux they had toiled down a long grade into the wide dry valley of the Crazy Woman. Mister Skye resumed command, keen-eyed and cold sober after giving parting presents of tobacco and shot and powder to Man-Afraid-of-His-Horses, and watching the Sioux war party trail east toward its Powder River village. James Method rode at his usual position, scouting forward and to the west, while Victoria scouted ahead and to the east. James had also become the principal hunter, something he did with ease and caution, never felling his game until he was certain there were no hostile parties within earshot. He favored buffalo, which grazed this up-and-down country in small groups, but when luck failed him, he could usually find a deer, and once an elk. He had a chance at a sow grizzly with a cub, but chose to avoid the dangerous animal.

All the long day the men of the party, mainly Cecil Rathbone and Clay Sample, along with Alfred, Silas Potter, and sometimes Alex Newton, took turns with a pike and shovels cutting a notch in the far cutbank that would serve as a ramp for the wagons. Alex Newton, soft and corpulent, swiftly blistered his hands and complained continuously. Silas Potter worked grimly, though his thin frail body kept him from achieving much. The real burden fell upon Clay Sample, who worked the pike into the hardpan, and Cecil, who shoveled the loosened earth away. Mister Skye helped occasionally, although he had the larger responsibility of keeping this party guarded and safe while it labored.

By the end of this hard day, with only a pitiful cut in the far bank to show for brutal labor, Alex began to complain about James Method, off scouting and hunting and lazing in the June breezes, instead of turning his powerful young body to the hard task of hewing out a wagon road. The black scout was unaware of it until he rode into camp at the end of the day bearing a heavy load of hump ribs, tongue, and liver he cut from a young cow.

"We employed Method because he's a strong young man and can do these things. I'm a minister of the Gospel and not made for such things. But you send him off lollygagging each day . . ."

"Mister Method is my choice," said Mister Skye bluntly. "Who else is there? Father Kiley can no longer do it."

"Yourself or young Alfred," Alex replied. "Maybe we don't need a scout at all. Your younger squaw could do it, keep an eye out . . ."

All of this was a peculiar and petulant argument coming from a man who had dug into the far cutbank less than an hour and had then pleaded blisters and fatigue. Even as Newton complained, Clay and Alfred Sample and Cecil Rathbone continued to chip away quietly and patiently.

Method had scarcely returned to camp when he felt Alex's glare, not to mention the frosty gaze of Silas Potter, and he wondered about it. The teacher's frozen gaze he was used to; he had rarely seen the frail white scholar smile or laugh. But he felt discomforted by the Reverend Newton's probing stare.

Then Mister Skye enlightened him. "Mister Method, they'd like you to help shovel. I suppose I'll have you do that in the morning, and I'll scout myself. After the nooning, we'll switch."

"Ah'll shovel," he said. He didn't mind. He'd let his lithe, powerful body work up a fine sweat. "Oh, Mister Skye, there's been another storm boiling up over the Big Horns, and flashing lightning I can even see from here, and Ah expect this river's going to flow hard soon enough."

The guide nodded.

Method turned over the meat to the women and stopped, as he did each evening, at the wagon where Father Kiley lay. "How goes it today, Father?" he asked.

"Is that you, James? I wish I could tell you better, but I can't. The pain never stops, and sometimes I think it's worse than ever. Victoria tells me there is lots of, ah, drainage from my eyes—from my eye sockets. I am reconciled to blindness, but Lord help me, this pain . . ."

"Ah'm sorry. Ah was hoping for better news."

"Tell me about your day," said the priest hastily.

"Ah saw something strange, and thought you'd know since you've been here a lot, or maybe Mister Skye . . . It was maybe two valleys over to the west, toward the Big Horns, still in this dry country and on a little creek Ah could jump across, with a lot of cottonwoods along it . . . good camping place. Ah dropped the cow buffalo right there, an easy shot, the wind right, and no sound carrying far out of that little bowl . . . And when Ah rode up, that cow was lying in some ceremonial place that gave me the shivers. There was twenty, thirty human skulls all in a circle, facing out, with signs of old paint on them, and some kind of rock pile with a stick in the middle, and paint-pictures on the stick, and other things, totems and amulets . . ."

"A ghost place," said Father Kiley. "Some village or some tribe lost a lot of people there, probably from ambush or war. They believe the spirits still haunt it. It's a taboo place where they never come. If I saw it, I could probably tell you what tribe. They all leave their marks. If you shot that buffalo cow in the middle of it, you'd better not tell Mary or Victoria, because they'll think that cow had one of the ghosts inside it. They'd no more eat that cow than shoot themselves."

"Ah thought it was a fine camping place. Would other tribes stay there now?"

"No, never. That's a place of terror, spirits haunting and lurking in the night, terrible things. No."

"Ah felt it, even in broad daylight, lots of sun, and the blue mountains with their white peaks just a little away. Ah got the shivers cutting her up."

From the campfire perhaps fifty yards away and far out of earshot, Victoria was staring at him and at the meat. It was not over the flames, but lying untouched in the grass. Then she walked to him in her fiesty way.

"Sonofabitch, that meat is no damn good," she snapped. "Where did you shoot it?"

"Nice little valley over west."

"What was there?"

"A few buffalo."

"It gives me damn bad feelings. That is bad-medicine meat. You get that damn meat out of this camp, way out, down the river and let it float, see? No good."

"That's fresh meat. Ah didn't even shoot it until a couple of hours ago."

"You get that damn hump meat out. I got the doe still hanging and we're gonna have that."

"Perhaps you could explain, Victoria," said Father Kiley softly.

"Nothing to explain. That cow got bad spirit in it. I stare at the ribs and I see old grandma Absaroka woman there. Sonofabitch, she's been dead ten, twelve winters now. I know her, that one in the meat."

"Surely you were imagining—"

"I see what I see. Now go get that dead Absaroka spirit woman and take it away or we all die."

There was no resisting her. She had the same sort of frantic power he had seen once before in an old black fieldhand at the plantation he had fled.

"Ah'm coming, grandmother," he said. Meekly he picked up the day's offering, wrapped it in a small tarpaulin, and carried it out of the camp, Victoria glaring at him all the while. Mister Skye noticed, and angled after him as he plunged deeper into the cottonwoods and away from camp.

"What was that all about?" Mister Skye asked.

"Victoria said the meat was evil, said she saw a ghost in it, and Ah have to remove it."

"Where'd you shoot that cow?" he asked sharply.

"Few miles west. In a place with some skulls in a circle. Ah confess, Ah didn't tell her that."

Mister Skye nodded. "I know the place. That is a place no Indian goes if he can help it. There was a slaughter there, whole Crow village wiped out, almost, by Arapaho wandering north of their usual haunts. Caught them at dawn, with the young warriors already gone after buffalo. If you saw a rock cairn and a marked stick and a few other things, that was Crow medicine there. But there's not a plains Indian who'd go near the place knowingly."

"Ah felt it, felt the evil, Mister Skye."

"Who can explain it, eh?"

"Ah don't understand Indian religion."

"Mister Method, I've been here in this wild land almost twenty years and I don't understand it either. But I respect it. Makes my hair stand sometimes. There are plenty of times when it's no good at all. The shamans will say good medicine is coming and then there's a disaster. But there are other times, mate, so help me, one of them has a dream, and they go to a shaman to have it interpreted, or they simply declare what is going to happen in the future, and then it happens exactly as they dreamt it. How do you explain that? I can't.''

''Ah think there's earth spirits and heaven spirits, and maybe the Indians know the earth spirits. Ah remember where Ah come from, there was an old woman, fierce old woman, one of the field darkies living in a shack, with wire gray hair and hot brown eyes and a thick nose, and all bent over and frail from a hard life picking cotton all her days, and she had it, the knowledge of the spirits and the future, and the power to change things. Ah was lucky, a house boy for the master, always living easy . . . But Ah used to sneak off and visit her down there and listen to her angry talk. She never just said something; she spit it out, made it snap out of her teeth. Ah'd take her the stuff Ah snitched from the big kitchen in the big house, sweets, leg of fried chicken, good stuff, so she liked to see me. She told me things then . . . she told me where Ah come from. Ah didn't know who my pappy was. Ah'm lighter so Ah thought maybe it was some white man, but the old woman said it was the master himself—and Ah was half-brother to the white boys Ah played with. She told me lots of things that were true. She told me Ah'd escape when Ah was older, and Ah did. Ah got a good education reading books and studying on the way the masters lived there in the house, and Ah had saved a few pennies and what all, and some castoff clothing, so Ah got a black suit and a boiled white shirt and a Bible one day, and ah got a stagecoach ticket—they wouldn't let me sit inside because Ah was a darkie—but Ah sat on top in my suit and white shirt and cravat with a Bible in one hand and a valise in the other, and rode away and no one stopped me. Ah was Reverend

Isaac Horne . . . Oh, Mister Skye, it was good to get
free. The masters treated me right kindly—Ah was
lucky—but still they owned me, could sell me or my
children, and Ah couldn't go anywhere because that slave
collar was around my neck, invisible but real . . . That
old woman told me it was going to happen. She told me
lots more, too . . ."

James Method suddenly remembered another story told
by the old grandma down in the shack, and his heart
lurched.

"You and I were both slaves, mate. I was press-ganged
by the Royal Navy at age fourteen, just a few blocks from
my parents' house near London. Never saw them again.
A slave in the bowels of a warship for years, until they
thought I wouldn't try to escape, and then I did, yonder
to the west where the Columbia River nears the Pacific
. . . Jumped over in fog, so the watch couldn't see me,
nothing but a belaying pin . . . Oh, it felt good, even
though I half starved for a month . . ."

But James Method wasn't listening. He had remembered still another of the prophetic stories the sharp-
tongued angry granny spat out at him in the shack beside
the cottonfield . . . a story with skulls in it and a storm,
and something else . . . something that would transform
his future.

"I suppose we've hauled the buffler meat far enough
to satisfy Victoria, mate. We'll leave it here for the
wolves and coyotes. They'll start a chorus tonight, eh?"

"Maybe Ah should take it back to the place where the
skulls are," Method said suddenly.

"You seeing the ghost spirit in it too?"

Method shrugged. "Ah think maybe she's right; that's
not buffalo at all."

Mister Skye looked exasperated. "You want to haul it
a quarter mile back and put it on a horse and haul it back
to the valley of the skulls, do you?"

"Ah think Ah do."

"That must be fifty pounds of buffler."

"Ah still think Ah do."

"Leave it," said Mister Skye.

Method shrugged, and they walked back through a loose growth of cottonwoods along the creek bottoms. But his mind wasn't in the present; it slipped back a few years, trying to remember what the fierce old granny in the shack had told him, what she had said would happen at a place with a circle of skulls that would give him the shivers . . . There were so many stories, and he couldn't quite remember this one. But he knew what he would do.

Back at the camp beside the Crazy Woman, the hostility grew so thick he felt it physically. Victoria squinted at him and muttered as she sliced a haunch of deer. The Reverend Alex Newton looked flushed and angry, and glared at him as if he were responsible for the blisters and the hard labor. Silas Potter, whose perfunctory courtesy had usually made tent-mate life easy for them, peered owlishly at him, bursting to criticize but not saying whatever it was that burned in his eyes. It was something James felt, and rightly or wrongly, he knew, they would turn their grievance into a racial thing: he had been sent by Mister Skye himself out to hunt and scout, but he knew that they were turning it into something else in their minds, darkies were lazy, darkies avoided hard work. He laughed within himself, thinking of the field-hands in the blazing sun of the cottonfields, doing brutal stoop labor because they'd be whipped or even killed if they didn't.

Well their opinions didn't matter. That was the magic of this wilderness, this vast somnolent country a thousand miles from the rim of civilization and organized life. Here he felt free in a way that not even freemen were free back there. Nothing could stop him from doing what he would. If he could survive, find food and shelter and friends, he could live here in perfect freedom all his days, forever beyond sheriffs and slave auctions and whips and masters and murder. So he smiled, said nothing this evening, and waited.

Only Mister Skye sensed anything, and now and then the guide stared at him with hard eyes.

It turned into a rumbling night as distant storms over the Big Horns flashed and growled, and the tendrils from them blotted out the stars. The growling of the heavens made them all uneasy. The Newtons, unused to camping and irked to have no wagon to sleep in, fussed with their tent and ran trenches around the side of it to carry rainwater off. Alex handled the shovel easily enough, blisters or not. Silas Potter also battened down, hoping to fend off water so that it didn't soak his bedroll, and James lackadaisically helped out. The Samples would sleep in their wagon tonight, high and dry. As for Mister Skye's lodge of carefully smoked cowhide that would turn any rain, the squaws always erected it in a place that would shed water well. That was a part of the Indian heritage and intuition of Victoria and Mary, and it had been done without a conscious thought. James watched Silas nervously anchoring the tent with extra ropes against the harsh winds that would rise in the night. Silas was too busy to notice James casually loading his gear in his saddlebags, or slipping his saddle and carbine sheath out into the night, or carrying his bridle off to the herd.

The horses and mules were restless and ready to bolt. A night like this could scatter their stock over vast areas. Clay headed out into the herd, bridles in hand, but the mules turned skittish and dodged him. He tried a horse, only to have it rear wildly as he approached. He called for Alfred to help, and then the rest of them. James grabbed a halter and a picket line. Alex and Cecil did too, cautiously circling the nervous animals. Several horses burst into a restless trot, and then stopped a hundred yards distant. Mister Skye, bareback on Jawbone, stood there, blocking passage. Cecil caught Magdelene and bridled her; then the others caught horses. The mules proved more difficult, but at last they too were picketed. There were not hobbles enough to go around, so only the better horses were hobbled, and at last the camp was ready for a stormy night. James drifted back to his tent, feeling strangely isolated and restless as he shifted more gear to his hobbled horse.

From his usual station near the lodge, Jawbone watched him narrowly, and James wondered if he'd shriek. Jawbone had been their night guard. Nothing approached the camp, four-footed or two, without Jawbone making a terrible racket. But would the demon horse permit a departure?

Then at last the campfire dimmed and the missionary party abandoned itself to sleep and silence. But the night muttered and roared and threatened. James did not wait long. After an hour or so he slipped out into the gusting dark—the stars were obscured so there was awesome blackness—and found his old bay horse. After saddling and loading, he set off into the night, leaving the sleeping camp behind him. Trusting the instincts of the horse because he couldn't see, he steered it north along the riverbank toward the spirit meat, and more by instinct than by senses found it untouched on the sand spit beside the creek where they'd left it. He wrapped it in burlap and lifted it to his overburdened horse and forded the creek through belly-deep water. The bay scrambled up a steep bank and then they were out, a jolt of lightning revealing the peaks of the Big Horns. He hadn't the faintest idea how to find the place of the circle of skulls, but he would try.

The ride that should have taken twenty minutes took hours. When he became utterly lost he rode to a ridgetop and waited for the lightning to give him a single blinding glimpse of the land, and in this way he wandered westerly, over several ridges. It began to rain lightly, and he dreaded the lightning when the storm was overhead. Still he pushed onward, his horse edgy and afraid between his legs. It was not his horse, really, but the missionaries' animal, lent to him for the journey, and that made him feel bad. But this seemed familiar. The storm was part of it, part of the old granny's story that was hissed out at him in harsh sibilants long ago. And in the story no harm came to him because of the storm. Still, the eerie rattle of lightning and the thunderous roars, and the hiss of light forking the black frightened him, and he wondered if the old granny was evil. Evil, leading him to his doom now. And then suddenly a flash revealed the place of the skulls down below. Rain pelted hard now. He felt the cold water sliding through his clothes, draining into his saddle beneath him, slithering down his neck. Another flash revealed the dead buffalo cow. He slid from his bay and undid the meat and returned it to the cow, reverently fitting it as close to its place in the carcass as he could, and when he looked up she stood there.

# Chapter 14

Astride Jawbone, Mister Skye stared at the buffalo cow carcass and the replaced meat. It had not been touched by wolves or coyotes or magpies, as if the animals, too, knew this place of the skulls was taboo. He looked for hoofprints, a trail, but knew there'd be none; the rain had washed everything away. Method was gone, vanished into thin air. Not an uncommon thing in this wild and lonely land.

"Bon voyage, mate," he said aloud, and turned Jawbone back.

His party had become smaller and more vulnerable with Method and his steady courage gone, and Father Kiley blinded and helpless. What would he do with the priest? Take him to Fort Benton up on the Missouri? And what would they do with him? Skye didn't know. There were no answers for a question like that.

When he left the camp the men were gouging the gumbo clay bank on the far side of the creek. The going became easier because the rains had moistened the soil for a foot or so, and the pike could work large chunks of it loose. But it still looked to be a labor of several days. He rode north, thinking that there was no particular need to cross just there, and maybe he could find a good ford at some place well below where Method had hunted.

It was a fine cool day, and the water beading on grass and leaves glinted in the sun. The air, washed of its dust, looked transparent. The brutal summer heat, which had made the digging such an ordeal, had temporarily gone. He pushed along the west bank of Crazy Woman Creek, beyond where he knew Method had scouted, hoping to find a crossing. Two miles yielded nothing but then the land flattened and the valley widened. Three miles north of the camp, he found a place. A rough one to be sure, but passable. The water flowed high from the rain, but the bottom was hard under Jawbone's feet, and the banks would not be an obstacle for double-teamed wagons. The river bottoms yielded their secrets to his keen vision—how often people in the wilderness looked but didn't see, he thought. Especially porkeaters, greenhorns from the east. He rode to the west lip of the valley and studied the country. It looked passable for wagons too. Then he turned back to the camp to share the welcome news.

He found Cecil, along with Clay, hard at work cutting the notch in the bank.

"Any sign of James?" asked the minister, leaning wearily on his shovel.

"Yes, some sign. He replaced the meat he took from a buffalo cow yonder to the west, and then vanished. Rain wiped out his tracks."

"It sounds like hoodoo," Cecil said. "Will we ever see him again?"

"I have no more idea than you do, mate."

"Was it the heathen religion? Why would he take buffalo meat back?"

"To undo what he had done, I suppose."

"It's paganism, Mister Skye. I never would have guessed it of James. He's lost to us."

"I think he was killed or hurt by the lightning," said Clay.

"No. He made it to the place of the skulls and returned the meat. There was no sign of trouble between here and there, mate."

"It was the devil at work," said Silas Potter.

Skye paused. "The things we don't understand aren't rightly the devil's work," he said slowly. "A man follows his own music. I will wager he's alive, and I'll wager he is doing what he must."

Cecil sighed. "He's gone, whatever the reason. A good man gone, and I'll miss him. Now we're a man short."

"Oh, I'll miss him so!" cried Esmerelda.

"Well, could be you'll meet up with him soon. That's a thing about this big country. It's not that people vanish in it, but that people reappear, show up when you're not expecting it."

But Cecil and Esmerelda looked crestfallen.

Silas was aflame with righteousness. "It's good riddance," he snapped. "He heeded the powers of Satan, and we must drive him from our midst."

"Pack up your gear and get ready to roll," Skye roared, cutting off Potter. "There's a crossing about three miles north."

They stared at him.

Cecil blinked. "Almost hate to give this up. This little cut in this bank has taken a day and a half of our lives, and now we're leaving it half done." He sighed. "Good labor and honest sweat gone."

"You should have found the crossing earlier. Or James should have," snapped Silas.

"Mate, hindsight is a fine thing, and makes us wise after things are over. Now if James hadn't disappeared and set me to wandering west and north, you'd—ah, Clay and Cecil—still be digging here for another day or two."

He turned Jawbone away, angered.

Late that afternoon they crossed Crazy Woman Creek with little difficulty and rolled another five miles over barren rolls of prairie, and made camp in a swale beside a small chokecherry and buffaloberry-lined spring. From their protected valley they could not see the Big Horns looming to the west, but the great mountains were ever-present now, brooding over the western reaches of the great plains.

In his lodge that evening Skye relaxed in the soft glow of a tiny fire that served for light rather than heat. Mary had arranged the robes into fine beds, as she always did, and played with young Dirk in the flickering light, laughing with him as he drew stick-figures with charcoal on a piece of smooth bark. Skye looked at her warm flesh in the soft light, and the shining braids of her jet hair, and her young curves beneath her dotted calico blouse, and he wanted her. Later, when the fire had died a little more, he would have her, and she would be glad, as always. He looked at his boy, who seemed to thrive under her care, and displayed the warmth of her flesh and darkness of her people, but his own blocky shape and squinting pale blue eyes.

Victoria busied herself with the last of her packing—she was always ready to travel at dawn, or in any instant in danger. And then she sat back, close to Mister Skye, because she was his sits-beside-him wife and had that privilege.

"Tell me about the black man," she said. "Tell me all the things you have not told me."

Skye grinned. "Mister Method shot that cow buffalo in the Place of the Forty Skulls," he began.

"I knew it!" she cried.

"Cow landed right in the center, near the cairn and stake."

"Ah!" she cried. "That was a spirit buffalo cow. The spirit of old White Buffalo Cow Woman was within her, and he shot it. Truly, I saw her face in the hump ribs, and so I knew!"

"Sometime just before the storm or during it, he left here, picked up the meat, and took it back there. I don't rightly know how he did it, unless the lightning helped. But it was there, the meat, placed as close and as reverently as possible to the carcass."

"Ah!" she cried again. "Now I know. The spirit of

White Buffalo Cow Woman was pleased that it was no longer roaming in the air looking for a home."

"But it is a dead home; it's still a carcass," objected Mister Skye.

"Yes, but the spirit is happy, and perhaps it entered into the breast of James Method."

From across the fire, Mary objected. "But there cannot be two spirits in one breast, Crow Mother."

"Ah! Who knows? Perhaps Mister Method is following the spirit to its new home. That is what I think. He is going to a village of the Absaroka, the village of White Buffalo Cow Woman and the chief, Many Coups."

"You think he's heading toward the Crow, eh?" Mister Skye asked.

"I am certain of it. We shall see him shortly, but things will be different for him. I do not know what the spirit of the Absaroka grandmother will bring to him, but it will be something good for bringing back the meat of the spirit cow that he took."

With that she would say no more, and rolled comfortably in her robes, the top one the softest albino buffalo cow hide and ideal for summertime.

"Bring me Dirk," he said, and Mary lifted the sleepy boy into Mister Skye's lap. He always enjoyed these moments. He was old enough to be a grandfather many times over, but this was his first and only child.

"Ah, my lad," he said in English. "You know the words of your mother, mate, but not those of your pap. It's time I teach you the poems and the stories and the songs of my people."

"I want the English words," Dirk said, "but I'm sleepy now."

"Go to sleep, mate," Skye said, handing the boy back.

Mary flashed a smile. In a moment the boy would be sound asleep in the cool air, and in another moment she'd slip out of her calico, and she and Mister Skye would lie together in the robes.

He never said a word. She always knew. She aroused him as no woman ever had with her lithe young beauty.

Let the missionaries howl, he thought. Let them rage. He was a happy man with Victoria and Mary, and what was not permitted back in civilization was of no consequence here. He was a savage now. A British press-gang had seen to that when they started a chain of events that brought him in middle years to this warm lodge high on the steppes of North America, where a beautiful and fiery woman now awaited him.

The guide grew ever more dissatisfied with his party. Just beneath the surface lay cauldrons of bubbling hate. In a time of crisis, they would all fall apart rather than hang together, and that might cost all of them, himself included, their lives. At the heart of it was Silas Potter, whose contempt for the others writhed inside of him like a snake. Ever since Cecil had joined the Sioux scalp dance, Silas had refused even to talk with the senior missionary. Just as bad, he avoided Esmerelda or glared at her, and was uncivil, if not rude, to Father Kiley and almost oblivious to the man's distress and blindness.

Alex Newton had become the other dissident and troublemaker, nursing a rage that his wagon had been abandoned and his body comforts reduced because of it. And, like Silas, appalled by the conduct of his father-in-law, who seemed to grow more boorish and barbaric the farther they penetrated the wilderness.

Though things seemed amiable enough on the surface, and the business of the day proceeded with polite and distant courtesy, surface courtesies were not unity, and Mister Skye wanted and needed unity here. Under pressure from hostile Indians, or weather, or most any calamity along the way, they would go their separate directions. Even Clay Sample seemed to be harboring antagonisms as the caravan pushed its way north and west.

The footsore oxen, rested again while the party dug at the cutbank of Crazy Woman Creek, were pulling the wagon with the organ and Father Kiley in it. Clay Sample's mules, though gaunted, showed no sign of failing.

And the span of mules pulling the carriage made easy work of it.

But all was not right. Mister Skye stopped Jawbone and waited for Potter, who rode a horse regularly now as eastern foodstuffs dwindled and the loads lightened.

"Mister Potter," he said, "I'm about to go out on a scout. You'll come with me."

The young man's face flamed.

"You don't even ask," he snapped.

"If I'd asked, you'd say no, and I mean to have you come, mate."

"I'm not the slightest bit interested in scouting."

Jawbone snapped his teeth at Potter's saddle horse, and the animal hurried along beside Mister Skye, no matter that Potter tugged on its reins.

In twenty minutes they were half a mile north and west of the wagons, riding up and down long swales and shoulders, with Potter sullenly following, a pained look stamped on his face.

"First watch the ridges, mate. Trouble usually sits on a ridge out here, and what may look like a small rock may be a head peering from the other side. And then watch the brush and the stands of trees and the banks and the coulees, all of which are hiding places, places where deadly men lurk to surprise us."

"I'm sure you do your job adequately, Mister Skye. This is unimportant to me."

"You might feel differently about it if fifty warriors boiled out of that draw over there, and came for your scalp."

"That's what you're paid for."

"Do you dislike me, Mister Potter?"

The young man rode silently for a while. "Let's say I don't approve of some things."

"Disapprove. Yes, that's the exact word, I think."

"I don't dislike you. Some of your conduct I deem improper."

"I imagine you do," said Mister Skye. "What do you disapprove of? My two wives? My taste for whiskey? My camp and trail discipline? My buckskins? This evil horse I ride? Or is it that I'm a white savage, armed with rifle and revolver here, and a pair of knives to boot? Perhaps it's because I'm a killer, a killer of human beings who may or may not intend to kill me. Or is it that I'm not of your denomination, and damned because of it?''

Silas Potter chose silence. Skye let him brood awhile, and then started in again.

''You're not even speaking to Cecil. He and Esmerelda danced a heathen dance, so you disapprove of them. And you disapprove of his plans to better the lives of the Blackfeet. Does the man set in authority over you offend you that much? You talk only to Alex Newton, but you disapprove of him, too. He's self-indulgent and a shirker. And Henrietta you dismiss as self-indulgent also, and mindless. Neither do you visit with the priest. You disapprove of him so much that you barely feel his tragedy. Don't you suppose Dunstan Kiley would welcome a little comforting? If you had been blinded and tortured by some Cheyenne, and lay helpless in a black world in a bouncing wagon, would you welcome some kindness? And what about Mister Method? He was scarcely gone before you were saying good riddance. Did you disapprove of him also? Perhaps you felt the African was beneath you and lacked your intellect?''

Silas looked pained. ''You don't understand, and I doubt that I could explain it to you because you lack the . . . the . . . ah, scholarship. I merely uphold the loving standards of church and civilization. I'm afraid if I elaborated them, it would be beyond you.''

''Try, Mister Potter.''

''I'd rather not.''

''Well, mate, if you won't, I will. And you'll be my captive audience, eh?''

''Go ahead. You disapprove of me. I uphold the laws of God, so you will heap whatever abuse on me you will. The more you condemn me, the more I serve God. I'm not interested in your opinions—not yours or Cecil's or anybody's. I'm interested in what is true and holy and good, but I don't expect you to understand that.''

''Am I keeping you here against your will?''

''Yes.''

''That happens in life, doesn't it. I was a prisoner for nigh onto eight years, and bullied about by people who were called sir, or lord, or mister. Now you're my prisoner for a hour or two, Mister Potter. I suppose you can't suffer me because I'm an uncouth sailor and a ruffian and violent man.

''Or maybe it's my drink. A true weakness, Mister Potter, and one you are free of. I get a fine edge to me, and over I go—at least when the nectar of the gods is available, which isn't often in this vast wilderness. Now there is a weakness. I abandoned you to your fate, and failed to guide and guard you. But not entirely, Mister Potter. For those squaws you privately scorn are better and wiser on the trail than I am, and this horse beneath me is worth ten guards and guides, and they are all more faithful than I am.

''Or perhaps it's this new Sharps and this Army Colt, with which I am always prepared to commit murder. This Sharps is a killing machine, sir. I can load a paper cartridge in it almost as fast as I can discharge the Colt. I am very good at it, Mister Potter. I have killed men in multiples of ten, and so I can understand your disgust. It disgusts me, too.

''And my lovely Shoshone, Mary, I take to bed and she builds a fine lust in me, just as she does in you, Mister Potter.''

The young man reddened.

''Oh, those things don't hide themselves, my friend. Those glances, those trips to the creeks when Mary is bathing, the heat rising from you as your eyes dog her. No, Mister Potter, your lusts are no secret, except maybe to yourself. What bothers you is not that I have a second wife who is beautiful and half my age, but that she inspires your lust, and that ruins your notion of yourself as the keeper of the flame.''

"I am pure," Potter cried hoarsely. "It is the Tempter, not I; the Tempter I wrestle with."

"Why, that's as good a name for a stiff as any, mate."

"You don't understand. I don't want your dirty squaw. I have nothing to do with her."

Mister Skye stared. "You don't command your own ship?"

Silas Potter glared hotly. "I can't explain it to someone who doesn't even have the rudiments of theology."

"Well, friend, you and your Tempter leave Mary alone, or I'll break your bloody neck."

Silas turned to ice. "I told you I have nothing to do with . . ."

Mister Skye was amused. "Nothing to do with any of us."

"—Nothing to do with certain episodes that gave the unfortunate appearance of, ah, misimpression that . . ."

"I know a dozen young ladies in the Crow villages who'd be enchanted with even you, Mister Potter. I will make certain arrangements. Oh, those Crow girls! You and your Tempter will have a high old time . . ."

"Are you done with your ravings?"

"Yes, that's all."

Mister Skye smiled.

Silas stared at him, not quite believing it, and then yanked his horse toward the wagons. And Jawbone let him do it.

# Chapter 15

He caught a glimpse of her in the flickering blue lightning and then blackness closed again. He supposed he had imagined it. He was soaked now, chilled to his bones, and eager to return to camp if he could make his way back. In the arc of one lightning bolt he had glimpsed a young Indian woman, her black hair parted and braided, her skin clothing black with water and hanging heavily on her slim figure. And that was all. He waited for another flash, more curious than afraid, but it did not come.

It was just an image in his head, he thought. He fretted. Why had he come here, and why had he felt such a compelling need to return the meat to the cow buffalo here?

Another blinding bolt, chattering and then booming, and he saw her again and she was closer. She said something and beckoned but he hadn't the faintest idea what she said.

"Who are you and what do you want?" he asked.

He heard a soft reply in a tongue he didn't know. He

had some notion she was handsome, maybe even beautiful, but he dismissed it. She was saying something, but his thoughts were upon finding his way back, or maybe finding shelter until the storm was over.

Then her hands reached to the bridle and she tugged the reins, saying something. She wanted to take him somewhere. All right, then, maybe she has a shelter. He gave the reins to her and mounted, and let her lead the horse where she would. What had the old granny said? *This was how he would find his woman.*

He felt the horse walking beneath him through a black void, going in a direction he didn't know. Was this woman a demon carrying him off to hell? He thought of Cecil Rathbone and his faith in one loving God; and he thought of old Mattie in her shack, angrily invoking the spirits of rocks and trees and frogs and telling him what his future would be. James felt himself slipping away from Cecil and Esmerelda—the others he cared little about, sensing they didn't care much for him, an intruder in their white caravan. No, he thought, that wasn't quite right. He cared about the Jesuit, Father Kiley, and he could not fault the Samples, who put him at ease. But now in this wild night he felt the Rathbones and their faith slipping away, and Father Kiley grow distant in his mind, even as the spirits of the earth-things rose before him. He felt the spirit of the horse beneath him, and the magnetic pull of the woman who led him through utter blackness. And the anger of the heavens, and the arrows of lightning and the rage of thunder, seeking him out but not finding him because this was not his time to die. He wondered whether he would slip away from all the white things, the civilized things, he had absorbed in the master's house, and return to the African life. His grandmother and grandfather had come from there, herded in the bowels of a clipper ship and barely alive when they landed on the Carolina coast and went to the auction block and were sold naked, both of them to the father of his master.

For a moment he hated all whites, even the Rathbones

who had been unfailingly kind and not at all patronizing either. But that passed. He had few grievances. All the while he was a slave, he had been treated well, save for the fact that he was property that could be bought or sold. Still, he was drifting away. God and the gentle Jesus they had taught him about were sliding away, and he felt fierce and attuned to every tree and drop of water, and especially the silent woman leading his horse.

They were climbing a long gulch with water running in it, he sensed. The hoofs struck rock, and the horse occasionally pulled up over low ledges. How the woman knew where to go he couldn't imagine. Ahead flickered a tiny light, and he wondered how a fire could prosper in a deluge like this one. Then its light reached out and he could see the silhouette of her ahead of him, and could even see his horse and its ears before him. The fire illumined a yellow hollow of rock in a cliffside, with a ledge over it. And it illumined another Indian woman, an older one, standing in its light.

It seemed warmer under the shelf of rock, and the gusting air didn't penetrate here. He dismounted and stared. The older woman stood tall and lithe, much taller than the younger one, whose figure was fuller. The older woman was dry, and had a green trade blanket drawn around her doeskin-clad body. Her black hair was shot with white, and on her face were several disfiguring scars. She smiled gently but there remained a fierceness about her that was palpable to him. He gazed at the young one, then, the one who'd brought him here. She seemed perhaps twenty, with a fine golden flesh and eyes that shone in the firelight.

"We were expecting you," said the older one in fluent English. "This one"—she pointed at the girl—"had a vision. Four times she dreamt the dream, and then came to me with it. I am Pine Leaf, a medicine woman of the Crow people. And before my medicine came to me, I was a warrior of the Crow. But I will tell you of that later. This is Gliding Raven. She does not speak your tongue, but she will learn."

"Ah'm James Method," he replied uncertainly.

"Ah, James. That is a name I know. You are wet. Take off your clothes and I will dry them at the fire."

He stared. "But Ah'm . . . Ah can't . . . You're women!"

"There is a fine, soft, well-tanned buffalo robe there for you to wrap in. There's another robe here for Gliding Raven."

"But Ah . . ."

"You whites don't have any sense. Do you want to shiver in those things?"

"Ah'm not exactly white . . ."

"You were a slave of theirs, like my friend Jim Beckwourth."

It struck him funny: hours ago he rode with a party of puritanical missionaries, and here he was about to peel off his shirt and britches and boots. He laughed easily and pulled off his sopping gray readymade shirt, and then felt stricken by modesty and turned his back to them and pulled off the rest. Someone behind him laughed and gently wrapped a fine buffalo robe over his shoulders.

When he turned, the girl stood naked, stepping out of soaked skirts, and the sight of her warm flawless flesh, her tawny breasts in the firelight, her lean and supple legs, lit fires in him, punched him until he felt breathless. But then she wrapped her own robe about her, and peered shyly at him from the brown curly hair of her soft robe. She laughed too, as shyly as he had laughed, and they seated themselves around the fire. But the image of her burned in his mind and prodded at his body, and he did not sit easily.

Pine Leaf wrung out the clothing and propped it up on sticks she cleverly arranged into a drying rack, and then sat down between them. James Method's heart pounded.

"Gliding Raven is a beautiful woman, yes?" said Pine Leaf, and that didn't help James at all.

"The most beautiful Ah've ever seen," he replied hotly.

"She will be yours," said Pine Leaf solemnly.

He could scarcely imagine it. Even now visions of her poured through him. He wanted her. This would be his life. Gliding Raven and himself, a thousand miles from white men's civilization.

"Listen to me, James Method, for now I must talk of things sacred to the Absaroka people, and of your future, and of Gliding Raven's vision that brought us here, far, far from our village where the Big Horn River, as the whites call it, meets the Yellowstone."

James could barely listen; his glances slipped to Gliding Raven and her golden bare throat and shoulders that gleamed in the firelight.

"Four times did Gliding Raven have a medicine dream. In it she saw a black man kill White Buffalo Cow Woman in the place of forty skulls. Four times the spirit of White Buffalo Cow Woman came to Gliding Raven and told her to come here at once. And bring to our village the black man, who would become a great warrior for our people, and would bring us knowledge of the whites, who are coming more and more, and tell us how we might live with them in peace. I won't tell you the rest of her medicine dream yet, but it is a good vision, good medicine. Gliding Raven told me her dream, and I saw that it was good for the Absaroka people and that she must travel a long way, seven camps, to come here so that her medicine would happen. I decided to come with her. We would like to take you back to the Absaroka village."

"Ah'm ready," he said.

"You must not touch Gliding Raven even though you want to," Pine Leaf said solemnly. "First you must become a brave warrior. When you have counted coup, or taken a scalp, or have stolen horses from the enemies of the Absaroka people, especially the Siksika, the Blackfeet, and give one of them to Gliding Raven's father, he will declare a great feast and will give you his daughter."

James Method was amazed. "Marriage?"

"Yes. But first you must become a warrior. Then you

will be named Seven Scalps and you will have Gliding Raven. She is very eager to have you. Her eyes shine and her body hungers for you, James Method. But that time has not yet come.''

All of this happened too fast and he thought perhaps he should get back on his horse and strike out for the wagons in the dying storm. And then he looked at Gliding Raven, and knew he wouldn't. He'd been smitten with something, love or lust or both.

"I am Pine Leaf, and now I will tell you about me, and about my friend Jim Beckwourth, who became a great warrior of the Crows, just as you will be . . .

"I myself am a warrior of the Absarokas, and sit high in the councils of our people. When I was young I vowed not to marry until I had taken a hundred scalps of the Siksika. I took many scalps, but not a hundred, so I have not married. I fought in many battles, and if I was not as strong as some warriors, I was faster, and deadlier with my bow, and I could make my ponies run the fastest of all. My medicine is strong as a woman warrior, and now it is strong as a prophet, and many come to me with their dreams and visions, and I see what is to be seen.

"Among us lived a trapper, Jim Beckwourth, who became a great warrior, and we gave him the name Antelope in honor of his deeds. He looked like you, and was my friend in battle, and I shared his robes for a while. He taught me your language. When I saw you, I knew the Absaroka people would have another great warrior among us, and that White Buffalo Cow Woman had sent for us to come welcome you.''

"Ah've heard of Beckwourth. Our guide, Mister Skye, has told me many a tale of the beaver-trapping days around our camps at night—of Beckwourth and Bridger and Broken Hand Fitzpatrick, and the Sublettes and many others . . .''

"Skye? You've come with Skye?''

"He's taking some missionaries to the Blackfeet.''

Pine Leaf pondered that. "He has many enemies among the Siksika. And he has always been our friend and ally. Why does he take these white people to the Siksika?''

''That is his business now—taking people where they want to go.''

''That is not good,'' said Pine Leaf. ''We will not let these people take their medicine to our enemies. They must share the white medicine with us first, so we may have the magic of powder and guns and the eyes that make faraway things close.''

''Ah'm not so sure Ah want to go to your village. Ah broke free of them just a little ago, and Ah want to sort things out. Ah've never been free before. There's nobody to tell me Ah can't do anything. But here you are, telling me Ah have to go join up with you Crows and become your warrior and take scalps. Ah've never taken a scalp in my life and Ah don't intend to start . . . In the morning Ah'm going to ride right out of here, and maybe Gliding Raven'll come with me.''

Pine Leaf shook her head solemnly. ''You will come with us. The spirit of White Buffalo Cow Woman has spoken.''

The glitter in Pine Leaf's eyes told James she meant it, and meant to enforce it, and probably could. She smiled slightly, as if reading his thoughts. ''I am large for a woman, but not the size of a man. Perhaps you would like to test me in battle? Any kind of battle?''

He shook his head. These two had his life planned out for him and called it medicine. Still . . . what spirits had inspired them to come to the place of the skulls and find him? They had come perhaps two hundred miles from their village, maybe more, just for this. He thought life as a Crow slave would be less free than the life he had in the south. For a moment he wished he had the protection of Mister Skye, who had taught him how to live in freedom, but now he was on his own, with two Crow women who consulted hoodoo spirits to guide them. He stared first at Pine Leaf, standing resolutely, a quick reach from her bow and quiver and lance; and at Gliding Raven, who was, he knew, the very woman, golden and black-haired, that the old granny had spat and raved about in the shanty. She lounged in her curly-haired buffalo robe, wrapped carelessly about her so that her amber thighs glistened in the firelight.

Something within screamed at him, warned him not to trifle with the earth spirits of these people, but to love the one God. But it was too late. The image formed of Alex Newton glaring at him; of Silas Potter's frost and politeness, and of the others' indifference. He sat in his robe, tugged two ways. Then he thought, who is God, if he let Father Kiley be blinded even while the Jesuit was doing God's work? This God he had grown up with seemed weak. The medicine of these Crow women was not weak. Had he not felt the call of the old woman's spirit? Hadn't these women glimpsed the future, coming here to escort him?

He peered into Pine Leaf's eyes, and found her watching him alertly.

"If you make a slave of me," he said softly, "Ah'll fight you, even if Ah die. Ah will not be a slave again. Ah'll not be the least among you, either. Ah'll be a man among you . . ."

Pine Leaf laughed easily. She sat down and lifted his old percussion rifle and carefully dried it while he watched distrustfully. The fire dimmed, and she did not renew the tiny blaze with more sticks.

"We have a long way to travel," she said.

In the dark, sleep didn't come. The clouds cleared, and the uncurtained sky paraded its stars. So much reeled in his head: what was medicine, what was God? Were they the same, or different? What was the devil? Was medicine the same as Satan? Who was Gliding Raven, and what would she be like? The image of her firelit brown body and jet hair and black eyes lit blazes within him. She lay there, a few feet away.

Then in the dark a form drew close. "It is Pine Leaf. Take me, and then you will not think about Gliding Raven," she whispered.

She was agile and firm and fiery, and soon he lay exhausted, slipping into a troubled sleep at last.

In the morning he found Gliding Raven dressed in her dried doeskins, preparing a small breakfast from jerky and a few roots. Elkteeth and quillwork decorated her dress. Her necklace was of polished hollow bone. By day she was even more beautiful than she had been at night, and he could not help but follow her with his gaze. She grew aware of it, and smiled at him shyly. There came to him a determination to have her, to wait for her, to win scalps for her, or whatever he must do. Her tawny flesh looked not so different from his own, but her jet hair hung blue and straight.

Pine Leaf had their ponies ready, and had saddled his as well. "I will scout ahead," she said, and slipped toward a nearby ridge, while James and Gliding Raven walked their mounts side by side. They had not spoken a word. He knew no way to communicate with her. He had not learned the sign language of the plains tribes. Then at last he decided to teach her the words he knew, and perhaps learn her words. And so they traveled, each of them pointing at something, eyes, nose, horse, water, and supplying the word, sometimes laughing at bungled pronunciation, but learning all the while. Pine Leaf acted as their eyes and ears, and they rarely saw her.

Once she rode back swiftly and steered them into a thick stand of cottonwoods, and a while later they could see mounted figures, tiny on a distant ridge, heading west. They were not discovered.

Each night they made camp in a well-selected place where Pine Leaf supposed they might find some safety. It was a giant country, with great swells of prairie running limitlessly to far horizons. Always the Big Horns loomed to the west, blue and inviting during the hot afternoons. Some nights Pine Leaf came to him; other nights she chose not to. It felt good, but not what it would be with Gliding Raven, whose image lay always in his mind now.

They made thirty or forty miles each day, traveling

with caution because this was a land hunted by many tribes, most of them enemies of the Crows. On one occasion Pine Leaf led them by night, explaining that they were circling around a large Lakotah party to the east, warriors who would enjoy nothing so much as torturing James and two Crow women to death.

Between the language sessions James brooded about medicine. What empowered Pine Leaf to know the things she knew? How did she know of enemies she had merely felt but not seen? How did she know this trip would be safe? Was medicine stronger than God? Pine Leaf seemed to know everything, including what James and Gliding Raven were doing, and the words they had exchanged. The graying medicine woman paid homage here and there to things she considered sacred, an arrow buried in a cottonwood at one place; at another, a small cairn of rock, with vermilion daubed on one rock.

By the sixth day they were rounding the northern end of the Big Horn Mountains. So adept had James and Gliding Raven become with each other's words that now they made simple talk. She was teaching him, as well, the sign language of the prairies, and he knew the signs for friend, and peace, and food, and other helpful things. They rode in the basin of the great Yellowstone River now, Pine Leaf said, and in the heart of the beautiful lands of the Absaroka people, who roamed a country of towering mountains, rushing rivers, vast prairies teeming with buffalo, all of it blessed by a warm dry climate.

Then on the seventh day, Pine Leaf led them into the great village of the Kicked-in-the-Bellies band of Crows.

# Chapter 16

There was only night. Dunstan Kiley's world had shrunk to the bed of a jolting wagon that bounced and rolled him hour after hour, until the day's journey ended. He had learned to tell day from night. By day, birds sang and temperatures rose, and sometimes he felt the hot summer sun heating his black clothing. And by day people came to him: Victoria to feed and clean him, Mister Skye to talk occasionally, and the Rathbones, who tried to bring cheer but could not, because he'd fallen beyond cheer. The little Sample girl, Miriam, came regularly too. James Method came also, until he disappeared. They told him Method had simply vanished the night of the heavy storm, leaving no trace, but doing a heathenish thing, taking meat back to the buffalo cow he had killed.

Like the darkness, the pain never ceased. He suffered an endless ache in his eye sockets, and it had become a part of Victoria's daily ministration to clean away the suppurating flow from them and wrap new bandaging. Each day she washed the soiled bandaging wherever there was water, and reused it because there was little cloth to be had. She had applied powders and ointments of her own devising, and muttered frequently when they failed to heal. On occasion Father Kiley saw blinding white flashes that scorched the inside of his skull, but these came infrequently and only punctuated the blackness.

His fate appalled him. He was alive, but useless, and a total burden on others. He had no notion what he would do, where he might go, or how he might relieve these people of the need to care for him. He thought of suicide, but that would be a grave sin. He thought of continuing his priestly duties, but that seemed impossible. He couldn't even read to say the Mass or perform other offices. He thought he knew them all by heart, but now his mind rebelled and blanked. He could not be a priest.

The sky was black, as it must be in hell, he thought. For surely hell must be the same as blackness, a place of no light. He tried to imagine the throne of heaven, the faces of saints, the look of his parents in Ireland, but the images were fleeting and laced with pain and lightning. He thought especially of the Virgin, in her blue gown, smiling gently, but her image diffused and vanished in his aching head. He thought he had a duty to perform, forgiveness of Wolf-That-Circles and the other Cheyenne whose names he didn't know. But the war chief had died, and Father Kiley found himself beyond forgiveness or anger, beyond hate or love in his extremity. He had come to believe that the Cheyenne were inspired not by malice, but by curiosity. Like all the plains tribes, they had heard much of the religion of the whites, who seemed to have medicine beyond anything the Indians had ever imagined. And so they had tested it, tortured the white holy man to see the medicine with their own eyes. See whether he would be immune to pain and fire and death. If he were ever to minister to Indians again, could he resume his holy offices without hatred or fear? He didn't know. And now he knew only the awful present; future and past had vanished into the night.

Day by day the small party rolled north. He sensed

approximately where they were: a little east of the Big Horns, and up at their northern end now. Perhaps near Goose Creek. It was a land of vast shoulders and long coulees which became palpable to him as the faithful oxen dragged his wagon up long slopes and down the far sides, the wagon pressing into the breeching of the wheel yoke, or sometimes skidding downslope upon chain-locked wheels.

One morning immediately after Victoria had given him breakfast, Mister Skye came to him. "Are you well this morning?" he asked.

"I no longer know what sick and well mean," the priest replied. "My head always throbs; the rest of me is the way it always has been."

"I thought I'd take you scouting with me, Father."

He shrank from that. "On a horse? Blind on a horse? Unable to see what's ahead or steer the animal?"

"I've got him saddled up. You've a Santa Fe saddle with a Spanish horn on it, something to hang on to if you need it. Do you good. I thought I'd lead you with a halter rope."

It sounded terrifying. "I couldn't—" he began.

But Skye's big hand was lifting him up and drawing him across ground he couldn't see.

"Now, mate, you're beside your horse. I'll put your foot in a stirrup and get you settled."

The priest paused. "If this is unbearable, will you bring me back when I ask?"

"Perhaps. I might cheat a little and leave you in the crow's nest a little longer than you want."

"Crow's nest?"

"The little platform at the top of the mast of a sailing bark. Even in a calm sea it'll swing twenty or thirty feet as the ship rolls. There's many a sailing lad who'd rather go on bread and water in the brig than be put up there in a storm."

The priest smiled wanly. "I think I shall have to re-name my horse Crow's Nest."

He felt Skye's hands guiding a foot into a stirrup, and

then he swung up, finding the saddle horn with his hands. His free foot probed for the other stirrup, and then was guided into it by an unseen hand.

"I fear to bring this horse close to your terrible Jawbone," Father Kiley said.

"Nothing to fret about. Jawbone's as mannered as I want him to be."

Then they rode, and he felt the horse swaying under him. He gripped the horn desperately. "I hope this ordeal won't last long."

Mister Skye replied gently. "Father Kiley, getting back to the business of living is going to be nothing but ordeals. I had a notion that this might be a little first step. Here's your hat. You'd better wear it against sunburn."

They rode quietly awhile, and after a few minutes the priest's dread of it lessened. He found he could stay on the horse, even when it gathered its muscles to leap a small crease in the grassy hills, The sun bored in hot upon his black broadcloth suit.

"We're north of Goose Creek, heading north," Mister Skye said amiably. "The blue Big Horns jutting up to our left. We're about a mile ahead of the wagons. We're rolling along pretty smoothly now. Few days and we'll be in the Crow camps. They're Victoria's people, and have always welcomed me and my parties."

"I have stayed among them," said Father Kiley. Once when he had been traveling with Pierre de Smet, they had stayed with the Crows awhile, and had been appalled by them. Never had he experienced such a bawdy and licentious people.

"I expect to find James Method there," Mister Skye said.

"Why? What would he be doing there?"

"Big medicine."

Medicine was a word the priest had come to dread and loathe. It was testing medicine that had blinded him; medicine that kept these western Indians blinded to his teaching and purposes.

"It's a pagan thing," he muttered.

Mister Skye said nothing for a while. Then, "There's a ridge ahead I'm going to climb and scout. Leave you here for a moment. You just hold your horse. I'll be back when I can. You're in a grassy wide valley. There's no cover here. I'll hand you the halter rope now. If your horse wants to follow, just pull hard on it until you twist him into a tight circle."

The priest felt the halter rope thrusting into his hands, and he took it, suddenly afraid. The horse turned, wanting to follow, and he pulled the rope. The horse circled, and sidled ahead, and he knew he was being taken somewhere. He thought to cry out, but didn't. Silence was vitally important when scouting, when trying to see without being seen. The horse kept drifting, and he grew afraid. The horse continued to drift, and he knew he was edging away from the place where Mister Skye had left him. Then came the nightmares—being lost or abandoned, helpless, blind in utter wilderness, wandering and stumbling to his death. Never had he felt so alone.

"Lord have mercy!" he cried, and knew at once what to do. He simply dismounted, sat down in grass, holding the halter rope in his hand. And waited. If Mister Skye didn't return, he'd remount somehow and let the horse drift. There'd be a good chance the horse would rejoin the wagon herd.

The throbbing of his heart slowed. He could hear his horse cropping grass close by. In blackness there is little time, and he lost track of it, not knowing whether Mister Skye had been gone minutes or hours.

"I am a weak Christian," he said to no one. Here he could talk to the wind and the sky. "I have little faith."

He waited he knew not how long, then heard the swift pulse of hoofs in grass, friend or enemy, coming death or coming life.

"Get up fast," said Mister Skye softly. "Yonder beyond the ridge is a whole village moving. Don't know what, but likely 'Rapaho, on a buffalo chase."

Father Kiley leapt to his feet, found his horse, felt for

the stirrup, and pulled himself up and poked around with his free foot for the other stirrup.

"We're going to have to run, Father. Find cover before their scouts, their wolves, find us. Yonder half a mile's a crease in the land, a coulee full of brush, and that's where we're going. We're going to run, and you'll have to hang on."

He heard Jawbone plunge away in a hard gallop. He kicked his horse, and it leapt ahead, almost yanking him from the saddle. Then he was galloping through a black tunnel, his hand locked to the saddle horn, faster and faster, in a whirlwind of terror. The horse leapt over something, perhaps nothing but a crease in the ground, lifting him high, and when he landed he careened to his right. But he held on, deathgripping the horn.

His heart thudded, and he knew a fear almost as terrible as the fear of torture. Then he thought: why am I afraid of the death I hunger for? What will be, will be . . . and he formed a small helpless prayer on his lips, even as the wild horse thundered down the black tunnel. He calmed. Brush whipped his legs. Ahead, he heard Jawbone slowing. His own horse slowed as well and then stopped, its sides heaving. He reached forward to its neck and found it soaked.

"We're here, Father," said Mister Skye quietly.

But Dunstan Kiley was unable to talk. He trembled on the trembling horse.

"We're in a draw full of chokecherry. I think we made it. I should be seeing their scouts along the ridge anytime now," Skye said, so quietly his voice carried only a few yards. "I don't rightly know what that village was. But it wasn't Crow. I know Crow on sight. They're moving west to east ahead of us. Should pass ahead of our wagons by two, three miles. Likely they'll spot the wagons, unless we're lucky."

"Blind on a galloping horse. Blind and no reins on a galloping horse," Father Kiley muttered.

"Be glad you didn't have reins."

"What now?" asked the priest.

"We wait. I'm going to slip off Jawbone and hold your horse. Don't want him whinnying."

There came a long silence. Then Mister Skye spoke, even more quietly. "Three of their scouts on the ridge. Half mile."

Another long silence. The priest sat helplessly on his horse, blackness around him, danger approaching. "Mother of God," he muttered, and it became a prayer, too.

"Quarter of a mile." The priest felt Skye's hand on the muzzle of his horse, ready to pinch the animal's nostrils.

"Quietly, smoothly, slip off your horse," whispered Mister Skye.

The priest hastened to do so, stepping into crackling brush.

"You were too high."

The silence pulsed like a heartbeat.

"One's coming down here, dropped off the ridge. That run of ours left tracks. Broken grass, hoofprints."

There was another aching silence.

"Gros Ventre."

Bad news. They were a wandering people, closely allied with the Blackfeet, and murderous enemies of all whites. The Gros Ventres could show up almost anyplace.

"He's picked up our tracks now."

"Where are the others?" the priest asked.

"One's up on the ridge watching. Other's gone, other side of it. Can't talk anymore. His horse knows we're here, but he's not looking at his horse."

The silence stretched out. No birds of summer sang on the breezes. A stick cracked somewhere ahead. The priest peered into black horizons. His horse jerked as he leaned upon it, and he felt Mister Skye's hand clamping its muzzle.

The priest waited for the cry, the arrow, the rattle of hoofs, the shot that would end his nightmare. Nothing.

A horse whinnied, just a few yards ahead. Another

whinnied far off and higher. He felt Skye wrestling with the muzzle of his horse.

Skye's breath was in his ear. "He's onto us," the guide whispered. "He's got the other one up on the ridge coming down. We're in a jackpot, mate. If I kill them, I'd bring the whole Gros Ventres village down on the wagons."

"Mister Skye," whispered Father Kiley, "my life is nothing to me. I'm going out."

He didn't wait for a response. He found the halter rope and mounted, presumably in plain sight now of the warrior, wherever he might be. He turned his horse in the direction of the sound of stalking, and rode forward, crashing through brush, waiting for the fatal arrow. None came.

He held one hand high over his head and rode, he didn't know how far. He guessed fifty yards, until the brush stopped scraping at his legs.

He lowered his arm, and sat upon his quiet horse, reciting in Latin the Pater Noster. All was darkness, but in his soul he saw light ahead, blinding light.

He discerned voices now, harsh sibilants of two men talking. He felt a hand upon his coat, a finger finding the bullet holes and the undamaged flesh beneath them. Hands gripped his head, and he felt hands untying Victoria's bandages, first the outer leather casing she had contrived, and then the cloth pads over his draining eye sockets. The pads were pulled away. He felt dry air reach into the holes where his eyes had been.

"Ayaaah!" exclaimed a low voice.

He heard a furious jabber of low voices. The language was Algonquian; he knew that. These would be the Atsina, then, one of two tribes the French trappers called Big Bellies, Gros Ventre. He knew little of this tongue, but he knew the one word that came to him over and over, medicine.

Would he live because of medicine? He didn't want that. He didn't want to survive because of medicine but because of—faith.

"I have no medicine," he said to them in English.
"You are wrong! Wrong! There is but one God!"

Silence then. He sat tall in his saddle awaiting the
blow. The arc of an axe; the thrust of a lance; the jolt of
a war club, smooth rock bound by rawhide to a handle.

He felt the horse beside him again, felt legs brushing
his, hands grasping his head. The pads were pressed back
into his eye sockets; the leather wrapped over his forehead and tied again in back. Then the stir of horses. He
did not know whether he was being taken. To find out
he dismounted and held tight to the halter rope of his
horse. The sound of hoofs diminished.

"There is only God," he cried after them.

He did not know where he was. He stood quietly,
holding the horse, feeling the sun burn into his black
clothing. He was very thirsty. Perhaps Mister Skye was
dead. It didn't matter. He would mount his horse and let
the horse take him where he would; no doubt to water
eventually. He would wander alone until he died; of
thirst, of starvation, of exposure . . .

He waited what he thought might be five minutes and
then began to mount.

"Wait just a minute, mate," came a low voice from
behind. "They're not yet over the ridge. I'll be with you
in a minute."

He waited then. He felt an insect on his hand; others
hummed around his face, landing at the edges of his
leather bandaging. Then hoofsteps, and the felt presence
of Mister Skye.

"You're a brave man, Father Kiley," said the guide.
"You've saved us all; saved that whole missionary
party."

"I cannot claim such a thing. I sought only to die."

"Medicine," said Mister Skye. "That story about
Wolf-That-Circles got around fast. Stories do, you know.
Within a fortnight it was probably known to most tribes
on the northern plains."

"That's the last thing I wanted."

"It was medicine, mate, big medicine. They poked

their fingers into the bullet holes. They had themselves a look at your eyes. Big medicine, Father Kiley. They hightailed out as fast as they could and left you strictly alone. Left our whole party alone, I imagine.''

''You can't imagine how that grieves me,'' Kiley said. ''I'm grateful we are safe, but not by medicine . . . not with heathen belief . . .''

In fact the encounter had plunged him into a terrible despair. God had spared him. But for what?

They were traveling again now. It grew very hot, and Father Kiley shed his suitcoat and managed to tie it behind the cantle of his saddle. Mister Skye was leading his horse.

For a half hour or so Mister Skye said nothing. Father Kiley grew weary beyond endurance, and he focused upon one thing, the luxury of the buffalo robe in the shaded bed of the swaying wagon.

''Have you thought of your future?'' asked Mister Skye.

''I have none. Take me to Fort Benton, I suppose. Perhaps I can catch a river packet.''

''To where?''

''To wherever I am sent. The Society will take care of me. One thing we Jesuits are is obedient. We are soldiers.''

''Are you sure that's what you want?''

''I don't want anything, Mister Skye.''

Mister Skye was silent a long time. Then, at last, he spoke. ''I don't rightly know where I stand about religion. I think on it; read Scriptures now and then. Makes my head ache. I suppose I'm a pagan, but I wouldn't claim it. Things happen. I respect faith. I've seen miracles. But none ever happened to me. When I was pressed into the Royal Navy, I tried to pray. I prayed my heart out. I was a slave, mate, a powder monkey, and a young lad, and my prayers never netted me a thing. God abandoned me. I had to survive other ways, mostly by giving a harder licking than I took . . . But you're different, Dunstan Kiley. Call it Irish courage. Call it blind courage. Call it Jesuit courage. I can't rightly say, but for sure it's Dunstan Kiley's courage. Are you so set on going back to the states? I'm not much of a believing man, but seems to me maybe God has other plans for you, Father Kiley. Hope you'll think on it before we get into Blackfeet country and Fort Benton.''

''We were rescued by medicine and superstition, not by our Lord, Mister Skye.''

''Don't know that I agree with you,'' said Mister Skye. ''I think God's love is upon you.''

# Chapter 17

Pine Leaf pushed them at a pace that James Method had scarcely believed possible. They made forty or fifty miles a day, he guessed, and yet the horses showed little sign of weariness. He was learning from her. Frequently she rode well ahead of Method and Gliding Raven, peering over ridges, disappearing into cottonwood bottoms, reappearing miraculously beside them when they least expected her. He studied the old Crow warrior woman, hoping to learn how to traverse the vast country almost invisibly, as she did.

Whenever his erstwhile friends in the missionary caravan encountered deer or antelope, the animals would race over the nearest ridge and disappear, sometimes leaving behind them a distant sentinel to monitor them. But now somehow things were different. Frequently they rode close to a herd of antelope without triggering flight. The deer seemed a little more edgy, but from safe distances they, too, stood their ground while Pine Leaf, Gliding Raven, and James Method passed in silence.

The limitless land had its effect on the former slave as well, and he felt himself shedding cocoons and growing day by day. It was July now, and the blush of spring-green was fading in these arid lands. He had not known that the earth was so vast. For days they had ridden north, and the whole while a single range of mountains loomed in the west, snowcapped and blue. Frequently they forded cold rushing creeks fed by the mountain snows.

He surveyed the aching distances, the hundred-mile vistas, and felt free. He had scarcely known what freedom was. He was finding that the vast land, without fences, without barriers, without forests, without civilization, taught him about liberty. For here he could travel unimpeded in any direction farther than the eye could see. In the South the cottonfields had been hewn out of dense lush forest and there was scarcely a hill high enough to afford a view. The damp hot land was itself a prison, the forbidding forests were the walls of his slavery. On occasion a slave would disappear into the dank woods. Usually he was caught, but sometimes one or another managed to live semi-free, a hunted creature of woods and swamps. But James Method knew that wasn't freedom; it was slavery amid the dripping woods. The southland had reduced his vision, made him believe that all the world, whites too, was enslaved after a fashion. He had not dreamed of freedom, because he scarcely understood it. He had dreamed of escape, running away so that he could possess himself, own his body and shape his mind as he saw fit.

But here on the sunny, somnolent high prairies he understood liberty. He became his own master, yes. But more than that, he could travel in any direction or climb the majestic mountains with a purpose in life—a wife, riches, horses, land beneath his feet that was not the master's. Almost daily he shed cocoons as they traveled, finding his own will, riding through a world without walls. As fast as he learned survival skills from Pine Leaf, his confidence fleshed out within him, as if liberty required command, power over nature and will. He thrilled to it. One evening Pine Leaf had taught him how to use her bow and arrows. In time he would master that, and be able to bring down game without the telltale boom of his rifle, echoing toward unfriendly ears. She taught him things he thought he knew, but didn't; how to skin game swiftly, how to build a fire with nothing but the flint and frizzen of his rifle, plus a tiny fuzzy bit of tinder.

Something else, too, was transforming him. His two companions were people of color. Pine Leaf's umber flesh, weathered with age, was darker than his own. Gliding Raven looked lighter, almost golden. They accepted him completely. He had never felt that among the whites. The Samples had been courteous. His tent-mate, Silas Potter, had been painfully pleasant. The Newtons simply distant. Only the priest, the Rathbones, and Mister Skye himself seemed not to care. He was certain of the goodwill of these people, but at bottom, uncertain whether he was an equal. Sometimes they seemed to monitor their tongues as they spoke to him, simplify words—as if they were telling him that he was a product of darkest savage Africa, and they the product of a refined complex culture infinitely superior to his own. But that too had vanished here. The two Crow women did not patronize him in the slightest.

Another thing was affecting him. Years earlier the mulatto Jim Beckwourth had come to live with the Crows, and had become one of their great warriors and subchiefs. James had heard of Beckwourth, who still roamed the West, and still spent time in the villages of the Crow. So a man of his color had gone before him, and these women were perfectly familiar with him and at home with him. Pine Leaf had shared the buffalo robes with Beckwourth, even as she sometimes came to James Method's bedroll in the middle of the night.

All of this was swiftly transforming the former slave into a freeman enjoying liberty and acceptance such as he'd never known. That seemed to him the miracle of the American West. He knew that eventually the tide of whites would flood here, too, but he hoped it wouldn't be in his lifetime. He hoped he might be a freeman, in perfect liberty, for all of his days.

He grew aware of yet another side, a side that crowded into his mind only in the night. Where there were no laws and rules, there were no barriers to the evil in men's souls. He was free, but also at risk. Any passing party of Sioux or Cheyenne could capture and torture him or make him a slave. He could not own land by title and deed, and he could hold his possessions only by power and domination of others, because there was really no such thing as property in a wilderness, or even in the villages of these people. Like Father Kiley's eyes, everything could be taken away. He would need medicine, big medicine, to enjoy his new liberty. For the poor, the weak or sick, the unfortunate, the widowed and orphaned, this liberty he was experiencing could be the liberty of death. Who would care for him, he wondered, when he grew old and sick and perpetually tired, like the bitter old granny he visited when he was young. The master had fed his old slaves, even her in her shack beside the cottonfields.

Now at last the bulk of the Big Horns diminished in the West, and Pine Leaf steered them westerly across a rolling arid land dotted with silvery sagebrush. Gliding Raven's eyes danced with excitement, and she managed to tell James that soon they would be in the village of her people. He could never look at her without the stirrings of desire. And the longing in her eyes and the touch of her hands told him she felt all this too. He was, after all, her intended. The medicine had made it so, and who among them would resist that mysterious power they called medicine?

Pine Leaf had told him something of this power her people called medicine. It was more than power over nature and events. It was spiritual insight, healing force. It could be used for good or evil. Those who resorted to bad medicine were destroyers, casting evil upon the lives of others, enjoying power and control. There were few among the Absaroka people who did that, and they were feared and despised. The shamans, the medicine men, were sacred and holy people, who asked nothing but to help those who came to them with needs or hungers or fears. A person who had medicine, who interpreted dreams, helped others to find their spirit helpers, named others with good medicine names, was a respected elder whose counsel was sought in all grave matters, including peace and war.

Now they pierced deep into Crow country, and Pine Leaf relaxed her scouting a bit, and rode beside him more and more, answering his questions, translating for Gliding Raven. Through Pine Leaf, the young people learned each other's thoughts and hopes. Gliding Raven wished him to become a great warrior and a person of high repute among the Absaroka people. She wished to bear his sons and daughters, as numberless as the winters of life. She wished to make him fine clothing of soft-tanned elkskin, trimmed with red tradecloth and beads and porcupine quills. She wished to scrape and tan prime buffalo hides that he could trade at the post of the whites for new weapons and powder and lead, and iron cooking pots, and sharp iron arrow points, and four-point blankets.

All day they rode northward along a river Pine Leaf said the whites called the Little Big Horn. Actually they stayed clear of the stream and rode along the western lip of its wide, shallow valley, ready to disappear from hostile eyes in an instant. That night they camped at a tiny tributary splashing out of the low hills that were all that remained of the great Big Horn range.

Pine Leaf sat down beside him after they had filled themselves on a haunch of antelope.

"Tomorrow," she said, "we will reach our village. We will leave this valley and go west over the hills, and down into the valley of the Big Horn River, and there will be the village of the Kicked-in-the-Bellies band, the people of Gliding Raven and myself. I will present you to our people. I will tell them of the medicine that brought us to you. Already they know of Gliding Raven's dreams. Now they will see that her dreams were true and good. There are things you must tell me; things I must tell my chiefs and my council. Tell me again about the people you came with; the people who have Mister Skye with them. Why are they going to the Siksika? Why are they taking their white medicine to the enemies of my people?''

''Ah'm not sure Ah can explain it very well,'' he said. ''They're a kind of medicine people, just like you're a medicine woman. They have a vision, Ah'd call it, to bring their beliefs, their faith, their God, to all the people on earth. They've selected somehow the Blackfeet to bring it to.''

''Why them? They're dogs. I have taken many of their scalps and maybe I'll take more. Why not us? We want the medicine power. The whites have things we need now—iron pots, iron arrow points, wool blankets, many kinds of guns . . . power.''

''Ah can't say,'' he said, perplexed. ''That's what they had a vision to do.''

''Who?'' demanded Pine Leaf.

''Why, Cecil Rathbone. He's a good man. He and his wife. They are good people, straight as your arrow flies.''

''Why is Mister Skye taking them? His wife is one of us! He betrays us! And he hates the Siksika. He has almost been killed by them many times. And one among the Siksika has vowed to kill Mister Skye, has sworn the oath at their Sun Dance to kill Mister Skye. And yet he takes these people to our enemies. I don't understand this, and neither will my chiefs, my council.''

''Who is this Blackfoot that will kill Mister Skye?''

Pine Leaf hesitated. ''His name is Moon-Hides-the-Sun. There is no more terrible name given to any man. Moon-Hides-the-Sun was born the day it happened, when all the world was shadowed and we thought the end of all things had come. It is the most terrible name ever given. I am afraid of only one person in all the earth, and that is Moon-Hides-the-Sun. He has evil medicine that I do not have. It is said he has the strength of seven warriors. He could kill me, and maybe will. He is not a chief. He refuses to be a chief of the Kainah, the Bloods, of the Blackfeet. He has said that to be a chief would destroy his medicine, for he would be responsible to others. No, he stalks alone, no one knows where, striking anytime, anyplace, even here in the middle of the land of the Absaroka. So powerful is his medicine that the children of our people dream of him coming and wake up in the night crying. I do not understand why Mister Skye goes to the land of Moon-Hides-the-Sun.''

"Ah can't say, but Ah imagine you could ask him directly when he comes here.''

"I am sure we will. And if the answer is not good, I know my chiefs will not permit them to go north.''

They rode over the low divide, over hills serrated by coulees, scattering coyotes that denned there. At a promontory they paused to gaze into the wide valley of the Big Horn, not far north of the canyon it cut between the Big Horn and Pryor Mountains. Below them lay the great Crow village, somnolent in the afternoon sun. The tiny dark cones of two hundred or so lodges, grouped in concentric circles, were visible. The village horse herd grazed quietly in the lush meadows beside the Big Horn River. A faint blue pall of smoke hung over the village.

Gliding Raven's eyes glowed proudly, and she sought Method's eyes, to let him know of her pride and pleasure in her people. Pine Leaf touched the flanks of her brown pony and they began the long descent. They were spotted below, and the camp guards, the wolves, boiled out to greet them even as the village crier raced among the lodges announcing their arrival.

To Method, the lodges looked much alike, smoke-blackened at the top, around the windflaps, but golden at their bases, where the buffalo cowhide retained its original color. Some of the lodges were painted with medicine symbols, suns and moons and other designs.

One lodge seemed larger than the others, and he supposed it belonged to the chief. He found other structures here too, brush arbors resting on poles planted in the earth, to provide a welcome shade and relief from the midsummer sun.

By the time they rode into the village, great crowds had materialized, along with barking dogs and scattering naked children. Everywhere in this year of 1855 was the evidence of extensive trading with the whites. Many of the women wore light, patterned calico skirts. Before many lodges hung black cast-iron kettles. A few of the very old clutched striped trade blankets, even in the heat of high summer. Scarcely a male wore anything more than a breechclout and moccasins.

This was, Method realized, a happy occasion, and people danced and pointed and chattered about them as they rode past. He was plainly an object of great curiosity, and he met their stares with a dignified nod of the .head. All of this was medicine. Had not Gliding Raven dreamed just such a dream as this? Had not the great medicine woman, Pine Leaf, declared the truth of it? Had these two worthy women not gone many sleeps away to bring the black man to this village, where he would become a great warrior, and husband of Gliding Raven? What more proof did anyone need of the medicine vision of these two? And so they rode with honor through the chaotic village, with old and young streaming along beside them on their way to the chief and the elders, who were gathering before the lodge of the chief.

James Method relaxed. It had seemed an alien thing at first, this village and these savage people, so unlike his white masters and the civilization that had enslaved him. These Crow were not handsome at all, plain-featured, ill put together. That made Gliding Raven's incredible beauty even more unusual, he thought. Ahead was the great lodge, and the chief, wearing his ceremonial bonnet, with other headmen beside him. James felt a little uneasy now. He had come into the far west with a party en route to the Blackfeet, mortal enemies of these people. Would it be held against him?

Beside him, Gliding Raven cried out and steered her horse into the crowd, and then slipped off it. Her parents stood there, and she hugged them. They stared at James, and he at them, these two graying people who would become his in-laws, his family, because the medicine proved true. Then they were lost from his sight. Pine Leaf beckoned him to come to dismount, as she did, before the village elders.

The chief was speaking, and James understood little of it. But then Pine Leaf translated. "Many Coups, chief of the Kicked-in-the-Bellies, welcomes you to our village. He praises me, and praises Gliding Raven, for our great medicine, and for bringing us a great warrior who will be like Antelope, Jim Beckwourth . . . You and I are to come into his lodge now to smoke the pipe."

"Tell him Ah'm glad to be here in this great land of the Crow, and this great village which has taken me in. But tell him Ah know nothing about war and fighting; Ah don't know about this warrior business."

Pine Leaf hesitated a second, and then translated.

The chief replied. "It does not matter what you were; it matters what you will be," Pine Leaf translated. "You cannot go against your own medicine."

With that, Many Coups and his elders filed into the great lodge, and Method and Pine Leaf followed. He was beckoned to sit down in a place close to the chief, a place he supposed to be of honor, Pine Leaf beside him to translate. But Many Coups was extracting a long pipe, its bowl made of some sort of red stone, and its wooden shaft decorated with raven feathers and small talismans. It grew very quiet. The light fell mellow gold, piercing through the translucent cowhides. Not even the raucous noise of the village seemed to penetrate here. Slowly the old man with the seamed cheeks and crow's-foot eyes tamped tobacco into the long pipe, and then lit it with a brand from the tiny fire at the center of the lodge. He puffed quietly until the tobacco glowed and its fine aroma filled the lodge. Then he saluted the east and west, the north and south, the earth mother and the sky father. Solemnly he passed the pipe to James Method, who didn't have the foggiest idea what to do, so he did exactly as the chief had done. Not until the pipe had circled the council, ten elders plus James and Pine Leaf, did anyone speak. Many Coups asked a question of Pine Leaf.

Beside him, the graying medicine woman began to speak. It took a long time, and he realized she was supplying the council with her story of the journey. At various times their eyes rested on him. Then the tone of her voice changed, and she was explaining something else, and now their eyes settled searchingly on him, and he heard the word Siksika mentioned, and supposed she was telling what she knew of the mission party.

Then she asked him a question. "They wish to know how Many Quill Woman is faring."

That mystified him.

"Victoria," she said. "Mister Skye calls her Victoria."

"She is well and happy. She feeds Mister Skye and scouts, and cares for the blinded Jesuit."

The who? That was news to them. This blackrobe Dunstan Kiley they knew, and the other one, Pierre de Smet, but surely Kiley had eyes?

James realized that these people did not know the story of Wolf-That-Circles and Dunstan Kiley. So he told them the story, Pine Leaf translating.

"Ayaah!" they cried. "That is news. That is great medicine. Blind and filled with medicine. It is a holy thing, worthy of great respect. Soon we will honor this great blackrobe."

Then came the hard questioning, and Pine Leaf struggled to convey answers. Who were these missionaries, shortrobes with wives? Why did they choose to take medicine to the Siksika dogs? Why was Mister Skye guiding them to the enemies of his own wife? Why was Mister Skye braving the terror of Moon-Hides-the-Sun? Why, why, why?

All of this James Method answered as best he could. Before he was done they had his life history, his escape from slavery, the help of these Methodist missionaries, who he named and described, one by one. As best he could, he explained the white men's faith, the purpose of missions, conversions, and the changes of habit and life they hoped to bring to the Siksika.

"It is beyond my understanding," said Many Coups. "If they bring their medicine to the Siksika dogs, why do they expect them to stop making war?"

"Perhaps the blackrobe, Father Kiley, can explain it to you, Chief Many Coups. Ah can't. Or maybe the headman, Cecil Rathbone."

The chief nodded solemnly. This would be a matter of high policy for his council. For a while they debated among themselves, and none of it was translated for James. But he knew it concerned the missionaries, and whether to prevent them from heading north. There seemed to be many opinions, and none of them prevailing among them.

Then at last the chief called a halt with an uplifted hand, and turned to address James Method.

"You are welcome in the village of the Absaroka people," Pine Leaf translated. "You will be my guest in this lodge for a day and a night, and then a guest of the parents of Gliding Raven, her father New Lance, and her mother Iron Kettle Woman. You will live in the lodge of Gliding Raven, and her brothers, and her parents, until it is the time of your medicine. In the time of your medicine, as it was dreamed by Gliding Raven and pronounced by Pine Leaf, you will in time take seven scalps. And that is now your name among us, Seven Scalps, according to what she has perceived from the hidden side of the world that is open to her because of her virtue. When you have counted coup, or stolen the horses of our enemies, then will New Lance give his daughter to you. And until then you will not touch her."

He smiled gently and dismissed them all, save for James Method and Pine Leaf. While his three wives prepared a buffalo hump roast, along with wild onions and herbs, he questioned Method further; indeed, well into the twilight. And when James Method fell into the robes given him, he felt that the chief knew every scrap of information about him there was to know. And as he drifted off, he felt free.

# Chapter 18

They struck the Big Horn River in mid-July and found no sign of the Crows. Mister Skye scouted to the north as far as the Yellowstone, while Victoria scouted south. When she returned that hot evening, she had information. Her village, the Kicked-in-the-Bellies, had indeed camped some twenty miles upstream, but were no longer there. The grass for miles around the village had been grazed to the roots, and the village had moved to new pasture and a cooler place. She was quite certain where that would be, a creek the Absaroka called Arrow two or three days travel to the west, that white men had come to call Pryor, after a sergeant in Lewis and Clark's Expedition. It was a sacred place of the Absaroka people, she said, for a little to the south rose three small conical peaks, the medicine place of her people. The center of these three low, matched peaks was the place of the vision-quest, where Absaroka youths went to discover their spirit helper, and their adult names, and their role in life.

To the south of these peaks lay the Pryor Mountains, long blue hulks split by a gorge, and teeming with the wiry mustangs that formed the foundation of the magnificent Absaroka horse herd. The way there was almost level, no obstacle to wagons once the Big Horn River was crossed. But the river itself was a formidable barrier that would require the building of a raft. Its silt-laden water ran cold and deep and swift as it approached the Yellowstone, and the deepest channel of the river in some seasons flowed eight or ten feet deep. The banks here were flat and gravelly, and that would be a blessing. Also, they'd find abundant cottonwoods that could be cut into giant logs. These, lashed together, could raft wagons from the east side of the river to the west.

Cecil Rathbone wondered whether between them they had enough rope to lash a raft together and provide a guy across the river, so the rafts wouldn't be swept downstream. There was no help for it but to set to work, and the next day he and Clay Sample hewed heavy limbs from giant cottonwoods, while Alex and Silas yoked oxen to them and dragged them to the shore. It took a day of hard chopping in blazing summer heat to cut and trim enough limbs for the raft. Mister Skye helped when he could and scouted and hunted for meat the rest of the time. Game was scarce here, where hunters from the great Crow village had scoured the country.

They were desperately shorthanded, Cecil thought. Alex Newton and Silas Potter between them equaled less than one hardened frontiersman. Method had vanished. The Jesuit lay helpless. Someone had to make meat, especially since the stores of food brought from the east had been eaten, and there was only Mister Skye to do it, and Victoria to guard the camp against surprise. Fortunately, young Alfred Sample pitched in, and seemed almost a man. It fell to the boy to lash the logs together in a shallow eddy of the river, and to guard them zealously against the reaching fingers of the swift current.

In the late light of a brutal day they completed the raft, and anchored it tightly to shore. Tomorrow they would cross. There was nowhere near enough rope for a guy from shore to shore. They would have to yoke oxen into teams and swim them across, pulling the raft, three round trips, one for each wagon and the carriage. And they would have to drive the entire loose herd across, and hope for the best.

Mister Skye rode in when the sun lay low, without meat. Nothing. Antelope and deer had vanished. No buffalo. Elk fled to the mountains this time of year. For men who had hewn and cut and dragged themselves to exhaustion, that was the hardest news of all. Cecil felt his stomach cave in as he watched Mister Skye unsaddle Jawbone.

"Sorry, mates," was all he said.

No sooner had Mister Skye returned than Victoria and Mary disappeared. Mary handed her boy, Dirk, to Esmerelda, muttering something she took to be a request to look after the child, and then the two Indian women disappeared into the lush growth along the river.

"What have we left?" asked Cecil.

"I have a little flour and salt. There must be some tallow. I think I could manage some sort of fry cakes."

"That sounds as splendid as a rib roast right now."

Dirk stared at them solemnly, understanding a little of his father's tongue. He was a quiet child, as stoic as his parents. Cecil admired the uncomplaining boy, even as Silas and Henrietta and Alex approached.

"What are we going to eat?" snapped Silas. "You'd think he'd have the foresight to gather game back a way, rather than wait until we got to this hunted-out area."

"Would have spoiled fast in this heat."

"Maybe Alice Sample has something," Henrietta said crossly.

"I'm sure Alice needs everything she has for her own very hungry family, dear," said Cecil.

"Are there fish in that river? I despise fish, but I'll eat a dozen tonight," said Alex.

It was a moot question.

Cecil saw the priest sitting quietly on the dropped tailgate of his wagon, and thought to let the man know of their distress.

"We're short of chow this evening, Father."

"So I gathered."

"We've a little flour. Esmerelda might manage some simple cakes if we can find some lard."

"I need nothing," he said. "I've sat here quietly all day while the rest of you have labored. Some water, and I'll be filled. For you I'll ask for loaves and fishes."

The thought struck Cecil then. Had he lost faith? Had he failed to ask?

He wandered back among his people.

"All along I've opposed this incompetent, demonic guide," snapped Silas Potter sourly, "but no, we had to go ahead, had to have him, and now he's left us to starve on the banks of a river many hundreds of hard miles from help."

Cecil placed a gentle hand on the young scholar's shoulder. "No, son," he said. "We are never far from help."

"Piety won't fill my stomach," Silas snapped. "This whole mission has fallen to pieces. Where's that lazy Method? Gone! What does a hard, powerful man like Skye do, when we have a heavy raft to build? Take his leisure on horseback, allegedly hunting for us. What do his squaws do all day? And now even they've vanished, heaven knows where."

Alex chimed in. "This is unbearable, Cecil. When we reach the Crow village, let's see who we can hire. Surely we don't want to employ this bumbling Skye anymore."

Cecil thought for a moment to lead them in a prayer, or a hymn, but thought better of it. They'd become so sullen their hearts were not open. He stopped briefly at the Sample wagon and Alice smiled wanly at him. They had, it seemed, almost nothing either, and the children were cross and even Clay sat sullenly. He spotted a small rise a few yards away, and repaired to it, wondering whether its rocky, striated top might harbor rattlers. But he found none, and sat down, feeling the day's heat rise from the yellow sandstone. And there in the deepening shadows he prayed for loaves and fishes.

Below him Mister Skye had lit a small fire near his lodge, and Cecil wondered at that. Heat hung thick, and there was no food to cook. He had taken Dirk back from Esmerelda, and was playing with the boy, laughing and roaring, while the child chattered like a squirrel, somehow impervious to the gnawing hole in their bellies.

Cecil resolved to show the same fortitude, and decided to ignore the howl and growl of his belly and go pass time with the lonely and alone priest, whose spirit Cecil had come to admire. But as he rose and stretched, he spotted Skye's squaws toiling down the riverbank toward the camp, each burdened with unidentifiable things in bundles and bags.

The others stared sullenly, lost in self-pity, but Cecil grew curious and trudged over to them. Victoria was laughing, and Mary grinning.

"More damn vittles than we can gather," Victoria said. From the bags they pulled quantities of roots, carrot-like but white, and scores of small bulbs Cecil recognized as wild onions. There were other greens he supposed were herbs, and indeed their fragrance lifted to him in the evening breezes. Gently wrapped in Victoria's brown shawl were scores of wild asparagus, each cut with her Green River knife. In Mary's hand was a small pot with surprising contents: ripe, red, lush raspberries. And another bag bulged with some berries of a variety Cecil didn't know.

"Sarvisberries," said Mister Skye. "Chokecherry and plum coming along, but still too soon."

Over the guide's campfire water boiled in a large kettle. It had mystified Cecil before, but now he understood. Swiftly the women cleaned the roots—breadroot, Skye explained, an Indian staple collected by them in large quantities—and the onions and dropped them into the kettle. Next came various herbs, and finally Victoria dipped into one of Mister Skye's parfleches and extracted several handfuls of buffalo jerky, which also went into the stew, whose aroma now galvanized the famished company. While the great stew bubbled, Victoria and

Mary cleaned the berries, reserving the raspberries for the children, and the tart sarvisberries for the adults.

The hungry company demolished the whole kettle of stew, and the berries as well, pronouncing it the finest meal they had had during their whole exodus. But not before Cecil invited Dunstan Kiley, who was led to the feast and was sitting quietly beside Mister Skye, to say grace. Esmerelda watched him, and wept.

At dawn the Indian women took the white women with them in search of another meal from nature's providence. Even Henrietta, inspired by her brush with hunger, was eager to go, and to learn. Cecil walked to the riverbank, to study the wide, rippling, quiet river in the long light of the new day. It seemed peaceful enough, wending its way through silent shadowed hills. But he sensed its power, its strength-sapping coldness, its cruelty, and once again he wondered at his own folly in coming here with wagons. Had he been crazy in his zeal to do God's work? Here, in these lapping waters, lay grave jeopardy again. The wagons, perched on their high wooden wheels, were top-heavy. A ripple, a wave, a gust of air, could capsize them, and if they tipped, they would spill the essence of his dreams, the tools, the Bibles, the organ, into the swirling river, and it would all end.

He had met and conquered rivers before. What man on the nation's westering frontier hadn't? Each stream was a separate problem. Each wreaked its havoc its own way, and only the canny observer might hope to anticipate and deal with the troubles. So he had come here in the utter stillness to meet his enemy. God gave him brains to deal with life's hard moments, and he intended to use them. To trust in God's providence, yes indeed, for that was part of it. But also to use himself and his skills and intuitions too. There was, he thought, too much of the other thing in the world—declarations of trust and faith that really masked indolence and foolishness. Hand in hand with it went the wrong kind of humility, the kind that avoided trying and striving. Cecil had the other kind, that came upon him after he had thrown himself at a knotty problem and failed. That gave him some sense of his outer boundaries, his folly, and that was where his kind of humility began. That was the river where he met God. He feared he might really be arrogant, insisting on trying, striving, pushing himself beyond his former limits. Had he not read of saints who trusted God more, and simply became God's instruments? He admired them, but he wasn't that kind. He was God's unruly servant, and now he had a river to tackle and a cottonwood raft, and some oxen to pull it.

He threw a small stick into the water to measure the flow. It vanished into the dark north swiftly. He trudged downstream to see how the banks lay a quarter, half a mile that way. The crossings would not be straight across but at a long angle, driven by the current. It looked good. The river bent east slightly, driving its current gently toward the far shore. But the shore was thick with brush, and passage might have to be hacked through it. He guessed the river ran seventy or eighty yards wide here.

He closed his eyes a moment, trying to visualize what might happen. They'd haul the wagon onto the raft and lash it. They'd double-team the oxen and hook the tugs to the raft. But how would they do that? Drive the oxen into the current and hope for enough shallow water so the oxen could stand while being hooked up? He decided to take a horse and just measure depth a bit. The more he knew, the more he could avert catastrophe. Then what? Someone riding a horse, riding a swimming horse, would have to whip the oxen. And then what? Why, that cold current would whip the raft downstream, swinging the oxen, pointing them away from the far shore, until the whole team was swimming upstream against the current, until it grew exhausted and the end came to the oxen, the raft, and all within it.

He knew then what not to do.

Instead he would take advantage of that gentle curve that threw the mainstream toward the far shore a few hundred yards down. There were willows here, and he'd cut some fine flexible poles from them, and he'd put the men on the raft, poling hard until they lost the bottom. He'd tie the last of the rope to the raft, too, about fifty feet of it, ready to be thrown to horsemen down at that curve where the current swept ten or fifteen yards from shore. As for the stock—the oxen and mules, the horses and milch cows—they'd swim free, with no lines to entangle them.

Only then, after he had envisioned his plan with whatever shrewdness he possessed, did Cecil J. B. Rathbone submit it all to God. "This is my best thought," he said. "Now show me your way and let me be humble enough to receive it."

He waited quietly in the somnolent dawn light, and then walked back to camp. While the women cooked he found his axe and began to cut long willow limbs and trim them until he had four or five poles, running two or three inches thick and ten feet or so in length. He was ready for the day, though there was one more river still to cross, the stream that separated his thinking from that of others.

After the meal he assembled his people and explained his purposes, and his reasoning. He would put the men of the party on the raft with poles; he would ask Mister Skye to cross the river and wait on the bend of the far shore, to catch the rope tossed to him and, on Jawbone, draw the raft to safety.

As he expected, both Silas and Alex thought it was madness. "Why," asked Silas petulantly, "float the raft free when there is all the power of the oxen to draw it across?"

And Alex, who abhorred the hard work of poling, added, "What if we miss the far bank? There we'll be, stuck on a raft and no way to get off and whirling down the river—clear to New Orleans."

Mister Skye said nothing, but saddled Jawbone and rode down the river a way, studying it. Ten minutes later he returned with his verdict. "It'll work," he said. "Best plan there is."

That settled it. Clay Sample, having weighed it all, announced in favor. But he had a question.

"We've got to cross that raft three times. How are we going to get it back for the next crossing?"

Cecil saw the answer at once. "The oxen will pull it back this way, slanting upstream into the current to get here. They won't be fighting the raft coming this way. We'll drive them across first, and throw the harness in the first wagon over."

And that was the way they tackled it. Mister Skye doffed his leggins, and in his breechclout swam Jawbone over and trotted on down the far shore. Victoria swam her pony, and continued up the far side to a distant ridge to do sentry duty there. Mary swam with her, with Dirk clinging behind. The Samples' wagon was eased down to the riverbank and laboriously levered up onto the rough cottonwood logs and lashed down. All the party's harness was thrown into it. Alice and Miriam nervously chose to go too, hoping to stay dry.

They hazed the oxen into the water, cracking whips and prodding with their poles, and watched the heavy beasts swim toward the far shore, drifting downstream as they did. A few minutes later they clambered up a muddy slope and shook themselves heavily and began to spread into the brush there.

Following Cecil's example, the men doffed their shirts and shoes, except for Alex Newton, whose corpulent body rather embarrassed him, and who chose to remain, as he muttered to himself, decently clad. Cecil, Clay, young Alfred, Silas, and Alex each grasped a pole and heaved the heavy raft into the stream, scraping bottom a way. Then they slid clear, poling furiously, sweeping downstream toward the curve. For a brief while the poles touched nothing, and they stood helplessly. But the raft angled the right way, drawn by its momentum and the current, and Cecil soon found his pole touching a soft bottom again, and he pushed hard. Mister Skye sat on Jawbone, belly deep in the eddying water, waiting a hundred yards downstream. It was easy. As they drifted close, Cecil tossed the rope. Mister Skye plucked it from the water, and set Jawbone toward shore, pulling mightily, helped by the poling. The raft bottomed somewhat sooner than they had expected, ten yards out, and the jolt sent Alex Newton careening into the cold water. He sputtered and stood, mad at creation, his black suit drenched. The laughter didn't settle his temper any. Cecil himself jumped off, wondering what sort of bottom they had. It was mud rather than the gravel he'd hoped for, but not muck. They could offload the Samples' wagon and drag it out with the oxen, cutting a path here.

It was well past noon before they had crossed the Big Horn, but Cecil's plan had worked, and they had no losses, though there had been a bad moment when a milch cow mysteriously turned around, halfway across, swam back awhile, got confused, turned into the current again and was swept far downstream. They found her alive and safe on the west bank a mile down. On the last trip across they rafted the other wagon, with the organ and Dunstan Kiley in it, and Cecil took time to explain to the blind priest what they were doing and why.

"I can pole," said Kiley.

"I'm sure you can," replied Cecil, "but you've got other rivers to cross."

By early afternoon they had reassembled their caravan and rolled toward the village of the Crows, Victoria's people, and the old woman's eyes shone bright in the July sun.

# Chapter 19

On Arrow Creek, hard by the cool slopes of the Pryor Mountains, James Method waited uneasily for the arrival of Mister Skye and his erstwhile colleagues. One glance at him would tell them much: he was attired now in breechclout and leggins, and fine elkhide summer moccasins all made for him by his future wife, with the help of her mother. Around his neck hung a sacred medicine bundle that Pine Leaf had given him, saying she would explain its contents to him in time, as he came to understand the Absarokas and their medicine.

Daily the great woman warrior instructed him in the uses of bow and arrow, lance, battle axe, and knife. She taught him how to ride his horse lightly and to jump off of either side and other things about horses and horsemanship he'd never known. Once she told him that her people needed a great leader, for their numbers had dwindled because of white man's smallpox, and many of them had succumbed to whiskey from the trading posts, and fallen into filth and degradation.

She met his gaze then and told him that he might be

the very one who would restore her people to their former numbers and courage. Gliding Raven had brought a great gift to the Absaroka people. Perhaps it was so. In less than a moon—he was thinking in Indian terms now—he had become a new person. He felt ready now to join a Crow war party, and do the things that would win him Gliding Raven. The Kit Fox Society, one of the most esteemed of the warrior groups, had invited him, and the invitation was a great honor. It all showed in his eyes, and the way he walked, and the assurance of his words. In scarcely half a year he had ascended from slave to uneasy companion of westering whites, to free warrior, on the brink of triumph among the Crows.

Mister Skye's party rode into the large village one afternoon, announced by the crier and escorted by the wolf warriors, village guardians and policemen, cavorting children, yelping dogs, and all of the curious. James stood well back among them, watching the fearsome bulk of Mister Skye in his black silk stovepipe hat, riding his terrible blue horse. And Victoria, greeting friends and relatives with joyous cries and hugs, and the Shoshone Mary, with the boy, smiling quietly from her pony at these occasional allies of her people. Behind them came the missionaries and their wagons and loose stock, staring at the Crows and being stared at in turn, curiosity and pleasure on Cecil J. B. Rathbone's gaunt and homely features, fear on the faces of the Newtons, and taut loathing radiating from the rigid pale face of Silas Potter. Behind them came the Samples, a little afraid, quiet, and self-possessed.

But it was Father Kiley who drew the stares and nudges now as he sat on an improvised seat at the front of his wagon. He had been known to them as a blackrobe colleague of Pierre de Smet, and now the story of his encounter with Wolf-That-Circles was familiar to them all, and they stared and pointed, and wondered what lay beneath the leatherbound bandages wrapping his upper face. Crow warriors stared thoughtfully at the white shaman whose medicine was so powerful that it felled Cheyenne right and left.

Victoria spotted her venerable and widowed father, and leapt lightly from her pony and into his embrace, and then the embrace of her stepmother. James Method stood near, and he could not yet understand the rapid Crow chatter of their reunion, but he could sense its joy and the love these people radiated. Victoria embraced not only her father, but those of her Sorelips Clan kin, sisters and cousins all, united in a powerful tribal faction.

As Mister Skye rode by, a man so terrible that there was always a notable space around him where others feared to penetrate, his small obscure eyes spotted James and held him in his gaze, instantly absorbing all that had transformed him. Then, faintly, he grinned, acknowledging it and approving of it. James felt suddenly that in Mister Skye's eyes, he had increased in stature, had come into a kind of manhood, an inheritance of the free western lands. He felt a kind of warmth, and even nostalgia about all the months of the trail, and Mister Skye's canny guidance came back to him. He had won manhood.

At the great smoke-darkened lodge of Chief Many Coups, this slow cavalcade halted. There the village elders and medicine men gathered, along with its esteemed medicine woman Pine Leaf, in whose austere lodge hung fifty-eight scalps of the enemies of her people. The chief gripped his raven feather-bedecked ceremonial coup stick, a badge of office, and studied this strange party brought by his friend and ally Mister Skye. And it lay in the chief's face, James thought, that these were odd white men and white women. The Absaroka women had scarcely seen a white woman, and now they crowded around Esmerelda and Henrietta—who looked like she might scream—and the Samples, fingering the cloth of their dresses, observing styles and stitching, boldly examining high-button shoes, poking at skirts to discover white petticoats. Only Esmerelda enjoyed it, and that perhaps was because she was studying the dress of her

Crow sisters, the finely-wrought moccasins decorated with beads or fur trim; skin skirts and blouses worked so soft that they were velvet; hair parted into dark braids, with carmine paint down the part and on the cheeks, and trade ribbons in rainbow colors gaily tied to the braids.

Cecil, dressed in his Sunday-best black broadcloth, which seemed less and less appropriate to his gaunt frontier-hardened frame, drew up beside Mister Skye, before the chief and subchiefs and great men of the village. Many Coups raised a hand and addressed them in the Crow tongue, while Mister Skye translated softly. They were being welcomed, he said. Next would be a smoke. He and Cecil and Dunstan Kiley would sit with the elders in council; the rest were welcome to the village, and were invited to make camp at a place that would be designated, and to turn their stock over to the Crow herders.

Now at last Silas spotted James, stared icily, and nudged Alex and Henrietta, who simply gaped. James nodded amiably, seeing at once an impenetrable barrier forever between him and these whites. Esmerelda and then Cecil spotted him too, but in their gaze was curiosity and finally small grins of delight in reunion, while the chiefs and Mister Skye exchanged greetings according to the great protocol of the high plains.

Then Mister Skye turned to his party. "These lads here will take you to our place here, mates," he said. "We're among friends and allies. Many know English. The trappers—Beckwourth, Bridger, and a score of others—have stayed among them. The Absaroka are the finest warriors and horse thieves on the northern plains, and will take special care of the livestock of their guests, for it would bring dishonor to them to lose even one animal of any guest in their village . . . You'll have no need to cook a meal, for you'll be guests at great feastings this evening, and all the while we're here.

"Now, mates, some of us will smoke the pipe with the chiefs and elders. Mister Rathbone and Father Kiley and I, as well as our lost and found friend there, James Method"—the Samples, who had not yet spotted him, gawked—"are invited to counsel with our hosts. We'll be along in a while. There are many here who'd like to enjoy your company, mates, so welcome them at your wagons."

With that, he dismounted from Jawbone, and left the horse standing in its own pool of space, untouched by any Crow, who well knew the medicine powers of that awesome animal. His new Sharps rifle lay in its saddle sheath at Jawbone's side. Way was made in the crowds, and the others turned their oxen and their wagons and drove them off down the creek a bit, accompanied by the flocking curious among these people. Esmerelda glanced fleetingly at Cecil, with a look that said she wished she might stay and be with him, and then followed the others. James waited until Cecil and Mister Skye had led the priest into the chief's lodge, and then ducked through the east-facing door himself.

"Well, mate," said Mister Skye, wrapping a brawny arm about Method's shoulders. "I knew it, and I know what's been your good fortune. If you've got Pine Leaf for a sponsor here, you've got a fine life ahead of you."

"Is Mister Method here?" asked Father Kiley.

"I am beside you, Father."

The priest said nothing, but grasped James's hand warmly.

They were seated according to custom, having carefully walked around the central firepit. James was familiar with the smoking ritual now, but waited impatiently as this ceremony of peaceful intention and hospitality unwound, and Mister Skye had presented his hosts with twists of tobacco, powder and ball, and vermilion paint, treasured things all.

Then there came silence. James became aware that Many Coups was assessing the two white medicine men across the circle from him, his shrewd eyes first upon Father Kiley, and then upon Cecil J. B. Rathbone. The priest sat quietly, unaware and waiting. With some frontier aplomb, Cecil sat quietly as well, and met the chief's steady and penetrating stare with a direct gaze of his own, obviously aware that upon his conduct here rested the fate of his long exodus. When at last the chief spoke, Mister Skye translated.

"Mister Rathbone," said the chief, "your purposes have been made known to us, but we would have you tell us in your own words. The taking of your sacred medicine to our ancient enemies, the Siksika, has caused controversy among us. There are some here who say you insult the Absaroka people. Others say you are the enemies of my people. Others ask why you do not bring your medicine here to us and stay among us. Others—our great woman, Pine Leaf, especially—say that you have no real medicine; it is false and weak and evil, and if you want to take it to our enemies, then go and do it, for it will diminish them and make fools and old women of their warriors, and destroy their nation. I haven't yet made up my mind. I'll hear you and hear my friend Mister Skye, and then I'll decide what to do, after talking with my chiefs and elders."

It would be a long afternoon of theology, then, Method thought uncomfortably. And so it turned out to be.

Cecil Rathbone plunged in with a robust enthusiasm and a poignant innocence, describing the things he hoped to bring to the Blackfeet, the ways he hoped to transform them from warlike nomads to plowmen and ranchers, raising grains and fruits, and herding cattle. He would erect a church and a school, and introduce them to a loving, caring church and Lord who'd look after his Siksika children and keep them from harm and who, in turn, required submission, love, loyalty, virtue, and praise. He'd teach them to read and write, and some figures too so they could calculate, and with that they could do what whites do, manufacture what whites produce. When the Blackfeet no longer waged war, or caused turmoil or raided whites, then the Lord of Creation would pour his medicine upon them and help them endure all things, and bring them to Himself and no matter how they suffered on earth, their next life would be spent with Him in perfect happiness.

The chief then turned to Father Kiley, who had an altogether different message and interpretation of the faith. Quietly the Jesuit addressed his unseen audience, droning on, as if reading from his missal or reciting a homily, seeing his words on the screen of his mind. The anguished priest began at once to separate the purposes of God from the magic possessed by whites, cleaving the things of the spirit from guns and powder and the power to find metal and turn it into pots and bullets and arrow points and knives. Father Kiley's narration turned to stranger things, long suffering, submission, obedience, and love freely given to God, redemption through the sacrificed Son Jesus, born of the Virgin, baptism, the spiritual and the carnal, the schism between the reformers and the original church, orthodoxy, divine love for all God's creatures, Crow and Siksika and Sioux and white alike, miracles, sin, sacrifice, confession . . .

To all of this the chief and his elders listened solemnly, more bewildered by the conflicting strains of this white man's religion than comprehending. Sometimes the things the Reverend Rathbone and Father Kiley said struck the familiar. Was not this God similar to the One Above, the Great Spirit, or even Father Sun? But Father Kiley's narration became a mystery to them: why worship and love this God if there was no medicine to be found in it? He had talked much of suffering, purging the soul, enduring grief, being humble and meek. Why become groveling dogs and miserable crawling creatures, worse than the Digger people far to the west who lived naked in deserts and ate grasshoppers and lizards and ran from others?

Pine Leaf, great warrior and medicine woman, drove these points home, in a voice laden with scorn. The Crow were a great warrior people, strong, the terror of their neighbors, powerful because they stayed true to their medicine and heritage as the people of Absaroka, the raven. If these white medicine people wished to take their strange faith to the Siksika, and turn them into fools and weaklings, so much the better! Let them go do it, so the Absaroka nation might triumph!

At last Many Coups turned to Mister Skye. "Why is it, my old friend, that you take these white medicine people to our enemies? By marriage, you are one of us, friend and ally, and many times over many winters, you have fought these very Siksika at our side. Have you now a change of heart?"

Mister Skye replied in Crow, and this time Pine Leaf quietly translated for James.

Mister Skye was a law unto himself, and diplomacy was a thing that had been beaten out of his very soul by a hard life, brutality, slavery, and ultimately his force of will. So his words were not chosen for their effect on his listeners. James sensed he spoke with the force of truth, rather than expediency.

"I was brought up in the Christian religion," he said, "and I respect it, for in my youth I saw its effect upon many people whose tongues were true and works were good and kind and loving. But I was ripped from my nation, and thrown into another world, and in my time of worst trouble, my religion failed me, and I became a man of no religion. I make my own medicine. Since then I have learned of your medicine religion, and have seen its mysterious force, even as I have sometimes seen the miraculous force of the faith I abandoned. I have come to your medicine men with gifts, seeking to know my future and what will make me strong, and I have found them keen and wise, and somehow able to look into the beyond and see what is to come, or the spirits of those who have gone to the other side. They are holy men— and women—and I honor them. I am taking these missionaries to your enemies and mine, the Siksika, and I think they will benefit. I will support myself and my family by doing it. I think the missionaries will give the Siksika something good that the Absaroka do not have and will need when the buffalo are gone."

"The buffalo gone?" asked Many Coups sharply.

"The buffalo will all go, and when they go, the buffalo medicine of the Absaroka will go with it."

There was anger and scorn among the elders.

"The buffalo are as thick as rivers and beyond numbering," said Pine Leaf to them all. "They are the brothers and sisters of the Absaroka people."

The chief stood. "We have heard you. Now my elders and chiefs and medicine men will talk."

Mister Skye and Cecil Rathbone led Father Kiley through the flap door and into blinding low sun, and James followed. Pine Leaf stayed within.

Mister Skye mounted Jawbone. "Mister Method," he said, "I'd like to powwow with you. Bring Father Kiley when you come. His wagon is no longer here."

James slid his arm around the priest's and led him slowly toward the missionary encampment downstream a bit.

"Well, James," Kiley said. "I would guess that you have come to stay with these people."

"Ah am," he said. "Ah'm free, and Ah'm going to become a leader among them."

"I can understand that. Though I regret it."

James thought to steer away from that. "And how are you, Father?"

For a long time the priest didn't answer. "The pain is lessening," he said. "My headaches are fewer. But I have a long dark wait until I am released. I hope I have the courage not to offend my Lord while I wait."

"You have many years, yet."

"My misfortune."

He took Dunstan Kiley to his wagon and helped him in, and settled him upon his buffalo robe. Cecil hovered near, animatedly telling the other missionaries of the council and the unsettled future.

"Mister Method," said Mister Skye. "Let's go yonder to the shade, and palaver. I don't know what the others are seeing, but I'm seeing a bloody new man."

The guide listened gravely while James described the strange, compelling need that had driven him to take the cow meat back to the place of the skulls during that storm, and all that transpired after that.

"Thought something like that," Skye muttered. "You're a free man, on your own now, mate. I think you're where you should be."

None of the others approached him, sensing from the things he wore, and the change in his demeanor, that he had crossed some divide of the soul and was no longer one of them, no longer a black citizen of a white world. Silas Potter stared icily, as if James's transformation were a personal affront. But the rest were simply distant, intimidated, perhaps, by what they saw. He stayed there, curious about the fate of these people and the council's decision, but he hovered close to Mister Skye's lodge and Mary and Dirk. Victoria was with her people.

The answer came at sunset, borne by Pine Leaf. "My chiefs have decided," she said to Mister Skye, "not to stop you. You may take these medicine people and their poisons to the Siksika. Let them rot. It might have been otherwise but for your talk about the buffalo going away. They laughed at such a thing. I laughed too. Those were strange prophecies, Mister Skye, and your medicine is bad. Take these people to our enemies.

"But I have foreseen something else. You will have troubles from our enemies along the way north. Not the Siksika dogs, but one of the others, perhaps the Assiniboin. I saw this in the smoke of the sweetgrass burning. Your party is weak because of these spirit men among you, who will not fight or defend their wives. I will go with you a way, and I am taking Seven Scalps, James Method. He must prove himself a warrior to us, so that he may have Gliding Raven, and we may see his medicine. With your people, he will have his chance. I am no longer young, but I have not forgotten how it is to draw a bow."

Mister Skye nodded. "Your presence among us is the same as many warriors, Pine Leaf."

She nodded. "My chiefs are making a feast. Bring your people when it is just dark, and we will feed you buffalo hump, the meat of the sacred buffalo sister that you say will depart from us. It will never go away! And bring the great wooden many-flutes that James described to us. We would hear it. We have never seen such a thing. Tell the woman to make the sounds.''

"Her name is Henrietta Newton, and I will tell her. The Lakotah feared it. Will the Absaroka people also be afraid?''

"The Lakotah warriors are afraid of everything,'' Pine Leaf snorted. ''The Absaroka fear nothing.''

# Chapter 20

From the Crow village on Arrow Creek they struck west across a vast arid land, skirting the Pryor Mountains hulking like a tilted table to the south. In the hazy west rose vast and jagged mountains patched with white, even though July was upon them, and of a looming majesty that not even the Big Horns possessed. They looked to be the roof of the world, and Mister Skye confirmed that these Beartooths were a main strand of the Rockies.

Cecil and Esmerelda exulted in the wild windy land, exclaiming at the prospects from every prairie ridge they traversed. Even Silas Potter was enthralled by this incalculable wilderness the Crow people called their home. He perceived it as a country that was too harsh for settlement by whites. It would be beyond civilization, the permanent province of savage peoples, an island of barbarism in a civilized world. He had grown skeptical of converting these heathen people, or teaching them the ways of white civilization. Unlike Cecil, whose boundless frontier optimism led him to believe anything was possible, Silas had a sense of limitations. He knew he had a much more acute intellect than Cecil; he could foresee disaster, and he was sure the only proper course for this party was to admit defeat and retreat to the east.

The overnight visit to the Crow village had confirmed him in his belief. He had a scholar's eye for detail, and a student's ability to find meaning in all that he observed. What he saw, as he peered owlishly through the lenses of his spectacles, was heathen savagery. These Crow people hadn't even the decency to dress their boys, who ran naked, though he admitted even the smallest girl wore a little deerskin dress. If the Crow were as bad as this, the Blackfeet could only be worse.

The buffalo hump roast tasted fine, but other Crow food was odd, and he wondered what was in it. Strange roots. Henrietta's organ concert had been edifying. They had rolled the wagon into a central area near the chief's lodge and stripped back the canvas from its bows, and she had played fine hymns, such as "Rock of Ages." At first terrified children and some of the women had held hands to ears, or run away screaming as the organ thundered. But they had crept back, with wide eyes. Henrietta told him she regarded her playing as the beginning of a great conversion of these people, and that inspired her to strenuous efforts. Silas doubted that; doubted that the organ hymns were anything but a fearsome novelty within the savage breast.

She had played until the dark thickened and her hands and feet were worn out, and then stood and bowed. But the heathen had built fires and were assembling for a dance of their own, and the evening that began with correct and sacred solemnity turned into a savage, howling, unspeakable saturnalia. The heathen Crow men and women danced in a great circle, undulating toward each other, and back, flaunting their bodies and behaving in a matter most improper and carnal, he thought. He saw umber glistening flesh everywhere in the amber firelight, Crow men prancing in their breechclouts, women lifting their skirts. It was too much for Silas. It all evoked wild and forbidden thoughts of Mister Skye's Mary in him, so he fled to his bedroll in loathing and disgust, and demanded of God that He put a stop to such things.

Now their caravan rolled westward again, augmented by James Method, and that heathen medicine woman beside him. It was bad enough, he thought, that Method had reverted to utter savagery, wearing Crow skins, the tops of his tawny thighs in plain sight above his leggins. But the heathen medicine woman and warrior woman wore even less, a breechclout and a fringed skin shirt, her long fine legs straddling her horse and scandalously bare. Like Mister Skye, she had a shining rifle of the modern breechloading type in a decorated saddle sheath, and a quiver upon her back. A bow she always carried in hand. She stood almost man-tall, and her black hair, glinting blue in some lights, hung loose. For a middle-aged woman, she seemed amazingly lithe and young.

It was bad enough that they had the Romish priest with them. But now they had a Crow priestess as well, what any good Christian would call a witch, and an African who had defected to that side. Had Cecil Rathbone gone mad? Silas peered around him. In this missionary party the only acceptable people were the Newtons, perhaps the Samples, and himself. Rathbone had strayed, making common cause with heathens. It was time, he thought, to put a stop to it. He'd form a faction: Newtons, Samples, himself. Meet in secret and decide what to do— return east, separate themselves from these people of perdition, whatever. He would think on that.

One possibility was exorcism. He had not seen such a thing, but had heard of it. They could capture that priestess, Pine Leaf, tie her down and perform the rite. There were rituals in the Catholic and Anglican churches for it, bell, book, and candle, but he didn't know what reformed churches did. He would consult Alex Newton, who was a considerable scholar. Kiley, the Jesuit, might know, but Silas had no intention of consulting him.

They made excellent progress that day, over land without barriers, and that night they camped in the bottoms of a considerable river Mister Skye called Clark's

Fork of the Yellowstone. After the meal of venison, from the spike buck the Crow priestess had easily brought down with an arrow, Silas watched narrowly, and was rewarded for his vigilance. The woman had actually unrolled her buffalo robe next to James Method's and it became plain what their relationship was.

"Have you noticed it?" he whispered to Alex Newton.

"I have. I have only sorrow in my heart for James. The Crow medicine woman I pity in her ignorance, but I hold nothing against her. I am not sure one could call such a thing evil. One must know the laws of God before one can understand evil. Saint Paul argued just such a thing in Romans, I think. She knows no better."

Alex's temperate answer annoyed Silas. "We are missionaries on a sacred enterprise. We can't permit such things," Silas snapped. "It is pure evil, right in our midst."

Alex sighed. "We succeed or fail as apostles by being a shining light among them, not by avoiding them or scorning them," he said. "Sorry, Silas. We're among the people of darkness, the ones we want to reach. These are ones who have never heard the Word. We surely can't thrust the benighted from us, or exclude them from our love and caring."

"You mean you tolerate it, like your father-in-law," snapped Silas.

"I think you will want to reconsider that harsh indictment," said Alex. "Prayerfully, and with love of all men. Think about love," he added.

Silas spun away angrily. So then, he thought, I am alone here! I alone uphold the laws of God, without compromise! I am the only one left in this small and faithless congregation! They are all lukewarm, and I am a pillar of fire!

That restless night in his blankets, staring out upon the chipped ice of heaven, Silas Potter knew who he was. He was a prophet of God. He would be a voice crying in the wilderness. He would be a brother of the other pillars of fire, Jeremiah, Isaiah, Ezekiel, Malachi . . . !

He would cry out at their wantonness and idolatry, and be driven from their midst for it! He would be their lost conscience, and the voice of God, and be exiled and persecuted for it!

He drove the thought of Mary's nakedness from his vision, where it had crept, with fierce contempt, and then slipped into the easy sleep of the righteous. In the morning he would no longer be a soft-spoken scholar and theology student; he'd be an acid-tongued wasp, stinging right and left, shaming and chastising them all, a hornet of God.

With the dawn Silas was a transformed man. He peered about him with burning eyes, finding wickedness everywhere. It was a lovely place, a meadow turning golden, rimmed by cottonwoods beside the river. Meadowlarks trilled, but Silas didn't hear them. He had thought to anathematize Pine Leaf and James Method, because their hot sin of the night would be lingering upon them, but both had slipped from camp and were out scouting and hunting, even while the rest ate and prepared to cross the wagons over the bouldered bottom of Clark's Fork. Still, there was Mister Skye and his wives, and he would begin with them.

They camped apart. The cookfires of Mary and Victoria nourished Skye, the Jesuit, and now Pine Leaf and Method. Silas found them in a merry mood, Victoria full of laughter and chatter, for she had seen her people and this was the heartland of the Crow nation, and she had the greatest of Crow women, Pine Leaf, here with her. Silas watched her and Mary laughing, and scolding Dirk, all with a pounding pulse. And there was Skye off near Jawbone, and urinating in plain sight.

With a quickening pulse he approached, steering wide of the evil blue horse, that followed him with bright malevolent eyes.

"Mister Skye!" he said hoarsely.

"Yaas?"

"You are a bigamist and a sinner. Set aside your

younger squaw and stop using her. You are a transgressor against God. Repent of your ways!''

Mister Skye was taken aback. From the cookfire the squaws stared, not so much because of what they'd heard, but because of Silas's odd and imperious tone of voice.

Mister Skye laughed heartily, his beefy frame convulsing with it, and his silk hat darting in spastic circles.

''Mate,'' he said, ''if a couple of kings like David and Solomon could have lots of wives, I imagine the good Lord will spare me my two.''

Silas hadn't expected that from the man. Hadn't even known Mister Skye could read.

''I see you're familiar with Scriptures. The Gospels say—''

''Mister Potter, do you know what a good woman is? She's a bloody miracle. She's a joy and a blessing. I'm an old vagabond roaming the wilderness and all I can give a woman is a hard life and a lonely one. But yonder's my Victoria, who does for me, lifts my spirit, makes me laugh, serves me like I was King of England, Scotland and Wales, lord sovereign of Canada, Australia, India, and the rest. She treats me as if the sun never sets upon me. And yonder's my Mary of the Shoshone, beautiful creature, warms an old man's flesh in the night, hugs a man who needs hugging, raises our son Dirk, of our union, fills my lodge with her youth and vitality and warm smiles. And the pair of them fight like warriors in a scrap, rescue me, nurse me, heal my wounds, and all for the hard life I give them. That's called love, mate. Go find some yourself.''

Silas drew himself up with dignity. ''Love is all well and good. But the Scriptures say that to love God, you must keep his law.''

With that he stalked off, faintly alarmed by Skye's heckling bellow, but delighted with himself for getting in the last word, the true Word. Now there were others to reform, and he would be the sword of the Lord . . .

Next he pounced upon the Rathbones, who were

breaking camp and stowing their few small things in the carriage, and readying themselves for the day's travel.

He felt feverish now with the heavy sword he carried, and he wasted no time in holy rebuke, beginning with Cecil's wrongful concern about the bodies and livelihood of the Blackfeet and his unconcern about their spiritual life, and jumping from there to Cecil's derelict conduct on the trail, hiring Mister Skye and his bigamous squaws, welcoming the Romish priest, tolerating sin and evil, weakness and shame, and all the rest.

As he accused he felt an excitement, his voice rose and sharpened, and he felt it cutting like a stiletto into the burning souls of his listeners. He was opening their eyes, awakening the Rathbones, firing them up to duty!

The outburst took only ten minutes, and when at last he quieted, he waited for Cecil to argue. But against this Silas was armed with Scripture. He would cite chapter and verse for all that he had said, verses to rebuke the derelict cleric who had led this party to perdition.

But all Cecil said was, "You're perfectly free to go back east, Silas. I'm sorry you feel that way. You contracted to come with me, but of course I won't hold you to it, feeling as you do about Esmerelda and me."

Silas felt faintly disappointed. He wanted to throw verses like thunderbolts, and Cecil wasn't defending himself. But that was the same as admitting his guilt, so he knew he had triumphed after all. There were others here now. The Newtons had been drawn to this by the keen high pitch of his voice, and the sharp slash of his condemnations. They, too, watched him quietly.

"I have no intention of going east." he said, as loftily as he could, so they might understand his high purpose. "While I put my trust in Divine Providence, and would be safe enough, it doesn't suit me to return alone. My mission is to correct—to rectify—all that has fallen into evil here. But I will do this: as a symbol of my separateness, I intend to travel a ways behind you, the conscience in your ears. I will be with you but not of you, making straight the ways of the Lord."

"As you wish, Silas," said Cecil easily. "Esmerelda and I would like to enjoy your company at our campfire this evening. You'll be there, eh? I'd like to hear more of what you have to offer us."

Silas felt excited. At last they would listen!

"I will think about it," he said. "There will be certain conditions."

He knew then what it was to be intoxicated. He was dizzy with delight, floating on air, feeling a strange power within him, an invincibility, a high exaltation he ascribed to God, to some mystic joy that was the gift of God.

There was yet the priest of Rome to scourge, and now he swept toward the wagon where the Jesuit sat in his black suit and Romish collar, an affront to decent men.

"I heard you, Mister Potter," said Dunstan Kiley as Silas approached.

It surprised him. In blindness, the priest's hearing must have become acute.

"I'm glad you did," he cried. "We don't want you among us. You belong to a faithless church, with leaders that live like kings and princes, and charge money for God's gifts. And your order has persecuted millions, and spread lies. We don't want you among the godly. Your wounds are nothing but the wrath of God!"

Dunstan Kiley said nothing. Then, softly, "I have a small favor to ask, Mister Potter. Somewhere in this wagon are my things. Everything is in two packsaddle panniers. Would you find them for me?"

Silas paused, wanting to go on with his great indictment, yet compelled to comply. Wordlessly he clambered into the wagon and dragged the panniers toward the priest.

"In one of them," said the priest, "is a small valise of black pigskin. Would you find it for me, please? And one other small favor, if you would. Would you lower the tailgate of the wagon?"

Silas dug in the panniers, mystified and suspicious. He found the valise and handed it to the priest.

"What are you going to do with that?" he demanded.

"Why, I thought to say Mass. I haven't, you know. It's been many weeks. Even though it was all as familiar to me as the back of my hand, it vanished when I was blinded. But now . . . now I wish to say it. I think it'll come back, once I start.

"You will curse us all the more with your Latin mumbling."

"I rather hope to bless us. I am most bewildered, lost you might say. A priest needs the Mass as much as any communicant, you know. It is friendship and reconciliation . . . for us."

Silas hadn't noticed the approach of Mister Skye.

The booming voice startled him. "Take your time, Father. We'll be busy crossing the Clark's Fork for a while, and we'll take this wagon over last. Mister Potter, we'll be needing you now to help drive the livestock."

"I do not recognize your authority."

But the priest was unlatching his small valise and removing things. First a white stole, which he placed around his neck, and then a small silver chalice, and a silver plate. Feeling his way, he edged to the rear of the wagon.

"I believe the tailgate is still up?" he said softly.

Silas stared at him coldly, and then walked over there and lowered it.

"There you are."

"For a little while, it will be an altar," the Reverend Father Kiley said.

Silas didn't know what to say to that, so he left. He still felt a fervent exaltation, a wild ecstasy. He peered behind him and saw the squaws, Victoria and Mary, settle near the priest.

Let them see the show, he thought. They won't understand a word of it, and the lost can lead the lost.

He thought better of his rejection of Mister Skye, and decided to help with the livestock. A prophet must be stainless and fulfill every duty asked of him. He suddenly felt terribly alone. He was acutely aware that being the sword of God had cost him friends, simple companionship, something that was hard to come by here, over a thousand miles from even the westernmost reaches of the frontier. Well, he thought, that would be the price, the great price paid, the burden borne, by those few mortals elected by God to chastise a fallen world.

Cecil and Alex toiled among the oxen, dropping the heavy yokes over their shoulders and pinning them, attaching the tugs. Near them Clay labored, slipping heavy collars over mules, tightening surcingles, slipping on bridles, buckling breeching for the wheel team, running the long lines through rings, and leading a pair at a time to his wagon. How oddly distant they looked to Silas, all of them strangers going about their business.

Mister Skye forded the river on Jawbone, back and forth, sounding the bottom. Mary and Victoria had already packed Skye's mules, this time piling the skin lodge on top of one for the crossing, rather than tying it down to a travois. They all seemed distant, and he was alone.

He climbed the east rim of the river valley until he stood on a low promontory and could look over the tops of the green cottonwoods, off to the Beartooths ahead, and the blue Pryors behind, vast and lonely and silent reaches of a land unknown to man—almost, it seemed—a land unknown to God. A land that oppressed him and held him prisoner in its iron grip.

"Do You love me?" he asked.

# Chapter 21

The next day they ran into buffalo. There seemed to be only a few at first, until they topped a grassy shoulder and peered into a basin that was black with them. This prairie between the Beartooth Mountains to the south and the Yellowstone River to the north hindered their progress. Massive shoulders radiated from the mountains, and the humped earth broke the sweeping country into endless valleys and hollows, most of them pierced by cold creeks that collected into larger streams.

It brutalized the oxen and mules, this land of grades. Sometimes they toiled most of a day upslope, only to toil downslope after that, hard work with the heavy wagons looming behind them, pressing into the wheel-team breeching. In each of these hollows buffalo grazed, or lay in the grass, rising hastily, rump first, as the caravan clattered into view. Close to the cows spring calves gamboled, and out on the ridges stood the sentinel bulls, half blind but with keen ears and a good sense of smell. Usually the herd in a valley burst away, led by a dominant cow, as the caravan approached, and with it went the slinking gray forms of the wolves that preyed upon the buffalo, striking the wayward calf or the injured and lamed with bloody frenzy.

This vast herd seemed beyond numbering, but not the black river of buffalo they had seen once on the flat prairies of central Nebraska. The corrugated land divided them all into villages, cities of buffalo. That whole day they traveled among them, and not until evening did Pine Leaf kick her fine buffalo runner into a wild gallop, draw up beside a fleeing young cow, and unloose a well-aimed arrow deep into the heart and lung cavity.

The animal staggered, ran awhile more spraying blood, and slowly sank to its knees, a half a mile from the Stillwater River, where they would camp that night. Even as the cow fell, wolves watched from the distant ridge. Pine Leaf slid lightly from her heaving pony and stood beside the trembling animal, and lifted her arms to it.

"What is she doing?" Cecil asked Mister Skye from a distant vantage point.

"Praying to the cow she killed. She's asking its forgiveness for killing it, and thanking it for the meat she has taken to sustain our lives."

Cecil was quiet. "I can understand that sentiment," he said at last.

"Let's go help her butcher."

Pine Leaf and James Method had already begun the hard bloody work, slitting up the belly and releasing gray steaming entrails across the parched grasses.

"Boudins," Mister Skye said. "Life-giving water in there, for any man dying of thirst. We'll go for the liver now—try it raw, Mister Rathbone. It's a treat that every trapper relishes."

Cecil was horrified.

"Does something good. Gives a man strength. The Indians know it. A man eats that liver, and he's made new by it. There's some that say the buff, with the liver and the boudins, is a complete food, and a man needs no more."

Pine Leaf sawed at the tongue, severing it at last and

placing the bloody hunk on a piece of hide that James had industriously ripped in violent jerks and occasional flashes of knife from the carcass. Then at last the choicest parts lay exposed, the hump ribs, and the fine, juicy, fatty tenderloin of the buffalo. These they cut and hacked loose, set them on the warm hide, and then wrapped it all into a bundle and hoisted it to the back of Cecil's nervous horse, all in all some two hundred pounds of prime meat and hide. They were not far from the others, setting up camp beside the sparkling shallow river. A feast tonight and a feast for breakfast. Even as the party walked the last quarter mile to camp, the wolves, gray wraiths in the late light of day, edged closer to the carcass.

"Seems a waste, " Cecil said to Mister Skye, "taking so little. All the rest for the wolves and coyotes and magpies and crows."

The reasons were obvious, and Cecil knew them as well as any frontiersman could, so Mister Skye said nothing. Tomorrow there'd be another buffalo for supper, and maybe another the day after that. Victoria would grieve because they were on the move and she couldn't stake out the fine light brown summer hide, flesh the inside, scrape the hair off the outside, tan it, and repair a rotting hide in their lodge with it. If they had a more permanent camp she'd be at the carcass, hacking meat from it and drying strips into jerky on high racks that reached toward the fierce sun.

They spent a restless night, hearing the bark and howl of wolves and the cackle of coyotes that sometimes seemed to rise from the very edge of their camp. Once in the night they awoke to an ominous roar. Somewhere near, countless of thousands of buffalo rumbled through the dark, driven by some unseen menace. At times the earth shook with them, as animals weighing a ton and more trotted from somewhere to somewhere else. The whole night grew alive with noises. Somewhere downstream, there was a great splashing in the Stillwater. Once Jawbone whinnied softly, his warning, and Mister Skye prowled the moonless dark to no avail, his Sharps in hand.

The horses and mules were restless, itching to join the flowing movement nearby. Mister Skye nudged Cecil, who was awake anyway, and between them they hobbled some horses and hoped the mules wouldn't drift with the buffalo herd. The exhausted oxen lay quietly in the darkness.

Dawn was extraordinary. An eastern cloudbank turned rosy, and its reflected light turned the Beartooths red and salmon, so that the looming peaks just south turned into a wall of fire. They all rose early from want of sleep, and gaped. For Mister Skye there was only joy. Of all the grand vistas of the west, this place was among the dearest to him. Here was a land so breathtaking it drew him here, and he always looked for business that would take him here to this heartland of the Crows. The sun caught the prairie hills now, lighting flanks of the earth except where jackpine made black patches along amber ridges. Here and there the sun caught the tops of aspen and cottonwoods, igniting the leaves into glowing emeralds. He stretched, enjoying the clean cool air, the tang of the silvery sagebrush and the resinous ponderosa pine that encroached everywhere here upon the prairie grasses. Victoria came to stand beside him, exuding joy, for this was home, and other villages of the Absaroka people camped nearby, perhaps in the awesome valley to the west where the Yellowstone River ran south and pierced into the rafters of the world.

One of the oxen had died in the night, the previous day's brutal toil up and down the shouldered prairie too much for the weary, gaunted creature. Cecil and Mister Skye and Clay examined the rest, concluding that they'd have to rest soon. The wagons were in bad shape, too, after thirteen hundred miles of overland travel, jolting along where no road went. The iron tires rolled loose on the felloes because the dry air had shrunk the wood of the wheels.

"In two or three days we'll strike the Yellowstone,

mates, and we'll cross at a place I know of that's wide, shallow, and gravelly, with some islands. West of Sweet Grass Creek, which we'll follow north to the Judith Gap. On the north side of the Yellowstone's a fine flat with good grass and cottonwoods, and we'll rest and reoutfit there.''

For two days more they drove through buffalo. Once a stream of them flowed toward them, running between the wagons and the carriage, panicking the oxen, causing horses to buck, turning the mules frantic, and sucking the loose herd with them. Had the buffalo been stampeding, galloping instead of trotting, they would have demolished them, perhaps killing most of the small party. As it was a milch cow disappeared, and it took hours of sweaty riding for them to gather stray horses and mules.

They'd never seen such a land as this, and they exclaimed at the yawning vistas at every ridgetop, sucked up the sweet-scented air, sniffed the cool distant pine forests of the mountains, enjoyed the exploding scent of sun-hot sage, and drank water so sweet and clear and cold it seemed pure snowmelt. In every creek trout darted.

The buffalo thinned out at last as they turned down a valley Mister Skye called Jim Bridger's Creek. He took them north, through sage-dotted hills, toward the Yellowstone until one evening they emerged in its wide lush valley hemmed between cliffs of gray rock here, though downstream the yellow bluffs gave it its name. It felt warmer in the protected bottoms. Mister Skye and Pine Leaf redoubled their scouting, for this was a great avenue for all sorts of travelers, many of them intent on horse stealing, but some much more dangerous than that.

The next afternoon they crossed the Yellowstone easily. The river was braided here, running in small channels and rivulets through a bank of gravel with an island in the middle. On the far side Otter Creek debouched into the river, and just east of that lay a flat where Mister Skye chose to rest the weary party.

There was much to do. Not least of the problems was

the condition of their boots, virtually soleless and torn from the continental hike. The women set to work on the boots, cutting buffalo-hide soles and piercing them with awls so they could be sewn to the uppers. Clay Sample and Cecil set about repairing the wagons. Each wheel had to be removed and wedges driven between the iron tires and the felloes. In one wheel of the Samples' wagon there was a broken spoke that would need replacing with whatever hardwood they might find here, which turned out to be none, so they fashioned one of tough cedar, the alternatives being aspen, willow, cottonwood, and ponderosa. It would be a brutal job that involved pulling the iron tire off the wheel. There were cracked hounds to replace, worn bolsters, ragged harness to repair with rawhide or anything else at hand. The weathered, bleached wagon tops were torn and needed sewing up. Their clothing, too, had gone to rags, except for Father Kiley's. Some skirts and petticoats were beyond repair, and some of Clay's and Cecil's britches had gaping rents in them.

The footsore oxen and mules spread out upon the grass, closely watched by the Sample children. Pine Leaf and James Method scouted and brought buffalo meat into camp each evening. Through all of this Silas remained distant and icy, not deigning to talk with any of them, taking lonely walks, Bible in hand, a man set apart by his own will. He volunteered no help now, and made no repairs even though his boots were in worse shape than most, and his dark prim clothing was shredded. He had become a burning-eyed figure in rags.

After two days of repair and rest, they had visitors. There rode into camp one evening a party of eleven rough men, grimy and grizzled, black-bearded, sallow, armed with greasy muzzle-loading percussion lock rifles, and long cruel knives sheathed at their sides. Pine Leaf and Method came too, a rifle-shot away. The visitors rode in silently from the west, their dark eyes taking in everything at once with total knowing, lingering long on the women. Mister Skye watched them come, knew they were French-Cree breeds from the north, famous for their volcanic and mercurial tempers and ruthlessness, and knew he and his missionary party, the women especially, faced grave trouble.

From the corner of his eye he saw Victoria and Mary slip into the lodge, and knew two rifles would soon be poking from the doorflap, ready to fire if any of these strangers lifted a weapon toward himself. The others had paused in their work, Clay standing next to the dismantled wheel, Cecil and Alex rising from the pile of harness they were mending. From a little distance, Pine Leaf and Method sat their horses, rifles in hand. And he held his own Sharps in the crook of this arm. Jawbone stood restlessly, primed to bull among them and ruin their shooting. But it would not be enough. Not against eleven razor-edged feral animals.

"*Bonjour*," said one in front, with a sagging eyelid and a shining scar from the corner of his mouth to his right ear, just above his full black beard. His lips were smiling, but his opalescent pearl-colored eyes didn't.

About five of the rifles were a fraction of an arc from pointing at him. The others, not so carelessly, aimed loosely at the other males among the missionaries.

"It is a pleasure, *oui*, a pleasure to find company. The wagons! We have never seen the wagons in this land. We will make the feast, *oui*? Across the river are many buffalo, and we shall make the feast. Tonight will be a ball, a promenade, *oui*?"

Mister Skye said nothing.

"You don't talk? You don't understand, maybe? But you are Yankees, *oui*? What gallant women, what beautiful creatures you have brought to this feasting place. What manner of people are these, so far from home?"

His pearl eyes were upon Alice Sample and young Miriam.

Mister Skye studied the ensemble, knowing what he would find. He saw no pelts on their packhorses, and if they had traps, they were few. He saw no signs of vocation, no array of axes that would signify woodcutters supplying the occasional steamer that braved the Missouri to reach Fort Union far to the east. They were not hunters, making meat for some larger party, for there were no spare packhorses. They were creatures of prey, plundering whatever they happened upon in this vast and lawless land, for whatever wealth there would be— canvas, horses, mules, firearms, and women . . . who would be used brutally awhile and discarded when dead or dying.

They probably had Cree mothers and French trapper fathers, these Canadians. That mix seemed to splinter two ways, the better among them becoming substantial frontier citizens, albeit unruly and resenting British rule, and nominally Catholic. But the others . . . Mister Skye stared at these, seeing the offscourings loathed by the Crees, and loathed by the French. It could go two ways: they'd take over swiftly and begin a brutal bacchanal, especially after finding the whiskey. Or they'd wait until the small hours, slit the throat of every sleeping male, defile the women, plunder the wagons, and steal the livestock.

"I'm Jacques Spratt, my friend, and you do not speak, eh?"

There was nothing to say. Mister Skye surveyed them one by one. Spratt was built like a bear, but next to him slouched a wiry one on a dun mustang, the blue stubble on his cheeks suggesting he once had shaved. He stared blankly at Mister Skye from under the rim of a greasy felt hat that had been tan. He had killer-eyes. Mister Skye was familiar with killer-eyes. The ones with killer-eyes would kill humans with no more compunction than killing a mouse. This one's hand gripped a revolver rather than a rifle. In a sheath hanging from his saddle pommel was another.

On the other side of Spratt sat a fat one, oddly fair-skinned, with ruddy and chubby cheeks and a vacant, moronic look that suggested he might be the deadliest of them all.

The others, bunched behind, ranged from ones who

seemed pure Cree, with high cheekbones and flesh the color of rust, to a few who looked French. Their eyes were not upon him, but focused on Alice and Miriam, and Henrietta and Esmerelda, and sometimes at the lodge where the voluptuous Mary had vanished. It was plain to Mister Skye.

"No," said Mister Skye. "You will be on your way."

Spratt grinned. "We will have a feast," he said. He nudged his black stallion forward. "I will send a man to shoot the buffalo, and your squaws will get the wood."

"No," said Mister Skye.

"I do not hear your name, monsieur. And who are these others you bring here in this place by the river?"

From the wagon Father Kiley emerged. The breeds stared, first at his bandaged eyes, then at his black robes. He wore his cassock now, black with red piping, and he had found his crucifix among his things and now its silver glinted in the late sun.

"Mister Skye, if you will talk a bit I will find my way," said the priest.

"A blind priest," said Jacques Spratt. "A father sans eyes, who cannot see us. Now isn't that an entertainment? He will bless us and he cannot see what we do. We will eat buffalo before him, and laugh, and he will not see us. Maybe he will dance with us, *oui*? It will be a great joke, dancing in front of the blind father. Was there ever such a night? Ah, the things his eyes won't see!" Spratt laughed easily.

Mister Skye felt unhappy with it, but the priest was there.

"You are the French children," the priest said easily. "You've been a long time away from the sacraments. My friends, I will hear confession and then I will say Mass."

Jacques translated this to the others, and they laughed amiably. The fat one snickered.

"Father," said Mister Skye, "they've heard you now, and perhaps you can find your way back to the wagon . . ."

"I'll stay here, Mister Skye."

"Mister who? Who are these? A blind priest, and my

eyes tell me the others are the heretics. We have never feasted with heretics before."

He nudged his horse forward again.

"It might be bad medicine for you," said Mister Skye.

"Medicine? Now we have it all—the medicine, the heretics, and the priest." He laughed.

"Your medicine is bad," said Mister Skye. Pine Leaf and James Method had edged closer now. She had slipped her rifle into its saddle scabbard and held a bow and nocked arrow.

"It will be a fine evening. We will listen to the prayers of the heretic women. We like prayers," said Jacques. He swung his rifle toward Mister Skye, and kicked his horse.

The other breeds lifted their weapons, grinning.

Skye shot Jacques through the heart with his cradled Sharps. The noise rattled through the clearing.

Jacques Spratt gaped, his eyes clouded, and he began to slide off his horse.

Mister Skye danced sideways to distance himself from Father Kiley.

From his lodge two shots boomed. One caught the skinny one in the head. The other missed, but seared a horse across the neck. The horse squealed and pitched.

Jawbone shrieked insanely, and catapulted violently into the massed riders, biting and kicking and squealing. Horses careened and danced and sidled, spoiling aim as breeds attempted to fire.

Pine Leaf rode in like a wraith, loosing an arrow that struck one breed in the thigh, and loosing another arrow with blinding speed.

James Method shot a breed at the rear of the party who had steadied his horse and was aiming at Skye.

Mister Skye dropped his Sharps and plunged into the middle of them with his Army revolver in hand. He shot once, putting a ball into another breed.

Then one of them clubbed his arm, paralyzing it. The revolver fell. As it fell Mister Skye plucked a Green River knife from his waist and in the space of a heartbeat plunged it into the withers of a horse, slicing it around and across the thigh of a breed, leaving gouting blood in its wake, and threw it at another, burying it in the man's chest.

Then he pulled a breed off his horse and kicked him as he fell. Mister Skye's silk hat fell off and was trampled by a pitching horse.

A shot creased Mister Skye's left arm, and red blood blossomed there.

Jawbone kicked and bit. His teeth clamped over the arm of a breed and the horse yanked the man to earth and stomped on him.

A bullet grazed Henrietta, tearing hair and dazing her. She fainted.

Three of Pine Leaf's arrows plunged into horseflesh.

A breed's shot put a bullet into Jawbone's stifle. He shrieked and began to gout blood.

And then the remaining breeds careened away.

It was quiet. They all gaped at Skye.

Silas Potter stumbled forward, his eyes crazed.

"You killed him in cold blood. We all saw you. You are a murderer," he said.

# Chapter 22

Barnaby Skye ignored Potter.

Cecil came running.

Skye caught Jawbone, who was shrieking and pitching. Gouts of blood pulsed down his offside stifle. He held the horse by the neck, calming it, stroking it with big, rough, loving hands. Then he examined the wound, a clean one with entry and exit holes at front and rear of Jawbone's powerful thigh.

Mary arrived, holding a weapon on dead and dying French-Crees. Victoria ran too, bringing a steel needle and thread.

"It's going to hurt, mate," Mister Skye said, grabbing each of Jawbone's ears and twisting them slightly.

Victoria was afraid, and so he swiftly hobbled Jawbone's rear legs. Then he held the horse's ears again and braced himself against the wild animal while Victoria sewed furiously, jabbing the needle in and out of flesh. The gouting from the entry hole slowed, and she turned to the larger and messier exit hole. The horse flinched and shied at her slightest touch. She couldn't sew, and the bleeding was dangerous.

Mister Skye flipped his knife, red with human and horse blood, to Cecil. "Heat it in the fire, mate," he barked. Cecil grabbed the vicious knife and placed the blade over live coals. The blood on it hissed and burned and stank. Victoria pressed a cloth pad into the wound, stanching the flow a little.

As Cecil waited he noticed Mister Skye's own arm sheeted with blood, and a hard grimace etched into the guide's face. Seconds, minutes rolled by.

"Bring it, mate."

Cecil tried, but even the handle was fiery to the touch, and he yanked his burned hand back. Mister Skye let Jawbone go and grabbed the knife, which seared the flesh of his hand.

The horse shrieked as the flat of the blade pressed into the exit wound, cauterizing flesh and lifting a nauseous smoke into the air. Jawbone quivered and hopped, and at last broke free, dancing madly, but the job was done; the bleeding fried to a halt.

"Take him to water," said Mister Skye to Cecil.

The minister was terrified. "I can't . . . he'd kill me."

The guide threw an arm over Jawbone's mane, and whispered something in his ear, and the horse quieted and permitted himself to be haltered.

"He'll be fine, mate."

Victoria started slicing Skye's shredded buckskin shirt off to get at the vicious slice in his upper arm. He grew gray from loss of blood and pain, and sat quietly in the grass, clenching a stick, while she dashed water into the wound and began to sew, her fingers and the needle and thread red with Mister Skye's blood.

Then finally it too was under control, and he lay back in the grass, while she bandaged the long slice tightly.

"Whiskey," he muttered.

"Sonofabitch, that would kill you."

"Pour a little on the wound. Some say it stops the mortifying."

"I got better," she snorted.

He glared at her but said nothing. She brought him water instead. "Drink it all," she commanded. "Then I make some damn good stuff with herbs, make you happy and stop fever and sweats."

Cecil returned from the river, with the badly limping horse lunging along behind him, and released it near Skye's lodge.

He stared, finally, at the bodies. One twitched periodically. The others lay inert and lifeless. There were four. Four more human beings dead because of his mad enterprise, his idyllic plan to bring peace and harmony and God's love to these far-flung peoples. As he watched, Mary systematically gathered weapons and piled the possessions of the dead into a small heap. They had very little, but she found a pair of good boots on Spratt. She unlaced them and pulled them off. The others wore moccasins.

Cecil glanced toward the wagons and the other campsites. His dear Henrietta was sitting up, and Esmerelda holding a compress to her daughter's head. Pine Leaf and James Method stared at the bodies, one in particular, the one James Method had shot.

"Ah don't know how to do it," he said.

Pine Leaf said nothing. She slipped a small skinning knife from its sheath at her waist, and knelt beside the body, grasping a fistful of black hair. The knife slid around the skull, just above the ears and forehead. Then she yanked hard. There was a soft sucking sound, then a pop, and the dripping scalp hung free in her hand.

"It is yours."

"I can marry Gliding Raven now."

"Yes, if you wish. But this is not what New Lance would hope for, this scalp of this dog. It is a scalp, but it is beneath her. Bring a scalp of the real enemies, the Siksika, the Assiniboin, the Lakotah . . ."

Cecil watched, fascinated, faintly sickened.

Mary scalped the rest, including the one not quite dead, so they would arrive in the spirit land bare-skulled, their medicine taken from them. She did not keep the scalps, but threw them into the bushes.

Pine Leaf stood, lithe and strong, two retrieved arrows in her hand. "We will hunt the others now. Perhaps they are not far and we can send them all to the spirit land."

Method nodded, and the two mounted and rode off.

Clay Sample came to stare at the bodies, having prohibited his children from approaching. Alex hovered at a distance, peering at the carnage but not wanting to come close. And Silas Potter was present, peering feverishly first at Mister Skye, then at the bodies, bursting to say things.

Cecil looked at Clay. "Let's bury them. Lot of work," he said. "Perhaps Father Kiley can give them some sort of service."

The priest was sitting in the grass. "You will have to tell me what happened," he said.

Silas Potter elected to do it. "Skye killed their leader in cold blood. Then these other savages killed three more and wounded others. We are in the hands of bloodsoaked savages. We are in the hands of demons, we have taken a peaceful mission and soaked it with murder and every carnal sin, bigamy, lust. I anathematize you. I declare the wrath of God upon you."

From the grass Mister Skye peered grayly up at Silas. "In two or three more seconds you would have been disarmed. Every man here tormented, tortured, and eventually murdered. Every husband forced to watch the debasement of his woman. They would have had special fun with Father Kiley, because the weakened are particular fun . . ."

Cecil blanched, realizing how close they had come. Still, he grieved. Lost life, war, blood, injury. What more might happen in this wild land where there was no law of God or man, and bands like these roamed freely to prey where they could?

"It never would have happened if you all had bent a knee and called upon God. Submitted yourselves unto the Lord and his Divine Providence. Trusted! Offered faith and peace!'' Silas cried.

Father Kiley sighed, wanting to say something but not saying it. Finally he murmured, ''The Church holds that it is no sin to defend one's self and loved ones from mortal danger.''

''Your church is faithless!'' Silas cried. ''You are all far gone in evil. There was no danger. They wanted to have a feast.''

Cecil felt torn. A part of him lay on either side of the bitter issue. Mister Skye was right. Silas Potter was right. That priest was right. And everything that had happened was wrong, a mission soaked in blood and led by murderous heathen through a wilderness that usually smiled but could suddenly become deadly.

Clay found two shovels. He and Cecil hunted for soft earth, and found some near the river, a wet loam. No one came to help them. They dug and hacked and lifted the damp umber soil into a heap, and Cecil tried to make sense of life and death, of faith and Divine Providence, and self-defense, and couldn't, and it ragged him as he shoveled and sweated. No one came, no one watched, no one appreciated. At last they had hacked out a hollow in the earth about three feet deep and as much wide, and just long enough for the short breeds. Wordlessly they set their shovels down and carried the bodies one by one, Clay gripping arms and Cecil legs, and dropped them into the ground, cheek by jowl.

The more Cecil shoveled, the angrier he became, but he couldn't focus it upon anything. It was just anger, a hot resentment of death and blood, of division in his mission, of danger and bare escape. And then as he set his shovel down, he knew. He felt angry at God, who had permitted all this. God who had sent suffering instead of help to this mission that had set out to glorify Him and spread his Word. He had been angry at God before in his life, and knew it for the evil it was, his own impatience, and weakness.

''Let's get Father Kiley. These were probably his people, baptized Catholics. Perhaps he would welcome . . . words . . .''

Clay nodded. The sweat-stained pair of them trudged back to the meadow, where the priest still sat, Mister Skye still lay gray in the grass, and Jawbone stood with his injured leg cocked, glaring yellowly at the world.

Cecil knelt beside the priest. "We have them in a trench. Not covered yet. We thought you might want to say a word."

The priest nodded. "They were probably baptized," he said. "Let me get my—no, never mind. Just take me there."

They guided the Jesuit through the brush to the place near the riverbank.

"They're in front of you now, two steps, " Cecil said.

Father Kiley peered sightlessly into heaven, and blindly into the earth.

"Little children," he said. "We do not know your names, but our Lord does. He has loved you from the beginning, and loves you still . . ."

Quietly the priest talked of love and forgiveness and reconciliation; of hell, purgatory, and heaven. Of the baptized and the unbaptized. Of the sins we do from our own will and pride, and the sins that we would rather not do, but do anyway. Of Christ's judgment. Then the Lord's Prayer in Latin, and he was done. Cecil and Clay shoveled earth over the French-Crees, and stood quietly a moment.

Cecil trudged wearily back to the wagons, where Esmerelda waited. He took her hand. "I need to go sit on that bluff up there. Would you join me?"

They walked together, hand in hand, he sweaty from his shoveling, she floating with relief. They found a warm sandstone outcrop on the bluff, where they could peer down into the meadow and the wagons, and see Mister Skye's lodge, and the people there.

"I suppose we could laugh," she said.

There was nothing else to do, so they did. They sat upon their rock and laughed heartily, and all the questions and doubts that had been flooding his mind seemed to diminish. If anyone heard them down below, he didn't care, and neither did his bride.

Then they said nothing, and let the sweetness of being alive seep through them. He drew the sweet August air into his lungs and exhaled and considered the act sensuous.

Below, Victoria helped Mister Skye sit up, and then gave him a bowl of broth and a horn ladle. He swallowed slowly.

"The two who saved us were hurt badly," Cecil murmured. "I saw it all happening but I was too dumbfounded to help, to act. In the space of a heartbeat, it would have gone the other way."

"How do you now that?"

"It is a lesson of the frontier. I cannot say just why."

"Some will condemn Mister Skye."

"I will encourage them to leave us," he said, rising. She took his hand again, and they talked softly.

They rested six days more. Mister Skye recovered quickly, and his grayness disappeared. But Jawbone limped terribly as he hobbled through the succulent grasses. Even the switch of his tail to drive away the flies brought a shiver through his rump. He slept lying down, on his good side, which was something he never did.

The oxen and mules ate constantly and fattened in the cloudless cool days. In two days they completed repairs. Clay assembled the wheel with the new spoke in it. Worn harness was repaired. Oxen shoed. Clothing restored. Boots and moccasins resoled. Only Silas did nothing. His clothes were tattered and the uppers of his boots had torn loose in places. The boots of the dead Jacques fit him, but he refused them violently.

After that they waited for Mister Skye and Jawbone to heal. Or rather, Cecil did. The Newtons and even Clay Sample avoided the guide, and loathing filled their eyes. Then Mister Skye pronounced himself fit, and they rolled off the next morning. Cecil was itching to be on his way:

they still had shelters to build before winter at Sun River, and even now the days grew short and the night air sharp.

Mister Skye walked. Jawbone limped painfully behind, untethered. He had a sailor's roll, as if even this continental prairie pitched like a bark on high seas. From their camp on the Yellowstone he took them north through rolling brown prairie, just west of Sweet Grass Creek, with the jagged Crazy Mountains always looming blue on their left.

The oxen and mules pulled eagerly after their rest and they made good time, finding splendid camps in the creek bottoms each evening. One night frost nipped the grass but by day the air was cool and invigorating. At a point where the Sweet Grass swung west into the Crazy Mountains, Mister Skye abandoned it and took them over a low prairie divide into the Musselshell drainage.

Three days later they reached the Musselshell, and camped in its cottonwood-choked bottoms. On the north bank rose sandstone bluffs, but they were broken, and reaching the high prairie beyond would pose no problem. To the north rose two ranges Mister Skye called the Belt Mountains and the Snowies. He said they would travel between them, through a gap. They were now, he said, in Blackfoot lands, though the Musselshell was also a haunt of Crows, Assiniboins, Gros Ventres, Flatheads, Crees, and others because it was prime buffalo country. Indeed, they found buffalo traces everywhere: along the small river were hoof-cut avenues winding like twisting highways through the sandstone bluffs. Increasingly the prairie ridges were dotted with dark jackpine, long-needled and twisted. The dry pitch-laden pine made fine fires for the buffalo hump meat that James Method and Pine Leaf brought to camp each evening.

They found grizzly sign along the river, but they saw none of the great and terrible bears, and were grateful. One old Ephriam, as Mister Skye called him, had scratched his mark perhaps nine feet up the trunk of an old cottonwood. They crossed the river easily the next morning, and toiled north along a rising prairie that seemed limitless except for the distant ranges. Already the Snowies wore a cap of white along their flat crowns. Never had Cecil experienced a land so vast, so limitless, so silent. It gave him a sense of security. He was sure he could see a hundred miles, and hear movement almost as far.

Mister Skye began riding Jawbone again, but not all day. The horse favored its wounded thigh but was game for anything. There were two cookfires each evening now, and they reflected the schism that had befallen the party. At one were the Samples, Newtons, and Silas Potter, who grew more ragged and brimstone-eyed each day. The other served Mister Skye and his family, the Rathbones, and Father Kiley. More and more, James Method and Pine Leaf were at neither, eating privately out somewhere in the beyond. Faithfully they brought meat and scouted, but they grew apart. Each time James Method rode in, Cecil noted that he seemed more Indian. They reported horse-thieving parties in the area, but so far the travelers had not been molested.

One evening when they camped midway between the Little Belts and the Snowy Mountains, some of the women went berrying. A long coulee twisted sinuously northeast, running a tiny trickle along its bottom, and was laden with buffalo bush, the leather-leaved hairy shrub whose berries were nourishing and a staple in pemmican. With Victoria showing them what to gather and how to strip the berries fast, and Esmerelda and young Miriam Sample following, the trio toiled its way up the coulee and around a bend and out of sight of the camp.

At twilight they didn't return. By full dark there was no sign of them, and Cecil grew alarmed.

"They should have been back long ago," he said to Mister Skye.

The guide began to saddle Jawbone. "It's best that I go alone," he said. "I am used to night work."

Mister Skye's voice sounded so calm that it quieted

Cecil. Perhaps, he thought, the women were treed by a bear that was also gathering berries.

"Could they be in trouble?" asked Alice Sample.

"Aye, ma'am, they are in trouble."

With that he rode silently from camp. Blue afterlight lingered in the west, but it would be a moonless night.

From the campfire he saw Pine Leaf and James materialize, and ride off with Mister Skye up the dark coulee. That was good, he thought. Pine Leaf would have Indian-eyes, have that ability to pierce into the night and see the way a cat did. Cecil wasn't at all sure there was such a thing as Indian-eyes, but it was a common frontier belief, and it comforted him. Pine Leaf would see through the deepening dark.

It became a long wait. For an hour, at least, the missionary camp was unified, and beside the fire before Mister Skye's lodge they sat, Mary and Dirk, Cecil, Clay Sample and Alfred, and his own dear Henrietta and Alex, each silent and filled with a deepening dread. Silas lay in his bedroll, unaware of trouble.

It was close to midnight, Cecil judged from the position of the Big Dipper, and growing sharply cold when the searchers returned, slipping so quietly into camp that it startled them. There had been nothing, no sound, and then they were there.

Mister Skye lumbered over to them and hunkered down beside the embers of the fire.

"They've been taken," he said. "Captured. Pine Leaf says Assiniboins. Horse-thief bunch. She says not many, maybe ten, plenty of fresh sign, heading east toward the bend of the Musselshell. There's probably a village of them within a day's travel. We're going to pack up now, mates, and follow."

# Chapter 23

There were seven. There had been nothing but peaceful twilight as they gathered berries, and then they stood there, materializing out of nothing. They looked shorter and stockier than the Crows, and had yellower flesh. Seven young warriors in breechclouts, six with bows, one with an old flintlock fusil. They rode small dark ponies, with shaggy manes and tails that hung to the ground, horses the proud Crow would have scorned.

Esmerelda stared, her heart suddenly thumping. Miriam, beside her, unconsciously slid closer to her side. Victoria stood nearby, rooted to earth.

"Assiniboin," hissed Victoria. These were enemies of her people, but a weaker tribe than the Blackfeet. The Assiniboin lived along the upper Missouri to the east and were a long-separated branch of the Dakotah Sioux.

Most were youths, but there was one with graying hair and deep seams in his brow, and a cruel arrogant stare. Upon his chest lay a strange necklace with long objects hanging from the beadwork. Esmerelda saw that they were desiccated human fingers, eight of them, each perhaps taken from an enemy in battle. She swallowed. The necklace was great medicine. Did she have any medicine to match it?

The headman stared at the three of them at length, dismissing Victoria the Crow woman, and focusing on Esmerelda first, and then Miriam, with flat, expressionless eyes. The girl shrank under his unblinking gaze, and hugged Esmerelda.

Like Cecil, Esmerelda believed that life must be tried and tested. Even now, there was no surrender in her. How many times, in how many lives, had opportunity slipped away because someone had been afraid to try?

"Come along, Miriam dear, we shall walk back to the wagons."

With that she took the girl in hand and turned her back to the menace behind her, and they set off, with the berry basket half full. Thus it went for a hundred yards. She did not look back, though she wanted to, and the muscles of her back rippled with the anticipation of an arrow.

Then an arrow did hiss by, into the dirt before them. She did not stop. There was yet a half a mile to the wagons, and she would not stop. Her legs would move steadily, rhythmically.

She heard the soft crunch of hoof behind her and then a hand as hard as strap-iron grasping her dress and tearing it. She turned, and the flat-eyed one, the one with the dangling human fingers on his breast, was leaning over his horse. Their eyes locked and she saw mockery in his, but the face was as immobile as ice. He leapt off as lithely as a panther, and lifted her as if she were weightless, setting her on the small animal. Then he lifted the struggling Miriam and dropped her on the withers of another pony ridden by a young warrior. That pony had chalk-white handprints blazoned on its chest.

"I don't want to go," cried Miriam fiercely.

But they would go. Victoria, too, now sat on a horse, her doeskin skirt hiked high up her legs. Esmerelda felt the headman settle himself behind her, and steel arms grip her carelessly, and they rode off, trotting silently up the long coulee. When they topped out a mile or so east, another warrior joined them, making eight. It grew dusky, and colors faded from the world, prairie and the nearby Snowy Mountains alike turning gray. Soon it would be night.

Now at last the implications of this seeped through Esmerelda a little at a time. Captivity. It had happened often enough. Her fate—could be anything. But one thing she knew now; she was being taken farther and farther from Cecil with each step of the pony, across an empty land. Unrolling behind them would be tracks, broken grasses, horse sign, leaving a thread of a highway to follow, mile after mile, so long as it didn't rain or snow. She didn't know where she would be taken—this was an endless land, a sea of rolling grass that stretched beyond horizons. How would Cecil find her; how would Cecil free her, even if somehow he found the place, the dot, the pinprick in this endless universe, where she would be?

The horse felt uncomfortable beneath her, its sharp withers grinding upon her thighs. But she was imprisoned in this precarious spot by bands of steel, so she endured because it was the only thing she could do. It grew dark now. She heard Miriam weeping, poor little girl, a tiny life suddenly torn apart. And still they rode. When night settled she spotted the Big Dipper to her left, and the North Star, and knew they were trotting east, always east, farther and farther from Cecil.

It came to her she might never see Cecil again. It had been a good marriage. She was only forty-four, and had hoped for many years, decades, more; growing old together. Doing the work the Lord had given them to do. Seeing grandchildren soon, when Henrietta gave birth. Bringing Light to those in darkness . . . even the darkness of soul she felt hard against her back.

It grew cold, and a biting wind sprang up, and she wondered how these Assiniboin, and all the plains warriors, could ride nearly naked in chill weather. All through the jouncing night Cecil grew more distant. They never stopped. She grew desperate to relieve herself, and the suffering turned into anguish, but they never stopped. With each passing hour Cecil drifted away, growing smaller and smaller. Her own Cecil. She yearned for the familiar contour of his lean body and the blankets that covered them both, but he was not here.

She turned to her faith and prayed, but the thoughts and words came hard. Then she began to talk out loud to her captor. "I beg you to take us back," she said. "We have come into this land to do God's work, and not to hurt anyone. We . . . we . . . I trust you will treat us kindly. I am, I've been a good and faithful woman. I do not want another husband . . ." She thought she would cry, but refused. She would not cry. But even the most timid review of her future brought a shudder. Violated. Taken as a squaw. As a slave. Tortured. They loved torture, didn't they. Loved to see how brave a white woman might be. If she cried and screamed, they'd mock her. If she remained silent and defiant, they would say her spirit went to the Other Side with honor and courage. She grew afraid she'd weep piteously.

Sometime before dawn they stopped at a tiny creek running southward from the Snowy Mountains. The tiniest fraction of a moon had finally risen and lit the place with ghost-silver. She was dropped rudely from the pony and permitted to slip into the darkness. There were no bushes. Near her were Victoria and Miriam. They all walked then, and the movement of her legs felt good in the harsh night air. The air felt icy. Ever eastward they walked, and then after a half hour of it they mounted again, even as a thin line of light cracked the horizon. Now, on mounting, she felt tired, and the nervous energy that had propelled her through this nightmare had vanished. She slumped. If she fell off it didn't matter, but whenever she slid, iron hands clamped her straight again. And now her captor snarled when she slid. She was weary beyond experience, and thirsty and hungry as well. During their brief stop the horses had been carefully watered, but not the prisoners. She closed her eyes, slumped into herself, and tried to rest.

The black world turned gray again and the long mountains on her left became a ghostly presence. They loomed lower here, and tailing down, petering out into a long high ridge. Their captors angled ever closer to them, and now they started into the foothills, following a pine-dotted ridge. The sun burst in the east and painted the land orange. Now she could see Victoria riding resolutely with a warrior behind her, and Miriam, sleepy, her eyes burning black. Her thoughts turned to the child. Surely they would not harm her, a girl who had not yet budded. But she didn't know. Those things seemed to be a question of whim.

Esmerelda thought of that tiny, fragile trail unwinding behind them across the miles and leagues, that fragile thread that was the sole link between her and Cecil. They climbed steadily, and now the weary pony heaved, and its neck and withers were drenched with wetness even in the cold air. Steadily they rode upslope, attacking it at an angle. It was park and forest country now, ponderosas and grasses, with the trees becoming steadily thicker until they rode into true forest and topped the long ridge. On the north slope they quickly emerged into grassy benchland again, and before them was a wide valley running east and west, with a silvery creek glinting in its bottom. And in this valley, but far to the east, was a village of seventy or eighty lodges, blue smoke hovering in the long orange dawn light.

For a moment the warrior carrying Victoria rode close; close enough for Victoria to say, "Flat Willow Creek, what the whites call it. Sonofabitch."

The fist of the warrior she rode with smashed into her face.

Esmerelda had never heard of Flat Willow Creek. But it was a name, something she could write in charcoal upon bark and leave to be read somewhere. Even now she was thinking of sign, and wished she had thought of it sooner. There were things she might have done, petticoat she might have ripped and dropped, piece by piece, petticoat to say she lived. Petticoat to tell Cecil she loved him.

They jolted down benchland, plateaus, and cliffs, and into the bottom of Flat Willow Creek, lush with bunch grass turned golden now as August faded. And just ahead rose the cones of the village, the dogs and ponies, and the welcoming Assiniboin people, who rushed out now to greet the raiding party of young and inexperienced warriors under the tutelage of the greatest warrior of the Assiniboin, Killer.

They rode toward the center of the village, where there was a clear space, a sort of village square, surrounded by tall lodges with their windflaps opening to the east. Just outside the village stood high racks upon which countless strips of buffalo meat were being dried into jerky. They were met first by a pack of snarling curs, yellow and gray, half wolf or coyote, that snapped at the heels of the horses. On either side of the headman's lodge near the center of the village rose tall slender poles topped by sun-bleached human skulls, with tufts of hawk feathers dangling beneath, to tell the world that this was a man of great medicine.

Straight toward the center of this village they rode, followed by the clamoring mass of newly awakened people, who were enjoying this victory celebration even before they had breakfasted. The young warriors raised their thick buffalo-bull shields high to announce the capture of slaves, a valuable asset to this small band. Here were women to flesh buffalo hides and bring wood, and a girl to bring Assiniboin children into the world someday. Only the capture of horses would have been a greater victory for this horse-starved people.

At last they stopped before the chief's lodge. Esmerelda shrank from the sight of it, for every totem here spoke of death; black-haired scalps dangling from lances thrust into the grassy soil; buffalo skulls set ritually around a space before the lodge; and those human skulls on the poles . . .

Her captor lifted her and dropped her unceremoniously to the ground, where she fell to her knees because her legs had gone numb. The village women swarmed about her, and she realized she was perhaps the first white woman they'd ever seen. There were a few white women at Fort Laramie, an infinity away, but these were northern people whose home was largely in Canada, and the sight of her amazed them. She tried to stand, but a horde of women pinned her to earth, plucking at the fabric of her dress. She had worn that day a silk taffeta, her best dress, because her ginghams were worn and she hoped to find time to mend them. But the shiny taffeta was a marvel to these women, and they fingered and plucked at the lustrous brown cloth with fascination, and then began ripping it, wanting it to decorate themselves.

Some of them had bone daggers or fleshing knives, and now they began ripping and slicing. Esmerelda felt her bodice tear, and saw the small buttons fly to earth. Then she felt terrible rips that tossed her one way and another, savage tugs at her skirt, the sound of fabric shredding, the murmur and cry of these women as they stripped her. And they didn't stop at the taffeta. She felt the cool morning air upon her chest, and white things disappear from her. She pulled herself into a ball and hugged herself but still the ripping continued, and now the points of the bone daggers found flesh and drew blood from her arms and thighs and buttocks, and she knew she was naked, and eyes of all sorts were upon her, staring at the whiteness of her thin body.

She didn't cry. She sensed her utter helplessness. There was no contortion of body or cry of her mouth that might help her. The women stabbed and jabbed with knives now, to see how this white woman bore the sting of them, fascinated. They'd peel her flesh, burn her with glowing brands snatched from cookfires, see to it that she died slowly, she knew.

She blanked her mind to the pain. The only flight open to her was the flight of soul, of mind, into some other place, and by some miracle she succeeded in that. She

chose her wedding day, the day of her union with Cecil.
She saw her big, homely frontier minister, very young,
standing beside her. She heard the drone of the minister,
and saw Cecil slip a ring upon her finger . . . . and then
she plunged back in the now, and felt her fingers being
crushed, and some old crone of a woman yanking at
the plain gold ring and finally sliding it over unyielding
joints . . .

A sharp nasal command halted it all, and the women
slid away from the sport, clutching whatever treasures they
had managed to rip from Esmerelda. She lay alone on
the earth, bleeding from a score of pricks, ghostly white.
She huddled into the smallest ball she could make of
herself. But even that protection of the sheltering earth
was not to last. Her captor lifted her bodily to her feet.
Beholding her was virtually the entire village, men,
women, children, packed densely around the space of the
buffalo skulls before the lodge of the chief. She felt a
helplessness such as she had never known.

But she would not die! She'd fight to live, to survive,
to count the days until she could be with Cecil again.
And if he didn't want her because of these . . . these
shames . . . she'd live anyway, find a life, remember the
warm sun, the love of God . . . .

She stood erect, eyes closed, watched but not seeing.
Her captor let go of her arm. If this is what the universe
gave to her, then she would stand erect. She had nothing
left to hide, so she did not cover herself. She opened her
eyes and found herself staring into the flat agate eyes of
the headman, who was watching her with interest. Never
had she seen such a face. He had half a nose, the other
part of it having been hacked away in war, and indeed
his name, she would find out, was Cut Nose. He was
missing most of an ear as well, and terrible jagged scars
creased his torso. The lips looked thin and cruel, cheeks
hollow and cheekbones prominent and skeletal. But his
eyes transfixed her. She had seen eyes like that in rattlers, unblinking and deadly.

She peered around now. Victoria and Miriam were

nowhere in sight. Victoria would be an ordinary prize for these people. They might torture and abuse her, and work her like a horse. But Miriam's fate she couldn't imagine.

The chief, dressed only in his breechclout and fringed leggins, plucked a war lance from the ground beside his lodge, and leveled it at her, and then stabbed delicately at her belly. It pricked, adding to the blood that smeared her. She felt death upon her. So this would be the end, then. Gutted here, so far from Cecil, still almost young . . . But the chief withdrew the lance, his lips forming a small cruel smile, and nodded to her captor, whose iron clamp upon her arm pulled her off, through the gawking crowd, past the nipping curs, toward a lodge larger than most. He was followed by two proud young women, obviously wives of this the greatest warrior, and displaying their status with every step. There were four good ponies tethered here, Assiniboin wealth, and painted on the lodgecover was the story of Killer's exploits: Killer counting coup with his lance, Killer with his bow drawn. Killer on horseback among a dozen prone bodies, all of it painted in black and carmine stick figures.

She was pushed hard through the doorflap and into the gloom of the lodge. Thin light pierced here through the cowhide cover and the smokehole, but it was a shadowy place. Around the firepit at the center, cold now because the women had been cooking outdoors, lay fine buffalo robes and parfleches. Medicine totems hung from the lodgepoles; a doll, although there seemed to be no children here; and a stuffed ferret, the medicine animal of this high-caste warrior. He followed her inside, and the squaws followed after, their eyes alight with the fun of what would come. Esmerelda peered into their moon-wide faces, seeking sisterhood and sympathy, and finding none, but only the flat-eyed pleasure she had seen in those outside. She thought she should have been grateful for this relative privacy, but it no longer mattered. She crawled to a robe and lay curled in it, feeling hunger and thirst now. She'd had nothing for as long as she could remember, when the world turned upside down.

She saw an earthen pot of water. If she was given no help, then she must find help in her own actions. Something as simple as taking water might yet preserve her. She reached for the bone ladle, and drank. No one stopped her. She dipped it and drank more, the cool water welcome in her parched throat and body. She drank a third time, and felt better.

"I would like food and clothing now," she said. They stared.

"If I am to be your slave, then dress me and I'll be about it. Someday, I will be free. Someday, you will know the love and lash of God, even though you don't know Him now."

The two young women squatted at the far side of the lodge, waiting for something.

She peered up at her captor, and read his intent. It grew very plain. Not that, she thought, God spare me that. God spare me for Cecil . . .

But even as her heart cried against it, she knew it would happen, she saw it happening. And they would not even be alone, but it all would happen before his other—his wives. She wished she might go mad, be transported out of reality, away from this place. But she knew it could not be. She was strong, and her mind rode upon the troubles of life serenely. Perhaps that was why Cecil had been drawn to her, had married her. She had been a full match for his own frontier strength and character and that is why the marriage had been so good, so good . . . She felt strong, and her mind would not crack and break. She would experience what was to come with all her faculties, with the strength she had been born with.

If she closed her eyes, she could pretend it was Cecil, but it wasn't Cecil and she couldn't pretend.

# Chapter 24

It began with a wrangle. Both Cecil and Clay insisted on coming along. Mister Skye would have none of it. He wanted only Pine Leaf and James Method with him, plus two spare horses to bring the women back.

"Look, mate," he said to Clay. "If all of us go, there'll be no one here to protect these people, protect Mrs. Sample. I'm leaving this camp in the hands of my Mary, and I trust you'll obey her. But she may need help." He left unsaid the obvious, that neither Alex nor Silas Potter would defend themselves and others with arms.

Clay Sample pondered the thought of his wife here with so little protection, and reluctantly agreed, anguish written across his face.

"And that goes for you, Mister Rathbone. They need you here. Your daughter and son-in-law need you. Every man counts here. I'll add, mate, that we don't want to be slowed down. Every minute counts."

"Esmerelda is my wife," said Cecil. He plunged into the darkness and found his hobbled Magdalene and freed her. He would come along, Mister Skye realized, unless he was hogtied. The guide didn't like it. Not even a frontiersman like Cecil would know what his wife's fate was likely to be.

The four of them rode into a bitter cold night, up the coulee. No moon shone. At the head of the coulee, two miles east of camp, Pine Leaf slid off her pony and studied the ground on her hands and knees, smelling because she couldn't see.

"I do not know," she said at last. "I have not found it."

They spent the next hours making a wide arc, with Pine Leaf on foot, pausing every few feet to hunker next to the earth. They swung southerly first, and arced north, and at last she gave up.

"It hides in the night," she said.

Mister Skye had a decision to make—wait here, or go. To go the wrong way might result in more delay. But he had not lived life like that. "We will go east," he said.

They rode east through the night over rolling prairie with a wind at their backs. When a cloud mass blotted out the heavens, they rode by dead reckoning through an awesome inkiness. Mister Skye hoped the wind hadn't changed. The breath of it on his neck had given him direction. He wondered about Cecil, riding silently beside him. Had the man any idea of what to expect? The minister had said nothing, but neither had he shown the slightest sign of despair or remorse for having embarked on this perilous journey.

When dawn cracked the northeastern sky, they were twenty miles or so to the east of their camp. To the north, the Snowies began to glow like ghost mountains. They paused to rest the horses and to chew on some jerky from Mister Skye's kit. He thought the Assiniboin, if that's who it was, would likely be on the bend of the Mussel-shell, another day east. But now would be the time to patrol north and south and cut sign if they could, rather than risk going farther astray. They paused another ten minutes until it became possible to see, and then Pine

Leaf and James Method swung north, while he and Cecil swung south.

Mister Skye walked so he could study the ground. It was time to rest the wounded Jawbone anyway. He spotted nothing. The undisturbed prairie grasses and umber earth stretched endlessly south with no mark of passage other than buffalo trails.

"It's the needle in the haystack, isn't it," said Cecil. "I had not understood the size of this land until now."

"Not that bad, mate. Where people and horses go, they leave tracks."

Cecil walked silently, studying the ground a little to the left of the guide. "Tell me, Mister Skye, the exact truth. What is my wife's—their—fate?"

He did not want to answer that. "Bad," he said. "If it's the village of Cut Nose, worse."

"Then let us hurry."

But they found nothing. For two hours they walked south, spotting no sign of recent passage. Once they found an old trail, windblown hoofprints, brown-dried dung, and studied its direction, but it meant nothing. Then Mister Skye turned back to see what the others had found, riding now but studying the ground still, in case they had missed a clue.

James Method was waiting for them at the place where they had split. "Ah don't believe we have anything, but Pine Leaf asked me to come back here and fetch you. She's inclined to believe they're over beyond yonder ridge."

"Little Snowies," said Mister Skye. "We'll follow her then, mate."

At midday they found her. She seemed to materialize from nowhere in the root ridges of the mountains. And she was standing squarely on fresh tracks of several horses.

"Eight," she said. "I have studied them."

Mister Skye knew they were lucky. They had gained nothing from the night march, and would have been here before this in far fresher condition had they slept out the night back at their camp. But they had the trail. They silently followed it up into country dotted with ponderosas, and finally into forest, and topped a ridge. A half hour later they stood their ponies on a promontory overlooking the valley of the Flat Willow. And in the hazy eastern distances, where the creek valley bellied out upon plains again, lay smoke.

Pine Leaf sat beside Mister Skye, seeing what he saw. "Have you a plan?" she asked.

In truth, he hadn't. Ride in, find out if he could if the abducted women were there, bargain. If they bargained at all, he knew what they'd want. And so did Pine Leaf. "Let's tie the spare horses here," he said. "Or down a little, as close as we can hide them."

"It is a good day to die," she said. "I have taken many scalps from them, and they will want mine now. But I will live. While I waited for you, I closed my eyes and permitted the medicine vision to form. I saw what I needed to see. I will live, at least for today. I will be very strong, as I was when I was young."

Skye nodded. He, too, had taken the lives of these people, while fighting them beside the Crows. They angled eastward now, staying upslope in the trees for cover and coolness against the midday sun, and when the trees petered out they tied the two spare horses.

The village lay ahead, but too far for details to emerge. They were in range now of its patrols, the police warriors who were responsible for its security at all times. Mister Skye stared at Cecil, wondering how the minister would bear the burden, but found him resolute and set-jawed. And he stared at Method, the young untried warrior tasting freedom now, but perhaps not yet aware of the price of this wild freedom of the plains. Then they rode.

He rode with his Sharps across his lap, wondering whether to go in with it in hand. To ride into a village with the weapon in hand, and not sheathed, would be a warlike act. It would be countered by village warriors, who would have lances and bows in hand. Even to lift the Sharps to fire it would result in a dozen lances pierc-

ing him before he got off a shot. To ride in with weapons
sheathed would be a sign of peace and parleying, but
also a sign of weakness in the eyes of this peculiar chief,
Cut Nose. He sighed, and slid the rifle into its beaded
saddle scabbard. At the same time, he unloosed the thong
that held his Colt in its holster. Behind him, the others
followed suit. Pine Leaf returned an arrow to her quiver.

There would be, he reckoned from the lodges in sight
below now, seventy or eighty warriors, and they would
all be waiting. Indeed, an advance guard of greeters was
boiling out of the village below to escort them, or fight
them. So they had been seen now, and what followed
would be fate, or medicine, or the will of God, he
thought, his mind running through the beliefs of these
three beside him.

Of all the villages he hated to ride into, this was the
worst. He would even prefer to ride into the villages of
the Blackfeet who were his enemies, knowing that the
proud Blackfeet would behave in the protocols of the
plains, than into this village where Cut Nose and his
lieutenants, including the dreaded Killer, ruled by cruel
whim and trickery.

The greeting party consisted of ten warriors, all in
breechclouts and nothing else save a band across their
foreheads to hold their long flowing hair in place. One
wore a single eagle feather and was graying. Mister Skye
knew the man, and dreaded his presence. It was Killer,
legendary warrior of these people, whose whole life consisted of living up to his name.

Now they were arrayed in a line ahead, and Mister
Skye and his colleagues stopped. Killer smiled faintly.

"We have come to parley with the great Cut Nose,"
Mister Skye signed with his hands.

Killer's gaze rested not upon him, though the warrior
knew him and knew of his horse, Jawbone. It leveled
instead on Pine Leaf, recognizing her and anticipating
everything to come, with seventy of his kind beside him,
and only one Absaroka woman to contend with.

Mister Skye's hands flashed again. "These are white

medicine people. The white man here is a medicine maker, like the blackrobes. Pine Leaf of the Crows is now a medicine woman of her people. The darker man is a warrior of the Crow, but came with the white medicine people.''

Killer nodded faintly.

"We have come to get our women. You have taken my wife Victoria.'' Now at last Killer's agate eyes focused on the famous Mister Skye and the terrible blue roan horse that carried him. "You have the wife of this white medicine man, who comes in peace. We will take his wife back. And you have a girl, daughter of the white medicine people.''

All this Pine Leaf followed with her eyes as Mister Skye made the signs with his hands. The others all followed his hands too.

"What women?'' asked Killer. "We have no women. Come into the village and see. We will show you.''

Mister Skye did not answer.

He touched heels to Jawbone, and they rode quietly into the village, past staring, unfriendly people. Flanking them were the warriors who had met them, each carrying a bow with an arrow nocked in it, a sign of contempt and trouble. Villages bore the stamp of their leaders, and Cut Nose ruled by terror. Maybe, Mister Skye thought, it would end here. But not before he put a bullet through the heart of Cut Nose and a knife into Killer. It would be a good day to die.

They drew up before the chief's lodge and found him standing before it, a rifle cradled in his hands. There would be no smoking of the pipe here. He peered up at them with the flat beaded eyes of a rattler, and beneath those eyes was the remains of a nose hacked off on one side.

Mister Skye chose English: these people had traded for years at Fort Union, the old American Fur post at the confluence of the Missouri and Yellowstone. Since they had been greeted without the protocols of the prairies, Mister Skye chose to return the insult.

"We have come for our women."

"What women? We have none of yours," Cut Nose replied.

"They are hidden in the lodges. Bring them at once and we will leave peacefully."

Cut Nose smiled, a grotesque smile because the scars across his face twisted his lips.

"Peacefully. I see four of you. Are there more?"

Mister Skye said nothing.

"I see a great enemy of the Assiniboin, the warrior woman Pine Leaf. She has taken many scalps. I am glad she brought herself to us."

"She is a medicine woman now. Her visions told her she would live through this day."

"Perhaps today," Cut Nose said, smiling. "Perhaps not tomorrow."

Cecil caught Mister Skye's eye, and pointed. Among the silent spectators was a squaw wearing the bodice portion of Esmerelda's brown taffeta dress. The sleeves were gone, and so was the skirt.

"I see the clothing of our women worn by yours," said Mister Skye. "Will you lie again?"

It was as much an insult to an Indian as to a white.

"Perhaps the famous white warrior would like to look in our lodges?" Cut Nose replied evenly. "I have decided that you will be our guests. We will have entertainment. We will take care of your horses, and I will keep your weapons in my lodge."

"I think not."

A silence stretched.

"You are four," he said at last.

"It is a good day to die." He sat on Jawbone waiting, ready, cold inside. He would have time to shoot once. Jawbone's ears laid back, and he tensed murderously. The horse's medicine was well known to these warriors.

Cut Nose eyed the horse contemplatively. "It is a good day for sport," he said. "We will have contests."

"We have come for our women."

Killer stepped over to the chief and whispered something. Then he said, "The women for the horses. I myself want the medicine horse of Mister Skye. I will have his medicine, or I will kill the horse with this arrow in my bow. With such a horse, the Assiniboin will be rulers of the prairies. Four horses for the women."

Mister Skye stared. "I know the famous Killer who speaks. But surely, with all the warriors here, you will have the horses anyway when you kill us? No. We will have the women now and leave."

Cut Nose waved Killer aside. "We will have sport," he said. "We will test the medicine of the great Crow warrior woman, who says she will live through this day. Here are two of our enemies, two Crow warriors, the woman and this one we have never seen, with flesh the color of the grizzly bear. We will let them run, and if they outrun my warriors they will be free. We will take their moccasins first, and if their medicine is good they will run away. The warrior woman, Pine Leaf, is reputed to be the fastest runner among all warriors."

"She is a medicine woman, not a warrior, and her hair is turning gray."

"That is good. We will see if her medicine is good. Otherwise, we will torture them. These are Crow enemies of my people."

Pine Leaf laughed scornfully. "We will outrun all of your warriors," she said. "This one with me is Seven Scalps, and his medicine is as great as mine."

She slipped lithely off her horse. James Method uneasily followed her.

Cut Nose was delighted. "The Crow warriors will start here," he said, indicating a place beside the creekbank. "My warriors will start there." The place he chose was scarcely fifty yards distant.

Lazily Pine Leaf unlaced her moccasins. James Method followed suit, looking troubled. She handed them to Mister Skye, and then her bow and quiver. She had for a weapon only the small skinning knife at her side—and she'd need it, Mister Skye thought. The spare horses were three miles distant. If they made it to the horses, cut the tielines, they might escape. Still, he did not like this. That left only himself and the minister here.

The Assiniboin warriors clustered happily at their starting point. They dropped their bows and arrows and chose lances, fine weapons to throw at a fleeing target just ahead, deadlier than bows and arrows. By Mister Skye's count there were over fifty.

"When I spear the earth with this lance," called Cut Nose, "you will go." To his own warriors he said something in his own tongue, and they laughed.

"Don't wait," hissed Pine Leaf to James, and he nodded. Now the whole village crowded to the starting points beside Flat Willow Creek. Mister Skye studied the village. Perhaps this would be opportunity. In the chase would be every warrior, save for the police society of the Assiniboin, who would as always guard the village. Ten or twelve might stay; the rest would run.

It looked like certain death for Pine Leaf and Method, barefoot, a few scant yards ahead of the howling pack of warriors trained to run and run. And Pine Leaf lithe in her breechclout and shirt, but graying . . . She walked indolently toward their starting place, not deigning to look behind her, but James did. He was already sweated with anticipation and fear.

Pine Leaf sprang. Method looked momentarily confused, then sprang after her. The Assiniboin warriors, enraged, howled after them, lances in hand. Pine Leaf raced straight for the spare horses, as Mister Skye knew she would, but it was plain they wouldn't make it, not even running for their lives. As they grew distant to his vision, he could see the warriors steadily closing the gap. One paused and threw his lance, wanting to count coup before the others. It sailed close to James. Mister Skye slid off his horse unnoticed by all around him, and slid his rifle from the saddle sheath. Now the police society warriors were watching, but he didn't care. He clamped a hand over Jawbone's ear and issued a quiet command. Then he let go of the rope he used for a rein.

The horse shrieked, and plunged furiously toward the

pack of running warriors, now stretched out over a quarter of a mile with the slower ones dropping out of the race. The sight of the horse plummeting after the runners enraged Cut Nose, who turned to find Mister Skye's rifle bore pointing directly at him, though the rifle was cradled in Mister Skye's arms.

"I thought I'd even up the medicine, Cut Nose."

The runners and Jawbone all disappeared beyond a shallow ridge, and Mister Skye knew he wouldn't see them for some minutes, if at all.

"We'll take the women, now."

Cut Nose stared at the rifle, and then stared beyond. The village was far from being disarmed. Eight warriors of the police society remained, and all of them surrounded Mister Skye and Cecil now, with nocked arrows in their bows, or lances at the ready. Even the old men held drawn bows, another dozen missiles aimed at him.

Mister Skye laughed. "It is a good day for you to die, Cut Nose. The bullet will pierce your heart and send you to the Other Side before any arrow or lance touches me."

But some crept behind Mister Skye, and he could not watch them all. Cecil saw it, and turned his horse to face them, his own old percussion lock rifle at the ready. Still it would not be enough. An arrow pierced Mister Skye's silk hat and set it sailing. Mister Skye dodged sideways, and an arrow intended for him struck Cut Nose in the arm, piercing the biceps and running half through without striking bone.

The chief roared something, and the arrows stopped.

"You and your women will die. As slowly as we can torture them, and you," he snarled.

# Chapter 25

Cut Nose looked pale and in great anguish, slipping toward shock.

"Your medicine is bad," Mister Skye said.

One of the chief's three squaws ran to help him, a leather thong for a tourniquet in hand. Skye waved her away.

"Your medicine is bad today, Cut Nose. The spirit helpers have abandoned you. The One Above looks away from you. You saw it in your own visions. Taking the women was bad medicine. You saw it. The things in the medicine bundle around your neck won't help you now, Cut Nose. Evil is upon your village. Killer should not have taken the women. There will be no good medicine here until you give them up."

Near Cut Nose, an old shaman lifted a hand to his face. Cut Nose glanced uncertainly. Mister Skye understood medicine and used the knowledge ruthlessly among these dreaming, vision-questing tribes of the plains. Now he saw, in the gesture of the old one, that he had struck a nerve.

"Let the women go and tomorrow your good medicine will return. You have offended the spirit helpers and the One Above."

Blood leaked from the pierced flesh of Cut Nose's arm.

Then he barked a command to two of his warriors. They turned toward some distant lodges. Mister Skye eyed the far hills, wondering when the main body of warriors would return and give Cut Nose new courage, new medicine. So far, he had no inkling of what was happening out there.

They brought Esmerelda first, naked. She walked with her head low, her gaze fixed upon the earth. Dried blood smeared her. Cecil's breath exploded from his lungs. Then another pair of angry warriors brought Victoria, who was dressed and seemed none the worse for wear.

Mister Skye did not know where to look. He did not want to look at gaunt, violated Esmerelda, or at Cecil. He looked at the chief, who was paying the prisoners no attention. He nodded to a squaw, and she leapt to Cut Nose and began the task of extracting the arrow.

Esmerelda was brought to within a few feet of Cecil, but could not look up at him.

"Esmerelda," he cried softly.

Victoria was brought to Mister Skye. "Sonofabitch," she muttered.

His old wife looked unharmed, and he felt a surge of relief. They smiled at each other. She had been something the Assiniboins understood, a good Crow slave woman. But Esmerelda . . .

"Cover her," said Mister Skye.

Victoria wrested herself free of the guard pinioning her, and stalked resolutely past two of the chief's squaws and into Cut Nose's own lodge. Moments later she emerged with a fine doeskin dress. She handed it to Esmerelda, who took it but did nothing.

"Put it on her, Victoria," Mister Skye said softly. Victoria did, and somehow Esmerelda was transformed by it into a dignified beauty with averted eyes, the dyed quillwork and other rich-colored decor on the dress magically illumining her.

The guide spotted returning warriors on a distant ridge. Time was running out, if it hadn't run out long ago. Cut Nose saw them too, as he sat on the grass while his squaws worked on him.

Cecil finally nerved himself to say something, after clearing his throat helplessly. "My darling. I'm glad you're safe," he croaked.

"You don't want me."

"That is not true, God is my witness."

"It will never by the same," she murmured.

"What happened wasn't your doing!"

"Nothing will ever be the same."

Tears slid down Cecil's cragged cheeks. Mister Skye could not watch a thing so terrible.

"I will help you upon this horse," Cecil croaked, slipping off the animal. She did not respond, but let him lift her up.

"Where's the girl, Cut Nose? Bring us the girl," Mister Skye roared.

The chief peered up at him malevolently, sensing perhaps that his medicine wasn't all that bad today.

"You will not have the girl. She will be a squaw in a year or two, and bring children to the Assiniboin. You will not have the girl. We will keep your horses and the girl. You will leave with your squaws. That is my final word."

Even as he spoke those warriors who understood a little English led away Pine Leaf's and James Method's horses, and prodded Esmerelda with nocked arrows. Listlessly she slid off and they led Cecil's mare away.

"We will take the rifles, too," said Cut Nose.

"Whoever touches our rifles is dead," said Mister Skye. The bore of his was aimed directly at Cut Nose again. "Your medicine is worse now. We will take the girl. Now."

The gray-fleshed chief didn't reply. With every passing second the situation deteriorated. Now the whole body of the village warriors came into sight, and at least one was being carried. Some limped, hanging heavily on others. Jawbone had scythed through them, then.

"See, Cut Nose, how your warriors are hurt. The village medicine is very bad."

But the chief saw it differently. "Perhaps I will change my mind when they get here. Go now or die. Maybe you will die anyway," he said tautly. The women had withdrawn the arrow after cutting off its iron tip, and had stanched the blood.

Mister Skye pressed hard. "Cut Nose, American Fur will not let you trade at any post as long as you have that girl. They will hear of it soon enough. You know that. You will have no place to get powder and lead and iron pots and iron arrow points and blankets. You will be beaten by all your enemies because you have no guns."

"I have said what I have said," replied Cut Nose angrily. "Say no more or you will die! And the rest will die too, after we have tortured them all!"

He barked a command and two of the police society warriors beckoned Mister Skye's party. These would be their safe-conduct past the returning Assiniboin warriors . . . perhaps. Mister Skye debated a moment . . . and acceded. With Jawbone gone, he lacked choice. He nodded.

There was one last delay, while Cecil tenderly laced Pine Leaf's moccasins upon Esmerelda's legs, and then they walked, Mister Skye, Victoria, carrying Pine Leaf's bow and quiver, Cecil, and Esmerelda, between the two stony-faced warriors. There would be a bad moment, very bad, when the group collided with the returning warriors, Mister Skye knew. The two escorting warriors would kill them at that precise moment.

The two parties converged. Mister Skye made his decision. He'd go for the two escorts first. Each of them had trade tomahawks and lances and could murder the four of them in the space of a heartbeat or two. Next he'd shoot Killer, returning now with the other warriors and in a rage to see his captives released. The seconds ticked down. The others were staring, lances poised. They came within arrow range, then lance range . . .

On a far ridge Jawbone screeched, and it sounded like the howls of a thousand wolves. They all stared at the terrible horse pawing ground. It was big medicine, frightful medicine. And then next to Jawbone, riding the spare horses, Pine Leaf and James Method appeared, long black objects in hand. Mister Skye guessed they were sticks being held the way one holds rifles.

The escorting warriors shouted something at the other warriors and the groups passed in knife-edge silence. Among the Assiniboin were four walking wounded, some bloody from Jawbone's terrible teeth and hoofs. And they carried one, dead or unconscious, bleeding and with an arm hanging unnaturally. And so they passed, and after Mister Skye's group broke clear, the escorting pair abandoned them and turned back.

Mister Skye watched them narrowly, expecting surprise, but nothing happened. A few minutes later the four met Pine Leaf and James, and he took the measure of things. They had lost three horses and Miriam Sample. Jawbone had a bloody slice along his chest, where a lance had glanced by. It had not been a good day. His Victoria was fine, but what about Esmerelda, who peered vacantly into an alien world?

What would he say to Clay and Alice Sample when there were no words? Lovely Miriam gone, perhaps to reside there, perhaps to be traded again and again, north to the Crees, south to others. Some captive women had even ended up in Mexico. They would not violate the girl. Indians as a rule loved children, and would probably care for her very well. But it still might shatter the child, drive her to madness . . .

"What happened yonder?" Mister Skye asked James, handing him the rifle he had rescued in the village.

"Ah ran until my lungs and heart were on fire, and still they came on. Some lances came so close they caught my clothes. Pine Leaf was a little better, ahead. My feet stopped hurting and turned to ice. But there was one, just a few yards behind, fixing to throw and my shoulder blades were prickling when I heard the screech and it gave me heart.

"Jawbone, he came a-roaring. They were throwing lances at him but he snarled and attacked them, and knocked them over, and then got the one behind me with a wild bite . . . and then he turned and faced the whole bunch of them, pawing and screeching, and it scared them off. Only Pine Leaf and Ah, we didn't quit running . . . Ah don't rightly know how a horse can tell friend from enemy and do that."

"He picks it up from me. Everyone's enemy at first, until people have been with me awhile. The first week or two after we left Fort Laramie, I couldn't have sent him out like that. He wouldn't have separated you from the others."

"He's a smart horse."

"More a crazy horse," said Mister Skye. "And I have made him so."

They walked westward all day, made camp at the spring south of the Snowy Mountains, and walked most of the next day, with only Esmerelda regularly mounted. The rest took turns walking and riding. Pine Leaf's feet had been scratched and torn and bruised by the long desperate run; Method's too, and each step tortured her until Mister Skye thought to remove Pine Leaf's moccasins from Esmerelda, who rode horseback the whole way. She put them on gratefully, but there was nothing for James Method. He walked grimly, leaving small spots of blood in every print in the clay earth.

There was only silence among them and a sense of defeat because sweet Miriam had been lost. Victoria seemed the least harmed, and the food gathering fell to her. They took no meat, but she industriously gathered roots and berries as they trudged through early September chill, into the jaws of northern autumn. And then as the sun sank that second day, they stumbled wearily down the long fatal coulee, and into camp.

They were all staring.

"Mother!" cried Henrietta and rushed to Esmerelda, only to fall back confused at the sight of Esmerelda's face.

"What happened? Tell us!" Alex demanded.

Only Silas Potter seemed unperturbed, a faint knowing smile on his face. By the fire, Father Kiley sat quietly, listening.

Mary read everything at a glance, and soon she and Victoria were chattering.

But it was Clay and Alice Sample, with Alfred beside them, who concerned Mister Skye most. They stared as the party straggled in, and then looked behind, as if Miriam might be a little back from the others, and then came the terrible dawning.

"Oh, God," Alice cried.

Clay stared resolutely, awaiting news.

"Sis isn't here," said Alfred sharply.

Mister Skye stepped down from Jawbone. He did not want to say what he had to say, but it was something to be done.

"Miriam's alive, a captive of the Assiniboin. We tried hard to free her, but could not."

"She's alive?" Clay asked.

"I believe so. We didn't see her."

A terrible silence settled while they absorbed that. Then Clay asked, "Can we get her back?"

"It's possible they'll trade her for goods at some American Fur post. The company won't deal with bands that have a white captive. So, yes, there's a chance . . ."

"And if not?"

Mister Skye stared into twilit hills. "Don't count on seeing her again," he said softly.

Alice wept. "Why did we come, why did we come?" she sobbed. "No, no, no . . ." She slumped into the grass and wept desolately, her small hands clenching and unclenching. "She was such a good girl. Sweet and helpful. She never complained. I don't know why God wants to punish—to punish a girl . . ." Wetness seeped in sheets down her face now. "Miriam, oh my Miriam," she cried, choking and trembling. Mary knelt beside her and slid brown arms around her, but Alice Sample was beyond consoling. The muffled sobs continued, haunting the hills. "I have so little," she said, her voice muffled on Mary's breast, "I've never complained . . ." she whispered. "Oh, God, Miriam . . ."

Clay knelt beside her. "I'm going after her now," he said resolutely. "I'll fetch her, Alice."

She seemed not to hear. He stood and headed for his horse.

Mister Skye caught him by the arm. "You'll only give Cut Nose another scalp for his medicine tripod."

"I can't stand here and do nothing. I'll take a little gold, all I have."

"They'll take the gold and your hair and laugh. Mister Sample, you must stay and care for Alice and your fine son."

"Doesn't seem right. I've got to do something. Must do something!"

"Aye. We'll do something when we get to an American Fur fort. The traders have ways, mate. Ways that we don't have."

"I must do something!" But Clay's resolution was seeping from him as he stood in this prairie place so far from help and civilization. "Do something!" he said, but it was an echo.

Mister Skye slipped a thick arm around his shoulder and steadied him until his breathing changed. Alfred stood nigh, and he grasped the boy's hand in his own big blunt-fingered one. It was small and clammy. The boy took courage from it for a while and then returned to his mother, who wept softly.

"May I talk with you, Mister Skye?" asked Clay. Together they walked into the dusk, far from other ears.

"First, tell me what happened. The whole thing. Then tell me something that is heavy on my mind—will Miriam be . . . abused?"

Mister Skye related the story, and then addressed Clay's question. "Unlikely she'll be abused, Clay. She's not yet a woman. Most Indians love children and delight in them. This group though . . . a bad chief, a bloody chief, poisons a band and its traditions, like a bloody bad king poisons a realm. Possibly some squaws will treat her meanly, half starve her. They want her for a squaw, Clay. They want more people in that small band. Likely they'll be decent enough to her and wed her off when she's at marrying age. They might trade her, though. Slaves, white women, get traded. Sometimes the trade is good because the new owners trade the woman for goods at some post or other . . .''

Clay sighed heavily. "I'm not encouraged.

"I didn't want to encourage you falsely, mate.''

Clay's eyes turned moist. "We had a fine farm, rich soil, in the Ohio Valley, a place that prospered us. I've known Cecil a long time, and when the call came, I answered. We sold the farm, and put what we had into some fine mules and the wagon and a few things. Have you ever heard of Cincinnatus, Mister Skye?''

"Not rightly, Mister Sample.''

"Cincinnatus was a great patriot of the old Roman republic. A great soldier and leader, who despised power, and for that reason was entrusted with it. They came to him one day, when the republic was besieged, and asked him to save them. He loved his farm, but he answered the call. Some say he left his plow standing in the middle of that field, and went off to war. He answered the call, Mister Skye. He was a patriot, and when he was called, he didn't dally; he answered . . . and soon enough he'd rescued Rome, gave up his dictatorial powers and went back to his farm. He's my inspiration, sir. I'm a patriot not only of this Republic, but of the Kingdom of God, and when Cecil's call came, I answered.''

Mister Skye found himself admiring the man.

"I can't say as I left my plow in the middle of the field, but we sold out. Alice fretted some about it, but we came along to plant the Christian flag out here . . .''

"I am sorry it came to this," Mister Skye said roughly.

"It is worse, sir. We had six children, but cholera took

four after a trip to the river. Jonathan was the eldest and we lost him. And the three younger, Sara, Artemus, and Josiah.''

Mister Skye could not imagine what to say.

''Mrs. Sample will be wanting to go back, I'm sure. Alice has borne more than a woman can bear. I have no mind for it. We have no money to purchase good bottoms again. What would you suggest, Mister Skye?''

''No man can make that kind of decision for you, Clay.''

''I was called and I must answer,'' he said resolutely.

The camp was morose that night. Some had been saved, but one lost. And another so wounded of soul that perhaps she'd never be the same. Only Silas talked, and his talk didn't help anyone. ''It is the whip of God upon the sinful!'' he cried, until Clay finally cornered him and asked bluntly what sins Miriam had committed that had led to her fate.

''It is the sins of the fathers upon the next generation,'' cried Silas.

''There are those here who grieve,'' said Clay bluntly. ''Will you not comfort them, and me?''

''The voice crying in the wilderness does not come to comfort, but to discomfort.''

''Then be silent,'' Clay snapped. ''Or I will silence you with my fists.''

Father Kiley stood. ''Mister Potter! You are crucifying our Lord! My heart breaks for the Samples.''

Mister Skye observed that with a certain pleasure. The condition of his party was worrisome. It was gravely weakened by a lack of horses, and demoralization, and he knew they'd be no match at all for any of the wolves, two- or four-legged, in this land. Pine Leaf and James were out scouting, on mules because the remaining horses were worn down.

Cecil seemed lost in his own world. He had wrapped Esmerelda in blankets and then slipped into the twilight, doing something that puzzled Mister Skye. Cecil plucked the last of the fall flowers, those that had resisted the frosts, and these he gathered into a great bouquet. Then he sat down beside the small cookfire and braided them, losing a lot of the petals of the asters and daisies as he did. Then, when he had a crude garland completed, he awakened the dozing Esmerelda and slipped it over her shoulders. She sat up, still wearing the beautiful doeskin dress of her captors, and stared at the garland about her neck.

"That's my wedding necklace for you," Cecil said.

Then, one by one he summoned the others to the fireside. The Samples did not wish to come, having retreated to their wagon, but he sternly bade them. He brought Father Kiley as well, and seated him, and beckoned Mary and Dirk and Victoria. He asked Silas to join them, but the young scholar refused.

"You have no authority over me," he said.

Then Cecil stood in the dusk. "We will pray now," he said. "First for the mercies of God; next for his blessing upon Miriam and the Samples; and last for my bride, my Esmerelda, and our joyous union and reunion. But let us first remember that Miriam Sample is not alone now; Almighty God is by her side, and hears our pleas."

And so they did for a half hour. Mister Skye watched quietly from beyond the firelight. He never felt comfortable at night close to a fire. But he saw, in that space of time, the renewal of courage and hope among these missionary people, and he approved.

At the end, Esmerelda wept, and Cecil leapt at once to her side, his scrawny hard arm around her, clutching her blankets to her. The others slipped away, permitting them their privacy. Esmerelda wept for a while, and then fell silent.

"Hold me, Cecil. Hold me and don't let go. If you hold me, I know I will be all right."

# Chapter 26

The deeper they pierced into Blackfeet country, the more dour Pine Leaf became. James scarcely recognized the woman he had come to know in the land of the Crows. They were poorly mounted now because the Assiniboin had taken her swift Crow horse, and James's fine bay as well, leaving them only Cecil's spares, or mules.

"We will steal good Siksika horses," she said sternly, and from then on her efforts were devoted less to protecting Mister Skye's party than to hunting prey, a Blackfeet hunting or raiding party that could be jumped in the night. That such a thing was at cross-purposes with Cecil's missionary hopes did not enter her mind, or if it did she had dismissed it contemptuously.

It worried her, this lack of a good horse between her legs, and now it made her fierce and angry as she stalked through the Judith Gap and into the lush Judith basin with the eyes of the hawk, and the cunning of a lion, seeing everything before she was seen. She barely talked to James or tolerated his presence.

He knew her story now. She had told him some of it.

Mister Skye had confirmed and elaborated it. At the age
of twelve her brother had been killed by the Blackfeet,
and she had made a most sacred vow never to marry
until she had taken a hundred scalps of the enemies of
her people. She grew lithe and swift and graceful as a
puma, and tall for a woman. When she insisted on going
out on war parties, the warriors laughed at her, but hu-
mored her wishes, only to discover that she was fierce in
battle, making up in swiftness—she was a brilliant horse-
woman—what she lacked in strength. And she became
absolutely fearless.

She was also the fiercest of all Crows, haranguing her
people into battle, and performing such feats of daring
when it came to stealing horses and taking scalps, that
she rose high in the councils of her people, becoming in
time the third-ranking person in their midst. She never
won her hundred scalps, and never married, but she
eventually had lovers, including Antelope, Jim Beckwourth. Now, in the grasslands of her enemies, the old
flame burned hot again. She ejected James from her buffalo robes and ritually purified herself for war. Her temper turned hot and smoldering. James didn't mind. He
had tasted death a few days earlier, felt its breath on his
back, and if the Crow woman beside him was transforming herself into a dervish, that would be all the better.
Her very ferocity was transforming him into a fierce
counterpart. He thought she was beautiful, tall and perfectly formed, and as lean and graceful as a girl.

All this Mister Skye saw, but said nothing as far as
James could tell. Pine Leaf and James stayed in the camps
briefly, only to bring in buffalo hump and tongue, and
then rode off again, stalking ahead of the caravan.

They rode through an awesome land of lush tawny
grass and rushing cold creeks full of trout. The Snowy
Mountains formed a smooth white wall to the southeast.
To the west lay the Belts; to the east the pine-clad Ju-
diths; to the north the Moccasins and Highwoods. And
not far beyond lay the great Missouri, and the mouth of
Sun River, near the great fall. After entering this north-

•

ern empire, Mister Skye turned just north of west, and
the wagons toiled over country so thick with buffalo that
sometimes long processions of the great animals in their
dark winter fur paraded right through the wagons, scar-
ing everyone. This was a different country, somehow
even more limitless than before, with dizzying views that
ended in blue infinity.

Here Pine Leaf knew she'd find what she wanted, a
hunting party of the despicable Siksika, and she searched
now not for buffalo, but for humans, like some great
stalking cat. And the second day into the Judith country,
she found them. Violently she pulled James from his
horse and hid the animals in a grove of long-needled
ponderosa. At this point they were fully twenty miles
west of the wagons and Mister Skye. Far ahead were
nothing but tiny dots to James Method's vision, but to
Pine Leaf's they were mortals. Some wild anger radiated
from her.

"Siksika!" she hissed.

And so they proved to be. About a dozen men were
preparing to run down their prey on buffalo ponies. They
had crept up on a band of buffalo, mostly fine big cows,
staying downwind. And now they were mounting the fleet
buffalo runners, specially trained fast and daring horses
that would close on a running buffalo, narrowly avoiding
its horns, until their riders had loosed an arrow into the
chest cavity of the buffalo. They had to be fleet, because
buffalo could run with astonishing speed and pull away
from all but the best ponies. Leaving their packhorses in
the hands of a herder, the hunters plunged into the wild
chase, and instantly the band of buffalo broke into a trot,
and then a lumbering run as the Blackfeet swept in among
them, their cries drifting down the wind, pumping one
after another arrow into the animals. One cow with an
arrow in her swerved and the buffalo runner did too, but
a second too late and a horn gashed its flanks.

From their vantage point at the crest of a low grassy
hill, Pine Leaf muttered and chanted Absaroka words
that James didn't understand. The stampeded herd swept

a quarter of a mile away, but still Pine Leaf never moved. She was studying each hunter, one by one, mastering his habits and daring. James thought she was probably measuring their scalps as well for the cutting. His own heart thudded. Soon he would be taking a Blackfeet scalp—the scalp he needed to present to Gliding Raven's father— and bringing fine horses too. He would begin his Crow life rich in horses, all stolen from the Blackfeet, and there would be prize buffalo runners among them.

When it was over there were twenty-three black carcasses humped in tawny dried grasses in the space of a mile. The hunters dismounted from the winded buffalo runners, and brought up the packhorses to carry the precious cargo of prime hides and hump meat and tongue back to their camp. There would likely be women in camp too, who would follow with knives, and take more meat for drying into jerky. The hunters were jovial after their success, and James could hear their shouts sometimes on the soft breeze. Twilight came, and still Pine Leaf did not move, but merely muttered the fiercest of incantations, summoning medicine. James felt hungry. He wanted also to return to the wagons with meat before it grew dark, check in with Mister Skye and let them know there were Blackfeet nearby. But Pine Leaf shook her head.

"Tonight," she hissed, "we will do what we came for. We will take Siksika scalps. We will steal horses. And then we will go back to my people. We will fly to the south, and you will have scalps. You will kill one night-herder, and I will kill the other. We will each take a scalp. And then the horses!"

"Ah'd like to say goodbye to Mister Skye. Ah'd like to shake the hand of the others, Cecil Rathbone especially. Ah'd like at least to let them know . . . Victoria's one of your people, Pine Leaf."

"Yes she is. But Mister Skye always takes care of them. We will go south as soon as we have made our raid."

"But Ah'm afraid those hunters will find the missionaries and blame them for—"

"Maybe that is good! Maybe they shouldn't take the
white medicine to the Siksika!"

James didn't like that, didn't like abandoning the missionaries to a large group of vengeful Blackfeet.

"Ah'm going to go warn them. Ah'll be back here
before we raid." he said. "And return our horses here
to Cecil Rathbone."

She glared fiercely. "If you go anywhere, you will die.
I will take your scalp back and tell my people you were
against us."

She was fully capable of it, and that subdued him. It
also made him feel all the worse. He had never before
betrayed friends.

Even as they lay quietly behind the crest of the hill the
wind picked up out of the northwest, and a vast cloud
mass blotted out the stars and the last of the twilight.
The temperature plummeted and it grew so cold that
James longed to run, move, warm himself. But still Pine
Leaf lay in the grass, like stone, impervious to discomfort. When he could no longer bear the cold knifing at
him around his leggins and across his neck and face, and
up the sleeves of his buckskin shirt, he stood anyway. It
was pitch-black now. Even as he stood he felt the needles
of sleet sting his face, and smelled snow on the cold
damp restless air.

"If it snows we'll leave a trail of prints in it a mile
wide that they can read," he said unhappily.

"All the better," she snapped. "It will lead south to
my village. And they will know we did it. The snow will
save me an arrow that I planned to leave among them,
so they would know that Pine Leaf is not yet too old to
make war."

James groped his way back to the horses and untied a
small buffalo robe that he carried behind the cantle.

"We might as well get comfortable." he said. offering
her space in it.

But she scorned it. "It is good medicine to suffer. If

you are warm you are soft and sleepy. If you sting with the snow and the cold of the Man of the North, it is good and your medicine will be strong."

It snowed then, the flakes streaking horizontally into James's face. He ignored her and wrapped the warm robe tight about him, and sliding his rifle into its protection as well. In that fashion he endured more hours, until at last Pine Leaf shook him roughly and bade him mount. He had no idea what time it was, but he knew that the hunters would be long asleep in their robes. There might not even be any herd-guards on a night like this, and that would make the whole thing easier: take the horses, kill some Blackfeet in their robes . . . that thought repelled him.

He settled into the icy saddle and they rode off into the teeth of the blizzard.

"We will use knives, or my bow and arrow," she said. "Be silent! The rifle will awaken them all."

How she knew where to go through that tunnel of black snow he couldn't imagine. No stars. The night was pitch-dark. They rode thus for perhaps ten minutes, though it seemed an hour to James. And then their horses caught a scent and their rhythm changed. Their heads were up and alert, and he hoped the animals wouldn't betray them.

"We will need to saddle the good Siksika ponies and leave these," she whispered. "So we will unsaddle these just ahead. I don't need a saddle at all, but you do. If these ponies follow us, that is good. If not, we will leave them."

So, thought James, they'd need time to saddle the horses they would steal; and Cecil and Mister Skye would be short two more horses. In the depths of himself he suddenly didn't want to be a Crow warrior. He wasn't at all sure he wanted to marry Gliding Raven. He wanted to head back to the wagons and camp and comfort in this fierce September storm.

But Pine Leaf had already slipped from her horse, one of Mister Skye's packhorses, and was loosening the cinch. James sensed dimly they were next to a grove of pines, of the type that dotted this country. He stared hard, trying to orient himself, but couldn't. Then she led him forward, their moccasins treading an inch or two of snow, straight into the needling wind. That was the only orientation he had: getting back to his horse meant going with the wind rather than against it.

They topped a low rise, and the hunting camp lay before them. The wind plucked sparks from the remains of a fire, and around that pinprick of warmth lay inert forms wrapped in dark, snow-covered robes. Beyond loomed the horses on a picket line to keep them from drifting ahead of the wind. Pine Leaf paused, waiting. After an icy eternity, the faintest shadow of a horse and rider circled out of the inkiness, faintly illumined by the occasional flare of flame.

"He is for you. We will see if there is another," Pine Leaf whispered, her voice lost in the gale.

James grew numb. He had never felt colder, and he wondered whether his numbness was a matter of the heart as well as his blizzard-buffeted body.

And still they waited. Another came then. This one rode close to the fire, slipped numbly off his horse to warm his hands. He cradled his rifle in the crook of his arm and held his hands to the orange embers.

Pine Leaf studied him. "It is the same one. They have only one guard. They think no one will come because the Cold-Maker has come tonight. We will show them the Absaroka come anytime!"

She rose and nocked an arrow in her bow. "I will kill him. But first we must circle around and cut the horses free, and drive them so the Siksika cannot follow us. Then I will kill the one at the fire, and you will kill one of the sleeping ones and take his scalp. And you will count coup on the others."

James nodded. They arced around through darkness, until they came close to the horses, dark hulks with snow catching on their backs. They were alert, heads up. Pine Leaf stalked close, catlike, murmuring some incantation that seemed to calm the animals, then her knife flashed silver in the dark, and horses pulled loose and drifted downwind. One snorted. The guard peered into the blackness, seeing nothing through the driving snow. But he seemed to sense something, and stood up, rifle in hand, finger curled around the trigger.

He was crouched like that when Pine Leaf's arrow drove into his chest. He coughed, began to fall, and his finger pulled spastically on the trigger. His rifle banged thunderously, and in an instant the others sprang up, grabbing their weapons from their robes. But they saw no target, only a whirling wall of snow, and blackness beyond.

From out in the blackness Pine Leaf cried out, like the bark of wolves. James knew enough of her tongue to understand. "It is Pine Leaf, warrior woman of the Absarokas," she cried. "I have taken your horses. I am holding your horse, Moon-Hides-the-Sun."

That terrible news chilled James even worse. Which one of those ghostly forms, now shooting into the blackness where Pine Leaf's voice had come, was the most dreaded of all the Blackfeet? He didn't have time to worry about it because now they were spreading into the night in pairs, and one pair stalked directly toward him.

He shot one and darted to one side, knowing the other would shoot or drive an arrow into the place where his muzzle had flashed. He saw the one dark silhouetted form drop. There were more shots, and he heard a horse snort and cough, and a heavy thud. A horse had been killed, then. Now others glided toward him, drawn by his shot, but he dashed sideways and crouched low in the grasses, hastily pouring powder into his hand, digging in his pouch with numb fingers for a ball and a new percussion cap. It took forever. His fingers wouldn't work. He dropped a ball into snow. Half the powder lay on the ground rather than in his barrel. He couldn't even feel the caps he dug for. And then it was too late. Out of the blackness came a rushing form, with glinting steel in hand. James clubbed wildly and struck a solid blow as the stock of his rifle slammed into the shoulder of the warrior. The man staggered and came on. James leapt sideways again, and clubbed a second time as the Blackfeet warrior whirled after him. This time the rifle connected with skull, and the man went down with a thud. But others were coming. Wildly James dug for his knife. Violently he caught the hair in one hand and slashed a circle around the skull with the other and pulled. The scalp popped off and James tumbled back into the snow, just as three others loomed near. It was enough. He had his Blackfeet scalp. He crabbed back, and when blackness enfolded him he paused to sense the direction of the wind, his heart clawing.

Downwind. He had to get downwind. He was lost now but Pine Leaf and the horses would be downwind. He was sweating, even in the bitter night. At every quarter he felt the looming presence of Blackfeet about to rush him, like ghosts, like hobgoblins, like the creatures that old granny had hissed about in the long ago.

Somehow he had lost his rifle. He had his knife in one hand and the scalp in the other. He didn't pause to hunt for it in the snow, but ran now, with the snow, through the night, alone and without a horse and surrounded by vengeful Blackfeet, including the most terrible of them all. Then, far off into the left of blackness, Pine Leaf was laughing. "We have stolen your horses, Siksika dogs," she cried.

Shots racketed again from behind. But James veered sharply in her direction. The taunting was really for him, summoning him to come if he still lived. Now he ran, the white earth rising before him. He hit a tree branch and it slashed murderously across his face.

"You are careless, Seven Scalps. You were afraid, even though we have taken their horses."

"Pine Leaf!" he gasped.

Now he could see the dark bulk of drifting animals ahead, a great many of them.

"You have a scalp," she said. "That is good. But where is your rifle?"

"Lost it. Clubbed with it."

She led him fast to a place where black trees loomed.

"Here. I have saddled two. For myself I saddled the one that was owned by Moon-Hides-the-Sun. It is my prize. I am the greatest warrior of the Absaroka."

James fumbled into the murk, found the horse and his saddle and swung up. Beside him, Pine Leaf had already mounted.

"Now we must herd them," she said. "Fast for a little while. They cannot follow until daylight, and then they will run on foot after us if there is not too much snow. They will run down our trail, hoping to catch us, hoping we will be careless."

He could not see what they were herding, and marveled at her night vision. Occasionally a sharp word from her reached him through the tumbling snow. He felt less cold now, running with the wind. But a great quaking limpness filled him, and he hung weakly to the pommel. Thus they fled through the night.

Dawn came so imperceptibly in the overcast he scarcely noticed its arrival, but at last he could fathom the world around him. Ahead of them, making a great swath through a foot of snow, were seventeen, no, nineteen, ponies, some of them fleet buffalo runners. A little to his left rode Pine Leaf on a great gray horse. As the light grew, he saw the hulk of mountainous country to the south. They were probably traveling east because that part of the low cast-iron sky was slightly brighter.

And there was something wrong with Pine Leaf. She held an arm unnaturally to her side, and her fine buckskin shirt was soaked with dark blood.

# Chapter 27

When dawn was nothing but a gray pencil of light across the breast of the prairie, Mister Skye saddled up Jawbone, shrugged into his blanket capote, and set off to the west. Pine Leaf and James hadn't shown up last night. Perhaps they had holed up in the blizzard, but he doubted it. They should have been back in camp before the blizzard started.

Behind him the camp was awakening to acrimony. Alex and Henrietta had a blazing fire going to warm up, and were haranguing Cecil, not only about the night's miseries but about their destination.

"It's too late in the year!" Alex snapped. "We won't have time to build houses and make meat. We have a whole northern winter ahead of us. We must make for Fort Benton at once, Cecil."

Mister Skye didn't tarry to find out the result of that. He was in Blackfeet country and he hadn't heard from his scouts and the whole party would be in danger. It would be a miserable day, he thought. The sky was cloudless. A hot September sun would turn the snow to slush and bog the wagons. There was no spare stock now, and the skeletal oxen and mules would make only a few miles through the mud before giving out. Pine Leaf had been riding Victoria's horse. Method had ridden Mary's. There were no more spares, thanks to the Assiniboins. Not only were his scouts missing, but two precious horses.

He turned Jawbone northwest, the direction the caravan would go today, if it went at all. Victoria would whip them into action if she could, and she and Mary and Dirk would walk beside the remaining horse and mules carrying the lodge and their supplies.

Jawbone made easy work of the snow, except where it had piled up and Mister Skye found himself in two-foot drifts. He rode an animal that seemed all the more energetic when the going became hard.

A half hour later the sun cracked the east, sending long yellow light across a vast undulating plain. A snow-capped distant square butte suddenly bloomed in the light. He saw nothing; no sign of Pine Leaf and James. No sign of human passage anywhere. Then, an hour out from the wagons, he spotted movement off in the hazy southwest. He stopped at once, knowing his very immobility might prevent him from being seen. Jawbone froze beneath him, and together they watched a small dark mass of animals toiling toward them rapidly. Twenty minutes later he could tell it was a group of perhaps twenty ponies, and there were two riders herding them.

He waited patiently, still immobile. Let them exhaust their animals in the heavy snow; he would save his. At a half mile he knew it was James and Pine Leaf, not because he could make out their features, but because he knew how they sat. But Pine Leaf slumped. A raid, then, he thought, Blackfeet ponies, and a scalp or two for James.

They saw him now. He steered Jawbone toward them, watching the steaming breaths of the hard-driven ponies as he closed. It is not an easy thing to stop a driven horse herd, so Mister Skye fell in beside James and Pine Leaf.

Her left shoulder was soaked with frozen blood, and she looked ashen. Hanging from James's pommel was a fresh scalp, frozen red blood around the lip of black hair.

"Congratulations," said Mister Skye.

"Ah didn't expect to see you again."

Mister Skye nodded.

"Your two horses are here," said Pine Leaf.

Mister Skye had already seen them.

"Take another if you need it," said James.

"That would be incriminating," said Mister Skye. He turned to Pine Leaf. "Would you pause long enough to be bandaged?"

She stared at him gravely. "There is one hole, not two. It is above my heart, and it no longer bleeds. I am dead, but not until we have taken these ponies, and these scalps"—she had one too, he noted—"to my people."

Mister Skye stared at this graceful, legendary woman.

"I believe I know the horse you ride. He was a colt when I saw him last, and that scar across his withers is one I made."

"I took him from Moon-Hides-the-Sun."

"Is he alive?"

"We do not know who we killed."

Behind them lay trampled snow, winding off into the cold haze. As they talked, both Pine Leaf and Method glanced to the rear every few moments. But they saw nothing but the blue haze of September there.

"I will say goodbye, then," said Mister Skye. "I will sing the song of Pine Leaf whenever I am with her people."

She nodded solemnly. She would live for a while because she willed herself to.

"I saw this in the visions," she said. "And I am ready."

"Mister Skye, Ah want to—would you shake my hand?"

"I would, mate," he replied, and they did. James tried to say something, but couldn't. "You have your freedom, mate. And you'll have a fine wife soon. But it is the freedom of the wild, Mister Method. From this day on, there'll be a whole tribe of Piegans wanting your scalp. And what they want, they usually get.''

"How will they know Ah raided their horses, Mister Skye?"

"The songs that are sung in one camp echo in another, Mister Method.''

Mister Skye slid Jawbone into the herd, parting it as it flowed southward. From his kit he extracted a ball of thong, and with it fashioned a catch-line for his two horses. Leaning over Jawbone he tethered one animal, and then the other, and pulled them away from the herd. He held them still as the dark ponies, mostly winter-haired now, slipped past, along with his two Absaroka friends.

"Adios, Seven Scalps,'' he muttered.

It was quiet. He headed back toward the wagons, leaving behind him the tracks of three horses, blue-shadowed cups in the snow. Now he, too, peered into the north-west, looking for whatever might materialize upon the brow of a distant swell of prairie.

He had things to think through. Behind him were tracks through the snow that linked him to the horse raid. And which endangered his missionary clients. Still, none of the stolen ponies would be found among the missionary stock.

Moon-Hides-the-Sun would be somewhere ahead. And in a rage because his great horse had been stolen. Mister Skye considered that man, that fearless and cunning and ruthless fighter, as one more formidable than himself. And motivated as well by the searing memory of a pre-vious encounter that had cost him his medicine. Moon-Hides-the-Sun had come down the mountain from a vision-quest and announced to all his people that he would kill Mister Skye at Fort McKenzie. Skye had been there—that part of the vision was true—but when it was over, Skye had taken his medicine pouch, snatched his medi-cine feather, broken his medicine shield—which had a black moon in its center with sun rays of white emanating from it—and had sent the warrior into the dreamland for two weeks with a blow of a belaying pin about the ear. But it had been luck and would not happen that way again. To get his medicine back, Moon-Hides-the-Sun would do anything, including ambush from cover.

When Mister Skye returned, the wagons had not moved.

"Sonofabitch," said Victoria, viewing the horses that Mister Skye brought with him. She and Mary threw their saddle pads over them while Mister Skye briefly described his encounter with James and Pine Leaf.

"Sonofabitch. Tonight I will wail for Pine Leaf," she muttered. "Now you make these crazy-medicines go. I cannot make them go. I got damn mad and still they don't go."

She clambered up on her pony then, and off scouting. He walked over to the other fire, where the missionaries huddled trying to stay warm.

Cecil seemed cheerful, as always, but the others were surly.

"Did you find them?" Cecil asked.

"I did. They are heading back to the Crow Village. I have my horses back, and they have others."

"Will we ever see them again?"

"Not this trip, mate."

"Oh dear. Oh dear," cried Esmerelda. "He's gone? I do so wish we might have said goodbye. I am so fond . . ."

"He cared for me on every occasion," said Father Kiley. "Oh, how I'll miss that good young man."

"He took a shine to you, Father. But he's a Crow now, Crow in his soul, Crow in his faith. And a Crow in war."

Cecil pondered that. "The Blackfeet will be wrathful, and we may be in harm's way," he said at last. "We have a division here, and I pray we can resolve it amiably. The storm has been very hard upon my Henrietta and Alex, and all of us have suffered. It's melting now, but that seems to make no difference. Briefly, the Newtons and the Samples and Mister Potter wish for us to turn north for Fort Benton and winter on the Missouri.

They say—and there's truth in it—that we haven't time left to build shelter on Sun River, and lay in supplies and food.''

"We're saying more than that," snapped Alex. "Those of us who wish to go to Fort Benton will go, no matter what the rest of you do. Alone if necessary. My dear Henrietta is now only two months from her time. I insist that we make for Benton, so that she may be delivered in comfort and safety.''

Mister Skye nodded, and turned to Father Kiley, who sat near the fire huddled in his blankets.

"What of you, Father? Have you thought of your future?''

"Mister Skye," said the priest. "I am in the hands of God. Since I no longer have a life of my own, there is only His will. I have that at least. In the weeks since the blinding, I have come face-to-face with His will.''

"Fort Benton would be a place to shelter, and then be taken down the river. You'd be looked after.''

"My Lord will take me to where He wants me, if He has any use for me.''

Mister Skye peered off upon the vast white prairies, now blinding in the fierce sun. The sky looked almost black with blueness.

"I don't know whether you are surrendering your will, or surrendering your life," Mister Skye said.

"Only will, Mister Skye," The priest smiled. His bandages had been replaced by a leather patch that Victoria had devised.

Mister Skye returned to the fire where the mission party huddled.

"All right, mates. I've not brought you this far, so close to Sun River, to steer you elsewhere. You've toiled your way across a continent to build a mission at a place only sixty or seventy miles distant. Cecil Rathbone had a dream, and once you all were lifted up by it.

"But you're right, mates. There's not time to build a mission and lay in meat and go to Benton for supplies before the real cold and snow sets in. But there may still be two months of good weather before winter closes. Time to locate your mission and begin to build it, hew down the logs, put up your corrals, cut some prairie hay.

"You preach faith, mates, but you have little of it now. I'll take you to Sun River, leave the men to start the work, and take the women to Fort Benton. American Fur will shelter you all through the hard weather, and the presence of you women will brighten that post. My friend Alexander Culbertson, the booshway there, will be glad to have you. And of course Father Kiley will find the help he needs there. He can be taken downriver in the spring, on a mackinaw first to Fort Union, and then by steamer."

He did not wait for objections.

"Harness up, mates. It'll be hard going for the mules and oxen, especially when the ground goes soft. Harness up now, and we'll have a warm camp in the evening."

Slowly they stood, half shamed by Mister Skye's criticism, half inspired by the thought of Fort Benton. And in a while they rolled off, the weary ill-fed oxen struggling in the slop and soft earth, and the ribby mules doing just as poorly. The day itself turned golden and pleasant, with the sun slaying the snow until bright grasses lay exposed again. They stopped frequently to let the burdened animals rest and feed.

They came upon the remains of the stolen traffic, now an avenue of rotting snow piercing west by northwest, and Mister Skye turned onto it. The going was slightly easier, but heavy in the thoughts of them all was where this avenue might lead.

Late in the afternoon Victoria slipped over a prairie ridge, and rode straight to Mister Skye.

She sat hard and wizened and motionless in the saddle, and her brown eyes blazed. "Siksika," she hissed to Skye. These were the ancient and dreaded enemies of her people. "A whole band, Kainah, the Blood tribe, in a buffalo camp. They are as many as ants. Maybe there are a hundred lodges."

Not as many, Mister Skye thought, as some years earlier, before the smallpox darkened so many of the lodges of the Blackfeet. And not so formidable, now that whiskey had cut its terrible swath through their numbers, whiskey from American Fur, in exchange for the exquisitely tanned Blackfeet buffalo robes.

"What of the hunters whose ponies Pine Leaf and Seven Scalps stole?"

"That is where the village is, where the Kainah dogs all camp. The whole village came to the camp of the hunters, where the snow trail ends. The buffalo are upwind to the west."

Making meat first, Mister Skye thought. Making meat for winter while the buffalo were near, and then they'd head on down toward the Crow country for revenge.

"We will go in," said Mister Skye.

"Sonofabitch," she said in English. "If I go in there and come out, I will build a lodge and purify myself for four suns."

"Do that, Victoria."

Late in the day, a dozen or so warriors boiled over a ridge and stared at the first wheeled vehicles they had ever seen, the two wagons and burdened carriage toiling slowly toward them.

Mister Skye rode ahead to meet them, and soon the Kainah warriors gathered around him, knowing him, knowing his medicine horse. They were older men, powerful and graying, the Buffalo Bull Society, the ones who guarded the various bands of these people. They were not painted for war or looking for it. If anything, they were intensely curious about these wagons furrowing the muddy prairie, and what might be inside.

Moon-Hides-the-Sun was not among them.

"Who speaks my tongue?" asked Mister Skye. It would be easier to talk than to flash the hand-signs of the prairies.

An older warrior who was made of slabs of tawny flesh welded into a powerful frame spoke up.

"I have spoke it some at Fort Benton, and before that

at Fort McKenzie. You are Skye, and who are these that come?''

"Medicine men," said Mister Skye. "Shortrobe medicine men of the whites, and a longrobe medicine man."

"A longrobe? Has the longrobe Point returned?"

"Not Father Point, but a brother. The longrobe Father Dunstan Kiley."

"Ah!" said the warrior. "I have heard of him. He has great medicine. I am named Bull Elk With Locked Horns, but at Fort Benton they call me Locked Horns. Has this blackrobe come to bring us more of the white medicine?"

"The shortrobes have," said Mister Skye. "They have come to bring medicine to the Piegan and the Kainah and the Siksika."

Mister Skye remembered Father Nicolas Point, a French Jesuit colleague of Pierre de Smet. The good father had stayed for many months at Fort Lewis in 1847, teaching the Blackfeet and baptizing them. Now they supposed he was returning, or one like him, to give them the white man's medicine at last, the medicine to command thunder and heal the sick. Father Point had left at last, gloomy about his labors, for the powerful Blackfeet had shown little sign, except for the crosses they wore as totems, of abandoning their fierce ways and turning to a Christianized life.

There was much muttering among these Bull Society men, and at last Locked Horns addressed Mister Skye.

"We will take the medicine people to our village. But there is one among us who has vowed to kill you, and him we cannot control. And on this day he is very angry."

"Moon-Hides-the-Sun," said Mister Skye. "But his medicine is bad. I will give him a new name: Stolen-Horse Man. Tell him that I have said it; that his medicine is bad."

Locked Horns stared. "How did you know of the stolen horse? Was Pine Leaf of the Crow among you?"

"For a while," said Mister Skye. "Pine Leaf and

Seven Scalps. But they have gone from us and are returning to their village with many horses.''

''Ah! We will kill her. We will have revenge. We will steal more horses than she took! I myself will drive my lance through her!''

''You are too late.''

The news shocked Locked Horns. ''Is it so?'' he said at last.

''It is so. She lives, but will die soon from a Kainah bullet.''

''Is it known whose bullet made this great medicine?''

''It is not known.''

''Maybe it was a bullet from Moon-Hides-the-Sun! Maybe his medicine is good!''

''You will know when he tests it upon me.''

They rode then into the great village comprised of three bands of the Bloods, and all of the village gaped at the wagons they had heard of but never seen, and the white women they had never seen. Where the white warriors and trappers kept their women had been a great mystery among them, and some had said the whites had no women of their own. But now such women were here, two of them in the carriage and another in one of the white-topped boats of the prairies.

No Indians were handsomer, thought Mister Skye, even in the soiled clothes they wore to butcher buffalo and scrape hides and make jerky and pemmican. This village spoke of pride and power, with well-kept lodges of new cowhide, vividly painted, and signs of great industry everywhere, in ground-staked buffalo hides drying in the sun, and great racks of drying meat.

Mister Skye glanced behind to see how his missionaries were taking it; indeed, how Victoria and Mary were faring in this place of enemies. Esmerelda looked drawn, and clamped tightly to Cecil, but enduring. The Blackfeet women peered into her face curiously, cheerfully, fingering her dress and even pressing a finger to her soft fair cheeks. In the carriage Henrietta endured, more fascinated by her first encounter with the people she had

come across a continent to proselytize than afraid. But
Alice Sample seemed the worst off, pale and unsmiling,
and no doubt finding no differences between these Blackfeet and the Assiniboin. Of the men, Cecil and Clay and
Alex seemed calm enough, though young, Alfred peered
about in near panic. And Silas Potter, in his ragged
clothing, shuffled along arrogantly, his disdain for these
heathen stamped across his face and plain to every one
of his hosts. Men, women, and children of the amiable
Kainah stared thoughtfully at him, and said nothing.

Mister Skye resolved to watch Silas closely. There
would be trouble there. The camp was on the Judith River
and sheltered by abundant cottonwoods now turning gold.
The buffalo, he surmised, were four or five miles west,
within easy reach of hunting parties that rode out each
morning to slaughter as many as they could for the meat,
and hides now coming to prime. He peered sharply at
these people, looking for his ancient enemy Moon-Hides-
the-Sun, but did not see him at first. Not, anyway, before they pulled up before the Kainah chief and headman,
who waited patiently before the chief's lodge, which was
blazoned with yellow sunbursts.

The young chief, whose name meant Moose-
Bellowing-in-Water, looked as taut and skeletal as a
drawn bow. He had eyes that weighed a man for war,
and a cast of lip that showed arrogance and cruelty. He
stood measuring Skye for caskets and holes in the earth.
And next to the chief stood Moon-Hides-the-Sun, he of
burning eye and glowering face, a giant of bronze fully
a head taller than Mister Skye, and riveted of strap iron.

"You are someone we know, Mister Skye. But we do
not know these others. We are told they are white medicine people, shortrobes and the longrobe who slew the
Cheyenne. Some among us favor the white medicine they
learned from the longrobe Point, many winters ago. But
I scorn it and trample on it. The ways of the People are
sacred. Some say we will be stronger if we learn the
medicine of the whites, but it is old-woman medicine
that tells us to do woman's work, plowing and toiling. I

will not permit it here. Tonight you will stay; tomorrow you will leave—if you are still alive. Beside me is one you know, and he has made a vow."

"I know Moon-Hides-the-Sun and I know of his vow to kill me, and I give him now a new name: Stolen-Horse Man, because his medicine is still bad," said Mister Skye.

Moon-Hides-the-Sun snarled and turned his back upon them.

"Is your medicine good, Mister Skye? I will not stop him. No Kainah will stop him from keeping his vow."

"See how he has turned his back. He is afraid. He has become a slinking coyote because his medicine is bad and he knows he will die."

Moose-Bellows-in-Water smiled malevolently. "If you kill the great warrior, Moon-Hides-the-Sun, in the village of the Kainah, you will face others."

# Chapter 28

Victoria huddled under her robes all night waiting for the Siksika dogs to kill her. She was ready, Green River knife in hand. Let the doorflap open a crack, or a knife start to saw through the lodgecover, and she would spring up like a lion.

Jawbone loitered at his usual station outside, ready to shriek his alarm, but she doubted the horse was a match for Moon-Hides-the-Sun. Mister Skye slept easily near her, his black silk hat parked to one side, and just beyond his dark hulk lay Mary and Dirk, all asleep. But Victoria knew the heart of the Siksika dogs, and the perfidies and murder in all of them, so she kept her vigil through the night. It had been different with the Assiniboin. She slept soundly through her captivity, because they were beneath contempt, not demons like these raiders of the north.

Yesterday, their chief, Moose-Bellows-in-Water, had insulted Mister Skye, refusing to smoke the peace pipe with him. Later, from within the lodge of the chief rose the snarl of angry elders and she caught enough of it to know that some among them wanted to murder Mister

Skye and his whole party. Moon-Hides-the-Sun had vanished and was preparing himself to kill Mister Skye because he had made a vow. But others of the Kainah had come to sit beside the uneasy cookfires of the evening to talk with the white medicine men. Some of them had been baptized by Father Point in 1847 and still wore cross-totems around their necks as a part of their medicine bundles.

Dawn was visible through the smokehole, though inside the lodge it remained night. Victoria uncurled from her robe, her knife still in hand. She was not tired from the sleepless night. Many times she had thus guarded Mister Skye. But she was eager to be off this morning, to escape the village of these Siksika dogs. She peered out the doorflap, and saw nothing; only gray mist rising from the Judith River where the frosty autumnal air breathed over it. The Siksika dogs called this stream Otokwi Tuktai, Yellow River. She stepped outside. Mary joined her, and Dirk, still sleepy from his long night's rest. He was a good child, quiet and happy.

Mary took the boy by the hand and led him to the river brush for their morning ablutions. Victoria watched narrowly. There was no one else awake. The Siksika dogs still slept, and so did the missionaries in their wagons and tents. No sooner had Mary and Dirk gone to the stream than Mary's shriek pierced the morning quiet. Victoria ran. Behind her she glimpsed Mister Skye, struggling through the lodge door. Partly concealed by chokecherry brush was Moon-Hides-the-Sun, his powerful arm arcing down, the stone-headed war club landing with a dull thud upon something there. Victoria raced, frantic with fear. She rounded a bend and saw Dirk, scrambling into the brush, and Mary staggering backward, a terrible gash gouting blood above her ear.

"Ayahhh," Victoria cried.

Moon-Hides-the-Sun sprang toward Mary as she began to topple, and again the bloody club smashed through the dawn gray. But Mary cringed sideways at the last second, and the club did not find her skull. She fell heavily. He wheeled toward Dirk, smashing his war club into the brush to brain him, but the brush held, and Dirk scurried deeper. Victoria sprang at him, sliced hard with her knife, but he blocked her arm and his own war club snapped close. Then he spotted Skye and he laughed and trotted away into the awakening village, dancing among the lodges, his feet burning on the scorched earth of fear, and his head hitting the sky of his vow.

Mister Skye, dressed only in his breechclout, rumbled through the brush and beheld the carnage, paralyzed. Mary writhed on the ground, her head a mass of bright blood that was matting her sleek black hair. Alive. Victoria reached her, plunged to her knees, and cradled that wounded head in her lap, crooning, singing the chant of death. Mister Skye said nothing, his breath steady in the morning air, his powerful barrel-body gathering up a lion's strength inside. Then he sprang back to the lodge and dug through a parfleche, extracting a thing he always had with him, something he took in hand only when he went berserk.

He called it a belaying pin. It looked like a war club, but made of lathed hardwood, one end flared wider in diameter than the other. He had told her that when he rode the seas in great boats, the pin was used to anchor long ropes. He said the water warriors who rode the giant boats used belaying pins as clubs.

And truly they did, for she had seen him use one, and in his hands it was a lethal, balanced club and better even than a knife, and he could stun limbs and brain enemies with it. Now she saw him punch through the doorflap and into the dawn to begin his deadly search for the Siksika dog who had attacked his wife and son. The village was stirring. A headman had found Dirk and Mary and Victoria now, and was rushing to the chief.

Mary's spirit hovered above her, so Victoria stood, and followed her man. So too did Jawbone, his long ears laid back, his yellow eyes murderous and his teeth snapping. But Mister Skye sent him back with a harsh growl, and walked with a roll, walked as if he were upon a heaving deck of a great boat, stalking the killer. He had no weapon other than that wooden belaying pin. Moon-Hides-the-Sun had two—a glinting knife in one hand, and the bloody war club in the other. Mister Skye was a man turning gray; Moon-Hides-the-Sun was yet in his prime.

Victoria followed, ready to kill and be killed, but Mister Skye didn't see her. He saw only the retreating, prancing figure of the murderer ahead. Moon-Hides-the-Sun never stood to fight, but always slid away, dancing around lodges, bursting through knots of spectators, edging past the headmen and finally past the chief himself, who stared.

"Your medicine is bad, your medicine is bad, Stolen-Horse Man," said Mister Skye softly, so softly that the hush of his voice was deceptive. Still did Moon-Hides-the-Sun edge backward, avoiding the trap of the creek but slipping out now upon the meadows near camp, with a swirl of Blackfeet, still wrapped in the night's blankets and robes, trailing after him. The warrior was edging toward the horses. He would dash for them and run away, and Victoria understood it perfectly. His medicine was bad. Moon-Hides-the-Sun knew he would die unless he escaped.

But he hadn't reckoned with his chief. This was a shameful thing, this wild dancing retreat. Had any Siksika, had any Kainah, ever brought such shame to a village? Victoria watched rage build in the chief as he beheld the flight of Moon-Hides-the-Sun. Mister Skye had calmly cut off his retreat to the horses, and now the bad-medicine warrior pranced backward once again, and the whole village was ashamed. Squaws wailed and pulled at their hair. Never had they witnessed such a thing. Bad medicine. Worse medicine than the Kainah had ever known. Neither had Victoria seen such bad medicine, so shameful a thing as this. The giant warrior was no longer a man, but a caged thing caught between a vow and bad medicine.

Angrily Moose-Bellows-in-Water snarled a command,

and jammed his own lance into the soft earth, where it shivered from the blow. The Kainah warriors came running, lances in hand, forming an arc behind Moon-Hides-the-Sun until he could no longer retreat without impaling himself on a Kainah lance. Other warriors, including the angry chief, raised their lances to complete the circle of murderous points surrounding Mister Skye and Moon-Hides-the-Sun. Jawbone shrieked, but Mister Skye growled at the animal. Some feral flame lit the chief's face, and his lance throbbed in his hands.

And so the pair danced alone in the death-ring.

"Your medicine is bad," muttered Mister Skye, still stalking forward with a strange rolling gait as if the earth were heaving under him, the hickory club poised easily in his right hand.

Moon-Hides-the-Sun stopped retreating and suddenly bulled ahead, feinting with his glittering knife while smashing his war club into the space where Mister Skye would be.

But Skye parried. The knife struck hardwood with a crack and the stone war club whipped air.

He kicked as it arced past, and the blow collapsed the warrior's leg momentarily. The belaying pin smashed brutally across the warrior's elbow, sending a streak of pain through his arm, and the stone war club sailed free of his spasming hand.

The warrior ripped upward with the knife, just nicking Mister Skye's thigh, leaving a line of red.

"Ayahh," cried spectators.

Jawbone shrieked.

Now the warrior thrust and jabbed, spun and sliced upward, mincing from side to side. Mister Skye didn't dance. He stood quietly on the balls of his feet, his eye on the knife, the belaying pin parrying and blocking, the wide girth of its top protecting his hand from the whipping blade. The blade hit wood with clicks that rattled like grapeshot.

"Medicine is bad," muttered Mister Skye. He let the blade glide past him and whipped his bare foot brutally into the warrior's gut. As the warrior doubled up the belaying pin, propelled by biceps of spring steel, caved in his skull. Moon-Hides-the-Sun was dead before he hit the grass.

Victoria peered around her wildly, ready to kill the first Siksika dog that raised a lance. But the chief had lowered his, discovering something in Mister Skye's berserk eyes that terrified him, and the warriors lowered theirs. Beside her she discovered Esmerelda sobbing, and Cecil Rathbone clutching her. Across the ring of warriors stood Silas, wild-eyed and scornful.

"You have committed murder, Mister Skye," he shrilled. "The devil will have you."

Mister Skye was not winded, though Victoria thought she could hardly find enough breath. He peered silently at Silas, and then at the chief, and walked slowly toward the chokecherry brush where his family lay. Victoria followed him, and so did the others, in utter silence.

The boy had crawled from the brush and was hugging his mother, who lay inert, flies gathering in the matted mess of blood and hair. Mary stared up at Skye, her eyes open, and Victoria supposed she was dead, too. But she was not.

"Take me to our lodge, Skye," she whispered.

He lifted her gently, carried her as lightly as he might a bird with an injured wing. And he wept. Slowly he walked to his small lodge, his wet eyes peering first at the chief, and then one by one at the others of this Kainah village. He laid her on the tawny grass before the lodge, and Victoria hastened inside for a buffalo robe and her kit of herbs and medicines, and began at once to wipe blood and hair away from gouged white bone. Mary's skull was not broken; only the surface flesh had been lacerated by the glancing blow. She slipped into a muttering delirium again, but Victoria knew she would recover unless she got the brain fever. Mister Skye took his son's hand in his big one and led Dirk to her. He sat solemnly beside his mother, contemplating the blood.

For the rest of that morning Mister Skye sat cross-legged before his lodge, with Mary's head in his lap. He did not move until her breathing became normal, and she peered up at him with unfocused eyes.

The drums thumped at about the pace of a heartbeat, their fleshed hide membranes drawn taut over the wooden barrels and vibrating to the soft rhythmic strokes of the four drummers and singers who beat them. The thumping was not loud, but it penetrated, and it seemed to pluck at Victoria's own heart and govern its pace. The Siksika dogs were holding their sacred buffalo dance, giving honor to their father Sun for the good hunt. It was a fine afternoon under an azure sky. Later there would be a feast of hump roast and tongue, along with all the delicacies, such as buffalo brains, raw liver, soft nose gristle, and bone marrow.

They had been in the village two days, more or less prisoners, although none of the Kainah had attempted to disarm Mister Skye. While the great hunt continued and the men rode out each morning to the buffalo herd and the women butchered meat and fleshed hides, the chief and his shamans debated the fate of the white medicine men, and Mister Skye. There were those, the chief included, who wanted to torture and kill them all and show the whole village once and for all that the medicine of the whites was false and weak and contemptible. But there were others who feared Mister Skye and Jawbone, and who argued that the traders at the fur posts might retaliate, and the annuity goods coming from the Grandfathers in Washington might not be given them. In the chief's council were none who welcomed the white medicine or thought it would benefit the people.

Mister Skye was in no hurry to leave. Mary remained too weak to be moved. The slightest movement of her head set her to groaning. A bouncing wagon bed would be torture for her. Each day the chief had painted his cheeks with vermilion slashes, blood-red insignia of war, and had thrust eagle feathers into his hair, and had paraded past the missionary party, his embered eyes boring

into them all. The missionaries had met his evil with
good, offering small presents and smiles. How strange
these missionaries were, soft as the breast of a dove,
smiling at the one who would slaughter them. Victoria
spat. Sonofabitch, she thought, how evil it was to be
caught in this camp of Siksika dogs. Not even Mister
Skye felt at ease among these people he called Bug's
Boys, and he never stirred about without his Colt at his
hip and his Sharps in his arms.

Some few who had been instructed by the Jesuit Father
Point in 1847 had come to talk with the missionaries as
much as language barriers permitted. Especially, they
came to see Father Kiley, and touch him, and hear the
Mass he finally offered when they pressed him to. But
they were few, a handful in a village that clung to the
old tradition of the Siksika.

Now she watched the impressive buffalo dance, beside
Mister Skye and Dirk. The throb of drums was too much
for Mary, and she slept in the lodge. On the other side
of her sat the white missionaries, even Father Kiley, except for the strange one, Silas Potter, who roamed
fiercely among the spectators, unkempt and in rags. The
young scholar stormed toward Cecil.

"They are performing a pagan rite. You are watching
a heathen religion. The worship of idols. Have you no
loyalty? Will you continue to betray God?"

"Silas, Silas, lad, to watch something is not to partic-
ipate in it," Cecil said mildly. "And they are going to
do it anyway. Sit and learn. What you learn of their religion will help you teach them about the true one. Have
a seat, friend. This is a thing to enjoy."

"Satan stalks the earth; demons dance here," Silas
cried.

Cecil nodded. The sacred dance was throbbing before
them. Virtually every boy and warrior in this long riverside village was circling the Buffalo Woman at the center. Each of them carried a ceremonial quiver, beaded
and fringed, and a strung bow, and at certain climactic
beats, they all loosed imaginary arrows at Buffalo

Woman, who trotted her own small circle in the middle of the seething ring of hunters. Each hunter in turn stopped and proclaimed his successes, the cows and bulls he had killed, the gifts of meat and hide he had made to the poor and widowed of the village. It was a merry celebration for the hunt had been good and all the lodges were fat with comforts.

Victoria envied the Buffalo Woman, for she had won a great honor. Like the medicine woman who was chosen each year to conduct the sun dance of midsummer, the Buffalo Woman had to be a woman of impeccable virtue, esteemed by the whole tribe for her faultless conduct, and the gifts she bestowed on others. This one was a beautiful young matron with glossy black braids, wearing a dress of soft white doeskin and bone necklaces. Her face and shoulders were invisible, covered with an albino buffalo head, so that the Buffalo Woman seemed almost a living thing, staggering with each flight of imaginary arrows.

Thus they celebrated and thanked Sun for the bounty, with a nasal chant that rattled the windows of Silas Potter's soul. Restlessly he stalked around the dancers, at one point raising his Bible over his head, and stretching his arms toward heaven. He looked shabby and distraught, his pale flesh hard-blistered by outdoor life. Then with a violent cry, he forged his way through the line of dancers, walked slowly toward Buffalo Woman, stood before her as she danced her small circle, and seemed to gather his breath.

"In the name of God, I command you to stop!" he cried.

The spectators, curious now, stood up and watched breathlessly, half amused, half appalled by this sacrilege. But nothing happened. The dance continued, after a fashion, the drummers softly drumming and chanting, and the dancers watching the crazy one in their midst. And then Silas whirled, smashed into Buffalo Woman, and knocked the sacred albino buffalo head, used only in Sun ceremonies, to the earth. She reeled and fell.

"You are worshiping the golden calf," he cried. "I proclaim unto you the day of the Lord!"

With that he kicked the sacred albino head violently, breaking a horn, and again, mashing a nose. Buffalo Woman scrambled to her feet and fled.

Victoria clasped a hand to her mouth. She had never seen such a thing, such a sacrilege. Even if these were despicable Kainah dogs, she felt offended by Silas Potter's insult.

They grabbed him, the warriors of the Raven Carriers Society, whose dance this was, and pinioned him. Cecil leapt up, but Mister Skye dragged him down.

"If you so much as move a muscle, you'll die, mate," he whispered.

Victoria clutched her Green River knife, and peered narrowly about her, ready to kill and to die.

They dragged the shouting Silas before Chief Moose-Bellows-in-Water. He stood slowly, a cruel curl to his lips.

"Repent," screamed Silas. "Demons, you worship demons. I proclaim the Gospel of the Lord. Repent and listen!"

The chief waved a hand, and an iron arm clamped across Silas's mouth. He bit it. The Kainah chief growled things to the Raven Carriers, and they dragged Silas back to the place where Buffalo Woman had woven her graceful steps. Here they tied his arms behind his back with thong, and here they lowered the sacred albino buffalo head over Silas. And then the dance resumed.

The drummers again began their heartbeat rhythm, and the hunters again praised Sun and sent volleys of imaginary arrows into Buffalo Man. Then the drums quickened, and along with the pulse, so did hearts, and along with hearts, feet and legs of the dancers, whirling wildly, madder and madder, pulsing and throbbing . . .

Then silence. It became a terrible silence, loud with heartbeats, stretching beyond the horizon, longer than any silence Victoria had ever known. Then, magically in unison, each hunter reached into his quiver and withdrew an arrow. Every arrow in that great flight of arrows went true. None missed, to sail past Buffalo Man and into the Kainah on the other side of the circle. Most of the hundred arrows pierced clear through Buffalo Man, riddling his chest and abdomen like the quills of a porcupine.

And still Silas stood, not falling and not falling.

"I proclaim the day of the Lord!" he cried, and fell. The albino head cracked as it landed, and rolled away.

"Oh God, oh God," sobbed Esmerelda.

"Not you, Silas!" muttered Clay.

Alice Sample sobbed wildly, coughing and trembling.

Alex stood abruptly, gaping at the twitching corpse, and Mister Skye yanked him down. "But he—but he—but he came to serve God and Man," gasped Alex.

"Tell me!" cried Father Kiley. "For God's sake, have they killed him?"

"Murder," muttered Cecil.

"I had such hope that he . . . he'd settle down when we got here. We loved him, loved him . . ." wept Esmerelda.

Across the circle Moose-Bellows-in Water licked his lips.

"Silas, my Silas," Cecil muttered. "Were you a prophet and a martyr, or were you mad?"

# Chapter 29

Five chill days later they reached the wide Missouri at a place where it ran north and south between dun prairie bluffs. That morning they had steered their tired wagons down a shallow coulee, and by noon they were in the Missouri bottoms. They stared silently at the throbbing river and its clear mountain-fresh water, and knew they had one last ordeal.

They had toiled through these last days in deep silence, doing what had to be done but living inside of themselves. Mary lay in the wagon she shared with Father Kiley and the little organ, improving steadily but not yet able to sit up for long because the concussion made her dizzy.

The party had acquired a new member, Weasel Nose, a slim cheerful youth of about twenty winters, who had asked to come with them and learn the ways of the whites from them. Cecil was glad to have him, and set about at once learning the Blackfeet tongue from him, while giving him English words.

The very afternoon that Silas Potter had died with a

hundred or so Kainah arrows piercing him, the village packed up and fled that bad-medicine place, its shamans deathly afraid of what sort of white man's medicine might befall them all.

They buried Silas where he fell in that meadow beside the Judith, and Cecil scarcely knew what to say over his shallow grave. He brushed off his worn black broadcloth suit and put it on. He'd lost so much weight on this continental voyage that it no longer fit. And he picked up the worn Bible, bound in fine-grained pigskin, and talked about love, perhaps because love was the thing Silas Potter never found in this life, and the thing, Cecil believed, he had found now in the other. Father Kiley stood beside Cecil in his long black cassock, saying nothing but sharing wholly in the bereavement and farewell.

"Oh, how we'll miss the boy," said Esmerelda afterward. "He wanted love. Just a few more miles, and he'd have reached our place, our mission. And then he would have been all right. Then he would have remembered love, divine and human." Her sorrow was shared by them all, and seemed somehow fitting.

Then they drove the wagons four or five miles in utter silence before the darkness came, through a heavily grazed swath where the buffalo had been and where wolves still prowled.

Cecil felt grateful for Weasel Nose's company. All the others had turned into themselves. The Kainah youth bestowed names upon the features of the land. What Mister Skye called the Belt Mountains, Weasel Nose called Mapsi Istuk. What Skye knew as the Highwoods, looming to the north, the boy called Sitosis Tuksi. The boy was the gift of God, and Cecil dreamed of the day when he could deliver a simple sermon in the tongue of the Blackfeet.

Now, on the bank of the Missouri, Mister Skye was uncertain.

"Sun River flows in here somewhere above the falls, but I don't reckon just where, Cecil," he said.

"Weasel Nose might know," Cecil said. "If we can get him to understand what we're looking for."

Mister Skye's fingers and hands flew in the language of the signs, and eventually the youth nodded. "Kaksistukskwi Ituktai," he said, pointing north. His hands said Point-of-Rocks River.

They crossed the river right there, for want of a better place. The autumnal stream ran languidly between gravelly beaches. The unburdened wagons were floated across, pulled by weary yokes and spans of oxen and mules. What few goods that water might harm were slung under the bows, while the tools were simply permitted to get wet. The waters leaking into the boxes rose several inches into the organ, and Henrietta fretted about the bellows, but there was no damage.

On the far side they toiled up a coulee and out upon a great benchland of tawny frostbitten prairie. An hour later they peered into a wide, shallow scoop in the prairie, with a goodly blue stream coiling in loose bows in its bottom.

"Sun River," said Mister Skye gently, from his seat on Jawbone.

They were perhaps two miles above its confluence with the Missouri, gazing into a gentle valley that stretched westward across a vast flat land, vanishing into a country of buttes to the southwest, and the low blue wall of the Rockies far off upon the sunset horizon. It seemed a barren place, with only a few cottonwoods in the bottoms, their leaves blazing golden now, to soften the tawny expanse and the endless emptiness of this land.

Cecil stood on the lip of the benchland and stared. To this place they had toiled over fifteen hundred miles, from far Independence, in their wagons, on foot, or riding their horses and mules. Esmerelda drew close to him and slipped her arm into his, and squeezed it gently. A few feet off, Alex and Henrietta Newton, she big with child now, peered into the valley. And beyond them the Samples, Clay, Alice, Alfred and . . .

It was late in the October afternoon, and the long sun

lay golden upon the brown grasslands, making an unearthly light that seemed to pluck up buttes and ridges a
hundred miles distant and make them blaze. It was a
limitless land, somehow more vast even than the endless
slopes of Nebraska. It was a strange, mystical land, a
place of dreams and dreamers.

"So few trees," whispered Esmerelda.

"But endless sun, and a big sky," said Cecil.

"We will make it home," she said, "and build a home
for God."

"Was it worth it?"

"I don't count my trials," she replied. "But I ache
for the Samples. And I try hard to remember Silas, who
came with us so far. We have our work cut out. We
endured whatever was set in our path, but that's the past,
and there is only the future and our mission. Cecil, we're
the torch-carriers, bringing Light to the people we've
come to bless. Now we'll begin."

Cecil smiled.

"It's so—desolate," said Henrietta with an edge in her
voice. "You mean to say that we came all that way,
walked all that way—for this?"

"Cecil, I'm not sure this is much of a place. We were
misled. Let's think about this, eh?" Alex said cautiously.
There was disappointment lancing his words.

"Surely you didn't expect homes and gardens and a
church and a parsonage, Alex."

"I didn't expect there to be—nothing!"

"We'll build. Tomorrow we'll find a site and conse-
crate it. Alex, nothing of value was ever built without a
cornerstone."

"I'm not a mason or a carpenter," Alex muttered.
"And I hope that dear Henrietta may have some comforts."

"Tomorrow we'll begin," Cecil said.

In the morning they unloaded the organ and set it under canvas in a sweetgrass meadow near a band of cottonwoods. Cecil saddled up the mare and plunged along

the river clear to its junction with the Missouri, splashed across and plunged up the other side, all the while dismounting and poking and prodding the land and soil and rock like a child. Then at last he made up his mind.

"Here," he muttered. "Here's rock and wood and good soil and river water. We can dig a shallow well too, in this bottom land. Look at this soil! Not black, but soft and rich, with good grass. We'll put the church here. The school over there. Build some houses along this way to have the view and stay out of the wind."

They watched him amazed, tagging along, sensing their fate and comfort in his hands as he circled the land like a horse getting ready to roll, muttering, crying to himself, kicking dirt, peering at highwater marks on Sun River.

"Here's the rock!" he cried. "Alex, fetch Mister Skye so we can move it!"

Men and horses dragged the speckled boulder to a gentle rise, and planted it in soft earth there, in a sunlit place that gave a noble view. Cecil stalked around an oblong, driving stakes into corners. "Now gather around!" he cried, some wild delight in his features.

They consecrated the mission there, blessed the cornerstone, remembered those who had fallen or vanished along the way. Alice Sample cried. They sang a hymn while Henrietta played her organ. Cecil's voice sailed sonorously into the wild that was already his home, blessing the land here and the church and all that it might accomplish. It wasn't long, a half hour, and they were done.

Father Kiley stood to one side quietly, and when all was done and this place consecrated, he blessed it.

All that took a day, and early the next morning, after tearful goodbyes, Mister Skye and his family, Esmerelda, Alice and Henrietta, and Father Kiley left for Fort Benton, taking two yoke of weary oxen and the nearly empty wagon. Even as the wagon drew away, they could see their husbands and friends sharpen axes and swing them into the cottonwoods in the deepening distances.

The women wept and talked of turning back and enduring the cold and hardship with their men. But they didn't. Instead they tended Mary, who lay in the wagon still sick and weak from her concussion, and ministered to Father Kiley, who now rode horse in blind ease beside Mister Skye each day. They steered well north of the Missouri to avoid the giant coulees and claws of rock that sliced down into the river bottoms. The nights grew bitter, and stars were chips of ice.

Fifty miles and three days later they skidded the wagon, with locked wheels, down a steep grade and into the outpost, dominated by the log and adobe fort built by American Fur in 1847 and rebuilt nearby later. It had first been called Fort Lewis, but renamed Fort Benton, after the Missouri senator and patron of the expanding west, Thomas Hart Benton. In a great sprawl around the fort lay rude cabins of married engagés, as well as the smoking lodges of assorted Blackfeet and other tribes. The crude village lay hard upon the Missouri, backed by a towering yellow bluff that protected it from north winds.

"We are at Benton," said Father Kiley.

"We are, Father."

"And you're wondering what to do with me."

"It passed my mind."

"I can draw upon the credit of the Society of Jesus to some extent. I will need to be taken down the river."

"There might be a mackinaw or two going, Father. That'd mean sitting in an open flatboat loaded with buffalo hides and freezing. If you'd like my advice, I'd say get to Fort Union before hard winter if anyone's going and will take you—that's fancy civilization compared to here—and winter there. Catch the fur company steamer down the river next summer."

"That's a long time," said Father Kiley desolately.

The place throbbed with riffraff in buckskins and bright calicos, a motley throng from many plains tribes, Cree and Blackfoot and Assiniboin. There were breeds and whites. There were French trappers who had penetrated here long before other whites. One or two escaped slaves caught his eye, along with two or three pink-cheeked easterners looking utterly out of place. They in turn stared at the wagon and the women. They'd never seen a wagon this far west, and the women inspired smiles, curiosity, and lust held in abeyance by Mister Skye's murderous gaze and reputation.

He stopped at the narrow portals of the fort, beneath its looming adobe brick walls and the slit-windowed corner blockhouse that covered the riverside entrance, and left Jawbone and Victoria to protect the women and Father Kiley.

"Skye!" rasped the bourgeois Alec Culbertson, "I heerd you was in these parts. Have a toddy."

Mister Skye gazed wistfully at the jug and its amber paradise and shook his head. "In a bit," he said. "I've got deliveries to make."

In a half hour it was settled. There were quarters within the fort suitable for the missionary women, and Culbertson and American Fur would delight in their company through the hard winter, and sell supplies to the men when they came in for them. There would be no doctor for Henrietta's delivery, but some fine Piegan midwives.

"I heer ye got Kiley with ye," Culbertson said when the other was settled.

"You hear a lot, mate. Maybe you've heard something else. A white girl, eleven or twelve, taken prisoner by Cut Nose and his Assiniboin."

"Nay, nary a thing, You lost her?"

"She was with us, got took berrying. She and Victoria and the parson's wife, Esmerelda. We got the rest back but they hid her. We never got a peek, and I can't say for sure she's alive. But that band, Cut Nose . . ."

Culbertson whistled. "That's no place for a little miss. Hope to God she's alive. Hope to God she's dead."

Mister Skye nodded. Alec Culbertson understood the realities.

"I've got a man riding to Fort Union today. I'll send

the details along with him, and maybe they can trade her back. Maybe. It's happened. But never with Cut Nose.''

"Never with Cut Nose," said Skye.

He told Culbertson everything he knew, described Miriam as best he could, while the bourgeois scratched it all down, dipping a quill pen into lampblack ink furiously.

"It'll go with the dispatch," Culbertson said. "Wish I could promise more. How are the parents taking it?''

"Mrs. Sample bore five or six children. They have one left.''

Culbertson whistled, and shook his head.

"More grief than a man and woman can endure," Mister Skye added. "But maybe you'll hear. Word filters in here.''

"The Injuns are the biggest gossips I ever run across," said the bourgeois. "I got a couple of surprises for Kiley stashed away here, a pair of lady penguins," he said. "Go git the porkeater.''

Mister Skye glared. "He's blinded. If you hurt that man or pain his spirit, I'll wring your bloody neck.''

The bourgeois grinned.

Mister Skye wheeled out of the rough log room, and the trader bolted up from his copperplate records and quill pens, and began barking something at his engagés.

Mister Skye found the priest waiting patiently on the wagon seat. "Culbertson wants to see you, mate. Says he's got something for you.''

"I remember him well.''

Skye led the Jesuit gently into the central yard. Off to the left the door of the windowless warehouse yawned, and the smell of dusty dry hides burdened the air. He guided the priest around some manure, and past a water trough and hitchrails. The bourgeois's quarters lay on the north side. To the east were the quarters of the engagés, and to the west, the kitchens, where rich smells emanated into the yard. On the remaining side were corrals and stables.

Inside Culbertson's chaotic rabbit warren stood the

bulge-bellied factor himself, and two nuns, white and black, white and black, in a room made of leather and log and bare earth.

It startled Mister Skye to see nuns, immaculately cowled, here a thousand miles and more from anything resembling settled community. They must have come by fur company boat as far as Fort Union, and trailed the rest of the way here somehow.

"Dunstan Kiley," roared Culbertson. "You old varmint. I heerd you wiped out a passel of Cheyenne by wavin' your wand."

The priest went rigid.

"Arrgh, I got a leetle surprise for your old Jesuit hide."

A nervous sister tittered.

"Over hyar I got a pair of genuine, bottled and bonded Ursuline sisters."

Father Kiley peered where he could not see.

"I am Sister Monica, Father." said one of the women.

"And I'm Sister Jude," said the shorter one.

Something like a grin lifted the corners of Kiley's mouth. "Mister Culbertson," he said tartly. "Now that's a fine prank to play on a blind man. These ladies—these ladies are . . ."

"With your permission, Father," said Sister Monica. She took his hand in hers and led it to her face, and placed a finger on her white cowl.

"Here is the cowl across my forehead. Trace it with your finger. Follow it, like this, down the sides of my face. And touch my black cape. And now I will hand you my crucifix. We are Ursulines."

Father Kiley sobbed. There were no tears for the ducts had been burned from his head, but he sobbed.

"You are Godsent," said Sister Monica. "We have been sent by the order to see where schools and sisters and the Church are most needed. This is a place where the need is very great. Many of the French are here, and have received no sacraments, and are in great need of baptism and marriage and reconciliation."

Father Kiley was beyond speech.

"We have found a small log building that used to be a trading post upstream for a school and church. And beside it, a place for ourselves and the other Ursulines who will come. But we have no priest. I . . . I cannot tell you how valuable you are to us, how much everything we have started depends on you. I pray God the Society of Jesus will consent."

For minutes Father Kiley said nothing, his sanctified hands clasped by those of the two women. He sucked air into famished lungs. Then a change came upon him, and he stood upright, no longer stooped. The others stood transfixed.

"Mister Skye," he said softly. "I was dead and am alive, lost and now found. I was proud—I roamed the wild lands knowing how to survive in them, make meat, live free, needing no one, as independent as any of you men of the mountains. Now I am humbled. I am dependent on others for every mouthful of food I eat, for shelter. I must be led wherever I go. I cannot even—even—I cannot even take care of my bodily needs without help. And now, in my . . . humbling, I depend on God. On his church. On these religious . . . And that's not all, Mister Skye. I have always loved the thing Saint Paul wrote, that God can make all things work for the good. Even blindness, sir. Other priests might come here from duty, but I will be here from love, and a loving priest can tend his flock better than one who is only obedient."

"I won't forget you, Father," said Mister Skye. "And we'll remember Miriam."

Something like a grin lifted Kiley's face. "Sister Jude and Sister Monica. Find me a place where we may sing the Te Deum."

Later, Mister Skye clasped the priest's hands in his own and made his rough goodbye. He settled the missionary women in their quarters, and arranged for the pasturage of the oxen and storage of the wagon. At the last he shook hands with Henrietta and Alice, but Esmerelda hugged him fiercely and wept.

He found his women in the lodge, which they had set up on the west edge of the settlement. Victoria had gotten Mary nestled down in her robes. It would be days before she could travel horseback again, but he had things to do. He held her hand. She smiled and he kissed her softly. He hugged Dirk. He turned Jawbone out upon the short grasses. The horses and mules all needed rest.

He counted his last bit of gold. There would be enough for a little powder and ball, some four-point blankets for Mary and Victoria to sew into winter capotes, a trinket for Dirk, and a good earthen jug of Fort Benton lightning.

Victoria eyed him narrowly, and muttered, but Mister Skye, with a certain gleam in his eye and a fine, building dryness of throat, rolled toward the fort.

# Author's Note

Pine Leaf was a real Crow warrior woman whose prowess in battle was legendary. She was probably killed by the Gros Ventre in 1854, but I have exercised the novelist's prerogative and have extended her life a year. There is no evidence that she had the medicine powers I have given her here.

The Blackfeet buffalo dance described near the end of the book is an invention. Most plains tribes did have buffalo dances, but these were more commonly performed before the hunt rather than after it. The Blackfeet did, however, take pains to thank their most important deity, Sun, for buffalo and successful hunts.

The Reverend Pierre de Smet, S. J., proselytized the Blackfeet in the 1840s, and in the fall of 1846 held a Mass in a Piegan camp where more than two thousand lodges of Piegans, Bloods, Northern Blackfeet, and Gros Ventres had assembled, along with such Blackfeet enemies as Flatheads and Nez Perces. In the 1850s Father Albert Lacombe founded his famed mission Lac Ste. Anne and ministered to the Blackfeet. Later, when the

Blackfeet Reservation was turned over to the Methodists by the government, Catholics were excluded from it. The nuns in my story were in Fort Benton well before nuns arrived in the territory that became Montana.

The Presbyterians were the first Protestants to proselytize the Blackfeet. In 1856 the Rev. Elkanah Mackey and his wife Sarah Armstrong Mackey arrived in Fort Benton, but didn't stay long. Mrs. Mackey was the first white woman to arrive at Fort Benton, and the first seen by the Blackfeet.

In 1857, the government complied with its 1855 treaty with the Blackfeet to establish a model farm at Sun River, along the lines advocated by Cecil Rathbone in this story. It failed. The Blackfeet were not interested in abandoning their nomadic buffalo and war-oriented life, and it became yet another of the noble experiments that had to be abandoned.

The presence of the Bloods, a northern Blackfeet tribe, on the Judith River around October 1855 is historical. A large portion of the Blackfeet nation gathered at the mouth of the Judith to ratify a peace treaty and receive annuity goods in October of that year.

Thus *Sun River* borrows from history, even though it is pure fiction.

My profound thanks to Dale L. Walker for sharing his vast fund of knowledge about the nineteenth century British navy. And to W. Michael Gear and Kathleen O'Neal Gear for sharing their encyclopedic knowledge of the Northwest and tribal culture. When I sought help from these friends, I received it abundantly.